P9-BZT-646

FLESH AND FIRE

FLESH AND FIRE

BOOK ONE OF
THE VINEART WAR

LAURA ANNE GILMAN

POCKET BOOKS
New York   London   Toronto   Sydney

Pocket Books
A Division of Simon & Schuster, Inc.
1230 Avenue of the Americas
New York, NY 10020

First Pocket Books hardcover edition October 2009

POCKET and colophon are registered trademarks of Simon & Schuster, Inc.

For information about special discounts for bulk purchases, please contact
Simon & Schuster Special Sales at 1-866-506-1949 or business@simonandschuster.com.

The Simon & Schuster Speakers Bureau can bring authors to your live event.
For more information or to book an event contact the Simon & Schuster
Speakers Bureau at 1-866-248-3049 or visit our website at www.simonspeakers.com.

Designed by Renata Di Biase

Manufactured in the United States of America

10 9 8 7 6 5 4 3 2 1

Library of Congress Cataloging-in-Publication Data
Gilman, Laura Anne.
    Flesh and fire / Laura Anne Gilman.—1st Pocket Books hardcover ed.
        p. cm.—(The Vineart war ; bk. 1)
    I. Title.
PS3557.I4545F54 2009
813'.54—dc22
                                                                        2009012786

ISBN 978-1-4391-0141-4
ISBN 978-1-4391-2687-5 (ebook)

This book absolutely has to be dedicated to my agent, Jennifer Jackson, whose casual suggestion "write me a food- or wine-based fantasy" was meant in jest but triggered the idea that became these books.

ACKNOWLEDGMENTS

CREATING THE LANDS Vin ate much of my life for a year and more; thankfully I had the help of many wonderful, talented, and knowledgeable people from the United States, France, Australia, and Germany. I sent e-mails and made phone calls and cornered innocent wine folk in their offices, peppering them with seemingly insane questions—all of which they answered cheerfully and at length, with the affection for the topic that shines through every person connected with the wine industry. Like writing, wine-making is a profession of passion and aggravation, often in the same moment, and I thank them for sharing a window into their lives.

Any details that don't connect to the actual process were either changed intentionally, or I got wrong. Don't blame them.

Special thanks go, in no particular order, to:

Hannelore Pepke-Durix (Burgundy)

Robert Kowal, assistant winemaker at City Winery (New York City)

Rosalind Berlow (New York City)

Karen Miller (Australia)

Stéphanie Bouhin at La P'tite Cave (Burgundy)

Henri Emmanuel at Cave du Cabet des Cordeliers (Burgundy)

François-Xavier Dufouleur at Maison Dufouleur Frères (Burgundy)

Robert Eymael at Mönchhof & Joh. Jos. Christoffel Erben (Germany)

the staff at Domaine Bouchard Aîné et Fils (Burgundy)

FLESH AND FIRE

hen I preach, I remind myself that the Collegium was created for one purpose: that the world not forget Sin Washer, and how—and why—He came to us. That is our duty, our reason for being.

The story is a simple one, in the telling. Ages past, prince-mages ruled these lands. Some were good men, and some were evil, but all were arrogant with their power, and the emperor in distant Ettion, busy with his own rebellious court, did not rein them in. Bored, they battled each other, staging magical conflicts merely to prove their skills. Year after year, the contests grew more brutal, the need to win more overwhelming.

In those days, all spellwine came from the First Growth, whose vines were straight and tall, the flesh fruit ripe with magic, and only the quality of a prince-mage's harvest determined whose spell-crafting would prevail. Thus the people were taken from their other, necessary work, until entire regions felt the pinch of hunger and disease.

Distraught, the people cried out to their gods to save them. Of all the ten gods, only two heard and listened: Baphos, patron of the harvest, and Charif of the growing season. Taking the form of ordinary mortals, they came together to scold the emperor for failing in his duties. The emperor, troubled closer to home, told them to take their complaints to the prince-mages and discipline them directly. Baphos and Charif did so, gathering them together and warning them of the consequences of their actions. But the prince-mages, prideful and strong, did not listen.

Charif was annoyed at the reception they received, and Baphos soothed her, and together they created a child who grew to adulthood between the sowing and the reaping. He was named Zatim, and when he reached his full growth, he came before the prince-mages as well and spoke unto them with the words of his parents, warning them to cease or be destroyed.

The prince-mages refused to hear his words as well, and ordered him slain for daring to reprimand them, for such was their pride in their magic that they thought themselves equal to the child of gods. And so the killers came upon Zatim as he walked alone, and fell upon him with blades dipped in deadly spellwine. But as the knives pierced his flesh, it was not blood but wine that flowed from his veins, a more potent spell-wine than any mage could craft. The killers fell back in awe and fear, and he struck them down with a single word, for unlike his parents Zatim felt no affection for humans to soften his heart.

But his parents' voices came to him, reminding him that he had been born not to destroy but to protect, and he heard them, and heeded their wisdom. Lowering his hands, the wine-blood flowed over his fingers and down into the soil, spreading through every land, and where it touched the grapes, they withered and changed, the vines twisting under his anger until where once there was a single spellgrape there now were many, their pale yellow skin tinged with the red of his blood, and the prince-mages did not know how to use them.

And the common people rushed to Zatim's side, trying to staunch the flow and save his life, and in their concern his anger was tempered. He smiled and touched them as well with his wine-blood, and their sadness fled and they felt peace such as they had never known.

"See this," he said unto them. "See this, how I cleft the magic of the land from the seats of power. Let nevermore the mighty craft magic and use it against those they are sworn to protect."

And then he died, and those around him gathered the wine-blood from his flesh, and brought others before them and washed their hands with the blood as well, and so the peace was shared, and they praised the name of Zatim Sin Washer, who had stopped the prince-mages and saved the lands from destruction, and given them peace.

This is the story we tell, we Washer's Kin. We travel from the Collegium school to pour the wine-blood for those who are in need of comfort, and tell Sin Washer's story, over and over again, so that none will forget what we once were, and how we came to be as we are now.

THAT IS THE story as we tell it, and it ends there, but where legend ends, history begins, and no true story ends so cleanly.

In distant Ettion, in the year of Sin Washer's birth and death, the emperor himself was slain in his own bed, and the lands fell into chaos. A few prince-mages still tended their strange new grapes, but Sin Washer had spoken truly: each vine was now limited in scope, not the mighty powers of before. And so the age of the prince-mages waned, their attentions turning to more immediate, practical sources of power and strength. But the vineyards remained, and in their place the Vinearts, the vine-mages, arose to master the grapes, and craft them into useful things.

And so were Sin Washer's words proven true once again, for Vinearts must spend their entire lives learning their vines, and have no time to build armies or rule over men, and princes, busy with the ways of men, have no time to dedicate to the secret and subtle ways of vines.

For nearly fifteen hundred years, through surfeit and famine, prosperity and plague, we have abided by Sin Washer's Commands. But time passes, memories fade, and the hunger for power is a terribly human thing, and so we—even we Washers—were caught unaware. . . .

Prelude

*I*n the *hills* of southern Iaja, thunder had rolled through the night before, but no rain accompanied it, and the slaves were at work in the vineyards soon after sunrise. The sun had progressed to the third-quarter mark when a lean figure came to stand at the edge of the yard. A freshly picked clutch of fruit rested in his work-roughened hand, and he was studying the flesh of the fruit, letting the magic deep within it speak to him and murmur of potential and promise.

A soft cough sounded, overriding the gentle morning hum of insects in the grass and attracting his attention, as intended. "Master?"

Vineart Sionio didn't turn, but out of the corner of his eye he saw the slave, diffident but urgent, his hands fisting in the rough tunic that hung over his wiry body.

"Yes?" While he waited for a response, the Vineart placed a young green grape on his tongue and closed his mouth around it, crushing it and letting the juice coat his tongue. The taste was both delicate and sour, and it rose into his nasal passages. Not anywhere near ripe, still waiting for the heat of high summer and the cooler nights of Harvest, but showing distinct promise. His vineyards were still young, giving only limited yield. This Harvest might finally change that.

"Master," the slave said again, "there is a . . ." The slave looked down at his feet, falling silent.

Sionio was a young man, barely thirty and still building his reputation; although granted a Master's rank, he had not yet earned the right to name his House, his vines still known by the name of the nearest village. He was ambitious, though, and worked as hard as any slave when hands were needed in the yard. His slaves respected him and his magic to the point of caution, as was only proper, but he did not abuse them. There was no reason for them to fear speaking if there was something to be said.

"A what?" He turned then, and looked directly at the slave. "Speak. Stop wasting my time."

The slave flinched. He was bald, and had either lost or forgotten to wear his hat that morning. Sionio made note to speak to the overseer about that. He could not afford a single slave to fall ill, not now. "I do not know what it is, Master. But it is in the fields. And it is wrong."

Very few slaves could sense the magic that grew within spellgrapes' flesh. But they worked the vineyards every day of the year, season after season, and it spoke to them in its own fashion. They knew what should be there . . . and what should not.

Sionio did not hesitate. "Show me."

The soil was soft underfoot as they walked, the smell of the young fruit warm in the afternoon sun. If the weather held for another month, if no rot or infestation threatened, and Harvest went well . . .

Sionio halted his thoughts there. Weather was something even a Vineart could not always control, and so it could easily become obsession. Sionio was a more practical man; he worried over what he could affect, and left the rest to the silent gods and Nature's whim. Skill and craft were what made spellwine, and he did not doubt his strength in either.

They came to the vines the slave had been weeding and stopped. "Here, Master."

A quick mental calculation placed them in seventh square, second grouping. Sionio knew every square of the enclosure, its planting, history, and expectations. The vines here were only four years old, but they had a noble heritage, the rootstock coming from his own master's enclosures, and in another few years their fruit would contribute to a noble, powerful spellwine that would carry Sionio's name across the known lands.

"Where is this wrongness?"

"There, Master." The slave pointed, his sun-browned finger shaking slightly. Six other slaves stood by, looking up and down the yard nervously, three males, two females, and one so old its gender was uncertain. Sionio frowned at them. They should be weeding and pruning, not fiddling with their thumbs like useless citizens.

"In the soil." The slave who had brought him word pointed again, down at the base of a vine, but made no move to get closer.

Sionio looked at the other slaves again, more closely this time. Two of them had taken off their own straw-brimmed hats and were crunching them between restless fingers. They could not meet his gaze, not even the oldster who should have known better.

These slaves had been bought cheaply, all past puberty; the overlooked second string was all Sionio could afford at the time. Still, life here was better than on the slaver's caravan. They were not afraid of him, but of what they felt. Or, more accurately, they were more afraid of whatever was there than him.

Sionio pushed passed the slaves and knelt by the vine in question. A grape vine needed support to grow on, the woody stem not strong enough to support itself and the weight of its fruit. During the bare winter season, the slaves wove tendrils around waxed fibers strung between wooden posts, giving the vines something to cling to as they grew. Now, in the warmth of early summer, the small green leaves were clustered thickly around those ropes, protecting the grapes underneath from too much sun, rain, or animal predation.

Sionio's trousers, durable canvas styled after those worn by Iajan sailors, were quickly stained by the dirt as the Vineart dug his fingers into the soil. He reached toward the roots buried deep in the mineral-poor ground, until the soil reached the dark red mage-stain on the back of his hand. The senses that made him a Vineart, the ability that allowed him to craft the spellwines, rang an alarm. It was not magic that warned him, but some deep atavistic sense, an animal's warning of a predator, of something not right lurking nearby.

The civilized maiar, or princeling, in his city or fine country house might scoff, but Sionio knew better. Instinct did not lie.

The slave was right. Something was wrong. Something deep, something new. Something that should not be there.

"Go fetch a firestone, and a smudge pot," he told the nearest slave, the one who had fetched him originally. "And a vial of sweetwater."

The slave took off at a run, and the others backed up a few steps more, not willing to leave but not wanting to be close to anything that called for sweetwater, also known for good reason as grape-purge.

"Now, what ails you, little ones?" he asked, returning his attention to the grapevines in front of him. To the uneducated eye they seemed perfectly healthy, the leaves shiny and unfurled, each bunch thick and heavy, the grapes small and deep green.

Whatever rot lurked in the soil, it did not seem to have affected the crop yet. With luck, they had caught it soon enough, and Sionio would reward the slave who had alerted him.

Then a tremor under his knee made him look down in time to see tiny red bugs skittering under his hand, digging their way out of the soil. They scrambled over his fingers, trying to climb the rough cloth of his clothing.

Bud mites were normal pests. They usually came out only in the early morning, feeding on the occasional grape that burst in the night. They should not be swarming like this, not now, not in such numbers.

Sionio unhooked a palm-sized wineskin from his leather belt with his free hand, uncorked it easily with two fingers, and tilted it so that a few drops fell onto his tongue. Unlike the grapes he had tasted earlier, the spellwine was rich and fruity, sweetly pungent: the instantly familiar taste of vine-heal. It faded into his mouth, the vapor rising into his sinuses, and as he breathed, the spell was released, allowing him to *feel* the soil, *feel* the movements under his hands and knees.

"Sin Washer!" he swore, jerking back even as the ground under him rumbled, the dirt and bugs flying upward as the force of his query summoned something, a something that erupted from the soil like a volcano, and threw him onto his backside.

The wrinkled, blind head of a grub rose a full length into the air, the shape of it familiar to anyone who had ever worked a vineyard, if a thousand times larger than such a thing should be. The slaves, shrieking, scattered and ran as though the grub would devour them. In the distance, from the kennel by the sleep house, dogs barked a now-useless alarm.

Sionio got to his feet, his gaze never leaving the giant grub's form even as his mind identified the known facts. He might be young but he was not green. Faced with a threat to his vines, a Vineart did not react; a Vineart *acted*.

The leaves near where the grub reared its dark gray form had already faded to an ugly yellow, dying by sheer proximity to the thing, as though its very presence were a poison. Sionio suspected that, were he to lift the leaves, the young grapes would be withered and dying as well. This thing had to be stopped, now, before the blight spread.

He didn't need a vial of spellwine to deal with the threat: the grub might be huge but it was still a grub. Disgusting, and the size of the thing made it a creature of nightmares, yes, but any Vineart worthy of his vines knew how to deal with such a thing.

It would be easier with his tools, of course.

Even as the thought passed through his mind, there was a sound behind him. The grub turned as though it, too, had heard the sound, and a thin shriek rose into the air from its open maw. The slave had returned. Despite its obvious fear, the slave forced himself forward enough to push an object into his master's waiting hands.

A firestone, warm and ready. And a small clay pot marked with the sigil for sweetwater.

The smudge pot would have been useful as well, but these were the two things that he needed most of all.

Clutching the firestone in his right hand, he felt the crystalline globe react to his own body heat, doubling and trebling the fire trapped inside glass until the colors swirled and danced, impatient to be let out. The clay pot he crushed with his other hand, feeling the thick, oily liquid drip over his fingers and down his palm, tingling slightly.

To work magic, most needed properly prepared spellwines. But here, in the middle of his own vineyard, all a Vineart needed was already in place. Let princes and lords buy spellwines; a Vineart had a more subtle magic at his command.

Sionio spit into his left palm and then clasped his hands together, letting the juice from his mouth mix with the sweetwater and coat the firestone. The spit carried the magic within him, tangled with the lingering traces of mustus and fermentation. Mage-blood was not as potent as spellwine, but it was always present and ready.

"Scour, scour! Root and leaf, be clean! Go!"

A basic decantation, useful to prevent infestations of bugs and rot. The heated sweetwater mixture turned it into a flaming torch, exploding from his hands at the grub.

Magic that would have cleansed a midsized field of the most tenacious rot washed over the grub, making it scream like a horse in agony. The full body of the thing pulled out of the soil until it reached a man's height, almost as thick around and thrice as ugly as the most deformed freak.

And still it screamed, the ugly, bulbous head reaching through the flames to snap at the Vineart, the source of its agony. Blind, it still came dangerously close, aiming not for the Vineart's head but his hands, where the flames came from.

"Scour!" he cried again. "Root and leaf, be *clean.* Go!"

The decantation was a basic one, but he was no apprentice to miscast it or underestimate the power needed. It should have been a matter of moments before this was finished. Still, the grub attacked, despite the spell, and Sionio found himself pushed back one step and then another, until his back was up against the row of vines behind him, and he could retreat no farther.

What *was* this thing, he wondered, even as he grasped for another burst of magic, suddenly unable to concentrate through his fear. The thought occurred: grubs, even bastard monster grubs, did not appear alone. Was this nightmare beast an aberration? Or were there more, lurking below the fields, waiting to consume his entire crop? If he faltered now, might he lose it all?

The firestone flared again, driven by his own fear and protective anger. The vineyard was more than the source of his power; it was his livelihood, his life. It was everything he had worked for, from the beginning of his training until now. The idea that something as ugly, as horrible, and as ordinarily defeatable as a *grub* might put that at risk drove him forward again, his hands flaming bright enough to match the sun overhead. His normally calm features twisted with anger and determination as he reached out with those burning hands, reaching through his disgust and natural aversion to *touch* the grub.

The moment he made contact, he wanted to recoil, to let go, to wipe his hands clean of the taint. The skin of the grub was hot and slimy and *wrong*. This was no garden mutant, no horror of nature. This thing was *magic*, although how or why Sionio could not fathom. Such magic was not possible, could not be possible. . . .

Even as Sionio thought those things, he was chanting a new decantation. Not an apprentice's cantrip, but something far deeper, far stronger, and far more dangerous.

"Wither and *die*," he ordered the grub. "Lack of moisture, lack of rain. Overheat, wither, and die. Go."

It was less a spell than a curse, the sort that should never even be whispered in any vineyard, much less his own. Sionio poured everything he had into it, and poured that in turn into the body of the beast grub. The remaining rosewater on his hands slicked onto the grub's skin like pig oil; mixed with his spit, it had the same effect as setting a torch to dry grain.

A huge, high shriek nearly shattered the Vineart's eardrums at such close range, and the grub wavered, quivered under his grasp, and then collapsed, taking down an entire span of the vine-row with its fall.

Sionio fell back, the monster's death throes knocking him away, and he landed again on his back. He watched as the grub thrashed and writhed, and, finally, fell still.

An eerie silence fell over the vineyard. Birds did not sing overhead, slaves did not chatter, and even the wind seemed hushed. Distantly, as though through water, he could hear the faint sounds of something rustling, and recognized it, barely, as the sound of human bodies. His slaves, who had run . . . but not so far away. If he called to them, they would come back.

No. Not until he was sure the thing was dead. Slaves were not cheap, and good slaves, loyal slaves, were even more difficult to replace.

He got up and walked with steady grace to the monster's corpse. The sweetwater was gone, burned off his hands, and he could feel the depletion of the magic within his marrow. Sweetwater was dangerous to the user as well as the target. But this was still his vineyard, his lands, and so long as his feet walked the soil, there was strength here for him to take. Enough to ensure this thing was dead, and the immediate threat, gone.

The corpse was still and cooling. Dead. Even as he bent to check, the wrinkled gray form began to shimmer and shake. Before he could even jump back, sure it was some sort of trick, it imploded, leaving behind only a choking gray cloud of foul-tasting dust.

He had not caused that. Magic-born, and magic-sent, and magic-destroyed. Whoever had sent this monster against him wanted no trace left to be discovered. Who could do such a thing? Touching the grub, feeling its life-spark pulsing against his skin, enhanced by the sweetwater, had filled him with such dread, such disgust . . . magic should not cause him to shudder like that. Something lay beneath it, something dank and sour on the tongue.

He could ask no one. A Vineart would have no cause to attack him; they could not benefit from his vines, nor take over his lands. That was not their way; deviation from Sin Washer's Command to abjure power was unthinkable, unforgivable. And yet, it was a magical attack, so clearly another Vineart was involved. But who? Who could have created such an abomination of a spell? More to the point, who had bought it, used it against him?

Shaken, Sionio stood, and with a twitch of his hand summoned the slaves to him. Four came, four of the six who had worked this cluster originally. If the two who fled were not dead already, he would remedy that by nightfall. He rewarded betrayal as well as loyalty.

"Speak to no one of this," he warned the remaining four. "Speak of it, and die." No matter that he had defeated the beast, that his magic had been the greater force. The fact was that someone had attacked him— had sent this thing into his vineyard. Any whisper, any gossip that his grapes were tainted by the attack, and his reputation could be ruined forever.

The slaves dropped to the ground and, foreheads on the soil, swore their obedience. When he released them, they got to their feet and went back to work, joining the others farther away. They all nervously avoided the blasted cluster as though still expecting something else to emerge without warning.

Sionio walked to the end of the square and looked out over his lands. The ground around where the grub had fallen was seared, the vines dead where they had grown. But there was no further sense of wrongness: there had been only the one massive grub, burrowing in from below.

"Is it me?" he asked the now-still air. "Is someone spelling for me specifically? Or are others under attack as well?" If so, he had no way of knowing; the demands of the vines made Vinearts into solitary creatures, not prone to mingling with their peers, and their training made it difficult to trust others. There was not a soul he could turn to, not a soul he could ask for advice, now that his master was gone. That was the way things were.

Sionio stared out across the tops of the vines, a wave of green sloping down to a high stone wall. Odds were that this was a onetime event, a freak spell gone awry and out of control, the caster silent out of embarrassment or fear. Still, he needed to be certain.

A second wineskin was hooked to his belt, barely large enough to hold one swallow. It never left his person, too valuable to ever let out of his sight. Unlike most spellwines, this one did not fade as it aged, but grew stronger, and all he needed was that one sip.

Still, he hesitated. This was a spellwine of his own making, and difficult to craft. There would be no replacing it, not for years. But if he did not use it now, there might not be years left him if he were attacked again unawares.

Decided, he removed the skin and let the liquid within hit his tongue. It was thick and heavy, bitter and sweet like overripe berries left too long in the sun. But that sensation was overwhelmed almost immediately by the sweep of magic distilled into that potent liquid. This was different than any other spellwine: a simple command triggered its magic.

"Show me my enemy."

The spellwine complied and, in that instant of connection—and discovery—his enemy struck once more. Fatally.

PART I

Slave

Chapter 1

HOUSE OF MALECH: HARVEST

he boy focused on what he was doing, but not so much that he failed to sense someone pause behind him, too close for comfort. He managed not to flinch as the older slave bent down to whisper. "Nice job you pulled, Fox-fur. Who'd you sweetmouth for it?"

The boy grunted, not wanting to talk, even to defend himself. Talk got you noticed. Notice was bad. Keep your face down, your hands busy, and your mouth shut, and survive. Those were the unspoken rules everyone knew.

After a minute the other slave shrugged and moved on with his own assignment. Left alone, the boy looked up into the sky, his eyes squinting as he searched the pale blue distance. He hadn't sweetmouthed anyone. Luck of the pick, was all. He wasn't going to question it. He didn't question anything; he just did as he was told.

The brightness of the open sky made his eyes water. There was a bird—a tarn, from the banding—flying overhead in search of a careless or greedy rabbit. Every year they cut back the brush to the ancient grove of trees that marked the end of the vineyard, trying to keep the rabbits and foxes from the vines. They had built stone fences and decanted spells to keep humans away, but animals were harder to convince.

This field, and the rest of it, was part of the Valle of Ivy. The valley was cut into a chessboard of fields, half green with crops, the others brown and fallow, interspersed with the occasional gnarled fruit tree, and dotted with low stone buildings. In the distance a river cut through the fields—the Ivy. The chessboard and the buildings belonged to the House of Malech, one of four Vinearts established within The Berengia, and the only one currently ranked Master. His master. The slave knew nothing of the other Vinearts or The Berengia, or what lay beyond her borders. To imagine anything beyond the vineyard and the sleep house was as impossible as flying with the tarn overhead.

At the far edge of the fields where the boy was stationed, a pair of trees—not quite so ancient, but still wider around than a man could reach—created a shelter for two low structures built of pale gray stone: the slaves' sleep house and vineyard's storehouse, where the plows and tools were kept. Those, and the open form of the vintnery behind him, made of the same stone as the enclosure's walls, were the boundaries of his world. The other buildings behind the vintnery, across a wide cobbled road, might as well have been on the other side of the Ivy, for all he knew of them.

The boy looked away from the sky and downward. Every slave in the House of Malech was working today. Summer had been warm and rainy, but those days had given way to cooler, drier mornings, and the grapes had ripened on schedule, green leaves turning a dark red at the edges, the grapes darker red yet, their skin tight over plump, juicy flesh. He could practically feel the ripeness in the air, waiting. He had learned the hard way not to mention that to anyone, the way the ripening grapes made a noise in his head, inside his bones. The one time he had asked another slave about it, he'd got beaten until his skull had bled, and the overseer had kept him out of the yards for the day.

The tarn had disappeared while he'd looked away. Now not even a cloud marred the expanse of blue, the sun already high overhead and surprisingly strong for the season. A faint breeze came down off the ridge, carrying a salty hint that cooled the sweat on his skin just enough to make it noticeable. The boy shifted, making himself as comfortable as he could, glad at least to be out of the direct sunlight, out of the fields. In the distance, past the vintner's shed, beyond the dark gray bulk of the sleep house, two score of slaves, stripped down to their loose-woven pants, worked their way up and down the groupings of waist-high vines, carefully stripping the ripe bunches from each plant one handful at a time, bending and rising in tune to some unheard rhythm.

He had done that, for three Harvests before this one, once he was old enough to be trusted. Your hands cramped after a while, and every finger cracked and bled, but not a single fruit was damaged if you could help it; each straw basket on their backs, once filled, was worth more than the slave carrying it. That was the first thing learned the very first day a slave was brought into the vineyard. You learned, and you survived, and, if your master was kind, you might even make it out of the yards, out of the sun and the rain, and away from walking stooped all your waking hours until you slept that way, too.

His master was not kind, but neither was he particularly cruel, and the boy had made it out of the yard. Barely.

Barely was enough. He could sit, and his back did not hurt, and his skin was not blistered by the sun. The Washer who traveled their road would say it was because he let the world move him rather than trying to move it. He didn't see how he could do otherwise. But there was much the Washers preached that he didn't understand.

A harvest-hire guard stood on the top of a slight rise at the edge of the field, watching the activity. A stiffened lash in his left hand tapped an irregular rhythm against his thigh as his gaze skimmed over the area being harvested. He was there more for tradition than need. It was death to steal a clutch of grapes. Death to taste one. Death to waste one. Nobles could afford spellwine, and free men might drink of *vin ordinaire*: slaves could not even dream of either.

The boy shifted, feeling warning prickles in his bare feet that told him he had been still too long. He looked away from the guard, letting his gaze rest on nothing in particular, waiting. That was best, to simply wait, and not draw attention.

When a basket was filled to near overflowing with fruit, the slave carrying it would place it to one side of the trellis-lane. A younger slave, not yet trusted with the picking, would come down to fetch it, leaving an empty basket in its place to be filled in turn. That slave would bring the full basket down, away from the vineyard itself to the crusher, a great wooden monster construct twice as high as a grown man and four times the length.

That was where the boy waited. His responsibility was to monitor the fill level of the wooden crusher, making sure that the right amount of fruit was added, no more and no less.

The other slave had been right; it was a good job. It was also an important job, a sign that the overseer was not displeased with him, and he felt the responsibility keenly. But the truth was that it was boring, and his legs kept falling asleep.

An old slave, his wizened limbs useless for anything else, watched from the other side, sitting in a raised wooden chair to make sure that every fruit was placed into the great wooden monster and that no slave sneaked even one fruit into his mouth. He was also there to ensure that no fingers or clothes were trapped in the process. Every year at least one slave was maimed or killed that way, the weights and beams catching the unwary or the careless. The boy had worked six Harvests since the Master bought him and seen the results: slaves missing fingers and, in one case, an entire arm, crushed to uselessness and cut off before it could turn black and stink.

Two baskets were emptied into the maw of the monster, then a third. The old slave nodded at the boy, licking his cracked, dry lips in a way that reminded the boy of the lizards that sunned themselves on the low stone walls between the vineyards. The boy looked away again, focusing all of his attention on the crusher, as though that would make the old man go away. Harvest stories weren't the only ones told in the sleep house. The younger slaves knew to stay away from that one's hands in the darkness, or when they used the shit pits at night.

The slavers had men like that, too. He had been younger then, too young, and not as careful. But the slavers were past, done with him now that he belonged to another.

The other slaves might fumble under blankets or up against shadowed walls, willingly or not. Here the boy learned how to say no without saying anything at all, to evade reaching hands without giving offense, and even as those his own age began to look around with an interested eye, he felt no desire at all, not even to use his own hand, as the others did. Fortunately, hard work and a sudden growth over the winter had finally turned his rounded limbs into harder muscle, so a slave grabbed at him at his own risk now, and the overseer had shown no interest in flesh, save that it did the work assigned to it.

That thought in mind, when the fourth basket was emptied into the belly of the crusher, he darted forward and looked inside. A dark line, the stain of years of pressings, marked the three-quarter point. The boy waved his hand in a circular motion, and one more basket was dumped in, then the heavy door was slid shut. The boy stepped back, out of harm's way, as the crusher was turned upside down with a creaking, moaning noise, like a giant moaning in his sleep. Pressure in the form of giant bladders was applied, another slave working the bellows to fill the bladders until given the command to stop, and then deflating it again. Once, he had been told, slaves did this work with their feet. Too many grapes were lost that way, the process too slow. He wondered about the feel of grapes under the soles of his feet and between his toes, tread upon like dirt, and could not imagine it.

"A good harvest, this year."

The boy tensed, his shoulders hunching up around his ears even more than usual. He had been so preoccupied with his boredom and his prickling legs, he hadn't noticed the overseer leaving his usual post and coming to stand behind him.

Stupid, stupid, he thought, trying to become invisible. The overseer had never hurt him, but you never knew what might catch his attention, and unlike the other slaves, you could not ignore him, or make him go away. The overseer was all-powerful. Even the season-hire guards were scared of the overseer.

"We shall see."

The other voice was deeper, dryer, unfamiliar but instantly recognizable by the power it carried. Even the wind stilled, and all activity halted for half a breath, then started again even more quickly than before, as though hoping to make up for that lapse. Even the insects creaking in the hedge called faster, louder.

The boy's heart squeezed dry in his chest, and his earlier fear was nothing compared to the shaking of his knees. The Master was there. "Idiot," he whispered fiercely to himself. Of course the Master was there. The Master was everywhere. Every inch of the vineyard was his, and he was in every span of soil, every clutch of fruit.

He owned everything, controlled everything. Decided everything.

It was safer in the fields, no matter that your knees and shoulders ached, to only face the overseer and his whip, and not the Vineart. Like a rabbit sensing the tarn overhead, he froze, and prayed to remain unseen.

The grapes, sun warmed and ripe near to bursting, didn't care who was watching them. Under the gentle pressure of the inflating bladders, the blood-red skins broke, and the crushed pulp and bits of skin dropped through the grate at the bottom, while the remnant of stem or leaf remained within the belly of the crusher. Another set of slaves carried the bottom pan to a large wooden vat off to the side, and carefully poured the contents into a great wooden barrel. The pulp would—like the other crushings of the day—be taken into the shade of the vintnery itself, where, the boy knew vaguely, it would be run through one of the two presses, even larger than the crusher, to create the liquid mustus and, from there, somehow, magically, spellwine.

Working the press was the most dangerous job of Harvest. Even to breathe too deeply of the smell was not allowed to a slave. And yet, the desire he felt, to draw it into your lungs, to maybe feel the touch of the magic, was almost irresistible.

You resisted. Or you died.

The boy stepped forward again; no matter how wobbly his legs or anxious his breathing, no matter how much he wanted to remain still, it was his responsibility now to ensure that all of the pulp had been emptied out, that no stems or leaves were left, and the presser was ready for another load of fruit.

The process would be repeated over and over again, until all the grapes had been stripped from the vines, or the first frost settled on the fruit, whichever occurred first. If the slaves valued their skins, they would win over the weather.

The aroma of crushed grape-flesh tickled his nose as he checked the inside of the crusher. Even as he coughed, he felt something was wrong. It was a pressure like a storm overhead, only stirring in his guts: as when something bad went into the stew and everyone had to use the pits all night.

"Nothing, nothing, you felt nothing" he whispered, barely audible even to his own ears, and stepped back into place. He could feel the presence of the overseer and the Master at his back, although he dared not look to see what they were doing. If the grapes were precious, the steps between harvesting and mustus were even more so. That was the second thing every slave learned at their very first Harvest. The mustus was where the value of the grapes were determined. A good Harvest meant the Master was pleased and the winter would be a good one, with enough rest, and food, and perhaps even a midwinter festive with music, if gleemen traveled through the area. A bad Harvest . . .

There hadn't been a bad Harvest in years. The boy would have made a sign to avert even the thought, except it might have attracted attention.

A downward push of his hand to the aged slave indicated that the barrel was clear, ready for another load, and the cycle started again.

"All the signs are positive," the overseer said, as the slaves went about their work. The two men took no more notice of them than one might of oxen drawing a plow, and the boy began to breathe a little easier. "The fruit has run clear in the first crushings, and there has been no sign of rot in any of the fruit."

The boy risked a glance sideways, to gauge how close to danger he stood. The overseer was a short, square-shouldered man, head shaved and arms tattooed; a former oarsman who had come to the estate by way of a broken and badly set leg and a debt he could not pay off. He was brutal and unflinching, and he was feared more than anything in the vineyard save the Master himself. And the boy was still far, far too close to both of them, and had no way to move without drawing un-wanted notice.

The dryness in his chest moved up into his throat, and there wasn't enough spit in his entire body to keep his tongue from swelling from fear. His bowels were shivering, and his skin felt cold despite the sun's harvest warmth.

"Leave me to do the judging," the Master said, and although it was spoken mildly, the overseer bowed his shaved head to accept the rebuke. The Master was not cruel; in fact, he rarely entered the slaves' world at all, save when he walked the fields to inspect the crop, but he was the spell caster, the winemaker, the master of his fields, and not even a Berengian prince might challenge him without risk. He was the one who bought them from the slavers and they lived—and died—as his fortunes rose or fell. The overseer made sure they knew that—once bought, the price for slacking off was death, because the Master would not keep a lazy slave, and no Vineart wanted a slave trained by another.

"Wait," the Master said suddenly, holding up his hand, and every breathing soul froze. "Let me see a sampling from that crush."

"You, boy!" the overseer called, and the boy started before realizing the call was directed to another. The overseer never called them by name, although he knew them all by sight. "Bring the Master a sampling!"

The slave who had been waiting, crouched off to the side, for just such an order was a tiny thing barely a decade old, and without enough brains to be afraid. It bent a bare knee in obedience, and then ran to fetch the spoon off the wall of the vintnery. The spoon was crafted of purest silver, flat at the bottom with deep sides, and a long handle, and only the Vineart was allowed to touch it to his lips. The slave child wiped its pale hand on its smock, lifted the spoon off the hook with reverence, and then climbed up on a makeshift ladder of two planks set on bricks in order to be able to reach into the vat.

The boy held his breath, watching out of the corner of his eye. The vat, a great wooden barrel, was twice as high and four times as wide as the child, and dipping required perching on the rim and hanging on with one hand. The slave was tiny; there was no reason for the sight of it leaning against the side to fill the boy with a worse fear than even the Master's presence. And yet, a sense of dread filled him as he watched. Moving carefully, the slave child leaned forward and dipped the tasting spoon into the vat of flesh and juice, scooping out a bare mouthful into the silver depression. The dipper wobbled, and the slave child grabbed at the side.

"Sin Washer save us!" a voice cried out, quietly terrified.

The ground underneath was not even, or perhaps the slaves had not cleared the platform properly when the vat was wheeled into place for this harvest, or it might have been merest chance, or the silent gods' ill-wishing that caused the weight of the slave child to tip over the huge wooden cask; it teetered slowly before crashing down with a terrifying, sloshing noise.

"Right it! Right it, damn you!" The overseer strode forward, his short, thick crop slashing out at bodies he deemed not moving quickly enough. "You, and you! Move faster!" The slaves were throwing themselves under the side of the vat, using their bodies in vain to move it back into an upright position. Several others had grabbed containers and were trying to scoop the crushed pulp up off the ground before the valuable liquid soaked into the dry-packed dirt and disappeared.

In the chaos, only two forms stood still. One was the Vineart, his lean form aloof and above the fuss, even as the precious liquid was lost.

The other was the boy, feeling a light spray of moisture mist against his face and neck.

He licked his lips and spat instinctively, terrified that someone might have seen him possibly drink, however unintentionally. Yet he did not race to help save the spilled crush, even as a tingle of it sat on his lips, coated his tongue. He stood off to the side, his damp mouth open as though to speak, his body completely still, his dark gaze riveted on the scene, and did not move.

He *couldn't* move, not to save his own worthless life. His lungs could barely take in air, and the prickling in his legs was forgotten under the onslaught of sensations in his nose and throat. He should be panicking, but his thoughts were oddly calm, focusing on one single fact: there was something missing here, something that should be happening, and wasn't. It made no sense, and yet it *was*. He knew it, as well as he knew the feel of his own skin. Where others were panicking, he felt the desire to laugh.

The overseer noted him standing there like a wooden dolt, and jolted forward, his thickly muscled arm reaching out to grab him, shove him into useful work. The boy felt those fingers start to close on his upper arm, but the Master snapped his fingers and, as though yanked by a chain, the overseer backed off, glaring at the useless slave, but restrained.

The Vineart studied the boy, his eyes hooded and his expression thoughtful, then turned back to watch the attempted cleanup.

The boy barely noticed any of this, other than relief when the overseer backed off. He was too caught up in the attack on his senses, and the odd feel of something missing, to worry about his own safety.

Finally, the vat was righted, and the salvaged mustus returned to the container. It had been no more than a span of moments, but more than half of the liquid was lost forever, soaked into the dirt, the pulp and skins ruined beyond reclamation. The smell hung, tempting and damning, in the afternoon air.

Filled with a terrible rage that colored his face near-blue, the overseer grabbed the offending slave child by the ear and threw it down on its knees before the Master.

"Lord Malech, this worthless piece of shit awaits your judgment."

All of the slaves stopped once again, and watched.

The Vineart stared down at the slave, his long, tapered fingers stroking the fabric of his trousers thoughtfully. The boy, still frozen, staring at the now-righted vat, found his attention drawn away by that small movement. In style, the Master's clothing was not so much different from those of the slaves he owned; pants and a sleeveless tunic. Unlike their cheap, mud-colored garments, however, his were made of fine-woven cloth in a richly dyed crimson, the color of a sunrise, setting off his olive-toned skin. A heavy leather belt was wrapped twice around his hips, buckled with a metal clasp, with two leather bags and a smaller, short-handled version of the silver spoon hanging from it. He wore sturdy low-heeled leather boots on his feet, unlike even the overseer's bare and dirty toes.

"Kill it," the Master said.

No voice protested, not even the slave child; its fate had been sealed the moment the barrel was overturned. To waste, or cause waste . . . The crime was clear, and the punishment well established. The overseer nodded and drew back his whip, bringing it down on the back of the slave's neck with enough force to break it instantly.

The sound of the crack carried into the air, and—unlike the smell of the crushed grapes—dissipated there. The body collapsed, crumpled into something no longer human. Just meat.

Someone let out a long, shuddering sigh, and a sob was quickly muffled.

"Enough!" The overseer turned and glared at the remaining slaves.

"You, toss it into the pit, bury it with the rest of the refuse. The rest of you, back to work! The harvest will not happen on its own!"

There was a rustle of movement as all the slaves rushed to obey his orders, and then Vineart Malech raised a hand once again, a single ring glinting silver on his index finger. Every figure stopped cold, including the overseer. "That one."

All eyes turned to follow the Master's hand.

The boy's heart shriveled and dropped all the way down between his legs when he realized that finger was pointing at him.

"Bring it here," the Vineart continued.

The boy closed his eyes in resignation. He was dead. The Master was never wrong, and the Master never took note but to order death. He clasped his hands together and bent his upper body down, his gaze now on the ground as was appropriate for a slave in disgrace, but otherwise the boy showed no fear. How could one already dead, fear?

The overseer wrapped a hand around the boy's forearm, but he didn't need to drag the slave; he went calmly, almost willingly. There was no purpose to resisting. When he reached the Master's feet, he bent farther into the dirt, placing his forehead on the ground in full surrender.

In his abject pose, he could not see what happened around him. Vineart Malech looked down at him, then flicked his fingers at the overseer, indicating that the rest of the slaves were to be sent on their way. He could hear most of them scurry off, trying to become invisible so that whatever was about to happen would pass them by. A few tried to linger, but a crack of the overseer's stick made them rethink their curiosity.

"You."

"Master." The boy's voice had just broken a few weeks before, and he was embarrassed at the way it wavered on the first syllable, and then steadied in a firm tenor. "Yours is the hand and the will." The ritual words came to him, as the slavers had taught him the first night, reinforcing the lesson with beatings. Once his voice was back under control, the words were flat, neither terrified nor toadying, but merely expressing a response to a query. He had perfected that tone in the years since the slavers had sold him to the House of Malech, but until now he had used it only in response to the overseer, so he did not know if he had it right.

The Vineart apparently found nothing objectionable in the tone or the words, only his action—or lack thereof. "You did nothing to aid the spill."

"No, Master." He saw no reason to lie; the Master had seen him do nothing. He could hear the overseer lifting his stick again, prepared to beat him for his answer, but the Master stayed the blow.

"Why?"

The boy was silent, his body stiffening as though preparing for the inevitable blows to fall. Where a certain death had not shaken him, the question did. What could he answer? How did you speak excuses when you were dead?

"Why, boy?"

The boy bowed his head even lower, but had no answer.

The first blow that landed hit his backside, hard enough to shake his slender body, but still he did not speak.

The second blow moved up to the ribs, hitting under the thin top, and the stick came away bloody. He felt the blood dripping, but did not believe it. Could you still bleed when you were dead? The urge to laugh bubbled up again, and he wondered if he had gone mad.

"Boy?" The Vineart's voice had changed, from cool to curious, as though the slave's resistance had truly piqued his interest. "Why?"

"Master. I do not know why."

The third blow was directly between his shoulder blades and sent the slave sprawling flat on the ground. His body shook, but he did not move from the position, not even to lift his face out of the dirt.

They posed there, the three of them, in a motionless tableau, even as the slaves worked around them, casting frightened yet curious glances over their shoulders. He could practically hear their thoughts: The slave should have been dead by now, and yet wasn't. The Master was not one to hesitate to punish any infraction, any insolence or challenge. Why was the boy slave yet breathing?

Any change in routine was terrifying, even if it involved less violence rather than more. They wanted him dead, to make things right again. He understood. He felt the same.

"You do not know why," the Master said. It was a statement of fact, and so the boy did not respond.

"Do you have a name, boy?"

The question made no sense. Slaves did not have names, not ones the Master would know. Even the overseer was known only by his position, not the name he had arrived with. Nicknames, like Singer, Old Tree, or Fishtail, those were common. A name implied value. A name indicated worth.

It was a question, one asked of him directly. He had to answer it, somehow. The boy lifted his head from the dirt, expecting at any moment to feel another blow, this time on his neck, breaking it.

"Boy?" The Master's patience was clearly wearing thin.

The words seemed to come as though not from his own mouth but from a long distance away, lost and unexpectedly reclaimed. There had been a name once, back when he had a mother and father, and a home that did not smell of sea breeze and grapes, but horse and cold, snow and fire smoke.

"Jerzy, Master." He swallowed, having to force the name out after years of disuse and silence. "My name is Jerzy."

The Vineart nodded, as though this confirmed something he had expected. "What did you feel, Jerzy? When the crush spilled?"

What did he feel? The question again made no sense. "Nothing, Master."

"Nothing."

"Nothing, Master." He dropped back down to the ground, awaiting his punishment. What answer had the Master wanted?

"Ah. No tingle? No desire? No need to run your fingers through the liquid, to feel it touch your skin?" The words were like hooks, trying to pull something out of him.

"I . . . Master, I . . . there is something wrong with it, Master." The words spilled out of him before he even knew what he was going to say. *Idiot*, he thought again, and braced himself for the next blow, expecting it, at last, to be the deadly stroke.

The Vineart's expression didn't change, but he nodded once again, as though finally satisfied.

"Come with me. *Now*, Jerzy."

The Vineart turned and walked away, toward the taller stone building behind the vintnery that housed the Master's living quarters. The House of Malech. Forbidden territory to even approach, for a slave. The overseer aimed a kick at the slave in order to get him moving, but the boy rolled and was on his feet, nimbly avoiding the blow. The paralysis that had held him earlier was gone, and his entire body felt alive again. He was alive. He wanted, very much, to remain that way.

His face still averted, his shoulders hunched from years of habit, the slave followed his master away from the harvest and everything that had, until then, been his life.

The overseer's whipstick cracked in the air behind them, and his low growl sounded over it: the boy flinched, even though it was not aimed at him. "Back to work, you worthless bits of flesh! The sun's still up and there's fruit to be taken in! Stop wasting the Master's time!"

The boy, following blindly, almost mindlessly, felt the dry soil under his feet give way to sun-warmed paving stones, and then to the rougher cobble of the wide pathway separating vintnery from the Master's own building. He paused, risking one last glimpse over his shoulder. Already the vintnery seemed impossibly far away, the vineyard and sleep house farther yet. He felt no regret, no sense of loss to be leaving it behind. And yet, something made him stop.

Before the sleep house and the fields, there had been only the slavers' caravan. Weeks filled with endless hours of walking, of traveling from one market to another, praying to be chosen, to be overlooked, to die, to survive.

"Are you coming?" the Master asked, still in that same dry, incurious voice. "Or do you wish to stay in the fields?"

The vintnery was safe, in its own way. For the past however many years he could remember, it had been his home. But no, he didn't want to stay there.

Head bowed, the boy followed his master across the pathway, under the green arches of the entrance proper, and into the House of Malech.

Chapter 2

*T*hose few steps, and forbidden territory was suddenly, immediately, real. The path was smoother underfoot than the cobbled road, and up close, the boy could see that the green arch he walked under was made of vines similar to those growing in the fields, palm-sized leaves twined over a frame so thickly the wood could not be seen underneath. Unlike those growing in the fields, there were no grapes hanging from these stems, and the greenery seemed to rustle as he passed underneath, although he could no longer feel the breeze on his skin. Crossing those cobblestones, he might as well have entered a different land entirely.

Something tickled the back of his neck as he walked under the archway; that nonexistent breeze touching his sweat-damp skin like curious fingers, and he almost shuddered. Not unpleasant, exactly, but unexpected. Unexpected rarely meant good news, and his nerves were already twitching. Not for the first time he felt sympathy for how the rabbit felt when the tarn passed overhead.

There was no time to linger on that, or to gawk at the line of plants, twice his height and heavy with fragrant, dark red flowers lining the path, because the house—the House of Malech—demanded his attention. A tall stone façade, the same golden color as the path, was set atop a slight rise, with narrow windows glittering with colored glass on either side of the entrance. It was even more impressive—terrifying— up close. If a building could speak, he thought, this one would sneer at a slave coming so close to its walls.

Slowly he forced the nerves away and noticed that the great polished wooden doors were open, standing ajar as though they never needed to be closed against night or theft or weather. Maybe, the boy thought, they didn't. Not even a winter storm would dare enter such a grand structure without permission. He wasn't sure he should enter, either, but the Master went inside, not pausing to check on the slave behind him. Torn between uncertainty and the Master's certain anger if he fell behind, the boy followed.

The doorway did not strike him down when he crossed through it. Once inside the entrance he had to stop, completely overwhelmed. The hallway inside was more than three times the Master's height, and large enough for a handcart to travel through without scraping the walls. Those great narrow windows let in colored sunlight, sparkling off a gleaming, pale brown stone floor. What words he had failed him utterly, and he gaped like a fish.

"It's just a building, boy."

The Master's voice made him blink, and his jaw slowly closed as he looked around, trying to find something more reasonable to focus on. He looked at the Vineart, the tall, lean form somehow less terrifying here, but had to look away again quickly, for fear of being trapped by the Master's too-bright gaze. All he caught was the impression of a long, lean face, framed at one end by graying hair and at the other by a pointed beard of the same gray-brown.

The hallway was not any easier to comprehend. On either side of him, plastered walls were covered by richly colored tapestries depicting scenes of vineyards, while directly in front of him was a wide staircase made of polished golden wood, rising up to a second level and a smaller wooden door, this one closed. The door was easier to look at. A closed door he could understand.

Having determined that his slave wasn't going to pass out in shock, Master Malech turned around as though searching for something himself.

"Detta! Detta, attend me!"

The Master, the boy thought, startled, had a set of lungs you wouldn't expect, looking at him. Tall and slender, like he had been half starved and never quite made up the difference, and yet his call to the unseen Detta filled the entryway and echoed up the stairs as if it came from the chest of a much larger man. His voice sounded different here, too, although the boy couldn't say how or why.

The summons was quickly answered, as a woman came out from behind the stairs, wiping her hands on an apron tied around her midsection. The boy left off staring at his surroundings, and stared at her instead. If the Master was narrow, this was the roundest woman he had ever seen. Her face was round, her hips were round, even her eyes were round, and got even rounder as she noticed him standing there, a few paces behind the Master. He was still uncertain if he was truly meant to enter the building or if this was some strange test he was about to fail and finally be punished for his insolence.

"A new one?" she asked, but didn't wait for an answer. "It will be needing a bath, then. A solid scrubbing, if I remember rightly. Why you don't just throw them in the river before you bring them in; it would be much the same to them."

"Detta." The Master's voice was quieter now, again with a tone to it the boy didn't quite understand. A slave who spoke so to the Master . . . It was incomprehensible, impossible. And yet this Detta stood there with her hands on her rounded hips, her graying curls swaying as she shook her head and contradicted the Master without any fear whatsoever. Even when he thought he was dead, he would never have dared speak that way, or to look the Master straight in the eye like that.

Whoever this Detta was, she clearly was no slave and therefore had standing far above his own. He ducked his gaze back down to the stone floor, before he was caught and punished for that as well. So many things he didn't understand, rules he didn't know. He reminded himself that he should already be dead; what more could happen?

The woman made a disapproving noise. "At least the hair on this one's short, less chance of anything hiding in there. All right, come on then, you. I don't bite, although I will slap you if you cross me." She made a gesture, catching the boy's gaze. "Come forward then, what's your name?"

"Jerzy, mistress." Saying it the second time was no easier than the first, but at least his voice didn't crack this time.

"Well then, come along, Jerzy. I'll have the managing of you, for now."

"Master?" He wasn't going anywhere without permission, if not a direct order.

"Go with Detta, boy. She's quite right; you stink, and I doubt you've cleaned some of those crevices since you were a babe in arms."

The boy didn't understand what the Master meant, but he knew an order when he heard one. Bowing his head in obedience, he followed the woman Detta when she turned and went back under the stairs.

The arched doorway she disappeared through wasn't visible from the main entrance, but once he walked through it, another world opened up before him. Where the hallway was grand and slick, the hall he was in now was far homier, almost comfortable, and he was able to breathe more easily, without fearing he might accidentally touch something and ruin it. White-daub walls and reddish-brown clay tiles on the floor echoed the sound of Detta's steps back at them, and made him aware for the first time of his bare feet, coated with dust and juice. His toes wiggled against the cool tile, and he opened his mouth to ask a question, but Detta kept walking ahead of him, and his courage failed.

"Mistress?" he ventured finally.

"Detta," she said. "Just Detta. I'm no mistress of anything, save this household, and there's no need for titles for that, not for one such as you."

More words he didn't understand, but had to obey, somehow.

"Detta." He was just trying the sound of the word out now, not trying for her attention. She seemed to understand that, nodding in approval and walking through another arched doorway.

This one led to a large room, still with white-daub walls, but lined with plain wooden benches around a great table, light coming in through tall, narrow windows on the far wall. The clean and bright lines of it, so different from the large but dark sleep house, made him forget the question he'd meant to ask.

"This is the meal hall," Detta said. "If you're not dining with the Master in his study or the workroom, you'll take meals here with the rest of us—we're not grand enough to warrant a second hall."

Dining with the Master? The boy decided at this point that they were all mad and any moment someone would strike him for daring to be here at all, but until then there was nothing to do but play along.

And then they were through that room, into a space that was filled with noise, heat, and bodies, a huge table at the center, and a massive fireplace against the far wall.

"Roan, Geordie, you useless sacks, mind the spits! And you, Lil, I know those breads should be ready for the oven by now, if you weren't slacking. Must I stand over you every breath you take, make sure you don't choke on your own air?"

None of the workers did more than roll their eyes at Detta's shout, their work continuing at the same busy pace. This, at least, was familiar to the boy, even if the surroundings were strange. A kitchen was a kitchen, no matter how grand.

"Lil, I'll need hot water, and much of it. Soap, two cakes from the look of him, and . . ." Detta stopped and touched a finger to the boy's chin. "No shears for this one, and no razor. I doubt it's old enough to shave regularly yet."

He was, barely, but a sharp-edged rock had taken the growth off a few days before, and it hadn't grown back yet. The overseer did not like slaves with body hair that might be hiding lice or other parasites. It seemed Detta felt the same. Geordie was not only clean shaven, but had a shaved pate as well, and both of the girls had their hair cut short and tied back with red cloths around their heads.

There were no females among the vineyard slaves, but Jerzy often saw local girls walking along the roadway, going to and from market with their baskets and barrows, and the Players often had women in their troop, although no slave came close enough to do more than note their gender. Closer, the cook who worked the sleep-house kitchen had two young daughters who were kept under their father's watchful eye. Their laughter while they played sometimes triggered a faint memory, almost a dream, of a woman with dark eyes, and a younger girl child who cried silently, but he could not name them, and after a few years he stopped trying to remember.

"Tub's still set up from last night," the girl at the spit, Roan, said. "And a kettle's just been to boil. We'll have him scalded nice and pretty before he knows what's what." She smiled at him, and the boy blinked at her in confusion. He was to be scalded? There was too much new, too much out of his experience, and he was lost.

"Bet it's never had a bath before," Geordie, the other slave at the spit, said. A taller boy, dark skinned and dark eyed, his red cloth tied around his neck, his expression wasn't as friendly as the girl's.

"You hadn't, either, when you came here," the girl said, tossing her head so that her short cap of dark brown hair rose and fell like a sparrow's wing. "And you smelled."

"I did not."

"Like a cess pot," the girl replied. "I thought I'd die of the stink."

"I'll have Michel bring out the water," the other slave—Lil—said, ignoring the two spatting, even as they turned the spit, roasting a great slab of meat over the fire. She was pale as the stone, from hair to skin, and taller than any girl he had ever seen before. "And clothing?"

"Not for now. Let's see how things go before we know where he goes."

Lil raised pale eyebrows at that. "It's not sealed?"

"Master just plucked him from the field. Bath first, then the testing."

The boy breathed a little easier, knowing for the first time what was happening, if not why. There were always tests, to see what you knew, what you could learn. It was like being assigned a new task as he had been this morning; they would tell him what he had to do soon enough. But first . . .

"Detta?" He had to ask. "What do you mean, bath?"

"No!"

"Stop being such a baby and get in."

"No."

"Jerzy. In. Now."

The boy stared at the wooden tub, half as large as a wine cask and filled to the brim with steaming hot water, and considered balking again. A stream, yes. Standing under the rain with a handful of soap-weed, that was natural. This . . . was . . . unnatural. You cooked with hot water, you didn't wash in it!

But Detta stood behind him, her arms folded across her ample chest, and he had the bad feeling that if he refused, she would have no hesitation about throwing him in headfirst.

"You've nothing I haven't seen before and I doubt I'll be impressed now, boy child."

Her voice, more than her words, convinced him. Stripping off his tunic and pants, he dropped them on the floor of the small room and lifted his leg to cautiously step over the edge of the tub.

The water steamed around his leg, but didn't burn. In fact, it felt . . . good.

"There, now you know you won't die of it. All the way in."

Since the alternative was to stand, naked, in a room that wasn't as warm as it had seemed when he was clothed, the boy got all the way in.

"Now sit down, Jerzy."

Sit? He looked down dubiously at the water, then back at Detta.

"Sit!"

He sat. There was a low bench in the tub he hadn't noticed before, just long enough to rest his buttocks on. It was surprisingly smooth, as though hundreds of backsides had been seated there before and worn the wood down. Water came up to his ribs, and he felt a pleasant warmth soak into him.

Then something rough and prickly hit him on the back, where the overseer's whip had landed, and he yelped as much in shock as pain.

"Hush, boy. Those marks need to be cleaned else they'll fester, with the layers of dirt you've been rolling in, and I don't trust you to do it yourself."

Detta had a scrub brush in one hand, a bar of something white in the other, and was working his skin as though it were the inside of the crushing vat the day after Harvest.

"You'll take my skin off!" he protested, even as she grabbed his shoulder and pushed him forward to get a better angle.

"Then you'll grow a new layer, and it will be a sight cleaner than this one," she retorted. "Hold still, and we'll be done sooner than not."

But no sooner had she finished with his back than she started on his front, making him raise his arms and lift his legs so she could make sure pits and feet were clean. The boy submitted, knowing by now that he had no choice.

"Right, then. Almost done."

He lifted his head at that, barely daring to hope, and a bucket of more steaming water was dumped over his face, getting in his mouth and eyes and making him splutter.

"Once more, and be thankful your hair's short, else we'd have to wash it, and cut it, too."

Warned, he closed his eyes and shut his mouth, and the second bucket of water cascaded off his face and down into the tub without further insult.

"There you are. All done. Up and into the towel, then."

He stood up, and Detta wrapped him in a length of cloth. Some vestige of memory moved within him, and he stepped out of the tub on his own, rubbing down his skin until he was dry.

A glance back at the tub stopped him mid-rub. The water that had been steaming clear when he got in was now the color of the river's side pools after a bad storm, reddish-brown and murky.

"Told you you were filthy, my boy," Detta said, seeing where his gaze had gone. "All that, off your skin. Want to see what you look like now?" She didn't wait for an answer, but took hold of his bare shoulder and directed him across the chamber. "There you go."

Something glittered on the wall, like still water in winter, and the boy stared into it.

A boy stared back.

"Haven't seen yourself in a while, have you, my boy?" For the first time, Detta's voice was gentle. "That's you, yes. That's Jerzy."

"Jerzy."

The name was easier to say now. The name belonged to the dark-eyed, pale-skinned figure he saw in the mirror: naked, scarred ribs and protruding ears and dark red strands sticking wetly to his skull.

"It used to be brighter," he said.

"What?"

"My hair. It used to be . . . brighter." It was a memory, a scarce scrap of one: himself, much younger, a shining cap of curls on his head that a much larger hand tousled with affection . . . red, like a fox's summer pelt. Fox-fur. His sleep-house nickname made sense now.

"You get older, it darkens," Detta said. "Likely, you make it to adult, it will be dark like a paarten's pelt, and attract women the same way, all wanting to pet it." She stepped back and examined him critically. "You're older than I thought. Fourteen? Maybe. Doubt you even know. We need to put some meat on those bones first, to see how you'll turn out. Go on with you, get dressed. Sooner you're tested, sooner we know what to do with you."

Those words blurred the image of the younger boy and brought him back to the reality of his situation: naked and shivering in a room he shouldn't be in, facing . . . what? A test. He longed to ask about it, but knew better. Detta might seem kind, but he didn't know how far that might go. The wrong question and she might turn on him. The wrong answer and he might be back out in the dirt of the field, the crowded stink of the sleep house.

He didn't want to go back there. Not now. Not ever. In the brief span of a bath, everything had been turned upside down, inside out, and changed. He would do anything to stay here.

His tunic and pants were folded neatly on a small wooden stool the same polished sheen as the doors and floors. While he was bathed, someone had taken his clothing away and . . . done something to it. The tunic was still stained and the pants worn at the knee and backside, but they felt . . . cleaner somehow. He slid them on and discovered that the old, knotted lacing of the pants had been replaced with a new cord.

That one small thing made a lump rise in his throat, hurting when he swallowed, and he didn't know why.

He finished dressing without a word, and then turned to where Detta was waiting.

"Maybe you'll do" was all she said. "Master will decide."

He followed her out of the room, his scrubbed feet newly sensitive to the cool texture of the floor. This time they did not walk through the kitchen, but out a different door into a courtyard, open to the sky. There was a small fruit tree at the center of it, and a small stone well off to the side, but Detta led him past without a chance to look more closely, through another door at the other end, and they were through into another part of the building.

The floor underneath here was not stone, but polished wood, smooth and warm underfoot, and the walls were not white daub but a smoother, creamier texture, almost like clay. He felt the urge to touch it, but dared not. His skin might be bathed, but he was still afraid he might leave a mark, a smudge of slave on the clean surface.

They were in a small square room with three doors, all closed, plus the open doorway they had come through. Two of the doors had metal handles on them, the third did not. Tall yellow candles were placed in metal holders on the wall. They were thinner than the ones used in the sleep house, but with the same steady flicker that lit the way almost as well as sunlight. The familiarity soothed him momentarily.

"On you go, then," Detta said, pointing at the door without the handle. "Inside. The Master's waiting."

She was new, unknown and therefore dangerous, but he wanted her to come with him. Wanted it the way he couldn't remember ever wanting anything before, with a hunger that scared him.

He didn't say anything to her, didn't even look at her, just walked forward and reached out to push the door in.

It moved before he could touch it, swinging open in soundless invitation.

He stepped in, and it closed behind him.

"Good luck, boy," he heard a faint whisper, and then forgot all about it, staring in astonishment at the vision in front of him.

Bottles. Dozens of rare glass bottles, green and brown, racked in wooden frames taller than he was, wall to wall, each bottle bearing a small tag hung around its neck.

The wealth of the House of Malech, there in front of him.

The temptation was too great; he could no more resist than he could stop his own blood from flowing. He stepped forward, stopped, and then moved forward again, drawn to one wall in particular. His arm reached out, unworthy hands touching the wooden frame, not quite yet daring to touch the bottles directly.

Wine. Crafted wine. *Spellwine.*

"Sin Washer be gentle," he whispered, and let his fingertips graze the cool glass neck of one bottle. It was smooth, smoother than anything he had ever touched, smooth and rough at the same time, and the skin under his nails tingled at the contact.

"You dare, slave?"

He jerked back so hard his arm spasmed, and his bowels clenched in fear that he had disturbed the bottle, but he didn't dare even look at it to make sure it remained intact. He fell to his knees and cast his gaze down on the floor, not even bothering to beg for forgiveness.

And yet, a dangerous thought crept into his mind. The Master—Vineart Malech—had ordered him to be brought here. The Vineart had put him in front of temptation. If the Vineart would then have him punished for it, that was his master's right over a slave he owned . . . but it was unfair!

"You think you are worthy to be in the same room as my work? To look upon a decade of crafting—to *touch* the bottling of my genius?"

Years of training took over, and it was as though the Master's voice filled the room, filled his head until there was no room for his own thoughts, no thought save obedience and unworthiness. He bent his face to the floor and cowered, waiting for the fatal blow.

"Stand up, slave!"

The boy stood up, wishing for his dirt back, to look like every other slave, to be back in the field where there was a chance to remain unnoticed, unobserved. Unpunished. He had never heard of a slave being taken into the Master's home. He had never heard of any coming out, either.

"Why are you here?" that harsh voice demanded, like one of the silent gods suddenly taking an interest in mankind again.

The boy trembled, speechless. Was this the test Detta had spoken of, to answer the unanswerable? Was the Master Vineart insane? No. Impossible. There was a reason to all this, some reason he was too insignificant to understand. A game, maybe, the Master played to amuse himself. But he did not know the rules, could not play . . .

Once before he had played a game he did not understand, had trusted another, and it had landed him in a slaver's cart, carried off, stripped of who he had been, sold into the endless cycle of planting, waiting, and Harvest.

The Vineart had broken that cycle. Why? He could feel the strain of trying to chase down every thought, and forced them into some sort of order.

"Do you not have a tongue, slave? Was it washed away with your grime?" A shove accompanied the question, a rough hand on his shoulder that rocked the boy back and almost made him lift his gaze. Another slave touching him like that would be cause for violence. He stifled the urge, and merely absorbed the blow.

Another came, this one harder. "No spine, to go with the lack of tongue? Is this what I raise in my fields, useless lumps of flesh? Useless lumps that come into my home, covet my wine?"

The boy didn't understand, but the anger in his master's voice made him angry as well.

"No wonder your parents sold you. If this was the best they could do, I pray they produced no more after you! Useless even as a slave."

The boy shuddered, his skin practically rippling with the effort of remaining still and silent, and all control of thought and temper fled.

"Look at me, boy!"

A direct command, and he raised his head to stare up at the Vineart, looking at him squarely for the first time, fear and anger evenly matched. The dead have nothing left to lose.

He glared into a narrow face, olive-toned skin framed by long graying hair swept back at his neck. A mouth that was thin and stern, chin covered with a sparse, pointed beard, nose scarred across the bridge as though it had taken one blow too many, years ago. The boy hesitated, and then let his gaze lift higher, into the Master's eyes.

Cold and blue, staring directly down into the boy's soul as though he were Sin Washer come back from the heavens to judge them all.

Another shove, this one actually pushing the boy back down, and he fell on his backside with a solid, painful crash. The Vineart sneered. "Nothing there but flesh. No tongue, no spine, no brain. I wasted water, cleaning you up."

"Then why did you? Why ask my name, bring me here, dunk me in water, clean my clothes? Why did you do any of it? Why not just leave me in the field where I belonged? Why show me all . . . all this?"

The words fell out of him, without thought or hesitation. Jerzy's voice cracked, and he didn't care. He just wanted an answer, for once, before whatever fate the Master determined fell on him.

"Ah."

That one sound was so filled with emotion, the boy wasn't sure he had actually heard it.

He wasn't dead, though. Slowly, Jerzy began to understand that. The overseer had not broken his neck. The Vineart had not struck him dead with magic for his effrontery, for his insolence. Risking greatly—and risking nothing at all, at this point—the boy stood up, and looked again at the man in front of him.

"What is your name, boy?" the Vineart asked again.

"Jerzy." It came almost easily this time, the memory of the boy-who-had-been, the boy of shining red hair and clean limbs ghosting faintly in his brain.

His master smiled, and like that, that simply, his eyes transformed from ice into sunlight, not warm but clear and welcoming. "I am pleased to see you yet live, Jerzy. I was worried there, for a moment."

Utterly baffled, Jerzy could only stare as the Vineart turned away from him, walking over to the wall of bottles and selecting one. The others disappeared, as though by . . . magic. Had they ever truly been there at all? No, they must have. He had touched one!

"Have you ever tasted *vina*, the wine of those grapes you have spent years picking and crushing?"

The open-jawed gape of before was back, all other thoughts forgotten. The Master was insane. There was no other explanation. Slaves did not drink wine, slaves did not taste grapes. Slaves did not *dare*.

"No, Master." But the memory of the spray on his lips just hours before made him hesitate, and the Vineart noticed it.

"Hrm." Two simple clay goblets waited on a low wooden table, off to the side. The Vineart uncorked the bottle and poured out a small dose of pale red liquid into each bowl.

Jerzy's hand twitched, as though it meant to reach out and take one goblet. He stifled the motion, and prayed it had gone unnoticed.

"Take one."

A command, for all that it was gently spoken. Was this the moment, then? Some game the Master played, to bring him all the way to this and then . . .

His imagination failed. He couldn't think of what might happen then. So he took the left-hand glass and stepped back out of easy reach.

"Excellent. Why did you take that one?"

"I . . . don't know." He looked down at the goblet in his hand, the way the liquid shimmered and moved when he tilted the bowl. "There's something about it . . . but they came from the same bottle. They should be the same."

"But they aren't?"

"No." Jerzy waited, but the Master was better at it. Nervous, but not knowing what else to do, Jerzy lifted the rim of the goblet to his lips. But rather than sipping, he sniffed, letting the smell rise into his nostrils.

Warm berries and a hint of spice. A tang of something he didn't recognize, sharp and bitter, but not unpleasant, promising warmth and pleasure. Another whiff, and something in his blood stirred, making him breathe faster, and his skin begin to sweat. He couldn't know what he knew, and yet he *knew*.

"There's something in this . . . it's spellwine." Not juice, not even mustus. Spellwine. His voice barely contained the awe he felt, and his hand shook so hard that the Vineart stepped forward quickly to lift the goblet from him before he dropped it. But there was no condemnation, no anger in his voice when he asked the next question.

"And the other one?"

Jerzy reached out and took the other offering, and dipped his nose to the surface. Berries again, and spice, yes, like the cooks put in porridge, but this time the sharpness was quickly overlaid by an almost ordinary sweetness. He mourned the loss of the sharpness, and was repulsed by the sweeter odor, although it was not an unpleasant smell, of itself. A second sniff, but the feeling of movement within him did not return.

"It's not the same. It's . . . not spellwine?" But they had come from the same bottle; he had seen the Master pour it directly. "Something in the bowl. The sweetness. There is something blocking it. Blocking the magic."

He hadn't known anything could do that. He didn't know anything . . . but he knew this.

The Vineart smiled. "Congratulations, young Jerzy. You passed."

"Passed what, Master?" At this point, he was so confused, so turned around and exhausted by all that had been thrown at him, intoxicated by the mere smell of the spellwine, Jerzy didn't care about anything but getting an answer. "What is all this for?"

"For you," Master Malech said, looking down into the first goblet thoughtfully. For the first time Jerzy noticed a mark on the back of the Master's hand; a dark red drop, almost invisible against the olive of his skin, as though something had burned him there, years before, and long scabbed and healed.

The Master noticed where his attention lay and, with his free hand, he reached out and lifted Jerzy's left hand, turning it so that the boy's own palm lay exposed to view.

Jerzy stared at it like a new discovery; with the accumulated grime washed out of the crevices and out from under his nails, the skin looked pink and defenseless. "My twenty-third year," Master Malech said thoughtfully, touching the bright red mark on that newly washed wrist. "A surprisingly difficult vintage, that. I only bought two new slaves, I remember, although we needed seven."

Jerzy stared at the mark as well. He had almost forgotten.

A hustle from the slave-pen, given bare moments to take whatever belongings they cherished. He had only one, a now-ragged scrap that had once been a tasseled scarf. He wrapped it around his wrist and allowed the slaver to shove him back out again. The large tent they came to was overbright, and too warmly heated, and he started to sweat immediately.

The slaver presented him to the man: tall and lean, his face in shadow despite the lamps. Unlike the slavers, who smelled of sweat and tallow—familiar, comforting smells—this stranger reeked of something harder, sharper. The slave sniffed the air without thought, trying to identify the aroma.

The stranger laughed. "Yes, yes. He will do."

A slaver grabbed his shoulders, forcing his left arm forward, and the boy tensed even as the stranger sipped from a silver cup, watching him. The stranger nodded once, and the slaver unwrapped the scrap and let it drop to the floor. The boy didn't have time to mourn the loss before the stranger leaned forward and spat onto the boy's upturned hand. The slaver, no stranger to this process, held him still even as the boy screamed while the liquid etched into his skin. . . .

"And now, as grapes are pressed into wine, we press this slave into something greater," the Master said, almost to himself, letting go of the boy's wrist. "You knew the grapes in the crush were weak. You sensed the difference between the pours, and were able to think it through to determine why. And you have not allowed servitude in the fields, or the scorn and abuse of the overseer, to break your spirit. Magic, knowledge, and strength. Those are the three things that are needed. Three things that cannot be taught, only learned. The three things a slave must show, in order to become my student."

This time Jerzy did drop the goblet. It slipped from his suddenly numb fingers, and dropped a handspan toward the floor. . . .

And stopped there, caught by a simple lift of the Master's finger, with not a drop of the wine inside disturbed. Jerzy's breath caught. How had the Master done that? There had been no spellwine poured, no decantation . . . Jerzy had never seen magic *worked*, but the stories all said that it needed both spellwine and decantation in order to happen!

"It may not be spellwine any longer," Master Malech said mildly, not remarking on the boy's shock. "But it's still an excellent vintage. It would be a shame to waste it."

Jerzy, his hand shaking, retrieved the goblet and lifted it to his mouth, waiting until his master lifted the first cup in a salute and took a sip himself before allowing the liquid to touch his tongue.

It was . . . Jerzy had no words for it. Sharp and bitter, full and sweet, tingling on his tongue and making his mouth water. A smell like the flowers outside, the dampness of an old barrel, and the crack of air before a storm . . .

"Relax," his master said. His voice was stern but his eyes were gentle over that narrow nose, not cruel or cold at all. "There will be time for you to learn what you are tasting. For now, simply enjoy."

Jerzy nodded and took another sip, this time letting the liquid rest on his tongue and then swallowing the mouthful without trying to understand it. The bitter and the sweet melded, and he felt the still-tense muscles in his back begin to relax.

None of this could be real. He would open his eyes and still be in the slaves' sleep house, old Wax snoring in the bunk above him, the day-chime about to ring and another day in the field about to begin . . .

"It's real," Master Malech said, and Jerzy wasn't surprised that his master knew exactly what he was thinking. "Some confusion is normal, but it will fade, and soon you will not be able to remember living any other way. That is how it always is. Come. Let me show you where you will sleep, from now on. Perhaps that will help."

Jerzy nodded, put his goblet back down on the table with a twinge of regret, and followed his master out of the tasting room. The wine alone could not be to blame for the confusion buzzing in his head; if the Master said he could make things make sense again, Jerzy would follow him anywhere.

Chapter 3

alech, Master Vineart of the House of Malech, citizen of The Berengia, was amused. Harvest was a stress-laden, dawn-to-midnight affair, and when he woke that morning, he had not expected to spend half of the day away from his vines, or to enjoy the experience quite so much. But life, he had found, had a way of surprising even the most jaded and weary of Vinearts.

"This is . . . mine?"

The boy had a look of stunned wonder in his eyes, looking around the sparse bedchamber as though it were a palace. Malech did not allow the smile he felt to escape, but remembering other such looks over the years, all the way back to his own, gave him a sense of real pleasure.

"Yours, yes." Despite his emotions, his voice was dry, as befitted a master. He still owned the boy—Jerzy—but differently from before. Now it was not possession of body, but of soul, and desire.

The room he had brought the boy to was in the upper level of the House, above his own study, with a single window that looked out—by design—over the vineyards. Jerzy could not see the sleep house from there, nothing that might be a reminder of his previous life except the grapes growing into the distance. The floor was bare, the bed narrow, the single cabinet barely large enough for three changes of clothing, but as the boy possessed only the clothes he stood in—and Malech had no doubt but that Detta would burn them immediately—it would be more than enough room for now.

And from Malech's own distant memories of the sleep house, the large room no doubt seemed enormous to the boy.

"And I am to study with you. I'm to be your student." Jerzy sat on the narrow bed, making the frame squeak. His bare feet rested on the polished wooden floor, and Malech made a mental note to have an old rug brought in before the winter. It had been too many years since anyone had occupied this room, and he'd barely had time to have someone sweep it out after Jerzy passed the first test.

"Yes." He had explained it to the boy already, but it would take some time—perhaps even weeks—for the reality to settle in.

Vinearts did not appear full-blown from the earth, after all. It was an ironic gift from Sin Washer: generations of trial and error had proven that only the deprivations of slavery, the removal of all family ties and comforts, pushed a man to the point where magic would surface. Even now, he could not coddle the boy, or risk ruining him. The skills were inherent and easily proven by the first test, but the refining of them required a combination of elements. . . . Like the grapes themselves, a Vineart must be stressed to produce the finest results, grown in poor soil and subjected to the elements in order to shine.

Someday he would explain that to the boy and set him on his own course, to acquire and scour his own slave population for the ones he in turn would train, to carry on their tradition. But that day was years to come, assuming the boy survived. For now, they would begin as always.

"Detta will be in soon to measure you for new clothing. In the meanwhile, the harvest requires my attention. I will see you again at the evening meal, which is at tenth chime."

Not allowing the boy to ask further questions, he exited the room, closing the door firmly behind him. This floor held the sleeping quarters for his household—Detta and now Jerzy on this side, and the four kitchen children on the other, over the kitchen itself. There was also old Per, who cared for the grounds around the House, but the man was a bit strange and refused housing, preferring to sleep in his carefully tended hedges in all but the worst storm-weather. You never saw him, only the results of his work. Malech smiled ruefully; would that more of the world could function that way.

The main floor held the living areas: the kitchen and dining areas, the laundry, and his own quarters, his sleeping chamber and the study where he met the few and far between visitors of importance who came to the vintnery. Such an arrangement would not work in the cities, where persons of importance required more privacy, but here, on his own lands, the matter of concern was not privacy but protection.

The balance of power had not shifted in his lifetime, but Malech preferred caution in all things. The Berengia, his adoptive home, was not the oldest of the Lands Vin, nor the most fertile, but the spellwines it produced always found an eager market, and that gave its Vinearts greater leeway when dealing with secular powers.

Malech was not a superstitious man, and the silent gods had not spoken since the Breaking of the First Vine, but he often gave thanks that the five princelings of The Berengia were jealous of their independence, and suspicious of one another. Because they constantly warred on one another, Malech—the sole Master Vineart within their borders—was too valuable to offend and so did not have to worry about making accommodations or agreements. The price was that he himself had no ally to call upon, should anyone be fool enough to challenge him.

So far, that had never been an issue, but simply because no one ever had challenged did not mean no one ever would. His quarters were on the main floor not because they were finer, but the better to protect the rest of the House in case of attack. It was no matter of heroism, or sacrifice: those who lived here belonged to him, and he in turn belonged to them, service for service.

He paused at the main floor, hearing the reassuring clatter and voices from the kitchen, and then went on. The grapes were harvested and crushed in the shadow of the vintnery, where the vinification tanks were stored. It was there the mustus waited during the trial period, when the potential of each vat was determined, their fate decided. The true work of the House, though, took place out of sight, in the cool, stone-walled rooms below his study. It was there Malech went now, passing easily through a door that could not be seen unless you already knew it was there, down stone steps to a long passageway.

The workrooms were down here, the cellars where he tasted and blended, perfecting the steps that turned mustus into spellwine, where he stored those most potent bottles, the most dangerous spells. The House that was visible from the ground was barely half the property—while the main cellar opened to the side of the House, to allow for the casks and vats to be brought in and out, there was much more, hidden from the outside by both construction and magic. Jerzy would learn all those rooms and hallways, eventually. But there was one spell active in this level that no student, no matter how trusted, ever gained access to. The Guardian.

Greetings, Master Malech.

The dragon over the last doorway was the only other being who could move freely through every structure on the property, and none save Malech could command it. Carved from the dark gray stones of The Berengian hills, The Guardian had no taste and no sense of humor, but it was polite, if stiffly formal, and thoroughly loyal. Every few years the Vineart thought about carving a new guardian out of a more pliable stone, to make it more of a companion, but there was no real need, and therefore no time.

"Greetings, Guardian," he said in response. "What occurs in my absence?"

Little. The stone dragon uncurled itself from the arch over the doorway to the cellar, where it waited when not needed and followed him in. The size of a small dog, the fact that its wings moved up and down was merely a conceit of the dragon itself. *The slaves work without too much gossip, the weather holds fair for the rest of the five-day, and a message* *arrived this morning asking for a shipment of blood staunch.* It cocked its head and tilted its muzzle into the air. *We will need more, soon.*

The spell that gave the Guardian awareness—bought at immense cost many years before from the one Master Vineart capable of crafting it—did not also give it the ability to foresee the future, yet it often saw connections in things that Malech did not, and the Vineart had learned to trust its predictions.

"If I make more, something will be less," he said, but nonetheless made note of it. "The slaves do not speak of their missing companion?"

The dragon merely gazed at him with blind stone eyes. The dead slave was already forgotten, and while Jerzy's mysterious survival might cause some to wonder, by the next morning even that would fade. Even the dragon, who knew nothing of blood and flesh, knew this. Slaves lived day-to-day. Memory was the privilege and curse of free men.

"Who ordered the blood staunch?" Not that he cared particularly what princeling warred on another, and Detta would handle the sale, as always, but it behooved him to pay attention. Human nature's urge to spar and slaughter—and their resulting need of his healwines—was what made him wealthy, and the House of Malech so powerful.

Atakus.

That did make him pause. The island-nation of Atakus was better known for defensive stances than aggressive ones, and was almost obsessive about keeping their reliance on other Vinearts—indeed, anyone not of their island principality—limited. They could not grow healwines, however, and so were forced to import those spells. "Has anything happened there recently I should know about?"

There is no news out of Atakus, save that Vineart Jaban sent a negotiator *to Atakus two weeks ago.*

"His reason? The negotiator's mission?"

The dragon did not answer, meaning that it did not know. In truth, it was no matter to Malech: when Sin Washer broke the Vine, shattering the First Growth into the five elements of earth, water, fire, flesh, and aether, he wasted his divine breath commanding the inheritors of the prince-mages to stay off the seats of power. The Washers had a bag of fables and stories to explain it, but Malech saw it as simple practicality. The grapes of one region crafted a specific sort of spellwine, and another region produced something else, and it was near impossible to learn how to craft more than a handful, and even that required a Master's skill. It was for that reason more than any demigod's orders that Vinearts kept themselves busy in the yards, and out of the seemingly never-ending politics of the city rulers and the nobility.

Too, Vinearts did not feel the same sort of loyalty to a city or region other folk might: the slaver caravans traveled widely, and slaves might be bought anywhere, so it was rare for a Vineart to end up near the place of his birth. Somehow they almost always found themselves in the region where they were best suited, with the vines that fit their skills, when their years of study were done.

As though by magic, Malech thought, and almost laughed.

"No matter," he said out loud to the dragon. "Family squabble, paranoia, or civil unrest, I do not care, so long as they keep it out of our lands and pay on time. If they want blood staunch, then blood staunch they shall have." It was a simple-enough crafting, of the half-dozen different healwines he was known for; a young and simple red, without any subtleties. Despite his grumbling, he had more than enough in the cellars to supply all of Atakus and still maintain inventory until a new vintage could be made.

The room they entered was roughly circular, with candle niches in the walls at regular intervals, an oversized wooden chair with a leather seat, and a wooden desk with a surface that was bare and gleaming. Against one wall a mirror old enough to be tarnished around the edges was propped, its edges framed by gold and silver strands shaped into delicate grapevines. It had cost a fortune to make and ship and would require a year's earnings to replace, were it to break.

Malech sat down in the chair and leaned back, looking into the mirror. For an instant the surface reflected him from knees to forehead, the tail of the dragon dangling behind him as it took up a new position perched on top of the inner doorframe. He had not brought a student into his home for many years, and the weight of it was heavy on his hands. So much could go wrong, and almost all of it during the first few weeks.

He did not like to use the mirror—the sleep house left scars, both physical and emotional, no matter how long ago you escaped, and you learned to nurse them in private. Spying on another, without their knowledge . . . And yet, the mirror could give him advance warning, if the boy were to be trouble.

Malech frowned at the image, adjusting the fall of his tunic, then spat into his hand and placed his palm flat against the mirror. Feeling the spell pre-existing within the glass respond to his touch, he ordered, "Display Jerzy."

The boy was still sitting on the bed, staring out the window. His hands were moving slowly, as though he were arguing with himself, and the body language, even through the mirror's haze, was clearly that of a spooked animal not sure if it should freeze or run. He started, as though in reaction to a sound, and turned. A shadow fell over the floor, and he rose, not the way he might in response to a summons, but the way you did when someone with more power or authority entered a room.

Detta, then.

"Enough."

The mirror went dark, and then returned to showing the Vineart's reflection. Detta had been managing his Household for nearly as long as Malech had been resident. She could handle anything short of spell-wine and would come to him if she felt a hesitation or concern.

"The boy has talent," Malech said to the dragon. "He was able to sense the mediocrity of the crush without any training or experience, and then again to choose the correct cup."

The dragon swished its tail and lowered its head to its stone talons, waiting for the rest of its master's thoughts.

"Talent alone is not enough. In the end, Guardian, it is desire that creates a master vintner, makes him into a Vineart. A passion, not for power, or strength, but for the grapes themselves. Anything else leads to ruin."

The dragon had heard variations on this before, in the years since its carving. It had seen three students come and only one progress beyond that initial stage. If it cared enough, or had a sense of humor, it might have yawned.

Malech was quite aware that his audience was not captivated. He had long ago accustomed himself to speaking to, in effect, a stone wall. It was still better than speaking to himself.

Only time, and tests, would show if Jerzy had that passion, and if he could survive the training that would refine his crude awareness into the skills of a Vineart. At this point in his life, after four decades of mastery, Malech knew better than most how chancy expectations could be.

True, there was a spellwine, made from black-skinned grapes that grew only on the coast of Iaja that opened a small, specific window into the future. Wealthy patrons from every civilized city—and a few uncivilized ones as well—paid fortunes to possess a half bottle. Some Vinearts paid dearly for it as well, using it to predict Harvests and to winnow out their students. Malech preferred to rely on his own ability to judge skill and character and leave spell-use to his customers.

"And there will be nothing to sell them if I sit here all day," he said, regretfully standing up, feeling his knees and hips creak as he did so. Jerzy would take a few days to settle in to his new status and all that meant. Meanwhile, there was still Harvest to oversee, both the vines here and his secondary fields north and south. It was always a race to get the grapes in before the rains came, and he could not afford to be distracted. If one block was subpar so obviously, even in the crush, others might be equally poor as well. That would force him to rely upon previous vintages to make up the shortfall in spellwine production. An entire harvest of *vin ordinaire*, while still quite saleable, would not improve the standing of the House of Malech. He needed to know what had gone wrong, and how far it had spread.

"I am expected tonight at the northern enclosures," he said. "Earliest I will return will be tomorrow night, well after dark. Guardian, keep an eye on the boy while I am gone. Detta needs to mind the House, and I don't think he's quite ready to mingle with the kitchen children just yet, nor be left alone."

The stone dragon curled its tail around its head, a sign of pleasure, and beat its heavy wings once in acceptance. It might not have a sense of humor, but it did like to be useful.

THE GUARDIAN WAITED while Malech gathered his things for his trip, then, once the Vineart called for Per, the yard-man, to bring his horse around, beat its wings once and flew up along the external wall to the window of the room the student had been given.

The window was closed, so it tapped the tip of its tail against the glass, careful not to use too much force and risk breaking the expensive pane.

The face that appeared, with a startled expression and round open mouth, was not the boy's.

"Oh, you," Detta said and swung open the window. "Come in, then." The dragon barely fit, its wings scraping the edges of the window with a rough noise. The student was sitting on the bed, lacing up a shirt that was considerably cleaner than the tunic he had been wearing. The Guardian could not judge color, seeing things only in shades of gray, but the shirt had actual cuffs and a collar and was a size too large, making the boy's slender frame seem like a child's instead of a youth's. But the look on his face was an almost tentative joy in his new possessions that changed to something much less readable when he looked up and saw the Guardian hovering in the air in front of him.

"What . . . is that?" The boy's voice was quiet, not rising in fear or astonishment. The Guardian approved.

"That's the master's servant. You'll get used to it."

"It's . . . made of stone."

"You'll get used to that, too," Detta said. "Master likes to work in stone, that's why all the buildings are made of it. His parents were stonemasons, he told me once. Gives him some memory of before, I suppose."

"Before?"

"Before he was a slave, I suppose."

The student looked at Detta, the astonishment the dragon hadn't caused appearing now in his eyes. "Master . . . was a slave?"

The woman paused in her fussing with items in the dresser. "All you wine-crafters were slaves once, boy. Where did you think you all came from? Sin Washer made sure of that, so you'd have no other ties to bind you."

The Guardian hissed. Vinecraft was for the Master, and only the Master. The woman was speaking of things she had no right to speak of, too soon. Detta took the hint, and turned away to close the window. "No matter now. You're here, as is he, and this dratted beast no doubt has a reason to be here, so I'm assuming the Master sent him, yes? So he's to be your problem, not mine."

She gathered up the old tunic and pants, and made a face. "And these are going into the fire. Try not to ruin what you've got on now until we have a chance to sew up something a bit closer to your size." She paused at the door, looking back over her rounded shoulder. "Anywhere within the House is your home now, too, boy. Explore, learn where everything is. The beast will doubtless warn you if you're somewhere you ought not be. If you've any questions as to how things are run, you come to me. When the chime sounds for dinner, be there or go hungry. Tomorrow will be soon enough for you to start with everything else, I suppose."

And with those words, she left.

The student looked at the dragon, who had settled on the back of the single wooden chair in the room, the frame creaking slightly under its weight. Wings furled at its back, claws dug into the frame, and the long tail curled around the chair to keep it balanced.

"What do I call you? 'Beast' doesn't seem quite right."

The Guardian could speak to the Master, but this slender, dark-eyed student would not hear his voice any more than the kitchen children could, not yet. So it merely hissed again, air forcing through the narrow opening of its mouth, whistling sharply between stone fangs, and launched itself off the chair, heavy wings filling the small room as they spread to catch unnecessary air.

Jerzy flinched, but the dragon landed with surprising gentleness on his shoulder, those stone claws not digging in at all, the hard weight remaining above his delicate human bones, not resting on it. Its wings stayed spread, over Jerzy's head.

The Guardian rose slightly, even though the wings did not move, and the boy's entire body was tugged along with it. He resisted, and the Guardian tugged harder.

"I'm supposed to go with you?" The boy shrugged, clearly well used to being ordered around without explanation.

"All right," he said. "Let's go."

Chapter 4

The next morning Malech walked through the harvest shed of the northern enclosure, listening to that yard's overseer update him on their progress. This yard was planted with firevines, which ripened more slowly than healvine, but the longer growing season resulted in a powerful vintage that earned his House a nice sum. The Mariners' Guild bought out most of his stock every year, firespells being far safer to use shipboard than any open flame, and the remainder he shared with the local chandler to craft smokeless candles that princelings gave solid coin for.

Once all the grapes were picked and crushed into mustus, their potential had to be judged, and Malech alone could make the determination if they would become spellwines, *vin magica*, or be shunted off into *vin ordinaire*.

Inspecting and approving the mustus took most of the day, and it was midafternoon before Malech was able to approve the final batch and set out for home. Exhaustion made his body ache, but once in the saddle, the matter of the odd blood-staunch order from Atakus came back to him. Such things were normally left to Detta, who ran the House accounts, and dealt—quite admirably—with them. So why did the order remain in his thoughts? Perhaps thinking of the Mariners' Guild early that morning had reminded him, since Atakus was a major port for trading ships coming to and from the southern lands.

Was it the Guardian's comment about needing more blood staunch that was bothering him? A demand that could outstrip his stores was rare indeed; blood staunch was not a plague-wine, nor taken for fevers—it was purely to heal wounds. He had never run out before. Large quantities would indicate battles, disasters . . . not things one associated with the island-state of Atakus. And yet, the size of the order indicated just such a disaster . . . perhaps one yet to have happened, or a battle yet to be fought . . . His thoughts chased each other, making him progressively more uneasy with every step his horse took.

Fortunately the beast knew its way home, because he could not remember a moment of it until they were plodding up the track in the gathering dusk and Per was coming to take the reins from him.

"All is well, Per?"

The yardman nodded, ducking his head. Per never spoke, and at times seemed half as sly and wild as a marten. He had been a slave once, too, but his touch with the horses brought him out of the yards and into the stable. Perhaps it was another sort of magic, save no spellwine had ever been found to control animals.

Malech patted him on the shoulder, and went inside, pausing only to knock the dirt off his boots. No alarm or uproar met him, so the Household must also be calm. Good. Dinner, and then to bed. All else could wait until morning.

MALECH WAS UP before sunrise, as was his habit, and down into the workrooms with a mug of steaming tai in his hands, his dreams having been filled with flashes of fire and a sense of foreboding, no doubt brought on by his thoughts the night before. There was, he finally concluded, nothing he could do about any dire history to come, save ensure they were able to fill the order and replenish their stock.

For now, he needed to focus on the mustus in front of him, his ruby-red healgrapes. Four of the five vats made his senses tingle, indicating that they might have the potential. The fifth, like the vat that had spilled two days before, had no such tingle.

"Master?"

He had heard the inner door open, and sensed the arrival of the newcomers, without having to turn around. "Ah, Jerzy. Good. Thank you, Guardian."

The boy came down the three steps, his gaze taking everything in without a further word. The stone dragon, his escort duty done, winged quietly into the wooden rafters, watching the activity below with unblinking eyes.

"Welcome to the first step of the magic, young one," Malech said. He was aware he sounded like a pompous bastard, but it had been so long since he had been able to share this moment with anyone, he couldn't resist. Magic was a thing of wonder, the process from incantation to decantation, and too much of the world saw only the results, not the alchemical transformation.

Jerzy did not disappoint. He looked around slowly, still drinking every detail in, his dark eyes wide and his jaw slack with amazement. For the first time, in that expression of wonder, Malech saw the attractive boy-child he must have been, before the slavers took him and the sleep house beat him down. Malech felt a moment of pity. It was easier to be an ugly slave than a pretty one.

And now, what would the House of Malech make of him? What sort of Vineart might this boy become? It was not an easy life but better by far than that of a slave. And if the boy had never been sold? A question for the silent gods to answer, if they cared to. Were those with magic within them sold, or did exposure to magic create it within a slave? Either way, none came to the Vines save via slavers.

"This is where the pulp goes? After we crush it?" Jerzy's gaze went from the seven wooden tanks, twice times his height and three times his reach in girth, and then to the great wooden door that led to the outside.

"After the crush, and the clearing. This is where the mustus is brought."

Only the most trusted, most experienced slaves were allowed within the vintnery itself. Here, where the real work was done, even fewer had access, and then only to bring the barrels in and out through the sliding wooden doors.

"It is brought in here to these tanks, to sit until Harvest is done, and all the lots have been pressed. Then we sort the mustus into levels, and vinification begins."

"Vinification." It was another new word, and the boy said it carefully, enunciating every letter.

"This is where it all begins," Malech said again. "Can you feel it? Can you feel what waits?"

Some never did. He did not think the boy would fail so easily.

"Like . . . someone sitting on my chest. No . . ." Jerzy's eyes scrunched closed and he put his hands over his ears as he concentrated, trying to block out all distractions. "Like someone pushing from *inside* my chest. It doesn't hurt, but it feels strange."

Malech almost smiled in relief. "Yes. I sense it as something stroking my skin, lightly, as though with a feather. It's different for everyone, we're told. Learn that feeling inside you, Jerzy. Learn it so well you can recognize it in an instant, can hear it calling you from within the grape as it grows. That is the mustus calling you, the raw, unspecified magic, still seeking its form. So tell me . . . which ones push most strongly at you?"

The boy walked to the nearest tank but did not touch it, or come close enough to touch it, as though some force kept him just so far away. He circled it, taking his time, then went on to the next.

"This one; it almost shoves at me. Those two, less so. I don't feel anything from the other four."

Malech nodded, but did not confirm or deny the boy's findings. As he studied, his senses would grow stronger, and he would learn to make his own estimations and to trust his own judgment, not to wait for the confirmation of anyone else, even his master. Magic was not taught, but *grown.* There was no need to confuse the boy with philosophies, however.

"For the next two weeks the mustus will wait in these giant vats, stirred twice daily to ensure a flow from top to bottom, forcing the flesh and juice to mingle. That will be your task, to attune yourself to the feel of each vat, to learn its temperament, and what it would be best suited for." It was a deceptively simple step for such important results, and a Vineart needed to know every one of them the way he knew his own heartbeat.

Jerzy's eyes flicked to the vats again, clearly measuring them against his own height, and just as clearly remembering the fate of the slave killed for overturning the vat. Good. It would keep him alert and careful.

"You will use those rakes," and Malech pointed to the four long instruments racked along the wall behind them. "Twice a day. And yes, there will be more vats added as the rest of the yields are brought in. You'll wish you were back in the field by the time you're done."

The look the boy gave him suggested that he highly doubted that, and Malech almost laughed. He, for one, was thankful to have someone else to pass this chore along to. Not only would it free his time for more advanced work, but his arms would ache considerably less this year. A few weeks of this and Detta's cooking, and the boy would bulk up to better match his height and stop looking quite so fragile.

"When it is ready, we will transfer it to smaller barrels, and from there the final transformation." Some of it would be bottled immediately as *vin ordinaire,* sold to those with coin who desired the intoxication of near-magic, without the risks—or costs—of spellwine. Only then would the final, most important touches be put on each spellwine, refining and finishing each for specific results. "But that will not be for at least a month, and there is much you must learn in the meantime."

"More magic?" Jerzy asked hopefully.

Malech laughed, if a trifle ruefully. "Nothing so simple, I fear. You, boy, must be civilized."

* * *

CIVILIZED, JERZY LEARNED, involved many things, including regular baths. Once a week one of the kitchen children brought steaming water into the bathing room, and he, like all the others in the Household, was expected to emerge clean all over. After the first dousing, Detta let him wash and dry himself, although there was a brief but embarrassing lesson on how to clean his teeth and ears, and properly trim his fingernails and toes.

Lil took the shears to his hair after a few days, trimming it in the same style as the Master's, short at the front so that his eyes and mouth were kept clear, but longer at back, over his ears and neck. Another handspan of growth, she said, poking him in the shoulder in a familiar manner, and he would be able to pull it back and tie it at his neck with a thong the way the master did.

It would take longer than that to grow even a close-trimmed beard like the master's, however, she added, and laughed when he blushed.

Civilized also involved lettering. Every morning after breakfast, once the dishes and platters had been cleared and the kitchen children set off to whatever other duties they had, he was directed to sit at the long, polished wooden table with Detta, and she would show him how to recognize letters and then words, and eventually how to write them as well.

"It's a thing of power, same as spellwines," she said when he protested the time and effort after a particularly frustrating session. Where recognizing mustus came naturally, writing did not. "All part and parcel of what you're to become, boy."

Jerzy did not doubt her. He did not even think to doubt her, any more than he would have doubted the overseer, although he did not fear Detta in the same fashion. If this was what they wanted him to do, he would do it. You did not complain in the sleep house, no matter how bad things got. In the Master's own House, where he was well fed, and bathed, and had his own room with a bed and a warm blanket, Jerzy would have died rather than balked. But he still did not see the point to it, especially since Master Malech seemed to have near forgotten him those first few days.

A few days later, just as he was beginning to feel comfortable in his new bed, his new clothing, and his new cleanliness, if not quite with the gentle teasing of the kitchen children or Detta's brusque instruction, another lesson was added to his days.

"Jerzy," Master Malech said, making a rare appearance at the morning table. "Come with me."

Leaving his bowl on the table still half full, he followed the Master out into the courtyard, where a stranger waited. "This is Mil'ar Cai."

The newcomer was short and strongly built, with milk-pale skin. He had no hair anywhere on his scalp, and a long brown mustache tied with red and blue beads. His clothing was more colorful than anything Jerzy could remember seeing before: dark red pants that billowed over calf-high leather boots, a bright blue sash, and a brighter red shirt with sleeves that tied at the elbow with green ribbons that fluttered when he moved.

"Cai is from the Caulic Isles," Malech said. "Across the narrows, come to teach your body, as Detta instructs your mind."

"Ey," Cai said in a thick but understandable voice. "There's no magic grows in Caul, and so we use our brains, instead."

Master Malech chuckled, as though Cai had said something amusing, and left them to it. Jerzy stared at Cai, half fascinated but slightly uncertain.

"Master Vineart was right: you stand like a slave, not a man, and certainly not like a magician! We'll begin at once, and soon your body will have the right of it. Ready yourself, boy!"

Jerzy had no time to ask what he was to ready himself for before Cai had him in the air and landing hard on the morning-cool flagstones.

"Up. Again. Be ready this time."

The next time, Jerzy saw Cai come at him, and went limp in enough time for the fall to hurt less, although it still knocked the breath out of him.

"All right. Better. You know that much, at least." Cai pulled at one end of his mustache and studied Jerzy again. "So, now we know where to start."

Every other day, from then on, they met in the courtyard in the late afternoon, after Jerzy had taken his second turn in the vatting rooms, punching down the mustus. The Caulic fighter taught him how to stand, to bow to a greater, inferior, or a worthy opponent, and how to move across a room—"not as a slave but as a magician!" Cai insisted, over and over again, thwacking Jerzy across the backs of his knees with a short, thick cudgel when he moved wrongly or hunched his shoulders instead of standing up straight.

Once he moved to Cai's satisfaction, the soldier promised him, there would be more interesting lessons using the cudgel itself, to defend against a mad dog, a hungry beast, or an angry man.

Jerzy wasn't sure which he dreaded more, the frustration of Detta's instruction or the bruising of Cai's lessons, but each night he tumbled into bed, exhausted and sore, and thinking there was no way he could survive another day.

Worse, while he was learning letters and movement, the sunup-to-sundown madness of the Harvest went on outside. During lessons with Detta he would look out the window and see the Master striding through the fields, or hear him moving in other rooms, calling for something or muttering to himself. Often he was gone the entire day and night, checking the progress of his other yards.

It surprised him how very much he missed the feel of the grapes in his hands and the soil under his feet, until he was dreaming of it sleeping and awake. A week after he had left the yards, when Jerzy came down for the first meal, tying up his pants even as he stumbled into the dining hall, he found Master Malech already there, discussing the day's matters with Detta. Still caught up in his dreams, he blurted a request before he could wake up enough to be afraid.

"Master? May I go with you into the fields today?"

Malech stopped with his mug halfway to his lips, and stared at Jerzy with those clear blue eyes.

"I—I . . ." Jerzy felt himself start to stutter, and slammed his jaw shut, his courage gone as swiftly as it had appeared.

"You miss it already?" It didn't feel like a question, and so Jerzy did not answer.

"Of course you do. It's Harvest. Time enough during Fallow for you to learn your other lessons. Detta, would you mind terribly if I took this worthless child into the fields and put him back to work?"

Detta's round face was equally solemn as she considered Jerzy, who held very still, barely allowing himself to breathe.

"He has been distracted," she said slowly. "Much like another male in this household, when forced to look at figures and facts . . ."

Malech chuckled, the sound of water over rocks. "A true Vineart in the making, then. Put food in your mouth, boy, and be ready to go as soon as you swallow."

Jerzy almost choked, belting down his meal, and was ready before Master Malech had finished his drink.

The cobbles felt different underfoot through the leather of his shoe than they had barefoot, and Jerzy was aware of the fact, suddenly, that he walked differently in them. In the House, it wasn't noticeable. Here, where he had spent most of his life either barefoot or wearing the heavy wooden pattens inherited from an older slave, every step he took made him feel as though everyone were staring at him.

In truth, nobody looked as they walked across the road and down past the vintnery building. A new slave was in the spot Jerzy had been only a week before, but the bustle of activity had slowed considerably. While they passed, a wagon came up the road, drawn by one of the three thick-muscled white horses that spent most of their time in the enclosure behind the icehouse. A single driver held the reins, and the wagon itself held two wooden casks lashed to the frame. Jerzy's nostrils flared, although all he could smell in the cool air was the familiar scent of dirt and horse.

"From the southern enclosures," Malech said, watching the wagon turn off toward the great sliding door that led to the vatting room. "A light yield this year, but I have hope for it. That's what you were sensing in those barrels. Come."

Malech led him deep into the field, pausing occasionally to check a leaf here or a vine there to make sure that nothing had been damaged during the harvest.

"Even the most delicate of hands can pull too hard," Malech told him, lifting a vine that had come off the supporting stake and tying it back up with a piece of twine he took from his pocket. "There is stress that is good, and stress that is bad. Letting the fruit touch dirt—does what?"

"Increases the chance of rot, or animals reaching the fruit." Any slave knew that.

"And after Harvest, when there is no fruit to rot or be eaten?"

Jerzy looked at the vine in his master's hand, the twisted brown plant as thick around as his wrist and gnarled like an old man's face, and had no answer.

"The vine must be stressed, but it must also be respected," Malech said. "Lift it to the sky so air moves under the leaves and moisture runs freely to the root, and the fruit responds. Leave it hanging, discarded once the magic is taken, and the next year's harvest will be poor. Remember that always, boy."

Malech frowned, then bent with an ease that mocked his age and plucked a small cluster of fruit from a vine in the next cluster. The fruit was small but deep red and should not have been overlooked. Jerzy braced himself against the ire that would doubtless erupt from the Vineart at such waste.

"Ah." Malech did not sound angry, and Jerzy risked looking at his master's face.

"Here," and Malech plucked a single grape from the bunch and held it out to Jerzy, an offering.

"Master?"

"Place it on your tongue and crush it gently. Use the roof of your mouth, not your teeth."

His muscles froze even as he was reaching out to take the fruit, as his mind understood what Malech was saying, telling him to do.

"Master?"

"It's all right, Jerzy. It's all right, now."

Still uneasy, expecting at any moment to be knocked to the ground for his blasphemy, Jerzy took the fruit and did as instructed. The skin burst against the roof of his mouth and he tasted the clean clear juice running down his throat, tingling and itching and tickling all at once, the tingling of what he realized was magic fainter than from the barrel of mustus, but unmistakable nonetheless.

It was a revelation, a moment that etched into his memories, and no matter how many times after that he tasted one, no matter how many times Malech took him into the vineyards, the tingling was never so intense.

A week later, the Harvest ended with the usual feast. A long wooden table was set out where the crusher had been, and slaves and hire-workers mingled freely, filling wooden mugs with *vin ordinaire* and ciders. Detta and Lil had produced seemingly endless loaves of bread, stuffed with roasted fowl and cheeses, and a massive wild pig was roasting over a fire pit, Per watching carefully to ensure none of the younguns got too close. Cai, off to the side, was playing a thin reed instrument with two local farmers accompanying him on drum and tambor, and a few of the slaves, suddenly finding new energy, were dancing, arms linked in a circle.

It had been a good Harvest, and Master Malech was pleased, which meant that everyone was happy. The Vineart brought a mug of cider over for Jerzy and lifted his own in toast. "Warm days, cool nights."

"Warm days, cool nights," Jerzy echoed, and sipped at the tart liquid. They had no pear trees of their own, but a local brewer always brought over enough for the celebration every year. Some of it was sent to the other enclosures, where smaller versions of the feast would be occurring as well.

In earlier years he might have been among those dancing. Now it was as though he had never been part of it, and they did not see the young student any more than they acknowledged the Master. Slaves kept their eyes down and never asked questions.

"Master?"

"Hrmmm?" Those cool blue eyes weren't quite so terrifying anymore.

"Why are the healgrapes so dark red, but others are so much lighter?" He was thinking, especially, of the greenish-pink flesh of firegrapes. "If it's not—"

"It's not a foolish question, no, although if you'd listened to the Washer preaching, you would know that already." A Washer had come by on the last day of Harvest, as was traditional, to say a blessing over the depleted vines and take his customary cask of *vin ordinaire*, but Jerzy had been too busy to attend, working in the courtyard with Cai.

"All grapes are blooded, touched by Sin Washer's sacrifice," Malech explained now. "How deep a touch they received is shown by the color of their skin. The darker the skin, the closer to the source the origin grape was, and the more specialized it became."

Jerzy watched the dancers go around and around, laughing harder the faster they spun. "So a grape with a pale skin . . . is not as powerful?" That didn't feel right: the bonegrapes had almost no red to them, and yet they mended cracked and bent bones that might otherwise take months to set. And when he tasted one, the pulp on his tongue and the juice running down his throat, he *felt* the magic rising within.

Malech stared out into the sky, looking, as always, for a hint of weather change to come, even now with the harvest safely in. "Not less powerful, no. Less specialized, and therefore more difficult to craft into something useful. Legend says that the First Growth was pale and thin-skinned, easy to crush for its juice, ripe with limitless magic. We have no white-skinned grapes left; Sin Washer took them from us as you would take a knife from a baby."

"That is . . . a good thing?" The Washers said it was, when they preached Sin Washer's gifts, but Master sounded almost wistful.

"It is a good thing. But the knife is shiny, and the First Growth was powerful, and we all wish to grow up enough to be trusted with the things we are denied. The blooded grapes are enough for us, Jerzy. We have no other choice."

THE WEEKS AFTER Harvest passed, and Jerzy spent even more hours every day in the vatting room, now filled to capacity with mustus from all the enclosures. He moved the liquid within the vats with his long-handled rake, punching the thick surface down so that the skins and juice mingled and mixed. His arms ached, and the smell of the grapes would not leave his skin or hair, and even the fascination of being so close to mustus wore off after a while.

The advantage to vattage work was that it required no thought, and he could let himself consider what Malech, Cai, and Detta were teaching him, allowing it to sink into his understanding the same way the skins sank into the liquid, the magic swirling and deepening with every turn. Slowly, speaking into the quiet echoes of the vatting room, he built a new vocabulary, words taking on meaning, his speech patterns changing until not even Detta could find fault with his recitals.

It was not all physical or mental labor, however. Although Master Malech typically ate in his study while Jerzy took his meals in the hall with Detta and her kitchen children, one eve-meal he came to join them, sitting on the wooden bench next to Detta, eating off a wooden trencher and passing bread and a pitcher of *ordinaire* as though they were all of equal status. Michel, Geordie, and Roan were struck dumb, but Lil and Detta kept up with their discussion of the meats they would need to put away for the winter, and what spices Detta should order when the traders passed through town next. As though reminded by that thought, Malech reached into his pocket and removed three small green fruit. Jerzy had never seen anything like them before. They were shaped like hen's eggs, although the exterior was rough, but when Master Malech sliced one open, the inside was pink and juicy.

"They're called pieot," the Vineart told him, taking a slice and eating it with obvious satisfaction. Jerzy took a slice as well, watching to see how to eat it without getting juice all over his face. The moment the fruit hit his tongue, however, he forgot to worry about eating cleanly, as Cai had taught him, and instead gaped in wonder.

Master Malech laughed, while the others at the table busied themselves with their own plates and pretended not to notice. None of them took any of the fruit themselves.

"It tastes like . . ." Words failed him. It tasted like sunshine and straw, like bitter anjas traded from Leiur to the west, those meaty nuts that looked like the knuckles of a man's hand, but this carried a sweetness to it that Jerzy could not identify.

"It tastes like bonegrape," he said, almost in a whisper, as though suddenly afraid to identify it. How could a table fruit taste like one of the most essential of all healwines, second only to bloodgrape?

"There is a similarity, yes." Master Malech was openly pleased. "A Vineart must be able to identify flavors and scents, which means opening himself to new experiences. Good ones, and occasionally bad ones. This—" and he took another slice of the fruit "—is one of the better ones. They're from Iaja, a land warmer than our own. Like limon, with a harder, greener finish."

Jerzy had no idea what a limon was, but if it tasted like this, he thought, it must be wonderful.

STRANGE NEW FOODS and experiences, a comfortable bed, and only the occasional clip to the head when he made a mistake: Jerzy was not fool enough to doubt his good fortune now. You did not come under the slavers' hands without learning what would be expected of you the rest of your life: food and care, yes, but work, endless work, until your back broke and your arms failed. To have that suddenly, magically change . . .

And yet, it was difficult. Harvest might have been backbreaking as a slave, but now Jerzy crawled into bed every night, his arms aching from the seemingly endless vat-work, often sore across the legs and ribs from Cai's ongoing lessons, and his head whirling from letters and numbers that would not disappear even when he closed his eyes and slept like a dead thing until the morning chime woke him, and the now almost-boring cycle began again. In that, at least, the five weeks since the spill had passed very much like his life before, in a constant repetition of meals and chores. Worse, because after the promise of that first day in Malech's study, despite the constant exposure to the mustus, feeling that nascent power constantly pressing underneath his breastbone, there was no spellwine. No crafted magic.

Every day he thought that today might be the day he asked, and every night he fell into bed, the words unspoken.

One night, however, he woke quietly, immediately, the way a slave learned to, and realized that it had not been sunrise that alerted him. He lay on his back, arms holding the blanket to his body. The pillow lay on the floor; he had pushed it off the bed at some point during the night, as usual.

The single window was open. He had closed it the night before, against the lashings of rain coming down off the ridge. The rain was not a disaster now: Harvest was complete, with the grapes from all the fields gathered, crushed, and vatted, the soil protected and prepared, and the slaves set to repairing the stone wall of the enclosure before the weather turned colder. Master had seemed pleased, if distracted, and missed the eve-meal two nights in a row because he was off doing something with samples from each of the vats Jerzy had been punching.

The night sky was clear now, but the stars were blocked out by a thick gray shadow perched in the middle of the window.

"Guardian?"

It could be none other, to come in through the window without an alarm being raised. The soft thump of something landing on the floor, allowing the stars to be seen again, confirmed his guess. The Guardian had accompanied him everywhere the first few days, but he had seen it less recently as time went on. He rolled out of bed, picking up the pillow and replacing it on the cot, then turned up the lamp on the desk, raising the flame until the room was illuminated.

The stone dragon waited on the floor, patient as only an inanimate thing could be.

"I'm to come with you?"

The Guardian could not speak, and its stone muzzle could not convey expressions, but Jerzy nonetheless got a distinct sense of "what else?" from the creature.

"All right. Let me get dressed." It wasn't cold yet outside, but for all that the House was grander than any sleep house, it still had corners where a chill could and did linger once the sun went down. Detta had given him three pairs of pants and two brand-new shirts, plus a sleeveless jerkin and a quilted jacket that actually fit him across the shoulders. He put on a pair of those pants, a shirt, and the jerkin, and picked up the hard-soled shoes he was supposed to wear when outside, just in case. Lastly he wrapped the leather belt once across his hips, fastening it with the dragon-head buckle that was a smaller version of the Master's own.

Whatever Master Malech had in mind, he was ready.

Chapter 5

The House was silent, even the usual night-quiet sounds hushed. Guardian took him down the stairs by Master Malech's study and through the stone hallway to a room he had not seen before, one with walls that seemed rounded at the corners in a way that confused the eye and made him slightly dizzy. Unlike the rest of the workrooms that held only tables and stools and cabinets of tools, there was actual furniture here, and a tapestry on one wall. What caught and held Jerzy's attention, however, was the large mirror leaned up against the opposite wall. Jerzy knew, now, how much the simple looking glass he had used on his first day cost, how very rare it was, so the sight of this one took all of his attention, and it was only when a cough sounded before him that he realized that his master waited there, seated behind a wooden desk, a glass of *vin ordinaire* in his hand.

Jerzy didn't know how he knew it was *ordinaire* rather than *magica*, but he knew it, the way he knew his hand was attached to his wrist.

"Good evening, Jerzy."

"Good evening, Master Malech." Even after these weeks studying with the Vineart, it was still strange to see the Master and know that he didn't need to avert his eyes or fall to his knees or fear being cuffed by the overseer for insolence. Stranger still, to see his master relaxing, his quilted dressing robe over dark gray woven pants and an open-necked shirt of some deep blue color, his feet bare against the cool stone of the cellar floor.

Jerzy came all the way into the room and took what seemed to be the expected position on the wooden stool placed directly in front of the desk. The seat was worn smooth, and the height was just enough that he could tuck his legs underneath comfortably. He thought it might have been made for him, except the sheen of the wood suggested that it had been carved long before he had been born.

Guardian flew up into the ceiling, settling on a scarred wooden beam, its stone tail dropping straight down like a sculpture, save for the occasional twitch of its pointed tip.

"Are you ready, Jerzy?"

Ready for what? "I don't know." He might have lied, but what was the point? The room was cooler than expected, and he was glad he had taken the time to dress warmly.

"A fair answer, considering you don't know what is in store. Nicely diplomatic. Your lessons are beginning to pay off."

Jerzy didn't know what Master Malech meant by that, either, so he just sat quietly and waited.

Malech placed his glass on the table in front of him. "The Washers tell the story of how Vinearts came to be: the guardians of a limited, reduced magic, the heirs of our forefathers' foolish arrogance. How we now, by Sin Washer's Command, turn inward and husband our vines rather than power over men. We are more than what the stories claim, and less. We are not the mages of generations past, no. And yet, a Vineart crafts more than spells, Jerzy. He crafts solutions, possibilities. Some are good. Some are . . . not good. Some heal; some cause harm. None of them are anything more than tools. A man who drinks a spellwine and kills another man, is he any different from the man who takes a knife and kills? No. The responsibility for the action is the same.

"There are those who say that we who craft these tools are responsible as well. That it is our hand that kills . . . and our hand that heals, as well."

Malech paused and looked at Jerzy, as though expecting him to say something. So Jerzy asked the next question that came into his head. "Can spellwine make someone do something they don't want to do?"

His master touched his bearded chin with a forefinger, his dark blue eyes half lidded and his expression thoughtful. That wasn't, Jerzy realized, the question his master had expected, but the Vineart answered it anyway. "In the southern regions of Altenne grows a spellwine, a healwine they call Lethá. It fogs the mind, but you must drink deeply and allow it to take effect. Can a spellwine cause a man to do a thing he does not wish? No. Not even a Master Vineart can do that, not with the most potent of grapes, no matter how deeply he might drink."

"Could the prince-mages do it?" Jerzy held his breath, sure that this time he had asked a forbidden thing. No matter that Malech himself had spoken of the old vines, the First Growth of the prince-mages; merely to mention them was to receive a lecture from the Washers about the wages of arrogance and prideful folly.

His master, however, merely said: "The old vines . . . We have no idea what they could truly accomplish, left with only legends that grow into impossibilities with every generation. I suspect the prince-mages, yes, could force another to do their will. But those wines and the prince-mages who crafted them are long gone, and not even the scholars of the Altenne can bring back their knowledge."

Malech leaned forward, his dressing gown falling open as he rested his hands on his knees. His intense gaze held Jerzy motionless, his eyes, in the dim light, seeming to glow from within. "But there is much knowledge we have reclaimed. Much we can do, within our limited modern scope. And I will teach you this, as my master taught me, and you will add to the knowledge."

"Yes, Master."

"And what will you do with that knowledge, once it is yours?"

Jerzy blinked. Things had happened so quickly, he was still dizzy, half expecting it to end as suddenly as it had begun. He had certainly not thought about that, never looked beyond the day, the week, the thought of the learning itself so overwhelming there could be no room for anything else.

Malech was waiting for his answer, and so he said the first thing that came to mind. "Use it to learn more."

Malech leaned back, and rubbed his close-cropped beard with one long finger again, this time with obvious pleasure. "Then let us see what you are capable of, young Jerzy. Let us begin with the source of our magic."

He stood, and walked to the wall. The stone gave way before him, not sliding away but simply disappearing. Jerzy didn't have time to gape, Guardian's tail thwapping him hard between the shoulders and knocking him off the stool to get him moving as well.

Stumbling to his feet, he rushed into the misty hole in the stone, holding his breath and hoping that the wall would not suddenly return when he was halfway through.

"The first mage, in the days when the world was young and full of discovery, drank of the mustus and felt the magic stir within him. But he did not understand what it was until he gave himself over to the mustus, took it into himself, and let the magic change him."

It was only then that Jerzy saw the wooden vat in front of them. Taller than Master Malech, and wider than three men could reach around, it looked like the vats in the vintnery he had spent weeks punching down, but it . . . felt different. The air around it felt different.

"In you go."

"Master?" His voice squeaked, and his eyes flicked back and forth from the Vineart to the vat, but the thought of running never entered his mind. Where would he go? Instead, he slipped off his leather shoes and pulled the shirt over his head, folding it and handing it to Malech, who took it with grave courtesy.

There was no ladder, no handholds on the vat. "How do I . . ."

Even as the words came out of his mouth, he felt himself rising into the air, as if someone had taken him by the back of his pants and lifted him.

"Sin Washer, save me," he whispered, but before he had a chance to panic, the invisible hand had brought him over the rim of the vat and dropped him in.

The mustus went up his nose; that was his first realization. Sweet, clean, and suffocating, pressing against him even as his feet touched the bottom of the vat. He knew how to swim, at least enough to keep from drowning in the stream, but his arms and legs remained still, his brain fogged and unpanicked.

Drown. Drown yourself. Breathe in and breathe out and let the liquid enter your lungs.

It was impossible, but Malech's voice urged him to relax, to give over and allow the must into his skin, his veins, his lungs, to trade out blood and bone for sweet juice.

He trusted his master. Trusting, he breathed in.

MALECH WAITED, STANDING easily by the vat, his body relaxed in a way that was not mirrored in his mind. Minutes passed, and he wished for the glass he had left in the other room. *Vin ordinaire* was not spellwine, it did not go through the final specification to bind magic to spell, but that cask had a pleasant kick to it that made time pass more easily. Yet this was no time for kicks, pleasant or otherwise. If something were to go wrong . . .

If something were to go wrong, his student would die, drowning horribly, and the entire vat would be ruined.

A Vineart did not form attachments, not even to those within his own House. A Vineart stood alone, as they had since the days of Sin Washer and the breaking of the Vine. And yet . . . the boy had potential, even more than any of his students before. There was magic fermenting in him, and a steady, careful hand could raise him to a magnificent vintage. If the boy did not falter, or fail.

"Rest easy, Jerzy. Trust the grape. Trust yourself. This is the first step, the most important step, and you cannot go further without first taking it."

INSIDE THE VAT, Jerzy felt the mustus leaching into his skin, softening him, blurring the lines between juice and flesh. Once the shock wore off, he knew the liquid: this mustus was from bonegrape, the healgrape that grew higher on the ridge of the southern vineyards, where the cooler air swirled around its leaves and kept the juice tart and pungent. Picked, and pressed, and placed into this vat, waiting . . . for him. He knew it, and it knew him. Time ended, his lungs stilled, his limbs faded. Blood was mustus, and mustus, blood. Magic swam with him, into him, touching the magic the Master said was within him, and suddenly . . . he understood.

Not all. Not much. But there was a connection now where before there had been only confusion and frustration. He felt the magic in the mustus the way he had in the vineyard . . . and recognized it within himself.

A Vineart was not merely one who knew how to craft magic into spellwines. A Vineart *was* magic . . . and spellwines were *him.*

Surfacing, gasping as cool air replaced the liquid in his lungs, spluttering and coughing, Jerzy grabbed blindly, his fingers closing around the smooth metal band of the vat's rim. He hauled himself out, throwing his legs over the edge and dropping down onto the ground. His pants made a sodden noise against his legs, and his skin prickled in the suddenly cold, dry air. A rivulet of mustus ran down his face, and he licked the drop off his lips without hesitation. It was clean and sweet and sang on his tongue.

Malech stood before him, his face solemn, his deep-set eyes cast into shadows, looking at him consideringly. "Give me your hand."

Jerzy didn't have to think, but lifted his left arm, presenting his hand, palm up, to his master. Those long fingers touched his palm, tilting the hand down. A sense of dislocation: the last time Malech had done this, he had been smaller, shorter, and his hand had to reach up.

Malech's thumb stroked the skin over the mark, and Jerzy's eye was drawn down to it, only to discover unmarked flesh. Before he could react, Malech turned his hand over, and presented Jerzy with it. The simple bright red brand that had identified him as a slave was gone, but a darker, rounded weal now rested on the outside of his wrist, as though a drop of wine had spilled from a cup and landed there, staining his skin indelibly.

On Malech's left wrist, a similar, darker stain mirrored his own.

"You . . . did that."

"Not I," Malech said quietly. "The vines know their own. It is done, and sealed. Your true training will begin after lunch. Go wash yourself; you're going to be very sticky in a few moments, and the insects will flock to you in an annoying fashion."

Jerzy stared at the mark, wet hair plastered to his forehead and dripping into his eyes, and then looked up at his master. The Vineart smiled faintly, his angular face not softened at all by the motion, and then he turned and left.

Jerzy breathed in deep, trying to keep his legs from wobbling as the aftermath finally hit him. Picking up his shirt and shoes, he followed Malech out through the hazed-out wall. Malech was nowhere to be seen, but the Guardian still sat on the beam overhead, its tail swinging gently as though pushed by a breeze. Its pointed muzzle turned to watch Jerzy as he walked through the room and out the door, but the Guardian did not move to follow him.

The stairs seemed far steeper and longer than usual, and when he came to the first landing, Jerzy stopped and stared at the light that was streaming through one of the narrow windows.

Guardian had woken him at night. The sunlight in front of him reached well into the window, striking the halfway point on the stone floor. The day was half over, and he hadn't even noticed.

Your true training will begin after lunch.

His slave-mark was gone.

Finding a burst of speed somewhere in his exhausted legs, Jerzy raced up the last flight of stairs and burst into his room, tossing his shirt and shoes onto the narrow bed, and stripping his wet pants off as quickly as possible, draping them over the windowsill to dry in the sunlight. Naked, he grabbed more clothing out of the drawers and started to put them on.

He stopped, one leg halfway in, and reconsidered: was it better to be on time, or clean?

The feel of his skin, starting to get sticky, decided him. The clothing was left on the bed while he used the pitcher of drinking water and a clean shirt to wipe the worst of the mustus off his skin, then the rest of the water was poured over his hair until it felt decently cleansed.

He would have preferred to go stand in the stream and let the cold water run over his body, but there was no time for that, much less go in search of one of the kitchen workers to have them heat water for an actual bath. Master Malech was waiting.

Chapter 6

PRINCIPALITY OF ATAKUS

The Principality of Atakus was not grand, by most standards; the island was small, and had only one Master Vineart to call its own. But that was Master Vineart Edon, and his delicate, dry wines were renowned for their control of winds. Seafaring lands paid whatever gold required to carry a cask of that spellwine on board every ship in their fleet, and to have their captains trained in their use. Whatever other spellwines Atakus needed, that gold could and did buy.

More significant to the Principality was the fact that those spells, cast over the whitecapped waters surrounding Atakus, had kept them safe from storms—and pirates—for five decades and more. The only visitors who came safely into the royal port of Atakus were those who were welcome . . . or who flew the red flag of parlay and negotiation.

Such visitors were greeted in the roofed courtyard on Mount Parpur, off to the side of the royal residence. The matching building next to it was the main royal residence, which also doubled as the Hall of Governors, where local leaders came to discuss matters of governance with their lord and master. Simply built, two stories high and studded with garden courtyards within and external views that carried for leagues in every direction over endless crystal blue waters, the white marble structures could easily be mistaken for places of worship, not government.

The prince of Atakus was an old man, whose seven grown sons were all put to work in the massive bureaucratic system, and two of his three daughters were solitaires, warriors who gave up all claim to House or family. His oldest and only remaining daughter, Thaïs, stood by his side during the daily workings, and was nicknamed "Wise Lady" for her political acumen by those who heard her speak. As a female she could not inherit his throne, but whichever son took over when he died would be wise to curry her favor, or risk disaster.

Current odds among the betting citizens had the second son as favorite, since the eldest showed more skill for paperwork than leadership, but it was the fourth son who was most often called to court, and was often seen, heads bent together in close discussion, with his sister.

This bright, cool day found the two of them seated beside the flowering hedge garden outside her sleeping chambers, on a white marble bench bathed by the morning sunlight. Thaïs was not a beauty, but had a grave dignity that won her a few serious suitors whom she had, so far, put off. Her long, thick black hair was tied up with a string of pink pearls and her body wrapped in a dark red dress of simple design. Her brother Kaïnam was more slender, his equally black hair tied at his neck with an unadorned cord, and his red trousers were matched by a plain white jacket without collar, fastenings, or lapel. Both were barefoot, their embroidered court shoes abandoned in the grass. A small white-and-black cat prowled at their feet, snatching at insects.

They had spent the morning with their father as he held court, listening to the thoughts and complaints of his governors, as he did every three-month. But this session had been different.

"It might be coincidence."

"It might. But it isn't."

"It might also not affect us at all."

"You are an idiot." She said it with affection, but in a matter-of-fact tone that did not allow argument.

A messenger had arrived the week before, from Ekai, a small territory off the main island. Ekai had no true government, no ruler, and was important only for its deep fishing harbor and a sunward-facing hill of ancient vines. That land was held by Jaban, the Vineart trained by Master Edon, who by training and common bonds looked to Atakus for guidance and protection. The messenger had carried a scroll written in Jaban's own hand, and presented it personally to the prince, who had then brought the subject up for discussion at this day's Session.

"Three ships destroyed, along with a royal ransom in spellwine," she reminded him. The Wise Lady had read the report, as her brother had not, and she felt the truth in it. "Driven to disaster by unruly winds, within our territory—waters protected against exactly such a thing. Kaïnam, think it through. How can it not affect us?" She pushed the cat away gently when it pounced on her toe.

"One man's report is not a fact," her brother countered, his usual dry, almost mocking tone moderated by the seriousness of the matter. He scooped the cat up in his arms and petted it until it went muscle-slack, purring with pleasure. "The winds are not always controllable, and if they were fools enough to use open flame rather than firewine to fill their lanterns . . ." He shrugged. Fire was a force of nature, and Nature commanded even magic; not even a Master Vineart was proof against that.

"They were seasoned sailors; we have no reason to assume that they used open flame." That was a fool's mistake, unthinkable for any shipmaster to condone. "But you are correct, we have no evidence, either way. A good point, thank you."

Their argument was less an argument than a sounding of arguments, in case her counsel was called upon. It was a role they were both accustomed to and normally enjoyed, but the loss of life—more, the possible implications for the much-vaunted benefits offered to ships using the Atakusian harbors—were sobering.

A horn sounded, thin and reedy, and they stood, him returning the cat to its grass hunt, both sliding their feet into cloth slippers quickly retrieved from under the bench. The short break was over; the prince and his advisors had returned, and the Session was resuming. Time to head back.

Inside the Hall of Governors, Erebuh son of Naïos sat on a simple wooden bench, the surface worn by generations of royal backsides that had warmed it. The prince sat up straight and stern, his once-black hair gone pure white, his skin tanned and lined with age and sunlight. Rumor had it that he had once spent a summer working a vineyard, far away. It could not be true, a royal son among slaves in the domain of a Vineart, but the rumor—and the aura of magic—still lingered on him.

The negotiator, Tomas of Eka, stood before the court once again, wearing a formal sash the pale yellow-green of unripe grapes over his travel-stained clothing. His boots were worn through, and he limped, as though there was a stone in the heel of one.

"My lord," he was saying as the two siblings reentered the court. "You have my master's petition. I beg of you, hear it and give me leave to return with an answer."

The ruler of Atakus studied the negotiator, not allowing any thought or emotion to appear on his age-lined face or in his dark eyes. "I have heard the report of this messenger of Vineart Jaban, and conferred with Master Vineart Edon."

Edon was an old man, older even than the prince, but his spellwines still showed the vigor of a man a third his age. He stood on the other side of the bench, a hardwood staff held securely in one clawed hand. It was forbidden for a Vineart to hold power, but not for one to stand with one who held power. Still, the Washers, while not speaking directly against either man, often preached pointedly about Sin Washer's Command, and the dire consequences of power mating to power.

Her father merely laughed and called the Washers alarmists and old women.

He was not laughing now. "Vineart Jaban tells us of disaster fallen upon merchant ships carrying spellwines from our ports, under our protections. Ships—seaworthy, tested ships, flaming like bonfires, all hands and their cargo lost."

There was a restless movement among the twenty or so gathered in the court's yard, but no one spoke up or indicated anything other than rapt attention to their prince's words.

"Master Edon has also heard these reports. He also hears from elsewhere within our domain of crops ruined by insects out of season, rot from nowhere, and rains that come down out of a clear sky."

Thaïs felt her back stiffen as her father spoke. She had not known of these events. A foul wind, even within Master Edon's range of protection, might be coincidence, as her brother said. A strange rain, a disastrous rot, a plague of pests, each might be bad luck or a poor season. Together, all in one year, all within their borders: that she did not trust.

"I do not trust this news."

Her liege lord spoke of the same mind. She had, in truth, learned at the knee of wisdom. And, she admitted to herself, paranoia. Atakus was small compared to the other Lands Vin, but their ports were well placed and much in demand—and eyed hungrily, every now and again, by ambitious princes. All that kept them independent was the strength of their Vineart. Edon had trained half a dozen students who, like Jaban, did not travel far from the principality, establishing their enclosures from Jaban's own cuttings, and owing him—and the prince—their loyalty. They might not be native to the islands, but they were Atakusian, blood and bone, by the time Edon was done with them.

Her father continued, his gaze touching on each person in turn, speaking clearly, so there could be no doubt as to his mind. "This may be a congruence of events. It may not. Our way is not to rush; we will assume nothing without further information. There is to be no panic."

As he commanded, so the governors would report, and the citizens would react. His decision made, Prince Erebuh turned back to the negotiator. "Vineart Jaban is dear to us, and we appreciate his sharing this information with us. Anything he needs of us in the wake of this tragedy, to make good his losses, we will supply. You may speak to our factor and discuss such matters with him, before returning to your home."

The negotiator bowed his head slightly in acknowledgment of those words, his eyes closing briefly as though in relief.

"As to what it all may mean . . . that is a matter for further discussion. At this moment, at this time, we will take no overt action." His gaze swept every person gathered under the white stone roof once again. "Make no mistake: we are on alert. We are on guard. If this was more than mere misfortune, if it is the attempt of outsiders to weaken our reputation, soften us for invasion or hostile negotiation, they will not succeed. We will not be weakened." The prince's voice rose in volume and deepened in tone, filling the air. His aged but still-powerful body, clad in a red tunic and robe of state, seemed to increase in mass, overpowering every other person in the court. "Our Vineart will turn the entire Harvest's work to spellwines stronger and swifter than any before, and they will ensure that we are protected, even as we use the resources of our island to discover who this enemy may be. So I command."

Master Edon looked gravely intent; no doubt this had been hammered out between the two of them during the recess. If Sin Washer had broken magical from secular power, he had also made them independent. A Master Vineart was bound to no one save the bindings he chose to accept, and even a monarch had no power to command him save he chose to be commanded.

There might have been other matters the gathered men wanted to discuss, but Prince Erebuh stood up and spread his arms in dismissal, indicating that this audience was over and done.

Afterward, the prince gathered his family and close advisors together in a small, private garden, as was his tradition. Freed from outside observation, the Wise Lady kicked off her slippers again, to her mother's obvious disapproval. But here, in this private space, she was not the Wise Lady, but simply Thaïs, her father's fourth and favored child.

Her father paced the outer pattern of the smooth stone patio, clearly not smelling the sweet Harvest blossoms or seeing the brightly colored birds dashing above them among the branches of the fruitwood trees.

"The winds were not caused by a spell." Master Edon's staff—never in evidence in public—was as smooth and worn on the handle as her father's chair, marked from all the years of his hand clenching it. His legs were bowed but his back was straight, and despite his age, any apprentice could vouch for the strength in his upper body—and the weight of that cane.

"It must be a spell," Erebuh said, clearly annoyed at his Vineart's insistence. "There is no other explanation."

"Must, my lord?" Master Edon was hairless, from chin to pate, but the place where an eyebrow might have been gave the appearance of rising in query.

The prince was as wily a creature as the Vineart, and merely glared at him, two sets of dark eyes staring at each other without flinching, as those strong-willed men fought, not with arms or words, but with the intensity of their personalities and the strength of their respective positions. Thaïs felt her heart tighten in anticipation of the storm gathering in front of her. A quick glance at Kaï, off to the side, saw he was equally intent on the scene.

Prince Erebuh was lord and master of these lands, but even he dared not push a Vineart too far. Likewise, a Vineart, no matter how powerful, rested only as secure as his relationship with the lord of the land. Even a Vineart had weaknesses, and even a Vineart must rest, on occasion. Better, much better for all within reach, for them to be in agreement.

"Must," Erebuh said again, not backing down. "Unless you, or someone else perhaps, can tell me of another force that might break our own spells—your spells—and wreck the sails of ships within our borders? Unless you can tell me of another force that can slip inside another Vineart's lands, and rot his crop so swiftly he does not notice until it is too late? Unless you can tell me how salt rain might fall from a cloudless sky?"

Edon stood his ground. "I can tell you, my lord, that there was no tinge of spellwine in any of these things. I am old, and have tasted almost every spell in existence, and would know them, even at a distance. This . . ." He paused, and shook his head. "This woke me in the night, stirring the aether in a way I have never encountered, but I could not name its source."

Erebuh did not blink, and the tension in no way receded, but somehow everyone knew that he had accepted the Master Vineart's words, at least for the moment.

"Then if we do not at this moment know how, we must go on to the second question: who?"

"The second question should be why, not who." Thaïs knew she should not interrupt; even as the Wise Lady her place was to advise when asked, not bring herself directly into the discussion. But the words came from her mouth without decision or hesitation.

Her father and Master Edon both looked at her in surprise, while the others gathered in the garden took a step back, all pretending that they had not been listening intently to the two men speak, seconds before.

"No," Edon said, heading off whatever scolding her father might have given her for interrupting. "Let the girl speak."

Thaïs was well into childbearing years, but to Edon any woman short of a crone was a girl. She took no offense.

"If Master Edon says that it is no spell which causes these things, then it may be man caused, or it may be freakish behavior of Nature. Either way, we have no way to predict or defend against it. Nature most especially must be taken in stride, if it is her will we suffer. The cause, either way, is less important than the result, that we are weakened. And so you ask: who would benefit from this?"

She did not wait for them to answer, and did not insult either of them by answering her own question. Any of the lands around them would benefit, were Atakus to fall.

"So you ask instead why?"

"Why, and why now. What has changed, this year? What has created a situation where another might be able to take advantage of our weakness? If this is man caused, why would they fall upon us first, rather than a weaker force? If this is Nature, why would we be the only ones affected? That question will lead us to the culprit faster than listing our enemies in order."

She knew, in her bones, that she was right, but Master Edon was shaking his hairless head, his fingers holding his staff lightly, confidently.

"The girl has wisdom, and I do not dispute her. And yet, she is wrong. Not in her logic, but in her conclusions. Neither the who nor the why is what is important, not immediately. If this is not magic, then it is mankind. And if it is mankind, it may be defeated by magic. We must determine the how, if we are to mount a proper countermeasure."

Thaïs chose her words carefully, knowing how quickly both men could turn to anger, and that she, however dear, would be the nearest and most obvious target. "More of the world is seen by your eyes," she acknowledged. "Yet might not such a countermeasure be better aimed if we first understood why it is required?"

Her father listened to them both, then held up a hand to stop Master Edon from responding, and instead turned to a third party. "Brother Joen. Will you give us Sin Washer's counsel on this?"

Brother Joen stood from where he had been waiting on a small marble stool, seemingly admiring the dance of a tiny bird over a flowering bush. His red-dyed robes swept gracefully around his legs as he moved into the discussion. A young man, handsome, if too pale to ever be mistaken for an Atakusian, his steady brown-eyed gaze and soft voice speaking of Sin Washer's love had soothed many an argument in the court since his arrival two years before, and for that alone the prince prized him, even as they argued over his reliance on Master Edon.

Thaïs did not trust him, not for his sake but the sake of the Collegium he represented. She had not trusted his predecessor, Brother Siyu, either. The Sin Washer had died centuries ago, and His legacy seemed often to be in the accumulation of connections and power more than the distribution of emotional or spiritual ease. She kept that thought to herself. Wisdom came in many forms, and silence was often the most useful.

"The Collegium acknowledges the Vinearts' wisdom and experience," he said, his voice as soft and smooth as ever. "Sin Washer Himself poured the holy wine upon our hands and so protected us from evil."

"I don't need schooling," the prince interrupted. "We speak not of sin but physical danger."

"All danger is sin, and sin danger," Joen replied calmly, but took the warning. "For now, the counsel of the Collegium is to assume no malice if there is no direct assault. In ancient days we might have assumed such events to be the work of the gods, but with Sin Washer's intervention they too have stepped aside, leaving us, as children must, to age into wisdom through our own experiences. As the lady Thaïs has said, this may be the acts of random Nature, and so must be endured, not defended against."

That was not what she had said, but Thaïs held silent again. She could argue with Master Edon, and know where she stood at all times. Brother Joen was a puzzle she had not yet put together, and until she had, she would not tangle with him, even in words. Perhaps most especially not in words. The Brotherhood might be all that was wise and noble, but they did not live and die here on Atakus, and Brother Joen might speak less from wisdom than some yet-unknown agenda that might not have her homeland's best interest at heart.

Call it not paranoia, but caution.

She looked up at that thought, and found Master Edon looking at her. In his aged eyes that had watched a lifetime of Washers come and go, she saw a similar thought. In this, at least, they were united. Atakus came first. The Collegium, for now, was not to be trusted.

*   *   *

THE NEXT MORNING, the wind freshened smartly off the cliffs, making old, retired sailors across the island lift their faces to the sky and long for open seas. Anchored at bay, a ship waited, its canvas wings furled and impatient, for the order to sail.

"NEGOTIATOR TOMAS!"

Tomas turned away from the clothing he was placing into his carry bag, the weary resignation on his face schooling itself into something more appropriate to greet the eldest daughter of his host, however unexpected the meeting might be.

"Lady Thaïs."

"You had hoped for more, from my father." She saw no purpose to pleasantries, but instead cut directly to her purpose. If you needed information, go to the source.

"I had no hopes at all," he said smoothly. "My only purpose was to bring my master's words to this court, to inform them of incursions and alarms my master felt they should be aware of. Prince Erebuh's office was uncommon gracious."

"Well said." She walked into the guest quarters, well aware that she should be doing no such thing. The small cottage Tomas had been housed in was on ground level, near enough to the royal residence that a casual stroll might conceivably bring her by, especially if she were struck by the desire to contemplate the bright red salt-berries that grew in profusion along the western cliffs. Nothing could explain her presence inside the personal quarters, however temporary, of a man not related to her, however. "Well said, but not entirely true. You came here wanting something. What was it?"

"Who is asking me this question?" he asked in return, watching her warily. His eyes were deep green, and alert as a bird's. Despite the poor condition of his clothing, he bore himself as a man of confidence and status. The way he parried her so smoothly only enhanced that contrast. He was no errand boy pressed into the negotiator's sash: no, her instincts were correct. This man had been sent for a reason.

"A concerned daughter of Atakus."

"Ah." He could read that sentence any way he chose to: it was vague enough to mean both everything and nothing. He turned his back to her, and went on with his packing.

"Vineart Jaban looks to Atakus in few things," she said, leaning against the doorframe. Having entered and made her point, she saw no reason to add to her risk by sitting down. "You supply your own food, both fielded and fished. Your men are decent warriors and better sailors. Vineart Jaban's spellwines fetch a fair price on the market, if not in the same category as his teacher's, and your population is reasonably healthy and thriving. The only thing you need from us is the continued protection of Master Edon's winds, to keep your own harbor safe. And that is the one thing that failed you."

"The ships were destroyed by fire. We do not blame a failure of your spellwines for that." A firespell was needed to protect against fire, and neither Master Edon nor Vineart Jabon crafted those. Vineart Pel, another of Master Jabon's students, did, but had they thought to carry any, if they used spellwines for lighting? Information they did not have. She made a note to mention it to her father, later.

"No?" she asked the negotiator. "But you expected us to be more concerned than we were. You expected us to do more than mouth concern and vague promises of heightened awareness?"

"I had no expectations." He reached over to the small table and picked up a shaped-shell cup of water, sipping it and then placing it back on the table. His throat moistened, he turned back to her, clearly about to issue a prepared speech that would lay his agenda out, or send her away, abashed. She waited to see which path he would choose. And that, in turn, would indicate what her next move would be.

Negotiation was both subtle and blunt, in turns. The skill came not in how you wielded each tool, but knowing which to use, when.

"Vineart Jaban fears that Atakus has become too . . . insular," Tomas said. "Too isolated, as damaged by their spellwines as protected by them. The fact that Master Vineart Edon was aware of what had been occurring reassures . . . but the fact that he does nothing, does not."

It was her turn, then, to say "ah," in understanding. It was not her father this negotiator had come to evaluate, but the Master Vineart. This was not a matter political, but magical, one Vineart to another. She had not known they played such games with each other. That was a surprise, but the way of the vine was closed to those of royal blood, by Sin Washer's Command. As such, their parries and counterparries were none of her concern. And yet, Master Edon *was* Atakus, in many ways. Unlike so many other nations, there was no layer of distrust between ruler and Vineart to stir the waters or rend the sail. Therefore, what concerned Edon, concerned her.

"And what message will you carry back to your master, then, if I may be so forward as to inquire?"

"I shall return with the message that was given to me. Atakus is aware of the situation, and will take steps as it deems suited, to protect the well-being of Atakus . . . and the lands that fall within its protection, of course." The last was crafted with delicate irony, and Thaïs shook her head, amused despite her concerns. He was no new-hewn negotiator sent on this task, no. Vineart Jaban had complimented them by sending the very best.

"As Vineart, Jaban is no indentured citizen of Atakus, to claim anything of us beyond the use and protection of his lands," she reminded him. "Our concerns sail together, true, but he pays no tax into our coffers, and for the honor of holding his lands, he pays only nominal tribute."

"Great tribute will be paid," Tomas said, and it was such an odd thing for him to say, his voice neither mocking nor promising, but somehow threatening, that she looked up at him quickly, hoping to catch his expression before it was hidden behind the negotiator's façade once again.

Because of that, she saw the throwing knife coming toward her, seconds before it landed blade first in her breast.

* * *

"Negotiator Tomas? We are ready to take you to your ship now." The young voice came through the doorway; a young male voice, full of cheerful humor. "If you miss the tide, we'll have to row, and you don't want to make us sweat now, do you?"

When he didn't get a response, the sailor shrugged, then pushed open the door, a little surprised when it opened easily, even more surprised when it stopped three quarters of the way into the swing, as though it had hit something heavy.

"Didn't know you had bags. I'll haul 'em down for you, if you want. Negotiator Tomas?"

The door wouldn't open, no matter how hard he shoved, so he slid sideways, some of his good humor disappearing as he narrowly scraped through. "Negoti—"

The words died in his mouth as he saw what had been blocking the door, and his hands moved together as though cupping water being poured from above. "Oh, Sin Washer, give us cleansing. Guards!" He backed out of the door, yelling at the top of his considerable lungs. "Guards, now!"

"My daughter is dead." The prince stood in the reception room of the guest quarters, not looking at either of the bodies still sprawled on the floor. He didn't have to look; the first glance had told him what was important.

"My lord . . ." The other man in the room was far younger but carried himself with an authority that marked him as a Vineart. He had arrived in response to an urgent summons, speaking for Edon, who was too old to travel that quickly anymore. He had been studying the room intently, hands clasped behind his back so as not to disturb anything even by accident, not touching, merely observing.

"Who killed them?" the prince asked, his voice demanding an answer without rising in volume or intensity.

'I believe . . ." The young Vineart had studied with Master Vineart

Edon for almost half of his life. He knew how to craft a handful of spellwines and could competently cast another dozen, but he had never seen a dead person before. It was disturbing him more than he cared to admit.

"Yes?" The prince had no patience for hesitation now.

"I believe that he killed her, my lord. And then killed himself."

The two bodies were both bloodied, but the girl's wound was a single blow, hard to the chest, killing her instantly. The man's were jagged, the blade going in several times before striking the final, awkward blow, as though the killer were resisting the act. The girl's face was still, almost serene in surprise. The man's was twisted in a rictus of rage and confusion. There was no evidence of anyone else having been in the room, other than the sailor who had called the alarm. The guards had taken one look and sealed off the entire quarters. By the end of that day the Vineart's student arrived, clearly having been thrown onto a swift boat and brought thence without delay.

"Why?" The one word was spoken in a steady, almost dispassionate voice, but underneath was the anguish of a bereaved parent given impossible news.

The young Vineart swallowed nervously, and looked around the room again, searching for some explanation. Something caught his attention that he had overlooked during his initial study. It might be nothing, and yet . . . He stepped carefully over the dead man and touched one spit-dampened finger to the rim of the earthenware pitcher of water on the table, next to a half-filled cup. "If it is fresh enough, perhaps . . ."

His fingertip ran along the rim of the cup, and the cloudy-clear liquid shaded into a pale yellow-green. The young man turned a shade paler and whispered something under his breath. He tilted his head as though listening to something being demanded of him from far away, then set his jaw and lifted the cup to his own mouth, visibly bracing himself and taking a sip.

He shuddered, and a pale blue glow surrounded his throat, running down the front of his body to his stomach, and then dissipating.

"I know not what happened here," he said, his voice shaky. "But this water . . . it has been tainted. Fouled. With . . ." He hesitated, almost unable to speak. "With magic."

"Who? How? Whose work is this?"

"My lord, we . . . we do not know." The student forced himself not to drop his gaze in shame and regret, no matter how much he wanted to. "It is magic, but of what crafting, what grape . . . we cannot say." Echoes of his master's voice, two days before. "We cannot identify the source."

The old man did not care how the two magicians had managed to share their thoughts and tastes across the distance, or that the young Vineart was shaken as much by the unknown magic as the deaths themselves. He still had four sons, and two daughters. He was still the ruler of a strong and powerful land. And, in that instant, he looked like a man who had lost everything.

"We have been invaded," he said softly. "Without a single blow or sound of warning, we are undone. Once word of this gets out . . . once other nations know that we are vulnerable, that my very own family . . ."

"It need not be that way, my lord."

The prince did not turn, did not look at the Vineart or in any way indicate that he was listening, but the student continued, speaking for his master in his cellar halfway across the island. "We can protect Atakus. We can stop whatever this unknown enemy intended. But you must allow us leeway, to do what must be done. You must . . . it is against the Command, in every way, what we would do."

The old man did not hesitate. "Tell me."

PART 2

Student

Chapter 7

HOUSE OF MALECH: FALLOWTIME

The months after his marking passed in a blur to Jerzy, with every waking moment filled with lessons of one sort or another. After Harvest, slaves spent their days preparing the yards for the dormant season, trimming back the dead vines and bundling them to dry for firewood. When they were done, the ground would be strewn with the remains of the crushing, mixed with pigeon shit, to prepare the ground for the cold Fallow season. Once that was done, they would spend the shortened days repairing whatever was given them to fix, or cleaning whatever was given them to clean.

In the House, though, the real work was only beginning. His early fears that Malech would teach him nothing, that he would be cast aside, seemed almost laughable now. He woke with the dawn, took breakfast in the dining hall with Detta and, occasionally, Master Malech, then

spent the rest of the morning alternating between working on his letters and numbers and map reading with Detta and being beaten into
competence by Cai.

"You are a lump of young tubers," the Caulian said in disgust after a
particularly slow response landed Jerzy flat on his stomach, spitting dirt
out of his mouth. "I would be afraid to let the likes of you out into a pen
of lambkins, much less a battle."

Jerzy flipped over onto his back, wincing as he did so. The yard where
they practiced had a layer of dirt, but underneath it felt like solid rock.
"I'm not going to go into battle," he pointed out reasonably. "Fight off
a wolf, maybe. Or a bandit, if one was foolish enough to attack the
House. But battles are for soldiers and solitaires, not a Vineart."

Cai picked up the cudgel Jerzy had dropped and weighed it in his
hand. He himself was unarmed, having taken Jerzy down with leg and
elbow. "Again thinking like a slave, boy. Power calls to those who are
hungry for power, and there are hungry idiots everywhere. Think you
forever will stay in this House, protected by Master Malech? A man on
horseback is a target to a man without; a man with food is fair game to
one who is hungry. I will not have you lose horse nor food for lack of
skill to defend."

"I don't have a horse," Jerzy said, getting up and accepting the cudgel
back from Cai.

"You will," Master Malech said. Cai stepped back a pace, his shoulders going back and his head inclining slightly in acknowledgment of
a superior's arrival. Malech acknowledged him, not looking at Jerzy. "If
you've done with the boy for now, I would take him off your hands."

"I release his sorry carcass to you," Cai said. "Boy, be sure to be back
here nextday morning, and be more ready to inflict harm!"

"Master?" Until now, most of his afternoons of study with Malech
had involved him standing by and watching as the Vineart sorted the
harvest and determined what it would best be used for. Had he expected great and wondrous things, he would have been disappointed:
like the hours spent punching the juice in the vatting room, there was

little outwardly exciting about the crafting of spellwines at this stage. And yet, he found it fascinating—and exhausting.

"Every day a little more," Malech told him that first day, too many weeks ago. "Patience is the greatest skill a Vineart may have. Patience, and a gentle touch."

He had tried to be patient. Something was different today. There was an air of excitement, or tension, about his master that made every nerve in Jerzy's body quiver. Today, he thought, might be different.

"Come" was all Malech said, turning and walking back through the back archway into the courtyard, and from there not into his study or the usual workrooms where Master Malech tested and blended the basic spellwines, lecturing Jerzy on the aspects of each particular spell, but down into the racking rooms.

Unlike the vatting rooms where Jerzy had labored, the spellwines here were stored in smaller casks placed on their sides, with tapholes at top and front through which samples were drawn and replenished. Air tunnels carved through the foundation brought cool air in from the outside and kept the stone walls and floor from becoming musty, while spell-cast candles placed at careful lengths above Jerzy's head gave the rooms a dim but clear light.

After the workroom, there were three rooms: the first and largest room contained five large wooden casks of the basic spellwine called heal-all, the second held three more casks labeled as healwine, and the smallest held two casks of the firewine, Malech's secondary specialization.

Today, Malech took him into the first room, and stopped.

"Tell me about healwine."

Jerzy had a moment of panic that crushed his excitement. "Healwine in its basic form is fresh and free flowing," he said, repeating Master Malech's words as perfectly as he could. "It's responsive, easy to use, quick to readiness, and quick to respond."

"So you have been listening. But have you been *learning*? No matter, we'll soon find out."

Malech placed Jerzy's hands on the side of one of the tanks, palms flat against the wood, just at shoulder level. "Tell me what you feel."

"The wood is cool, but not slick. I can . . . I can feel the pressure of the wine inside. It's heavier than the mustus in the vatting tanks, more powerful, but it does not press the way the mustus did. Master, if all the healwine is in these casks . . ." His voice trailed off, and Malech waited. A shiver went through the boy, as though something had passed over his grave, then he went on.

"Punching the wine: that brought the magic out, made the power of the juice come together with the strength in the skins. Filtering it, getting rid of the skins"—that had been the second step, the skins going into the fertilizing mixture the slaves spread over the soil to feed it— "allowed the juice to come out on top, for power to use strength, and not to be overwhelmed by it. Now . . . It is not pressing me because it is . . . waiting?"

He didn't stop for a response, certain for once that he was correct.

"You've taught me about five different kinds of healwine: heal-all, blood staunch, bone-heal, melancholia, and deep-heal. There are five tanks here, and three in the next room, and none of them are separately marked, so the next step must be for all of them, equally, and then . . . then they are crafted for each specific spell?"

As the words tumbled out of his student's mouth, Malech felt his face purse up in an unexpected smile. "Who knew such a mind lurked under all that dirt. Well done, boy. Well done. Yes, there is a process we have not yet discussed. Healwine magic cures or corrects ailments, creating the proper delicate balance in the human—or animal—body. But magic is not, of itself, delicate or balanced. Just as we created a balance between strength and power, now we must craft a delicacy into that power; to teach the magic where to stop, else it do harm where it might heal. Without that . . . What might happen then?"

Jerzy, his hands still flat on the tank, shuddered. "A heal-all, told to close a wound in the face, might close up the mouth as well?"

"An extreme case, but possible. And so, here is where your own abilities come into play. Feel the power within that cask, boy. That cask and only that cask, the magic speaking to you, touching back at you, and let your own magic rise to greet it, the way you have been greeting the smaller vials. There is no difference in power, no difference in technique. Do you feel it?"

"Yes. It . . . sings to me." The boy sounded surprised.

"Sing back to it. Sing to it of control and balance. Of a delicate flavor and delicate touch. The magic wants out, that's all it has ever wanted. Show it the way to get there."

Jerzy nodded, his face set in a fierce determination. Malech placed his hands on the boy's shoulders, feeling the muscles bunch and tighten in response.

"No, relax. Relax. There is nothing here that controls you; you control it." He softened his voice, making it as soothing as possible. The boy was quick and smart, but the lessons—and the scarring—of the years of slavery lay in all of them. Stress made for riper fruit—but delicate handling was what made a powerful spellwine—or Vineart. "Relax and listen. . . ."

Jerzy's muscles slowly softened, but the tenseness remained until Malech let go and stepped back, still giving instructions until he saw Jerzy's head lean forward, his forehead touching the side of the tank, and his breathing even out so that a stranger might think that he had fallen asleep in that position.

"Tell the magic that it must listen to you, in order to be free. Like a horse to harness, magic must know what is expected of it. . . ."

Even as he spoke, Malech reached out to the cask as well, not physically but with his other senses, overlaying the boy's efforts with his own. This was still his wine; he was the Vineart. Stress the vines, stress the Vineart. . . . But too much stress ruined both, and he could not afford to have the boy fail.

"Enough now. Relax, let go, let the wine settle, and release. . . . Good."

Jerzy sighed, and he felt those neck muscles tense up again. This time Malech removed his hands, allowing the boy his privacy. "Now," he said, keeping his tone conversational, "I want you to go into the workroom and do exactly that same thing on the sample there. Only this time, you will be the one to lay down a spell-structure, and see if you can convince it to take hold."

He watched carefully while Jerzy nodded, and turned, as though in a daze, and walked back to the workroom. Yes. Students, like vines, needed to be stressed. Like spellwines, they needed to be crafted. Balance was important in knowing which method to apply, and when.

"UP! UP, DAMN you!"

The Master's voice slammed into Jerzy's ear, tumbling him out of his narrow bed and onto the hard stone floor. He did not stop to consider that he might have imagined the summons: six months within the House had shown him too many wonders to doubt, and so he merely reached for his clothing, grumbling a little at the timing of masters who interrupted dreams just as they were reaching a good point, in this instance having to do with a faceless but nonetheless invitingly warm figure wrapped around his nether regions. Then something in the night air alerted him, and he stopped with one leg halfway into his trousers.

"Master?"

There was no answer, only a sense of impatience and . . . worry?

"Guardian?"

But there was no heavy flap of stone wings at his window, either. The Guardian, who had more than once been sent to fetch him while he slept, was elsewhere.

Something was wrong. He looked out the window, his gaze unerringly drawn to the nearest slope of the vineyard, and his breath caught at the flickers of light where there should only have been still darkness.

Root-glow.

Jerzy had no memory of getting dressed, or indeed of how he made his way from his bedchamber to the fields. For all he knew, he sprouted wings and flew there. Once on the ground, the sight was worse than he could ever have dreamed; all along the rows of winter-dormant grapevines the soil flickered with a sickly yellow color where the infection was attacking the roots, spreading even as he stood there, horrified, and watched.

Root-glow was a springtime infestation. How was it here, now, in the middle of Fallowtime?

"Take this." Malech appeared next to him, and thrust a wineskin into his hands, his words coming out as puffs of frost in the cool night air. His master was wearing a quilted jacket, cinched at the hips with his usual double-wrapped tool belt, and was pulling on fingerless leather gloves even as he spoke. "It's heal-all. Do you remember how to cast a clarification?"

Jerzy nodded, even though the Master hadn't waited for a response. "Take the downslope; I'll work uphill. Go, boy!"

A clarification spell was simple enough; in its most common form it was used with healwines to determine the truth of a story in court, stripping away the lies and elaborations until only the unvarnished truth remained. But that was on people. How was he supposed to . . .

The months of being drilled on soil, vines, and spell-crafting kicked in, and Jerzy understood. Strip the additions away. Strip away that which was not part of the truth, the original form. A vinespell was crafted to do a specific thing, focusing the magic within the wine, but the magic that existed within the grape was broader than any spell, and that magic could be manifested in a variety of ways—if you were a Vineart.

Even as he was uncorking the wineskin and taking a mouthful, Jerzy was already focusing his will on the liquid in his mouth, ascertaining the properties of the fruit, fresh and sweet, but with a surprising depth and structure to it. That was unusual for a heal-all. Not a young vintage, maybe five harvests back, when the weather had held warm and dry?

Now was not the time to play spot-the-vintage, he scolded himself. Too many hours had been spent memorizing the signs of blights and infestations for him to underestimate the danger. Root-glow, if not stopped, could seriously damage growth in the spring—and, in worst-case scenarios, require an entire field to be undone and replanted with new stock.

Around him, slaves scurried with sand and shovels, working to dig out roots that were already too infected to survive, trying to stop the spread that way. But it was too slow, too inefficient a way to save the vines, especially when the slaves had to beware touching the actual rot or risk a painful rash on the exposed skin. Root-glow was only lethal to plants, but everyone knew it wasn't kind to flesh, either, and the soothe-salve used for it smelled worse than the rash-blighted skin.

Holding the mouthful of wine in his mouth, Jerzy focused his awareness on the liquid, tasting the properties of the grape, the nature of the soil. He could recognize the specific spellwine, down to what yard the vines had grown in, and that allowed him to unlock the deeper magics within. Had this been a wine of another's crafting, it would have resisted him. But the crafting had been Malech's, and the magic recognized him, too. More, this was a spellwine from this very vineyard, soil-to-soil and vine-to-vine, and there was a special strength in that.

To the root, go. Once, to direct. Once, to decant. Once, to strike. That was the rule.

He could feel the magic summoned by his direction, sliding from his mouth, out and down the rows of vines, slipping through the thick, clotted soil to spread over the roots, waiting for decantation. What to say? Jerzy felt panic flutter inside him, making his stomach sick, and every thought fled his mind, leaving him helpless and near panic. Why hadn't the Master told him what decantation to use? He didn't know, he was only a half year removed from ignorant slave, and he had never done this before, never used a spellwine outside the working chamber before, he didn't know, it was too much; too much weighed on him!

These vines were his responsibility to save.

That thought staggered him, hitting like a blow to the gut, and then a slave shoved him aside, digging frantically at a half-mature vine, swearing as he did so, and Jerzy's paralysis was broken. It was too much, but to do nothing was unthinkable. He was no slave, to dig and grub—he was a Vineart.

"Restore to health." It was as clumsy a decantation as could be, yet all Jerzy could think of. Healwines. "Heal the vines. Go!"

Even as he gave the strike order, Jerzy swallowed the spellwine, feeling it rush down his throat and explode through his body. Ordinary folk didn't feel this, the intoxicating power flooding every nerve, making him shake in the aftermath, Malech had said. But he couldn't revel in it; this wasn't a training class. Even as the spell was cleansing and protecting the roots from invasion, the yellow glow fading and sputtering out up and down the row, Jerzy was moving on to the next grouping of vines, repeating the process over and over again as he moved downslope, slaves moving out of his way even as they kept digging at the roots that still glowed. His world narrowed to the wineskin in his hand, the feel of the rounded, sweet fruit in his mouth, and the flickering lights in front of him, his body moving mechanically down and down the hill, aware only of the darkness behind him and the lights ahead, until there were no more lights on the ground, only a pale glow overhead. He tilted his head back, and wondered blankly if he was supposed to do something about that glow as well.

"Young one."

Jerzy blinked, and turned to face the source of the voice. The overseer stood there, his hard face covered with dirt and worn with exhaustion. "The Master calls for you."

"But . . . I must . . ." Words felt strange in his mouth, and he was suddenly aware of a confusing dizziness in his body.

"Master calls for you," the overseer repeated, and then something strange flickered across his face, and his huge hand came down on Jerzy's bare shoulder. Jerzy was too tired, too confused to flinch, but the touch, while firm, did not crush his shoulder as expected. "You done right, young Jerzy. The field is safe. Let us handle the rest, like we know how. You go to the Master, now."

Still numbed and confused, Jerzy realized that the morning had come, his wineskin was near empty, and the buzzing in his head was not due to a swarm of insects but the pressure of so much magic ingested too fast.

"Yes. All right," he said. Tucking the wineskin over his shoulder, Jerzy stumbled around a slave still digging around the roots, although with less frantic energy, and headed back up the slope to where the Vineart waited.

"Master?"

Malech was looking out over the fields, and Jerzy turned to echo him. The vines were still brown, bare, and wizened, and it was almost impossible to believe that in a few months, pale green leaves would begin to unfurl and ripe fruit would hang low. The soil was innocently still, to all intents and purposes untouched except where spades had turned out root and filled the spot in with paler sand, to halt the root-glow infection.

"Out of season," Master Malech said, as though to himself. "Out of season and so fast. It could all have been gone. The entire yard, my oldest vines. Overnight, in the blink of the moon and the whim of the silent gods. All our care, our skills, are nothing in the face of such disaster."

"Is there no vine immune to root-glow?" Even as he asked the question Jerzy cursed himself for a sleep-addled idiot. If there were, would not the Master already have planted it? He deserved to be hit, for such ignorance.

"You pay a price for such an immunity," Malech said, and to Jerzy's relief there was no censure in his voice, only a weary instruction. "A vine might be bred to resist rot, or a particular bug, or to grow where rains come heavy or weather runs cold. And then?"

The night air was chilled, and he shivered despite the sweat, wishing he had thought to grab his quilted jacket as well. "To change the nature of the vine in such a way . . . it would change the nature of the grape as well?" Vines showed the nature not only of the roots but the soil they grew in. A spirit-healgrape grown in the dry sand of Malech's home-land would have different effects from the same grape transplanted to the Cerian Hills and their shorter, cooler summers, and neither would be the spirit-heal Malech grew in his northern fields. The magic itself would change, depending on the location and the Vineart. It seemed logical that changing the plant itself would have no less an effect.

"And?" No hint if he had answered correctly or not, merely his master offering more rope with which to truss himself.

"And only Sin Washer had the right to change the nature of the vines?"

The expected cuff landed then, although not as hard as it might have been on another morning. "The Sin Washer gave the vines into our care," Malech said. "We have dominion . . . but that dominion must be tempered with wisdom, else we have learned nothing from the fate of the prince-mages. And wisdom, boy, means considering the balance of the universe when making such a decision. A vine resistant to root-glow almost inevitably opens another weakness—one we would know nothing about until it struck. And then, our fields denuded and a full span of replanting to wait before a new harvest; what happens to a Vineart then?"

"Yes, Master," Jerzy said. His head spun from the wine and the cuffing and the lack of sleep, but he dared not show any of that until the Master released him from lessoning.

Malech stared at the vines a moment longer, his eyes deep set with exhaustion under shaggy gray brows, and then sighed. "Enough. I race ahead of your understanding once again. Tell me, what decantation did you use?"

"A restore-to-health," Jerzy said, grateful to fall back on his familiar role of student being quizzed. "I thought at first to strengthen-and-protect, but was afraid that it might attach itself to the root-glow rather than the root itself."

"Hrmmm. A fair enough concern, and a passable solution, if lacking elegance."

"Would not a rougher vinespell be preferred?" Jerzy knew he was exhausted, if he was challenging his master, but the question seemed a fair one. "This . . . root-glow is rough and ugly and seemed to call for blunt flavors, not delicacy. Is that not why you brought heal-all, not something more particular?"

"Hrmm." A pause, and then the Master laughed. "Perhaps you have been listening in lessons, after all. Go, get some food in your stomach, boy, and meet me in the workroom at the eighth hour."

Released, Jerzy staggered off back toward the house, feeling every hour of exhaustion in his parched skin and weary bones. Halfway there, he turned and looked back. Master Malech still stood on the rise, his long and lean form upright against the pale blue Fallowtime sky, so like the Guardian's stone-still form as to be carved of the same materials.

Shaking the thought off as useless fancy, Jerzy went in to break his fast. The kitchen was already roused, aware that there had been a disturbance in the night, and he found himself seated at the scarred wood table in the dining hall with a bowl of sweetened grain on the table in front of him and Lil pouring out a cup of steaming tai from the cast-iron kettle. She had been made cook the month before, freeing Detta to more efficiently run the Household and manage the business aspects for the House of Malech. The change had also affected their relationship; he was oddly more comfortable with her now, and she teased him less as a result.

"Here." Lil's red kerchief was slipping down over her sweat-beaded forehead, and she shoved it back into place with the inside of her elbow. "I made it extra strong and extra sweet this morning, and drink it up and no complaining. It will keep you going until you can fall over."

Jerzy hated tai, especially sweetened, but the girl was right—it would help him stay awake throughout the day. He took the mug from her hands and sipped, trying not to grimace.

"Take it all at once," Detta said, bustling into the room and sitting down to take her own meal. Unlike the others, she was dressed for the day, her wide leather belt jangling from the keys and pouches hanging from it, and her gray curls neatly combed and coiled. The uncertain hesitation Jerzy had once felt in front of the older woman hadn't quite disappeared—she was still as much a force of nature as Malech, and with almost as much power within these walls, but it was tempered now by the knowledge that Detta saw them all as her cubs to protect, even the Master.

"It ruins my taste," he said, scrunching his face to show his dislike of the brew.

"That's why you should take it all at once," she told him. "Sipping it spreads it on the tongue. Gulping it gets it into your throat that much the faster."

Jerzy was annoyed that he hadn't thought of that himself; it was so obvious now. Taking a spoonful of the grain, he chased it down with half the mug's contents, wincing a little as the steam hit the inside of his throat and rose up through his nose. The second gulp was more cautious, trying to avoid the gunk that waited at the bottom of the mug. Lil hadn't been jesting when she said she had brewed it strong.

"You were able to contain the infection." It took Jerzy a moment to realize that Detta was stating a fact, not a question. She had worked for the Master her entire life; she knew that if they hadn't, he wouldn't be here, spooning grain into his mouth and waiting for Lil to serve out the cheese roll he could smell baking in the oven.

"How did it get into the vines?" Lil asked, refilling his mug without regard for his protest. "Another mug, and then I'll leave you be. Doesn't Master have protections up against such a thing?"

"Of course." Jerzy felt a flash of annoyance that Lil—a serving-girl—questioned the Master so casually.

Lil wasn't at all abashed by his tone. "Then how?" She looked first to Jerzy, then to Detta. Detta shook her head, and looked at Jerzy, as though he would have the answer.

"I don't know," he had to admit. "Master Malech will, though." He scooped the last of the grains into his mouth and swallowed, then washed his mouth out with the entire mug of tai in one long gulp that left him coughing.

"Don't breathe and drink at the same time," Lil suggested pertly, taking the now-empty bowl and spoon away, even as he put the mug back down on the table and pushed his bench away. The cheese rolls would have to wait.

"Master's waiting for me. Don't know that we'll be finished in time for supper," he told Detta, who nodded as though she had been expecting such, and likely had. "I'll have Lil set cold meats aside," she told him, "for whenever you're finished, or famished, as comes first."

THE STEPS DOWN to the workrooms were steep and shadowed as ever, but after half a year's climbing up and down, Jerzy took them confidently, if not carelessly. Halfway down, he heard the sound of stone brushing against stone, and ducked even as the Guardian moved overhead.

"And where were you, all night we were slogging and spelling?" he asked, not expecting an answer. The stone dragon took its usual place on the mantel, curling its wings tight against its body, and merely stared at the boy. Jerzy didn't even know what the Guardian guarded—it moved from workroom to House and then back again, occasionally disappearing but never for long.

The boy shrugged and entered the workroom. The now-familiar smells of must and candle wax met his nose, almost overriding the memory of the tai on his tongue. Malech was in his usual spot, leaning back in the carved wooden chair and staring off, seemingly into space. Jerzy settled himself on the small bench, the surface after so many months a comfortable perch.

"Today we will continue with the crafting of heal-all, as we used up a considerable portion of our stores this evening past. Go fetch a half barrel from the last but one Harvest and bring it in."

Jerzy blinked disbelievingly at Malech, who met his gaze with a solemn, unperturbed look of his own. Clearly, today's lesson was not to be about root-glow. He bit back the questions still on his tongue, and did as he was bid.

MALECH WATCHED HIS student carefully all morning as they poured vial after vial of the jewel-red wine from the barrel and tested Jerzy's understanding of craft. It was a delicate process: only a trained Vineart could convince the liquid magic to accept a spell. It was that framework—the spell—that made spellwines viable, allowing someone other than its creator to use it. Without the spell, the wines were no better than a toy, an amusement. Properly incanted, they were powerful tools.

The gift and the training were equal sides to the crafting, and needed to remain in balance to create a balanced spellwine, an effective spellwine that would do as directed. That was the secret to Vinearts' continued survival: not that they could command the magic themselves, but that they had learned, over centuries, how to allow others to do so as well. And if those others never knew how very little of the magic inherent in a spellwine they in fact used, compared to what a Vineart might command . . .

Safer that way for all concerned.

All this went through Malech's mind as Jerzy focused intently on a vial, trying to sense the magic within and bend it to his will. Some might caution against letting him jump so swiftly from slave to blender, but Malech had seen from the very first that the boy was a fast learner, swift to comprehend and cautious enough not to overjump his abilities. And it had been a good Harvest; they had spellwine to spare, if the boy ruined a batch, or it came out too weak for use.

Still, the boy was not without flaws and weakness. He hesitated, looked too much to Malech for approval instead of trusting himself. He was a follower, not a leader. Neither of these things were fatal, but . . . For that reason so far the boy had handled only the heal-all, the simplest if most lucrative of Malech's craftings, although they'd worked the other healspells together, Malech guiding the boy's touch. By the time the vines flowered again, the boy should have the basics down cleanly. After next Harvest, he would start the boy on more complicated crafting of firewines, and then . . . if Jerzy survived that far, then they would move on to the most delicate of the three vines the Valle of Ivy was known for: a rare fertility-wine that grew only in a small enclosure along the coast and was vinified only once every two or three years, as conditions allowed. Growvines were the oldest variety, and required a steady hand, a delicate balance, and a mind strong enough to clear itself of all but goodwill and good wishes, else it turned into a curse. Grow-spells were nothing for a beginning student to touch.

It would be a shame if this promising boy were to fail before that point. Malech had grown fond of Jerzy, and this attack on the vine-yard—and it had been an attack, no mistake—would have over-whelmed most of those of his age and limited experience. Aware of that, the Vineart was alert to even the slightest sign of breakage. So far, save for a few carefully hidden yawns, the boy seemed the same as the day before. Curious, yes—only a Guardian wouldn't be curious!—but not flinching, not hesitant . . . and not overconfident, either, despite his success during the night before. The boy was taking the events in stride, and not shirking in the day's learning. Good.

He doubts too much.

He did well last night, Malech replied.

He doubts, Guardian repeated. *Doubt fails.*

Malech pushed the stopper back into the bunghole of the half cask, and turned to face his student. "Now. Quickly and clearly. What are the three applications of heal-all?"

The boy set aside his decanting glass and stood to recite, his eyes fixed at some spot over Malech's head. "To apply to a patient who is asleep or insensible: compose within the mouth and apply through the application of hands. To apply to a patient who is alert: compose with the mouth and apply through application of mouth to mouth. To apply to self: a patient must compose within the mouth and apply onto the wound particular."

"And the limitations?"

"Limitations are . . ." Jerzy's eyelids flickered as he tried to remember, his dark, almond-shaped eyes taking on a panic until the knowledge came back to him. "Healwine, in the hands of ordinary folk, affects only wounds visible or known. The healer must be aware of the injury and how to fix it. An unknown or unsuspected injury will not be affected. If an untrained ordinary were to attempt a healing, the spell would not work." A pause, and one hand whisked nervously at a strand of hair that fell over his forehead; then he continued. "A Vineart, using a basic spellwine, may heal all injuries known, even without healing arts. A more complicated spellwine might accomplish more . . . Master?"

The boy had done well enough that Malech allowed the interruption. "Yes?"

"You said the root-glow was out of season. So how did it get into the vines? Had it been there all summer? Could you have missed it, when we cleansed the soil after Harvest?"

The boy obviously braced himself for the cuffing a foolish question would normally earn, but did not flinch or show any other sign of uncertainty. Despite himself, Malech was pleased, both by the unexpected confidence in asking and the thinking behind the question. That didn't stop him from cuffing the boy across the nearest ear, for impudence, and then again in case the first cuff hadn't seemed serious enough. Jerzy's skin flushed a dark red to match his hair, then faded to its normal tones. For the first time Malech wondered where the slavers had found this boy, with that skin and doe-slanted eyes and his dark red hair. The slave caravans traveled everywhere, picking up trade as they went, but such a striking-looking boy child normally would have been kept by all but the poorest, most overrun of parents, in the hopes of his catching a wealthy patron's eye once he came of age. . . .

No matter. They all ended up where they were meant to be, somehow.

"You think I failed something as basic as a soil-cleansing?" Malech asked in return, his tone purposefully calm. The boy would have earned a third cuffing for such a suggestion. But not asking it would have been a greater omission, and an even greater disaster for them both. Guardian was correct, damn it. A Vineart could not doubt. The leap from a slave's obedience to Vineart's confidence was the most-often deadly one.

"If it wasn't there before, and it would not occur in the natural order . . . the vineyard was deliberately infected?" Jerzy wasn't asking his master, but rather speaking to himself: Malech could practically see the workings of his student's mind, puzzling over the question. "Who *could* do such a thing? Only someone who knew how quickly root-glow spreads, and yet, if they knew that, they would also know that it is easily contained and destroyed, so long as one is alert. . . ."

His eyes widened, and he looked up at Malech in a combination of satisfaction and alarm. "Master, they were testing you. Who was testing you? Who would dare, to endanger a harvest . . ." Those eyes narrowed again. "More, the vintnery itself would have been damaged. Your reputation . . ."

The boy's anger felt true, and it warmed Malech, even as he knew he had to contain it, before Jerzy lost the thread of his logic.

"My reputation is beyond the reach of anyone who might wish me harm. The worst they could have done was . . . bad. Yes. I am the best crafter of healwines"—no bragging there, simply fact—"and if there was another plague, or war, then the loss would be sorely felt. But there are other vineyards, as you well know. We would survive." Barely, and not easily, but no need to burden the boy with that knowledge, nor the fact that there were some to whom the deaths of others, absent ready healwines, might be reason enough for the action.

"As to who it might have been . . . the possibilities are open." He was not young, and had his share of conflicts with others, but the Guardian's warning echoed, and he hesitated. No, now was not the time to tell the boy everything. Some details he would hold close to himself, until and if the time came to share them. But a few cold truths would be appropriate, at this time and place in Jerzy's lessoning.

"Not all people hold our work in high regard, boy. There are those who say the Sin Washer meant to destroy the magic, not share it. That he was sent to destroy the *vin magica* entirely; that the juice of the grapes was meant merely to refresh, not empower."

"They say Sin Washer made a mistake?" Jerzy's voice held amazement, not horror—slaves were not taught piety in the sleep houses, but survival.

Malech laughed without humor. "Not in so many words. They frisk around it like lambs determined that there is no butcher, only grass and mother's milk forever. They say that his intent was subverted, his sacrifice made in vain, and so long as a single Vineart practices, the ideal kingdom of man will never come." He settled down into discourse mode, letting the recently poured vial of lesson-wine rest on his desk, abandoned for the moment. "They are few, and shouted down at every opportunity by the Brotherhood of Washers, but they have won a toehold in a princeling's Household here, a maiar's city council there.

"It was this group that first discovered root-glow, on the shores of a distant land. There, in the stalks of a native grain, it was a frustration, not disaster. But they brought it back, and loosed it among us, and it took years before we discovered the way to combat it, to limit the damage it might do."

"And you think that they, that some member of this group, set it on us? But . . . those are healvines!" The outrage in the boy's voice was mixed with a rougher emotion. Malech was amused—and gratified—to identify it as a possessive sort of anger on behalf of the vines themselves.

"These people believe that the prince-mages should have been eradicated, not merely split; that only a magic-less world is pleasing to Sin Washer. Even if it means losing the good that spellwines do, yes. Be calm, Jerzy."

"Why do we allow such people to continue?" The boy was almost spluttering in his upset.

Malech leaned back and fixed Jerzy with a stern glare. "Because it is not our place to stop them. Sin Washer's Command is clear on that matter. Were one such fellow so foolish as to strike at me, I would strike him down, and none might gainsay me. But we are not princelings, with armies or courts. We do not decide the law, and the law in this land gives them freedom to do as they will, so long as it harms no other man nor property."

Truth, if not the truth entire. Had these men thought to burn the vintnery itself, the law would have been his ally, finding the villains accountable for his loss. The vines, through Sin Washer's act, were none of man's owning. A Vineart might cultivate, and harvest, and make use of . . . but he had no dominion, no rights of ownership. Any man might grow vines and press a *vin ordinaire*, if he so desired. Few did, either fearing reprimand or through lack of knowledge, but in theory, any might.

That was theory beyond Jerzy's understanding at this moment, however.

"Master?"

His voice was so tentative, Malech sighed. Still, caution was not unwise for a student. "I haven't smacked you to the floor yet, boy; you might as well get your questions out now and stop being so mouseish about it."

The boy practically tumbled his words over one another, anxious to get them out before Malech changed his mind. "Why did you not hunt down those who did this, discover who they were and punish them? Is that not a personal strike, and allowed by the Command?"

An easier question to answer, that. "No spellwine can tell truth from lie, or good from evil, Jerzy. Magic is a thing of nature, not mankind. Healing or growing, raising the wind or damping a flame, those are things a Vineart may do, by Sin Washer's Command. This . . . such an attack, if it is such, is a matter of proof and courts. Vinearts tend to their magic and the princelings tend to their laws, and the world no longer rocks in the conflict between the two as it did in the days of the mage-lords. The Washers make sure of that."

"But, Master—"

Malech's voice cracked harder than his hand would have, and he took the time to make sure the blow landed properly. Caution was one thing. This line of questioning could only end in disaster. "Sin Washer came to us to save us from ourselves. I for one have no desire to require him to make a repeat visit. We are Vinearts. We compose our lives around the crafting, and we leave the governing to those who are born to that."

Jerzy was properly subdued, and took up his vial and wine again without further comment, settling at a table across the room to work. The Guardian, however, lifted its head up from its stone paws and looked down with those sightless eyes at Malech; a steady, thoughtful gaze.

You know that cannot last. Not if the rumors we are hearing are true.

Recent rumors come to his unwilling ears, of strange plagues and seemingly random attacks. Of vineyards damaged, their fruit withered, or eaten away by some unknown rot. Like the unusual order coming from Atakus, things that happened outside his lands were no concern of his, so long as it left him and his alone.

And when it begins to concern you?

Malech looked away from the Guardian, and focused all of his attention on Jerzy's careful, if halting, movements with the vials. It was a valid question the Guardian asked. He just didn't know what the answer would be.

Chapter 8

Three months passed from the root-glow infestation, and outside the barren brown ground was more often than not frosted with ice, the slaves huddled in the sleep house or working with the livestock. When the ground was bare, Jerzy worked mornings with Cai; they had progressed to riding lessons now, and Jerzy felt confident enough to stay on horseback no matter what the beast might do. The few times that snow covered the ground, he was given over to Detta, learning more of how a vintnery was run. Someday he would need to know these things for himself, Detta said.

Jerzy couldn't even begin to imagine that day.

In the afternoons he worked with Master Malech, more and more often crafting the finished wines, what Master Malech called *vina*, into balance. He had even corked a clay vessel of his own crafting, and spent several days floating on that sense of accomplishment, until Master Malech slapped him down with an almost impossible assignment, and he ruined an entire quarter cask of healwine trying to manage a bone-set incantation.

A week after that, by the time he'd woken, washed, and relieved himself, and emptied the pot of soil into the chute, the sun was warm enough to melt the window frost. The sign was clear: Fallowtime was ending. He walked down the stairwell to the dining hall, wondering if this would put an end to his lessons with Cai, and had barely sat down at the table when Detta dumped a question on him like a bucket of icy water.

"A message came from Beuville this morning. Winter sickness in town, all quarantined, could we send healwine and take payment after their crops are in?"

He checked himself, looking for Malech, as though the Master might have come in unnoticed behind him, then realized that yes, the House-keeper was asking him.

"Beuville is . . . where?" he asked, stalling until his brain caught up with his body. It had been a hard, cold morning, and simply forcing himself out from under the coverlet had taken all of his willpower.

"Half a day's walk to the west. They hold their charter of Prince Ranulf, but deal directly with us for their needs. Their workers built our press, when Master Malech came into residency."

"How serious a sickness?" That should have been his first question: he had not been born when the rose plague swept through the known lands, but he had heard stories that made his skin creep with horror, of bodies covered with petal-like blemishes, blood running from their mouths and anuses until they simply bled out, and not even the strongest blood staunch could stop it. The Berengia had been spared the worst, due to Malech's spells, but the fear of the plague's return haunted everyone, even now.

"Serious, but contained," she said reassuringly. "It's merely illness, not plague." Jerzy nodded, breathing again. Detta had been a girl when the rose plague had hit, and would not underestimate the risk.

"Do you trust them to pay?" he asked. Detta handled all money matters, and Jerzy knew Malech trusted her implicitly.

Detta shrugged, her rounded shoulders meeting rounded chin. "It's still a month and more until first crops will be sown; if they recover in time to man their fields, they should be fine. If not . . ."

"Send it," he said. "Unless Master Malech has a reason to say no."

"I always have a reason to say no. What disaster are you plunging me into this time?"

Jerzy flinched, and Detta shot Malech an annoyed look that he ignored, reaching past her to take a sausage link off the platter and, carefully, pop it into his mouth. She sighed and handed him a cloth to wipe the resulting grease stain off his fingers. It was only then that Jerzy noted his master was wearing a grandly embroidered half robe of garnet cloth over—unusually—clean black trousers and a white shirt with a vine pattern embroidered on the collar, a pair of soft leather shoes replacing his usual sturdy and scuffed half boots.

"Messenger arriving today?" Detta asked, while Jerzy gaped at the unexpected finery.

"Yes, curse them for bad timing, as I'd thought to—oh well, can't be helped. Pigeon arrived this morning. I'd half a thought to pitch it into the stew pot." He waved away the offer of a bowl, but accepted a mug of tai from Lil. "You were talking about offering credit?"

"Beauville's come down sick. Nothing serious, but we won't be getting the Players this year, as they're caught in it."

"Ah. Pity, that. Whatever they need, yes. If all else fails, I'll take their firstborn sons." He paused. "No, too many of those already. We can settle on sheep. They raise good sheep there, very tasty. That will be fine. Jerzy, go down to the workroom and continue where we left off yesterday. If you're making decisions about our livelihood, then you're comfortable enough with the process to be on your own for a short while without causing epic disaster. Do nothing to prove me wrong in that assumption." He glared at Jerzy over the rim of the mug, and then walked out of the room, his shoes making no noise against the stone flooring.

Jerzy looked at Detta, who looked away, holding her hand to her mouth. He wasn't sure if that meant that she didn't want to explain what was bothering Malech, or if she was hiding a smile that would mean the Master had been joking, and he wasn't supposed to know that she knew. Even after all this time, there was still so much about living in the House that confused him. "Messenger?"

"None of your worry, young Jerzy, if Malech hasn't seen fit to tell you."

That was true enough, so he did the only thing he could do. He finished his meal, and went down to the workroom.

The Guardian was already in place over the doorway, and on impulse Jerzy reached up to touch the tip of its tail where it dangled just over the lintel. The stone was cool and smooth to his touch, and Jerzy felt somehow disappointed, as though he were expecting something else.

The wine they had been using in the previous day's lesson on how to incant *vin magica* had gone slightly sour overnight, so Jerzy went into the storeroom to bring out another. As always, walking into the storeroom was a pleasant assault on his senses; the resting casks filled with wines emitting an array of smells, from ripe seaberries to the cool hints of winter nutmeats. More, the heady awareness of *magica* rising from those casks intoxicated his brain and made his mouth water. Normal reactions, Malech had told him. Normal, but dangerous. A Vineart controlled spellwine; he did not allow the spellwine to control him.

Shutting off as much awareness of the finished wines as he could, Jerzy pulled down a half cask of prepared *vina* from the storage rack and carried it back out into the clearer, less interesting air of the workroom. A push of the appropriate stone in the wall, and the door slid closed without a sound. By now, Jerzy no longer marveled at that. Like the bathing room, the Guardian, and having a bedchamber to himself, it merely *was*.

Creating magic: that still amazed him. Even more so when he was allowed to do it himself, without Malech's hand guiding his own.

A slave in the field, he had walked along the vines uncountable times. If there was a memory before pointed green leaves and woody vines, it was faded at best. Never then, the child he had been, could he have understood how simple the act was, to wring juice from grape, and decant juice into magic. How simple—and how . . . words failed him utterly.

How complicated, impossible, and astonishing, as drawing that first breath, or taking that first step, your body knowing what to do and then doing it. You could learn only so much through books and lectures and repetition. To create wine, much less spellwine, it needed to be in your hands, in your blood.

It ran through his head, like blood pumping in his veins. From mustus to *vina*, from *vina* to *vin magica*, and from *vin magica* to proper spellwine . . . he could not craft spellwine, not yet, not anything that could be released as such. Not for many years, Master Malech said. Already he was ahead of where most students might be, and with that he needed to be patient.

Patience again. Any time he displeased Master Malech, it was a cuff to the head and an admonishment to be patient.

The half cask Jerzy selected was from one of the southern fields, tested and proofed by Malech in the most recent Harvest. It had been in one of the vats Jerzy had punched down, reciting his lessons as his arms worked endlessly and the smell of the mustus rose into his nose and seeped into his skin. Transferred into smaller holding casks for vinification, the *vina* was ready now for the magic within it to be woken and directed.

Jerzy's hand did not tremble as he let the deep red wine flow into the decanting glass, and his voice did not falter as he reached inside himself, finding that deep, resonant voice within him that spoke to the magic of the wine.

There were three clay pots of spellwine filled and finished on the worktable in front of him, ready for stoppering, and his knees were slightly wobbly with the effort, when he felt the crash. The walls of the workroom were thick stone and kept sound out as well as they kept the cool air within, but the sound traveled through the ground itself, almost a physical shock. The sound that did cut through the rock was a high-pitched keening that had Jerzy heading up the stairs before he'd known he was moving.

Detta and the new kitchen boy—Geordie had gone on to another placement the month before—met him in the front garden, having come out through the kitchen door at the side of the house.

"The cart!" the kitchen boy said, pointing down the path out to the main road. Through the archway Jerzy could see a pile of splintered wood that used to be one of their transport wagons. All three of them could hear the low screams and moans as well as the alarmed cries of other slaves running up from the sleep house and the vintnery shed.

Master, what do I do? Jerzy thought helplessly, his head spinning from the chaos.

A dry voice sounded in the air around him, unexpected but so smooth and familiar that he barely started in surprise that his master could hear, and speak, in that fashion.

"Idiot boy, I can't be bothered by this now. Make sure none of them are permanently damaged. We can't afford to buy new slaves right now and we will need all the able bodies we have. And clear the road, so the other wagons can get through!"

The voice disappeared, and he was left with Detta and the kitchen boy staring at him. Jerzy realized, with a clenching in his gut, that they had not heard Master Malech's voice and were waiting for *him* to give orders. Detta's question that morning hadn't been a fluke: in Malech's absence, he was master of the House.

Jerzy was about to turn and go back to the cellar to grab a flagon of healwine when he realized that there was already one in his hand. His own *vin magica*, not specified yet, but still healwine. Still usable. But . . . he didn't know enough, he couldn't control it without the spell crafted in, and he didn't know how to do that yet, he had to go back, find something else . . .

"Jerzy, men are hurt!"

Detta's words snapped him out of his hesitation, and Jerzy moved, running down the path, the flagon held firmly in one sweaty hand, the other already pulling the stopper from the top. The wagon—one of the three used to transport barrels from the vintnery to the warehouse where the porters would then take them to their final destination and bring back much-needed supplies—had somehow, impossibly, broken in two.

The horse, one of the white, heavy-muscled animals, thankfully with the disposition of a boulder, stood quietly among the wreckage, the leather harness resting limply on its broad back. Three slaves lay to the side of the splintered wreck, and two were underneath, trapped against the cobblestones. One, Jerzy quickly determined, had been crushed under the metal brace and was obviously dead. The other was the source of the screaming, and there was a dark puddle of blood forming under him.

"Clear the debris," Jerzy ordered the nearest slave, a man decades older than he. "You, and you, help him. You"—he pointed at a younger slave who had been hanging back, staring in fascination at the wreckage—"take the horse back to the enclosure, have them check for injuries, and report back to me what they say."

The boy made an odd ducking move, then moved forward, slowly and carefully, to take hold of the leather reins and urge the horse forward. It snorted, a plume of warm wind in the cold air, and resisted briefly, then allowed the boy to take it away from the chaos, heavy hooves stepping delicately around the wreckage.

"Those other men?" Jerzy asked Detta, who had come to stand next to him. Her skirt was covered with dirt and blood, and her hands twisted in the fabric, but her face was composed and her eyes were dry.

"One dead. One with a broken leg. The other seems unharmed but is unconscious."

"Move the dead one aside. Get someone to splint the broken leg." He spoke almost absently, the orders a distraction from his main concern, the man being uncovered from the ruins of the wagon. He hefted the flagon and took a step forward. "I will see to the other slave when this one has been treated."

A path cleared. Jerzy moved to the bleeding slave's side, and went down to his knees in the wet dirt. The man's face was ashen under his weathered sun-browning, and his eyes were not focusing.

"Fox-fur? Thought you were dead. Are we dead?"

"Not yet," Jerzy responded. He didn't know this slave, didn't recognize the voice or the face. "Rest easy; we'll take care of you. I need you to concentrate on the pain now. Focus on it, make it everything."

"Not much trouble with that, Fox-fur." He closed his eyes and concentrated, sweat running down his face and mixing with the blood. Jerzy lifted the flagon to his lips and took a scant swallow, letting it roll and rest in the hollow of his tongue. Specifying, and a year or more of aging, and the spellwine would have aged and strengthened into a smooth flow of power. Now it was raw, rough, and untried—exactly like the one about to decant it.

Once to direct. He let the flavor of the *vin magica* rise through the roof of his mouth, learning the essence of it, then swallowed it, slowly, so slowly, feeling the magic fill his throat, coat his stomach, and rise through him until he was near dizzy with the power. The first step was simple: "Into that body, go."

His hands reached out to touch the slave, cool fingers touching fevered bones, bloody flesh. Would it work? Would the *vina* recognize the words? No time to worry, keep going. Second step. What were the words of the second step? He reached, searched, and found them, drummed by dry rote into his memory.

"Bind and seal, as before. Go!"

He could feel the magic surge from his hands into the slave, the torn and battered body rising off the soil as though struck by lightning. Jerzy's eyes hazed over with a red mist, as though the *vin* itself coated his sight, his mouth filled with the lingering taste, and his skin tingled from the power. Caught, he lost himself in the sensation.

"Jerzy!"

Detta's voice, urgent. Jerzy blinked, and the red mist receded. Beneath his hands, the slave lay in the road, a red haze of magic covering his entire body. The haze hovered, then sank into the wounds, healing him from bone on out, as Jerzy had commanded it.

"Good lad," Detta said. "Well done. He will live. Let them take him now, and you look after the other."

Lost inside himself, Jerzy let her lead him away, while slaves came to carry the injured man back to the sleep house, where a physic brought up from the nearest village would attend to whatever damage remained.

The second slave had been turned onto his side, a warm puddle of bile evidence that his stomach had emptied at some point. Long brown hair was plastered to his skull, and his features were slack, no obvious wounds bleeding or bones protruding, only an ugly purple shadow on the left side of his face and top of his shoulder. He wasn't in pain, at least. After the screams and moans of the other slave, Jerzy was relieved, and then felt guilty for that relief. Better the slave was awake and screaming than this motionless, soundless death-in-life.

"Can you do anything for him?"

The urge to say of course he could, to be confident in the face of Detta's doubt, welled in him and then faded. "I don't know. If I knew what was wrong, or if he could tell me . . ."

The slave's chest rose and fell, shallow but steady, and a hand held under his nose felt the faint exhale of air. Jerzy peeled back one closed eyelid, but the eye itself rolled back in the socket, unseeing. Death-in-life. Jerzy had seen it before, years ago, when another boy in the slaver's caravan had not woken up one morning. The caravan master had let him be for a week, but when there was no change, they had left him on the side of the road. There was no hope for ones like that; even if they recovered, the slavers said, there would be no use to be gotten out of him.

The weight of the flagon in his hand reminded Jerzy that he had an option the slavers lacked, an option and an order to do whatever was needful. He lifted the flagon to his mouth and took a sip. The acrid taste of the *vin magica* was familiar now, and the pattern of sip, hold,

and swallow followed without conscious thought. The magic slipped
through his skin and bones, filling his veins.

"Find the cause."

The direction was simple; the decantation less so. How could even a
Vineart heal an ill that could not be identified? If the magic could not
find the cause, no decantation could work—

Do not hesitate, or the vinespell will slip from your grasp. Malech's voice,
stern in memory, was like a cuff to the ear. The magic worked only
so long as the first flush remained; delay too long, and the second sip
would not be so potent. This was not a spellwine, not yet, but the dif-
ficulty was the same.

He needed to know the damage done to the slave, but only the slave
could tell him. The slave could not tell him. Therefore, the first step . . .

"Wake the mind."

"Go!"

The magic surged, obeying his will . . . and then faltered, fading even
as Jerzy forced it forward again. Any man might cast a vinespell, Malech
had taught him, but a Vineart *commanded* it. Only a Vineart could command *vin magica.*

"GO!"

The magic drove itself into the slave, making his limbs twitch, and
his eyelids flutter as though he were waking, but then the body flopped
back down onto the ground like a broken doll. The wine turned bitter
in his throat, and Jerzy gagged on his failure.

A moment of anger and self-disgust consumed him—if he had taken
a flagon of the Master's crafting, the decantation would have worked! It
was his fault, his failure.

Jerzy sat back on his heels and lifted his hands from the man's face.
His fingertips tingled from the residue, but the magic drained from the
rest of him as swiftly as it had poured into him, and he felt his body
quiver with exhaustion even as his mind worked sharp and cold, still
riding the thrill of magic through his system. His thoughts were sharp
and clear, and could not be escaped.

Failure. He had failed. The body lived, but the flesh alone was useless, and everyone knew that there was no place in this world for a useless slave.

"There is nothing I can do. The body has gone too far to be roused; even if the body healed, the awareness is gone." The words were for himself; Detta had gone off somewhere while he worked, and none of the slaves still working to clear the road would acknowledge that he was there, much less stop to listen to him, ducking their heads and looking away when they passed. The realization drained the last of the spell-fog from his brain.

Six months and more past, he had been one of them. Six months past, he too scurried past the Master, head down and eyes averted, trying to remain unnoticed, unpunished. Had he not sensed something amiss with the mustus that day during Harvest, one of the slaves on this wagon today might have been him.

Had it been him, he would not have the weight of a man's death on his hands.

"Jerzy?" Detta came to stand beside him. "Oh." Her voice was soft as her steps, and full of regret. "Should we . . . should I have someone . . . ?"

"No." Jerzy shook his head, only now noting that sweat had dampened his scalp and the back of his neck, despite the chill of the day. It was a small inconvenience, not even worth noting, except once he had noted that the rest of the world came roaring back in like a summer's storm; the sound of the slaves carting debris away, the creak of leather and thud of wood, the murmur of voices and a slight shushing of wind overhead through the bare branches of trees on the far slope. The sun was well over the vineyard now, but it cast little warmth on the scene. On a normal day, he would be at lessons with Cai, in the workroom, or the cellars, or walking the land here or at the Master's other fields farther south, to check on their progress and learn their cycle. He would rather be any of those places than here, now.

Leaning forward, Jerzy gathered the fading wisps of magic, and pressed his hand down firmly on the slave's fever-warm forehead. This required no decantation, only a whisper of magic. Healspells were crafted to end suffering, however that end might come, and to a body in this condition, the final ending required no command, but a merest suggestion.

Rising to his feet, Jerzy stared down at the cooling body, and prepared to explain his failure to Malech.

"I TOLD YOU I don't have time for this, boy."

It hadn't taken much to determine where Malech had gone; he hadn't been in the circular workroom, and his clothing was too fine to be in the cellars, so that left only the study, the room where Jerzy had been tested, that first day. By now the study was as familiar to him as any other room in the House, and the awe he had felt on that first day was replaced by an almost casual acceptance of its wonders. Unlike the cellar workrooms, the study was finely furnished, with a table and chair made of ancient vinewood that gleamed with polish, and where on his first visit there had been the image of bottles—now, he knew, shifted from the storeroom below in a bit of magic the Master had yet to explain— shelves of scrolls and books lining the far wall, away from the window.

Malech was standing with his back to the door, fussing with the silver cups on their tray. Silver cups for *vin ordinare*; metals debased *vin magica*, diluting their taste and leeching away their potency. For *ordinaire*, it did not matter. The expensive glass vessel resting beside them held a liquid of deep golden amber. *Ordinaire*, but not ordinary, that. The color only gave hint about what a wine might do, but that particular shade and depth—and the fact that Master Malech was using glass to serve it—told Jerzy that the wine was from the mountains behind them, where the gilded vines grew. No *magica* came from those grapes, but a minor Vineart named Bartelt picked them at the last moment of harvest and then dried them on beds of straw, making a sweet *vin ordinaire* that brought as much gold as any spellwine from the princelings and their households.

"Master."

Something in his tone must have alerted Malech, because he turned to look then. "How many died?"

"Three."

"And how many lived?"

"Two will recover by the morrow, most likely. One man's leg is broken, but he should be able to do sit-work until it is healed. The overseer sent for the physic to ensure it is set properly."

"So. Five slaves on the wagon, and three dead." Malech seemed to consider those facts. "You were unable to prevent the deaths?"

"I . . . two died in the accident. The other was in death-as-life. I could not tell what was wrong, to heal it. I had only *vin magica*, and the slave could not tell me. Master, had I thought to bring a flagon of your crafting, true spellwine . . ."

Malech sighed, his hand pausing as he reached for something on his desk. "I left you to your own devices because your work had been acceptable, Jerzy."

Acceptable. The word stung, on top of the burn of failure. He needed to be more than acceptable. A man was dead because he was merely acceptable.

Malech frowned at him, as though sensing his thoughts. "If the slave was unconscious and not to be roused, then there was nothing to be done. Some harms cannot be undone, some bodies even the most potent of healwines cannot cure. Not even Sin Washer could save a body from death, only prepare him for it. Slaves die all the time. They live, they serve, they die."

Malech's voice was not harsh, merely matter-of-fact, and Jerzy bowed his head in acceptance.

"The bodies have been taken away?" his master asked.

"Detta is seeing to it." They had an agreement with the physic—he handled minor ailments among the slaves, and in return he took away the bodies of those who died, no matter the cause, for his own studies. It was gruesome, but useful; they had no time or place to bury the bodies, and the slaves had no family to object.

"Then the matter is done. Consider it your lesson for the day. You have enough to occupy you otherwise?"

"Mil'ar Cai is coming back this evening," Jerzy said. The Caulian had been away for a week, traveling on his own business. "He said that he was going to bring me my own cudgel." Jerzy wasn't sure if he was excited about that or apprehensive. His own weapon in all likelihood simply meant that he would be hit harder, if he did something wrong.

"Ah, good, good." Jerzy suspected he could have told his master that the stones had started speaking, and the response would have been that same distracted approval. "Then I will see you in the morning. Now, if you will—"

"Lord Malech."

Detta appeared at the door, a man with her. Jerzy had never seen him before, a short, bald man wearing a long robe like those of the Washers, only a rough brown instead of Washer's red, and splattered with mud from the thawing roads.

"Lord Malech, as you requested . . ." Detta let her words fade away, and gestured to the man.

"Yes. Thank you. Come in, *meme-courier*, please." Malech waved the stranger to a chair, and turned back to the *vin*, pouring it into two glasses and handing the stranger one. "Jerzy, that will be all."

Clearly and obviously shut out, Jerzy bowed his head again in acceptance and left his master and the stranger to their discussion, the door closing firmly behind him.

There was no use in feeling as though he were being punished: if Malech had been disappointed in his actions, the Vineart would not have hesitated to say so. Jerzy would see him in the morning for lessons, as usual. And perhaps Cai would be able to tell him who—or what—a *meme-courier* was, and what his appearance meant.

Chapter 9

*T*o *Master Malech* of The Berengia, from Master Seth of
Iaja. Greetings, a query, and a warning."

Malech sat back, the now half-empty glasses of Bart-
let's gilded *vin* on his desk in front of him, and listened to
what the *meme-courier* had to repeat.

"Your communication came to my attention this week past, and I
admit that your words brought both comfort and dread. You are the
first I take into my confidence, and only because I am troubled beyond
my ability to handle, and as much as I fear creating worse problems
should word of this escape, I fear even more remaining silent. In the
past ten-month, there has been a marked increase in the number of
pests and infestations discovered in my lands, and I begin to suspect
that it is not mere foul chance but a part of something larger, perhaps
something we have need to look deeper into. . . ."

When the *meme-courier* finished his message, he stood silently, as
still as he had been during his recitation, waiting to see if Malech had a
response for him to bring back.

Master Seth was no fool. Infestations in their season were the normal course of a Vineart's life; for all their magical properties, the vines

were still mere plants, and subject to the crisis and calms of all growing things. For all that the wines could heal and force growth, call the winds or encourage rains, there was no true way to control nature's creatures or make them dance your tune; that was the purview of the gods, and the gods had been silent since giving them Sin Washer and setting them upon this course, millennia before.

Malech preferred life that way. To live in a time when gods spoke and miracles occurred . . . he could only imagine that it would be messy, and complicated, and all-around disruptive to the order of things. Malech approved of order, and routine. A well-run vineyard thrived on routine.

But he, Malech, was no fool, either. That was why, after the root-glow scare, he had sent carefully worded queries out into the world. This was the first reply. He suspected it would not be the last.

"This is my response," he told the *meme-courier*. "To Master Seth, greetings. Your words are well considered, and well heard. We have had only one such troubling incident"—no need to tell the other Vineart that it had come close to succeeding—"but that one was fierce enough to concern me."

He paused then, struck by a thought, all the more troubling for not having been considered before. How had the wagon happened to have broken, so suddenly, and without warning? Was it a sad accident, as sometimes happened, without dire import? Or had something—or someone—struck it down? And if so . . . how?

It was, he decided, possible that an outside force had somehow, for some reason, sabotaged the wagon. But unlikely. The wagons were of an age where such things could happen of their own, especially on winter-rutted roads, and his shame for not replacing them sooner.

"You were wise indeed to watch and wait, for we have no need of panic flitting through the villages." Or indeed, the great houses of the princelings who bought most of the spellwines and expected only per-fection in the vintages they used. Rumor of crop failures, even if untrue, might cause his usual customers to go elsewhere. "I shall, as you request, inquire discreetly and determine if this is merely a time of natural trials, or if there is, as you fear, a pattern and intelligence behind these incidents. I will inform you of anything I determine. Until then I remain, Malech, Master of the Valle of Ivy, The Berengia."

The *meme-courier* placed his hands together in front of him, cupped to indicate that he had received the message, and then pressed his hands together, palm to palm, and bowed. "You have honored me with your custom," he said, his normal speaking voice higher and lighter than the one he had used to deliver his message.

Pigeons were faster, for short messages, and a negotiator was for matters public or political, but a *meme-courier*, if you could afford one, was best for things of a private nature, and any Vineart working within Iaja needed to take care, for their prince was a jealous and controlling sort who meddled in affairs outside his realm. Unlike negotiators, who were often affiliated with the House or prince who retained them, and therefore often suspect and held hostage, the *meme-courier* guild had immunity to travel near anywhere, to take passage on any boat of any allegiance, pass beyond walls of any House and remain unmolested and unquestioned so long as they remained robed and neutral. Not even Washers could claim such privilege, although the Collegium had the ability to manifest their unhappiness with a seated ruler in ways more than spiritual, when pressed.

Malech was startled from those grim thoughts by the man's gentle shifting of weight from one leg to another, a polite reminder that he was still there. "You honor us with your skills," Malech replied, and with that formality, the *courien* was over.

Malech stood as the *meme-courier* left, then sank back down into his chair and picked up the glass, downing the remains in one hard swallow. He had spoken bravely in front of the other man, but the truth was that he was worried. The root-glow attack had not caught him unprepared; the only surprise was that it had taken so long to arrive.

His long-held policy of standing aloof from matters outside the Valle had protected him this long. But, perhaps, no longer.

An attack, directed against all Vinearts? Unlikely. Impossible, he would have said. More likely all this was merely a run of bad luck that life was occasionally heir to. Vinearts were merely men, after all. Skilled men, with the Sin Washer's blessing on them, but still men.

And yet, there were nights, too many nights in the past ten-month, that he had woken before dawn, still in his bed with a cold sweat upon him and a sense of foreboding in his mind. That something dark and dire was sweeping down off the hills, threatening all that he knew, all that he had built.

If others, too, felt that fear . . .

"Guardian."

Malech.

"Am I overreacting?"

There was a pause, weighted as stone. Guardian did not decide anything lightly; it was not its nature.

No.

No. He had not thought so, either.

"Up!"

Jerzy rolled out of bed before the Master's command registered, reaching for his trousers even as he tried to remember what shirt was clean, and where he had tossed his shoes the night before. An illuminated history of the Lands Vin slid off the edge of his narrow bed and hit the floor before he could catch it, and he swore. Books were rare enough; Master would have his skin if that book were damaged.

"Up!"

"I'm up!" he said irritably, pulling his shirt over his head and catching his ear on the lacings. "I'm up, but be still a moment and let me dress myself first."

The voice stilled, but there was a sense of impatience in the air that was even more annoying than the words, and the heavy shadow outside his window came closer, as though intending to come through the closed pane.

"Break that glass and Detta will not be happy with you," Jerzy warned the Guardian, sitting on the edge of the bed to first scoop the book back to safety, and then to slip on his shoes. After having to dig a splinter of wood from Jerzy's sole, the Housemistress had warned him against going outside his room without something on his feet. It still felt strange after so many years barefoot in the soil, but while the Master ruled the vintnery, even he did not contradict Detta within the House.

Fully dressed, he dragged a cloth through the pitcher of water and scrubbed his face with it to get the last sleep out of his eyes, yawned once for good measure, and headed down the stairs. Outside the window, the Guardian made its own silent way back down to its usual perch. In the weeks since the *meme-courier* had come and gone, predawn summons were more common than not, even after nights when they burned wax well into the darkness. There were times Jerzy swore he'd barely laid down before he was rising again, the lessons of the day before still jangling and disconnected in his head. Something was driving his master, and all he could do was try to take it all in, and keep up as best he could.

The new kitchen boy, Bret, was in the kitchen, stirring up the fire. Jerzy stuck his head in to sniff the air and see if the bread was ready yet.

"Nothing yet," the boy said, seeing the shock of red hair. "Someone's to bring it down to you when it's ready."

"Our thanks," Jerzy said. The usual orders were that you had to be at the table, at least in passing, to get fed. He didn't know if Bret was taking a risk or if the House-keeper had relented, but either way he was thankful.

The entire way to Malech's workroom could be plunged into utter darkness, and Jerzy would still be able to clatter down the stairs, familiar with every bump and curve of the stone, and as he passed under the lintel, his fingers curved around the tip of the Guardian's stone tail easily, giving it a familiar tug.

The Guardian, as usual, ignored him.

"What are the five qualities of firewine?"

"A deep garnet color. A nose of warm spice. A near-pure clarity. A strong structure on the tongue. A lingering finish of ash." By now, being hit with a test even as he was walking into the workroom didn't startle or stop Jerzy, and the information rose to his tongue without conscious recall. He rather suspected that was the point of these attack-questions, to see how he responded without warning. It didn't make sense to him—everything that he had learned until now, everything he had seen had emphasized the need for time and gentle handling when crafting spellwines. What need had a Vineart for sudden movement or stressful recall?

But asking that sort of question now, he knew, would result in a cuffing. Master Malech had his reasons. His only responsibility was to answer correctly and quickly.

"Good. Now go into the storeroom and bring me out a bottle of it."

Jerzy nodded, then waited for further instruction. When none came, he looked inquiringly at the Vineart. "Master?"

Malech scowled down at him, his narrow face creasing into lines of displeasure. "What? Go, fetch, you idiot clod!"

"Master, I have never worked with firewine before. Where is the bottle? How will I know it?"

The usual blow to the side of his head didn't come; instead Malech merely closed his eyes and shook his head in disgust. "If you can't tell firewine from healwine, get yourself back to the muck of the vineyards; you're useless to me."

Jerzy stared at his master in dismay. How . . . how could Master Malech expect him to . . .

Clearly, Master Malech did.

A tremor of fear swept through Jerzy's body, like a cold finger tracing his bones. A test. A new test, and if he failed . . . would Master Malech truly expect him to go back to the fields? To leave the House, go back to being a slave?

Yes. Master would. Like being able to sense the mustus, this would prove he had the right, the ability, to stay.

He could not fail. He *would* not. He had skills now, knowledge of the wines, of the flesh of the grape . . . Touching the mark on his hand for courage, he took a deep breath, and did as ordered.

The storage room was as familiar as the Guardian; the thick stones keeping the temperature cool no matter how the weather changed, the spell-lights that lit the walls and cast shadows into the corners and under barrels, the smell of *vina* and straw in the air, making it intoxicating to breathe deeply. The barrels and half barrels were stacked against the far wall, the wood slats ranging from a pale yellow to a deep, burnished gold, each strapped by brass belts that glinted in the spell-light. But that wasn't his destination today.

The finished bottles were stored against the interior wall, in rows up to the ceiling. Each bottle came from distant Avlina, where the Glassmaker's Guild was situated. Malech would use nothing less than their best for his spellwines. Normal folk used leather, clay, and wood, and even the House used clayware for daily liquids; this much glass in one place still took Jerzy's breath away.

Some of the bottles were new and clean, while others had layers of dust coating their surfaces. Each had a parchment tag around its neck, listing the vineyard they came from and the year of crafting, but to read through every single tag would be the work of weeks, if not longer. He had to find the right bottle, now.

Start with what you know, and build on that. He knew mustus, had near-drowned in it until he learned to work with it, to own it. The same with *vina*. It was in him, a part of him. He would know it anywhere, in any container, no matter how it was transformed. The magic in the barrels sang to him, distracted him. So. From there, where? He had tasted healwines, had worked with them, walked in the soil, the water, the air the vines breathed. He knew them now, too. If he shut them out, the way that he shut out the call of the *magica* . . . He touched the mark on his wrist, a reminder.

It wasn't easy, but it was simple, once he saw the process in his head. Like closing a door to keep down the cold outside, something closed in his head, and the pressure decreased.

The air was still intoxicating, but he could detect different strains in that aroma, sniff out particular elements, and almost, almost identify them.

"Firewine. Warm spice. Dry heat. Bitter ash. Strong structure." He almost sang the details to himself, his voice echoing against the stone walls and bouncing back at him. There were other elements competing for his attention, other spellwines stored here for Malech's own use, but he focused on the identifying marks of firewine, and found himself moving toward one section of wall, his hand reaching for a bottle stored just barely above his head.

Jerzy didn't know what to expect when the bottle came off its shelf and into his hand. Some spark of recognition, perhaps; the same flare of magic he'd felt from the mustus. Instead, he merely felt the cool weight of the glass against his palm and fingers, the glass heavier than he'd expected. There could have been water held inside the green surface, but somehow he *knew* that he had chosen properly, even without looking at the tag.

He checked, of course. Being sure and being willing to risk that surety against his future were not the same thing. He had to squint to read the tag, faded brown ink scrawled on the strip of curling parchment.

"Western Fields, The Berengia. 1395AW."

The Western Fields were actually south of them, on an eastern slope. That was where the firevines were grown. It wasn't quite as good as "Yes, you have selected properly," but it would have to do.

Carrying the squat bottle in both hands, Jerzy went back out into the fresher, thinner air of the workroom, and placed it down on the pouring table, a battered, scarred wooden bench stained with a hundred years of spills and drips.

Malech had turned away and was working at his desk, his attention entirely on the section of rootstalk he was dissecting. The carcass of a shiny black beetle the size of Jerzy's palm lay next to him, pinned belly up to a bed of wax.

"Master?" He waited.

"There is a pot of water in the corner. Burn it."

Jerzy blinked, then looked over his shoulder. Sure enough, a large clay pot rested on the floor in the corner of the workroom, filled to the brim with water.

"Burn the pot, Master?" Even as he asked, he felt the ghost of a cuff against his ear. Malech didn't have to hit him for him to know when he was being an idiot. Burn the water.

Malech didn't even bother to respond. This was still part of the test.

He looked at the bottle again. He had never opened a bottle of spell-wine before. Casks of must, half casks, skins . . . but never a bottle. It shouldn't feel so different from using a wineskin. Either way, the liquid was the important thing, not the casing. Still . . . it *felt* different.

There was a slender knife on the table. Jerzy picked it up and used it to slice away the wax sealing the bottle shut, then dug out the cork the way he had seen Malech do. His nose twitched as the aroma of the spellwine rose from the now-open bottle. Warm and comforting and just slightly acrid, the wine seemed to entice him, luring him into taking just one sip, then another. . . .

He resisted. Healwine was gentler stuff, even the purging spells were crafted to soothe rather than inflame. It waited for you to choose. This . . .

He raised the bottle and found that his arm was shaking. There was a small silver tasting spoon set into a niche on the desk, and he poured the wine into that, using both hands to steady himself, then put the bottle down and replaced the stopper. Feeling anxious, even though Malech hadn't said anything further, nor stopped whatever he was doing at the desk, Jerzy curled his fingers under the short handle and lifted the spoon to his mouth. The cup's surface was so shallow, he estimated that there was, at most, two mouthfuls of wine poured.

Two needed to be enough. He wasn't sure he would get a second chance.

The first mouthful slid onto his tongue, heavy and smooth, almost fleshy. The scent went straight up into his nose, bringing forward the memory of overblown red flowers, multipetaled, pungent, and spicy. He didn't know where the memory came from, but it matched almost perfectly. He cupped his tongue to hold the richness in, and for a moment almost forgot, in the sensation, what it was he was meant to do.

That was a danger with the stronger spellwines, Malech had said. They took over, made you stupid. An ordinary person might survive being stupid; a spellwine would not do anything beyond what it was crafted to do for him. But a Vineart could never afford to become secondary to the *vin magica,* or it would corrupt his own magic and soar out of control. Drunkenness was not allowed to a Vineart, for good reason.

Now, how to direct . . . Flame to water? No, not *to* . . .

"Flame on water."

He stared at the pot, and the surface shimmered, just a little, as though something unseen had disturbed it. The wine warmed in his mouth, the spice intensifying, becoming sharper.

The command was easier; there were only a few variations allowed for firespells.

"Burn safely."

"Go!"

The surface shimmered again, ripples forming, and then a fireball exploded on the surface of the pot, rising straight up toward the ceiling and sending pottery shards flying everywhere, even as water spilled onto the stone floor, hissing with steam. Jerzy ducked, his arms flying up even as he felt the spellwine slide down his throat and explode likewise in a burst of intensely ripe fruit.

"Washer's hands!" Malech's chair went skittering across the floor and crashed into a wall, even as Jerzy looked up from underneath his crossed arms to see if the fire had gone out.

No. It still shimmered and danced on the spilled pool of water, flickering over the shards of pottery, apparently quite content to remain where it was, rather than spreading to anything else in the chamber.

Jerzy looked at the blue-white flames, then looked around the chamber, and finally, reluctantly, looked up at his master.

"The last command is to be said softly, not shouted," Malech said, in a terribly mild voice. "A safe fire should be coaxed, led, never . . . hurled."

Jerzy swallowed, nodded, and committed that to memory.

"I'M PUSHING YOU."

Jerzy stopped with a jam roll halfway to his mouth. They had cleaned up the fire and water and pottery just in time for Roan to arrive with a tray of food and a carafe of tai. Malech had cleared off his desk—thankfully moving the pinned insect somewhere else—and they had settled down to eat. His hands were still shaking slightly, and to his shame, Malech had noticed.

"In the normal course of events, you would not have touched firespells for another season. You would have had a chance to see them growing, participated in their harvest, learned their nature before they were crafted into a potent form. . . ."

Malech exhaled, a gusty sigh that seemed at odds with his normally composed façade. "You did well, all things considered. A little abrupt, but the flame stayed where you sent it, and went out when you commanded it to do so. That is really all that a basic firespell needs. Well, a little more delicacy in touch would be appreciated, especially when used indoors. Fortunately I wasn't overly fond of that water pot."

Jerzy put the jam roll in his mouth and chewed carefully, as though the noise of his jaw working might cause Malech to stop talking.

"I'll try to be more careful, give you more information to start, but I need you to be able to keep up. The next few months . . . I need you to be ready." Malech picked apart a jam roll and left the debris uneaten.

"Ready for what, Master?" A risk to speak, but Jerzy couldn't help himself.

Malech looked up, his deep-set eyes seeming darker—or was it that his hair had become grayer? Overnight, it seemed to Jerzy, his master had aged ten years.

"I don't know, boy. That's what's worrying me. I don't know." He seemed to be arguing something with himself, then brushed the crumbs of the roll off his long fingers, the gold ring on his index finger catching the light. He tapped it thoughtfully, then turned to pull a large scroll off a shelf, pushing aside the platter of food to make room for it on the table. Jerzy grabbed his mug and another roll before they were out of reach, and leaned in to see what Malech was showing him.

It was a map, drawn in colored inks. Some of the shapes looked familiar to Jerzy, although he did not recognize the letterings or symbols drawn on them. "That's us, here in the Ivy."

"Yes, very good." Malech looked pleased. "And this is Iaja, and across this line here, farther north, is Oerta, where they grow the most unusual grapes; pure, dry and delicate, and half a bottle will call up the most amazing storm at sea; not even the finest captain can outrun it. Never annoy old Conna, boy. Even princelings walk carefully around him. Fortunately, all the bluster seems to be in his spellwines, and none in his moods."

Malech collected himself from memories, and continued tracing the lines of the map. "This is your world, boy. Each marker indicates the House of a Vineart of note, or their secondaries, and those sigils, the ones in green, are the rulers of each land. You need to learn them, boy. Do you think that you can do that?"

"Yes, Master Malech." Jerzy had no idea—there were so many!—but he dared not give Malech any cause to doubt him. The threat of returning to the fields was still too close, too raw, even if he didn't quite believe it anymore.

"A decade," Malech said, and it took Jerzy a moment to realize that his master was speaking not to him, but to the Guardian. "A decade, the boy needs, should have. And here I am, planning to cram so much into him in less time than a wine takes to age. Can he do it, do you think?"

The Guardian lifted its stone head from its paws and looked down at them with blind, unblinking eyes.

Yes.

Jerzy felt the voice more than he heard it, and *knew*, somehow, that it came from the stone dragon overhead. Like tasting must in the air, the essence of the Guardian was unmistakable.

"Yes. Well, if he couldn't, no doubt the vines would have left him to rot under the sun," Malech said. "But the crafting must still be done with care, no matter how hurried...."

The Guardian, its part in the conversation clearly ended, lowered its head back to his paws and was silent.

"Master ... why?"

Malech stopped speaking and stared at Jerzy, long enough for him to feel that same uncomfortable sense of uncertainty he'd felt that first day, almost a year past, when Malech had first tested him for magic. All that he had accomplished was suddenly dwarfed by a sense of everything he didn't know, the depth of his ignorance reflected in Malech's troubled expression.

Then the lines of worry in the Vineart's face smoothed out, and the calm, composed mask was back in place.

But now, for the first time, Jerzy understood that it was a mask. That more went on underneath than he had ever been given permission to see ... and that something between them had just changed forever.

"This world was once a terrifying place. You know of it, if only through Washers' stories. Great prince-mages battled against each other for vanity's sake, and the lands trembled with their might ... and the people suffered, and cried out to the gods for protection."

Jerzy nodded. Everyone, even slaves, knew that. Sin Washer came down and saved them, punishing the mage-princes for their arrogance.

"What the stories forget, or never knew, was that the land suffered, too, boy. It, too, called out for protection. There are some who claim that the gods responded not to our needs, but to protect the land itself."

Malech took a sip of his tai, grimacing when he realized it had grown cold and bitter.

"Grapes are like men: they grow best, most strongly, when they are placed under stress. Too much stress, too much harsh treatment, and they wilt and die. It is a balance we must observe, to bring out the best in the grapes . . . and ourselves." He looked as though he were about to say something more, then changed his direction.

"The Valle of Ivy maintains balance, and because of that our spell-wines have been sought after for their potency and consistency. Our princeling, Ranulf, and I maintain balance, so the people need not worry about power struggles between us, and live their lives untroubled by things greater than they. So it was ordered by Sin Washer, and so it has been for counted generations. But now . . . I hear whispers and see portents, boy. Beyond these lines—" he traced the boundaries of the Valle with his forefinger— "something grows. It grows, and it stretches its tendrils out, not merely to one region, but everywhere. The vines are sensing it, the stress in their soil beyond what is healthy or desired. Men? We know only that the world becomes a darker, more frightening place. Crops are endangered, and Vinearts scurry to make the best of what remains; princelings and maiars and kinglets all squabble and bite, each trying to blame the other. I hear of this, I sense it, and I know, no matter what I do, it will come, too, even to the Ivy."

"What is it, Master?" He was fascinated, caught by his master's telling.

"That, boy," Malech said, laying his palm down on the map and pressing down, as though to keep it still. "That is what we must discover."

Chapter 10

ATAKUS

The seas off the coast of Atakus looked the same as they had for every day of his life; blue-green, capped with white, stretching leagues in every direction into the horizon, the waves and wind tossing the smell of brine into the air. If an observer didn't know better, he would think that nothing had changed, and nothing ever would change.

Everything changed.

"Ah. There you are." The voice carried across the open courtyard, although the speaker barely raised his voice. "I've been waiting."

Kaïnam, Named-Heir of Atakus, had a grinding headache located just behind his ear and over his left eye. The cause of that pain raised one gnarled hand and summoned him across the small courtyard:

Erebuh son of Naïos, Prince of Atakus, Hereditary Lord of the Island, Protector of the Sea and the Isles Surrounding.

Before becoming Named-Heir, Kaïnam had no idea how much those words weighed on the back of one's neck, a yoke you could not, dare not, shake off.

His father sat on a white stone bench, resplendent in his red tunic and pearlescent shellstone diadem, and smoothed the cloth over one knee. Kaïnam came and knelt before him, both greeting and submission.

His father's hair was long turned white, but his voice and his hands were as steady as a much younger man's. "So. You have seen the scroll, had time now to digest the contents. What think you?"

Kaïnam wasn't fooled by the mildness of the question. As Named-Heir, his opinions actually had some value. Some only: and to be spent carefully, wisely. His sister would have counseled him patience and delicacy, especially in matters concerning their father.

His sister was dead. He had been but a student at her heels, and she was gone now.

Bereft of her advice, he stood now like a tested schoolboy, his teacher awaiting a response. The scroll in question had come that morning from Edon, Master Vineart of Atakus, the culmination of months of work and secret correspondence back and forth. It had taken Kaïnam a mere five minutes to form his opinion on the result.

"Father, you cannot think to approve this. It is . . . it's . . ." Diplomatic words failed him, and he blurted what was foremost in his mind. "Vineart or no, Master Edon has gone mad, and infected you with it as well."

"Mad? Perhaps. But you are not lord here yet." The words were softly spoken, with gentle affection, but a clear warning in the tone as well. "When you are, you will know that ofttimes things that are distasteful must still be done. Be they stone-sane, or mad as the wind."

The courtyard they stood in was part of the private garden outside the royal chambers. At his back was sheer cliff and deep ocean. At the other end of the garden was the bulk of the main building, and two guards loitered a discreet distance away. In all the years of his growing, the royal family had never required guards, nor even his father. Not here, on Mount Parpur itself.

All that had changed when the Wise Lady had been murdered by an honored guest, and his father had gone mad.

He missed his sister terribly. He had gone from fourth son, one of seven, to the heir-announced on the basis of her murdered regard, and the trade had not been a fair one.

"Master Edon has, as promised, delivered a spellwine that will protect us and our ships from any repeat of last season's attack on our ships, to protect us and those we have promised to protect. I see no reason not to make immediate use of it."

"No reason? No reason?" He knew that his voice was rising, becoming almost shrill, but he couldn't seem to moderate himself. "Do you know what using that spell will do?"

His father's voice was almost obscenely calm. "It will protect us."

"It will *destroy* us." By Sin Washer's hands, how could his father not see that? They had gone mad, Master Edon and his father alike. The attack, however startling, however disturbing it had been to realize that their waters were somehow suddenly vulnerable, did not warrant this. Not even murder warranted such a drastic measure.

His sister would have agreed. His sister would have known how to change their father's mind.

Kaïnam tried to modulate his thoughts and his words, but it was oh so difficult when what he wished to do was shake his father until the old man saw reason.

"We have always been isolated, by our own intent, but still we traded, still we saw the world—and the world saw us. We are one of the major—one of the only!—ports of resupply for ships traveling to the desert lands! To slip from sight, to disappear behind this curtain of magic, as Master Edon claims he can accomplish . . . the only purpose that will serve is to raise questions—of where we have gone, and what cause we might have had. If we are not alone in being attacked, if there are others suffering similar depredations—then in protecting us, you will turn us into scapegoats!"

Even as he uttered the last word, he saw that his breath was wasted, the look in his father's eyes no longer on their once-protected boundaries, but somewhere else, darker and less lovely.

"Scapegoat or sacrifice, which would you choose for us? No matter; my decision is made. At the filling of the moon, we will raise this curtain of magics, and Atakus shall slip entire from the world's view."

The Wise Lady would have known what to say, would have counseled them fairly, coaxed them from this madness, and earned her naming yet again. But that wise voice had been silenced by an assassin's blade, and Kaïnam bit his tongue, and did not argue further. Heirnamed could yet be un-named, and he did not trust his brothers with that responsibility. Not now. Not faced with what they faced, from the outside, and within. Not while his father and Master Edon held to this course.

His father stood, his sun-bronzed skin still firm and his shoulders still strong as a much younger man's. His eyes might carry more shadows these days than even a year before, but they still saw true. Kaïnam had to believe that. If he didn't . . .

If he did not, then all was flame and ruins, and he would have no choice but to do the unthinkable.

There was a pause, two figures standing, young and old sides of the same coin, the silence growing into something heavier, thicker than the salt-scented air.

"I will see you at the evening meal?" his father asked.

"Of course." He ate every evening meal with his father now, no matter how often they had conferred during the day. One food taster was more economical than two, after all.

AFTER HIS FATHER left, his guards accompanying him, Kaïnam found himself retracing a route, only recently familiar, to the guest quarters.

His guard trailed a discreet distance behind, only one and relaxed, here inside the very walls of the residence. Never mind that his sister had been killed within these same grounds. Kaïnam almost wanted to scold him for being lax, save that the laxness suited him in this moment and this instance. He wanted no eavesdroppers on this conversation.

The door he approached was open, as though the occupant had been waiting for him. Perhaps he had.

The robed figure stepped out, his body language casual, and they walked together along the open corridor, as though by chance meeting on their way to the same destination.

"I have met with my father," Kaïnam said. "He and the Master Vineart are in accord as to their intentions."

"You could not convince him otherwise?" Brother Joen paced alongside him in the corridor, his sandals slapping against the cool stone tiles like the lashing of a cat's tail. In contrast, Kaïnam's bare feet were silent as a whisper.

"Did you truly expect me to?" he asked Joen, keeping his voice low. The guard was distant and discreet, but even innocent words could often be misunderstood. "Do you think my father would not consider his actions and his reasons well before calling upon my advice?"

"You are his chosen heir. I had thought . . ."

Kaïnam watched the Washer as he realized where that sentence led, and tried to draw back his words. "You thought I had more influence on the old man, more say in how things were run. Is that why you have cultured me, after my sister's death? To wind your way into Atakus politics in that sideways fashion?"

Brother Joen blinked, his gentle face like that of a confused owl. "Kaïnam, how could you think . . ."

Suddenly, the weight of his new title was too much, and he could practically hear his shoulders crack. "Spare me the injured innocence, Brother Joen. It does neither of us honor. I know that my sister did not trust you, and you know that she did not trust you. In her absence, lacking another entrance, you sought to use me. That is how the tide is sailed. I will not deny that I used you, in turn. My father trusts the Washer Collegium, and to think that I am aided by one of its members soothes his mind and gives me a way to challenge him, sway him, without suspicions being raised as to my loyalties."

"You do not trust me?" This time the injury sounded real, and it amused Kaïnam that, of all he had said, that was what the Washer picked up on, and questioned.

They passed an open window, framing an ancient olive tree, and Kaïnam inhaled the spicy scent, taking refuge for a moment in the familiarity of it. The crest of the Principality was an olive tree main-masting a trade vessel. Even before vines, there had been olives. His family was as old as this island and survived the same way: by letting the winds and the tides roll by. This, too, was but a moment in the ages.

"Try not to take it too personally, Brother Joen. After the murder of my sister, I trust no one, least of all an outsider. We are no Vinearts, restricted from political games, and so we must learn to play them well. You—and by you I presume the Collegium as a whole—do not wish Atakus to isolate itself from the rest of the world, to shut our ports as Master Edon proposes. Nor do I. For now, we work in accord. But it will be work done in vain, at this moment. My father the prince has decided, and will not be gainsaid."

"A decision may be reversed. . . ."

There was no change in tone, no sideways look or inferring words, but Kaïnam stopped hard and brought a hand down in front of the other man, halting him in his tracks as well. Agendas were all well and expected, but he would not allow this. "Do not say what you might not be saying. Do not even *think* what you might not be thinking. I disagree with my lord in this instance, but his is the right of decision, by right of law and leadership. More, he is my *father*. Do you hear me, Brother Joen?"

"Kaïnam, I did not mean to . . ."

Kaïnam stared down from his additional height, drawing his spine up to make the most of that difference, presenting as regal an image as he could accomplish in bare feet and simple tunic. This must be nipped in the bud, immediately. "Do you hear me, Brother Joen? My allegiances will not be challenged."

The Washer, defeated for the moment, raised his hands up, under the arm held against his chest, and made the traditional cup-and-pour blessing motion. "I hear you, Named-Heir Kaïnam of Atakus."

Kaïnam did not believe him, and certainly did not trust him, not as an individual or as a representative of the Collegium, blessed be the Sin Washer's name. Still, the Wise Lady said more than once, you make do with the tools you are given, to make the boat you must have. So it would be with him. And so, smiling gently, he dropped his arm, and they continued on their way to the Session, where his father the prince would inform his people of how their lives were about to change.

Interesting times. Yes.

He almost looked forward to informing Brother Joen that the Washer would not be allowed to leave the island to tell the Collegium what had happened to the people of Atakus.

Chapter 11

HOUSE OF MALECH

Once *Master Malech* shared his worries with Jerzy, the pattern of life changed again. Jerzy's lessons with Cai were reduced to twice a week, and his time with Detta ended entirely. He now spent much of his time in the fields, performing midwinter inspections for Master Malech, while a slow but steady stream of visitors came to meet in private with the Vineart. Detta stood in the doorway watching them arrive and depart, her normally comfortable, confident face looking more and more worried. "It's not natural," she said more than once, in the manner of a woman who knows she won't be listened to. "It's not natural for him to be so partaking of the world, poking about like this. It won't end well, Sin Washer knows, it won't end well."

"Master knows what he is doing," Jerzy said finally, tired of hearing her worries that niggled deep inside at his own. "There are things going on that you don't understand."

"Is that so, young master?" Detta said, and Jerzy flushed, feeling a handspan high and twice as foolish. "I . . ."

But Detta had gone, back in through the half door that led from the road to the inner courtyard, leaving him standing alone with his confusion. He hadn't meant it the way it had come out, truly. He just . . . Jerzy sighed, and watched the most recent arrival hand the reins of his horse to a slave and walk up the path to the House, moving forward to greet him and direct him to Malech's study. He no longer stopped to marvel at the whisper of awareness that brushed him as he walked under the archway—an awareness he now recognized as belonging to the Guardian.

This visitor's arrival was a reminder that he, too, had somewhere to be, and things to do. While thrilled to be trusted with the monitoring of the secondary fields, Jerzy wished he could be in two places at once, the better to keep track of what was happening. Master Malech knew what he was about, no doubt. But having finally been allowed in to some secrets, Jerzy wanted to know them *all*.

AN HOUR'S RIDE later, and Jerzy's thoughts were still chasing each other like rats, and none of them were making him comfortable. "Off you go, boy," the man driving the wagon said, hawing the cart horse to a halt. "I'll be back to pick you up at dusk. Mind you be here!"

Jerzy hopped down off the wagon, remembering at the last minute to grab his carry-sack, and watched as the driver flicked the reins and the wagon moved off down the wide track. That wagon was a new one, built to replace the one that had cracked apart on the road, but it was no more padded than the older ones. As much as his thoughts were uncomfortable, Jerzy's body ached from the trip south, being jounced about on the hard bench and having to keep one hand on the railing to keep from falling over. The driver was a large man, the bench was small, and Jerzy was thinking on the way home he'd ride in the back with the bales and barrels.

The enclosure looked barren, almost abandoned, in its winter dormancy, and Jerzy had trouble seeing the potential in it, for a moment. In six months, however, it would be a hive of energy and activity. Firevine grapes were left until the last moment for harvesting, slaves often racing against the first frost to get the fruit in and crushed. In addition to checking for frost-damage, Malech wanted him to know every grouping of the slope the way he knew his way around his own bedchamber, so when the time for harvest came, he would be able to direct the action.

"You're too young for this," Malech had said again that morning, staring at him over a mug of tai. "Too young and too green yet. Unripe. But there's no choice, and so you'll grow to the occasion. Stressed to greatness, that is how Sin Washer made us."

Jerzy would be more reassured by that oft-repeated phrase if the Vineart had seemed more certain of that, and less trying to convince himself as well as Jerzy.

The morning sun was cool but bright overhead as Jerzy walked along the path that led to the top of the ridge. The vines were grown only along the top half of the slope, to catch the best of the sun and the most of the cooling evening breezes. The lower half of the slope, and the richer, less rock-studded soil, was given over to herbs and vegetables. Most of that produce went to Lil's kitchen, and the remainder to the sleep-house kitchens. The sleep house here was much smaller: only six slaves and an under-overseer lived here year-round. They were working the herb patch already, their forms bending and rising as they weeded and picked, tossing the clods of weeds to one side and placing the pickings—hardy winter vegetables—more gently into their baskets. The pattern of their movements was rhythmic and soothing, and Jerzy stood for a moment, watching them.

He couldn't remember what it felt like. Even the not-remembering felt distant, as though he had always been a Vineart, merely waiting to be brought forward, the past falling off him even as dirt fell from the roots of the harvested plants, even as the skin slipped from a grape and the juice ran free.

Stressed to greatness. He bent down and picked up a handful of soil, letting it run through his fingers, small pebbles making it feel different from healwine soil, the dirt clinging to the rough stones' surfaces, feeling dryer, more grainy against his skin. It was cold, and had a pulse running through the grains similar to his own heart's beat. He might be imagining that last, but he didn't think so. The vines here were almost as old as the main yard, and the older the vine, the more powerful the magic.

Jerzy knew that what he did here was important, that it was part of the learning he needed to accomplish, to reach the next step of his education, just as the lessons with Cai and Detta were important. Still, there was the knowledge that he was being pushed along, not because he had earned it, or deserved it, but because his master was otherwise occupied, and he was being shoved forward to fill a hole rather than advance his own skills.

And, he admitted to himself, he wished that Master Malech were here with him, walking the rows and telling him what he needed to know, instead of mewed up in the House with yet another visitor. From serene isolation, the House had suddenly become a hive of activity. There had been another *meme-courier* last week, and a robed negotiator the day before last, but this morning's arrival, a man on a strongly muscled white mare, had been different. Clad in fine leathers, he had worn a band of brass around each arm: the mark of a full-ranked member of the Cooperage.

Even slaves knew of the Cooperage. Originally they had merely been the suppliers of casks and barrels to Vinearts, crafting and selling their wares. Over time, Malech had told him, their wealth had increased to the point where they invested in shipbuilding as well, and now were among the wealthiest—and most influential—of the guilds.

Why had a Cooper come here? Could the guild know something that could add to the Master's fears? That seemed unlikely. Yet, if he was offering new barrels, then why had Malech not allowed his apprentice to meet the man, instead of shoving him to a field such a distance away that by the time they returned to the House, the stranger would doubt-less be long gone? And why wouldn't Malech tell him what these mes-sengers were bringing?

Stressed? Ignored, more like, and it all added to his feeling of being left out of the important matters, and now Detta was angry at him as well.

Still, it was difficult to remain out of sorts under the wide-open blue sky, the cold breeze bringing him the scent of the earth, the vines, and hardworking sweat, wrapped together in a familiar slap against his lungs. Jerzy slipped off his soft shoes and let his toes dig into the soil. Detta might frown, and Cai would howl about protecting his balance, but Malech would understand, and approve. Skin to soil told you more than your eyes ever could.

Stepping carefully, he moved into the topmost grouping. The vines were rough and brittle in the cold, and he had to move them aside gen-tly. A quick look at the brown stems showed that they were winding properly around the staves. Like Sin Washer, a vine grew from the soil, supported by others, and spread its bounty like a mother opened her arms.

"Boy," he called out to a slave who was working nearby, carefully re-placing a stave that had been damaged. "Any problems with foxes?"

"None, young master," the slave replied. He was older than Jerzy, with the same olive-toned skin as Master Malech, and sleek black hair and eyebrows to match. "Some of the usual burrower beasts, but we ate a few and they learned to pass us by."

Jerzy nodded at the slave's report and went on with his inspection. Every grouping, Malech had said, and so every grouping he would do.

"Serpents."

The Cooper didn't bother to nod, looking over Malech's shoulder at something fascinating on the wall behind him. "Sea serpents, yes. Wit-nessed and documented. Three ships lost this past season alone."

Three ships was a considerable blow. But that wasn't what had brought the Cooperage to the House of Malech. "There hasn't been a serpent sighting in seven generations, since the Spellstorm of Bradhai."

"Yes. We know."

Malech hated Coopers. They meddled in politics as well as craft, arrogant beyond the princelings of old, and claimed a price each year that bordered on criminal, protecting their craft with such violence no man dared break with them. If there were a way to bypass them, he and every Vineart would take it . . . but there was none. Clay and stone, glass and hammered metal had all been tried, but while casks of such material might make a drinkable *vin ordinaire*, you could not craft a spellwine thus.

There were other places a captain might go to commission a ship, and for better terms—but none were so seaworthy as a Cooperage ship. For them to admit to losing three in such a short period of time . . . he might have suspected the Cooper of creating a story of sea serpents to cover their failure, save that they had no need to tell *him*. Save that he had begun nosing about for things of just such an odd or unnatural nature, and a sea serpent, hundreds of years after the last one had allegedly died by the hand of Master Vineart Bradhai, was certainly that.

Still, this messenger of the Guild did not appear to be a man who would waste his time merely to discuss legends or rumors.

"A serpent," he said again.

The Cooper was a tall man, broad shouldered and flaxen haired, with the hands of a workman, and a nose that had clearly been broken and reset a number of times. No pretty negotiator, this one, but an active member of the Guild.

"A great gray beast, rising from the deepest waters between Jhain and Atakus, crushing the masts in its maw and slamming the body of the ship to splinters with an unending length of gray-scaled tail. Yes. A serpent."

It could have been a giant craw, or even a pack of great sharks driven into a frenzy. Time at sea made even the most stable of men chancy, and sailors were odd sorts to start. "And your clients? They have responded to this news . . . how?"

The Cooper deigned to look at Malech then. "The Jhain-hai has ordered all of his ships to patrol his shores, looking for the beast, with orders to kill it. They trust in spears, not spells, and will die as their ship-brothers did. We do not intend to be so foolish."

"And you bring this news to me. You think that I can craft a spell to kill a serpent?" Malech didn't laugh, although he found the idea bitterly humorous. Bradhai had been a master of his generation, and it had taken his masterwork—and a fleet of ships—to kill that pack of serpents. Most had died in that final storm, including Bradhai.

"No."

Malech wasn't sure if he was relieved by that simple response, or insulted.

"If this is a serpent—and like you, we have our doubts, Lord Malech—if something has brought the serpents back from destruction, it is nothing for one man, however great a Vineart he may be, to undo. That would require a mage, and we have none in this world any longer."

Malech made a quick heart-pour gesture of thanks, and noted that the Cooper did not follow suit. Interesting. The Cooper might simply not have been a pious man. Or he might wish for a mage to reemerge just as the serpents had. If so, he was more a fool than Malech thought: serpents, unlike mages, could be avoided or placated. Serpents could be taken out by spells. It had required a god to rid the world of mages.

"So what do you want of me?"

The Cooper leaned forward, looking directly at Malech for the first time. "The very thing you seem to need of us. Information."

JERZY WAS SURPRISED when he jumped down off the overseer's wagon and walked up the pathway under the arbor arch to see the morning's visitor standing by the nut trees, thoughtfully puffing on a pipe. A sense of excitement rose in him. The stranger had not left, after all. Perhaps

Master Malech had decided to include him in whatever discussions were happening?

Suddenly conscious of his dirt-stained feet and sweaty clothing, Jerzy meant to go on into the house without disturbing the visitor's repose, hoping to wash and change before the evening meal, but paused as he caught the scent of smoke rising through the dusk air and mingling with the flowers. It wasn't an unpleasant scent, just unfamiliar, and it made his nose twitch, trying to categorize it.

A voice came out of the shadows. "You must be the boy."

Jerzy bristled at both the words—Malech might call him boy, but he was near a man's growth now—and the lazy, almost dismissive tone in which they were said.

"I am Master Malech's apprentice, Jerzy."

The stranger stepped forward, looking him over. "Yes. You would have to be, wouldn't you? A fine young man, and a handsome face."

Jerzy's annoyance was replaced by something else at those words, a darker emotion that made him want to lash out, wipe that sneer from the stranger's hard-edged face. He stifled the desire. This rude stranger was nonetheless his master's guest and he had a responsibility—and a duty to the House—to mind his tongue. Suddenly the endless speaking lessons with Detta had a practical use.

"This face is attached to a rather dusty body," he responded politely, taking a step back as gracefully as he could and letting nothing of his feelings show in his voice. "I shall doubtless see you at the evening meal?"

"Indeed." The stranger took another puff on his pipe, and smiled at Jerzy, a slight, secretive smile that made the young Vineart want to back away slowly, alert to a sudden, unprovoked attack, as though the visitor were a wild dog. Instead, Jerzy nodded once, imagining the Guardian's gravity and slow dignity, and turned back toward the door.

Every step he took, he was aware of the stranger watching him, and an itch in the center of his back that had nothing to do with sweat or dirt.

There was a new tunic laid out on his bed when he got to his chamber, and a comb rather pointedly left on top of the rich red fabric. Despite himself, Jerzy grinned. Detta despaired of them both, from the Master's untidy gray locks to his own dark red tangles, but she never gave up. He picked the comb up and carried it with him to the washroom. He would try, again. But he doubted this time would end any differently than the last. Vinearts seemed to naturally have unruly hair.

Dressed in the new white shirt and a pair of brown trousers, leather half boots on his feet and his hair slicked down by application of comb and a dab of nut butter, Jerzy made his way down the stairs to Malech's study, hoping to report his day's work to his master before the meal.

"Come in, Jerzy," Malech's voice sounded before he could even raise his hand to the solid wooden door. His mouth twitched into an unexpected grin, the odd sensation catching him by surprise. No matter how many times his master did that, it still seemed, well, magical. Invited, he used his palm to push open the door, and walked in without hesitation.

Malech was also dressed in a crimson tunic, although his trousers were white and of finer material than Jerzy's own. He was still growing too quickly, Detta said, to warrant the expense of shatnez weave.

"Ah, good, Detta got to you in time. We will have a guest for dinner."

Jerzy almost said that he knew, but something made him remain quiet. His reaction to the visitor's comments lingered, making him feel off-kilter and uneasy, as though he had done something wrong but didn't know quite what.

Malech didn't seem to notice. He was pacing, nothing unusual for the Vineart when he was deep in thought, but tonight there seemed to be an extra quality to it, some added tension in the way he moved, and that added to Jerzy's sense of unease.

Not sure what to do, Jerzy ignored his usual bench and instead stood quietly next to it, his hands resting by his side, letting his thought return not to the encounter with the stranger, but the sight and scent of the grapes in the afternoon sunlight, the hum of slaves' voices as they worked, the feel of the warmed soil under his toes. He could feel his heartbeat slow down, and the unease faded, slightly.

"An interesting discussion, yes. The Cooperage has never been an ally to us." Malech spoke as though continuing a conversation he had been having with himself before Jerzy arrived. "But they are not adversaries, either. At least, not when my gold is not upon the table. And they, for once in their mis-spawned existence, seem interested in something other than their sole advantage. That is not a good thing, boy, not a good thing at all. It bodes something ugly stirring. I was right to worry."

Malech suddenly seemed to realize Jerzy was standing there, and shut his jaw with an almost audible snap.

"Master?"

"Too many years of working alone," the Vineart said, almost apologizing. "And you, quiet as stone when you choose to be. A good trait, that, but disconcerting to your master. So. We shall have company at the board tonight, as my discussions with Cooper Shen ran long today."

Jerzy held his breath, hoping that Malech's next words would tell him what those discussions were. Instead, his master went to the desk and sat down in his high-backed chair, leaning back with his long legs fitting under the desk, which had been cleared of the usual clutter of scrolls and papers. "So. In the time we have before the meal, tell me; how do the southern vineyards look?"

Jerzy stifled a sigh, sat down on his bench with his feet tucked under him, and gave his report.

AT DINNER, THE conversation gave no clue as to what the two men had been closeted over earlier. After so many meals taken in casual disorder, either in the dining hall with the others or in the workroom with Malech, the formality of that meal made Jerzy feel that, despite his fine clothing and clean hair, he had somehow wandered into someone else's life. Rather than the usual bread-platters, they ate off vinewood plates, the knots and burls sliced thin and polished until they glowed, with utensils of the same wood, tipped in gold, and Roan and Bret served them silently, without the normal back-and-forth chatter that enlivened group meals. Malech sat at one end of the table, with Jerzy at his left hand and the Cooper at his right.

Roan brought out grape leaves wrapped around goat cheeses from a village down the road, to be eaten with their fingers, and then roasted pigeons with a light-colored sauce of something tangy and sweet. Lil was, Jerzy thought contentedly, a much better cook than Detta had ever been. They drank only citron-scented water during the meal, not even a *vin ordinaire* on the table. It was as though Malech were showing how little he had to show off, that he had no need to impress the visitor by offering what were, to a Vineart, common drinks.

That was how Jerzy interpreted it, anyway. His master might have had something else entirely in mind, and neither of them could know how the Cooper saw it.

The Cooper, Journeyman Shen, was taller than Jerzy had thought at first, and had finer features. Compared to Malech's drawn skin and sharp bones, he seemed larger and more filled with life, however disloyal that thought might be. His conversation ranged over the things he had seen and done, with—to Jerzy's disappointment—none of it touching on what had brought him here to discuss with Malech.

"And how long have you been with Lord Malech, young master?"

Jerzy looked at the Cooper, flustered by the direct question and not quite sure how to answer. "As many years as I can remember," he replied finally.

"He has been at studies for slightly less than a ten-month," Malech said easily, before Shen could say anything. "I find him reassuringly adept, and surprisingly bright."

"But . . . so many years . . . ?" Shen looked confused, and then something seemed to shift in his memory. "Ah. That is correct. You choose your apprentices from your . . . worker population." There was a tone of something in Shen's voice that Jerzy didn't understand, and he looked to Malech for explanation.

"My slaves, yes." Malech was as blunt as Shen had been circumspect.

"It is a system that has worked for us for generations. The so-called civilized world may not understand, but it is not for them to interfere."

Shen looked as though he were going to argue, and Jerzy looked from Malech to Shen in fascination. Something silent and uncomfortable was going on between the two, but he didn't understand what. Being a slave was a bad thing? How else then could Master Malech have found him?

"I will bow to history in this regard, Lord Malech," Shen said gracefully, finally, and the meal resumed. Throughout the second course, however, Jerzy felt Shen's gaze turn to him more and more often, no matter the conversation, until he felt the intense desire to get up and leave the table, to avoid that regard. The Cooper said or did nothing offensive—in fact, he seemed more determined to bring Jerzy into the conversation, asking his thoughts and opinions when they discussed the recent blight of root-glow that had, apparently, hit a number of other coastal vineyards in addition to their own, equally out of season.

"It is my understanding that such a—it is a fungus, yes?"

"Yes."

"Such a fungus is normally spread by a carrier, not simply carried by the wind, especially if, as you say, the conditions were not usual. But to spread so quickly, it would need a carrier with entry to your yards. A bird, perhaps? Or foxes?"

"Or a man, is that what you are asking?"

Jerzy asked the way he would have asked Malech, seeking correction and instruction. Instead, Shen responded as though it were a viable suggestion from a valued correspondent.

"We at the Cooperage know only the results of root-glow, not the means. Lord Malech and I touched on the topic earlier, but only briefly. Might you think it possible for a man—or many men—to transport this rot somehow, from place to place?"

"Transport it?" Jerzy had the sudden image of a man with a woven basket over his arm, glowing from within, a look of overdone malice on the man's face, like a Player acting out the role of an ancient prince-mage, riding a horse that looked like a fire-breathing cross between the Cooper's mare and the heavy, placid wagon horses. The image was ridiculous enough to break through his astonishment at the question. "How? Root-glow cannot be contained, only killed. To handle it . . . you would risk . . ." Belatedly he cast a glance at Malech, and received a subtle nod of the head to continue. But carefully, his master's expression seemed to indicate. Carefully. "It prefers vine root, but an unprotected hand, one with an open scratch or cut in the skin, might also become infected. Untreated, it can kill."

Unlikely—Jerzy had never heard of such a thing happening—but vineyard slaves knew of the danger. Someone without that training . . .

"Ah." Shen seemed satisfied by that, and let the topic go, moving on to talk with Malech about the ironwoods of southern Iaja versus the more flexible but also more porous heartwoods of Caul. But it could not be put aside so easily by Jerzy, and the rest of the meal he worried at the idea. The thought of someone attacking their fields specifically, he could accept—that they did not know who might do such a thing did not mean it was not possible. But to arrange for someone to travel, up and down the coastline, carrying the root-glow in . . . in a basket like turnips?

Not impossible, no, if incredibly foolish. Who would do such a thing? He had asked Malech that at the time, and not gotten an answer that satisfied either of them. Finally, Jerzy put the thought away. It was something for Master Malech to determine, not himself. He should not have involved himself in the discussion at all. He was merely there to listen and, if he could, to learn.

After Bret cleared the table of the dishes and platters, Master Malech brought out a half carafe of gilded *vin* and poured them each a glass. The liquid shimmered in the lamplight, deep gold as a sunset and red as dawn, thick and sweet as honey. The three men let conversation lapse and merely enjoyed the treat with handfuls of roasted nuts to enhance the flavor.

"That," Shen finally said with a sigh of satisfaction, "was an excellent meal. My compliments to your cook. Now, if you will excuse me? I fear I am a servant to my pipe; anlikaroot soothes my digestion and allows me to sleep comfortably after such a repast, else I will be up all night pacing."

"Indeed. You might find the courtyard a pleasant place for such a stroll. Jerzy, if you would care to accompany our guest? I need to discuss a few matters with Detta before the evening ends. Shen, a good night. I will see you both in the morning."

Jerzy was very much aware that he was being asked to substitute as host for his master. There was no way to refuse, not without disgracing the House. So he swallowed his own hesitations, and rose from his chair as gracefully as he could to lead Shen out into the courtyard, leaving Malech sitting at the table, his glass of *vina* still in his hand.

Most of the time Jerzy thought of the courtyard simply as a way to get from one wing of the House to the other, or where he could lift a quick bucket of water from the well, rather than going down into the sub-kitchen. At night, it felt different somehow. The fruit tree cast moving shadows on the ground, and the bench looked as though it were carved out of silver rather than stone. The moon glowed overhead, almost dimming the scatter of stars, and the night insects were chirping and buzzing in a drowsy chorus. In the eaves overhead a pigeon let out a sleepy coo, quickly followed by the nearby hunting call of an owl, and then silence.

"Your master thinks quite highly of you," Shen said, after taking a long draw on his pipe. It was polished briarwood, and the curved tip glowed dark red with ash.

Jerzy blinked. "He hasn't cuffed me recently," he said in cautious agreement. "And only threatened to send me back to the fields once this month." He had deserved it, too, that time.

"Ah." Once again, the Cooper seemed taken aback. "I suppose . . . every apprenticeship must have its own form, and the work you do is dangerous in its own way. Some sort of barrier must be maintained. A shame, but understandable. I suspect that you would bloom, under more gentle conditions."

Shen's hand touched Jerzy's shoulder. It could have been a chance gesture, or a paternal sign of affection, but it felt . . . different. Familiar. Jerzy shuddered once, as though a breeze had struck between his shoulder blades. Acting purely on instinct he stepped back, moving away from the Cooper too hastily for it to be anything other than a rebuff.

"My apologies," he started, horrified that he had somehow insulted his master's guest, but the Cooper shook his head, the offending hand now safely at his side.

"No, boy. The apologies should be mine. I had not—" He laughed, almost ruefully, Jerzy thought. "I have enough of an ego to think that my advances are not displeasing, and I need to be reminded otherwise every now and again."

The words sounded sincere, but Jerzy's shoulders remained hunched and his skin twitched in memory, like a horse ridding itself of flies. The Cooper had meant no harm, Jerzy knew that, and yet the peace and comfort of the evening was broken.

After an uncomfortable attempt to pick up the conversation, Jerzy excused himself as politely as possible, retreating to the safety of his bedchamber. When he looked down again, the Cooper was still standing there in the darkness, the tip of his pipe still glowing. Jerzy shucked his finery and crawled into bed. He thought that sleep would elude him, but the *vin* and the rich food combined to drug him into a heavy, dreamless slumber.

When he came down the next morning, it was to the news from Lil that their guest had ridden out before dawn, while she was heating the ovens for the day, rather than waiting for a more formal farewell.

Malech met him in the hallway outside the study, after a subdued morning meal. "What did you speak of last night, to Cooper Shen?"

Jerzy could only shrug helplessly. "I . . . he . . . I told him that you were a good master. And he . . ."

Malech waited, his face giving no indication of his thoughts.

"He put his hand on my shoulder." It sounded beyond foolish, spoken like that. He had been touched many times in his life, often with violence behind it. Even Malech was still quick with a blow or a cuff when he answered too slowly or with the wrong response. Shen had not been harsh, or rough; he had in fact been gentler than anyone save Detta, in Jerzy's memory. He had done nothing wrong, committed no offense . . . so why then had his skin crawled when the Copper moved too close?

"For a touch, you offended him?"

Jerzy shrugged again, and almost welcomed the familiar blow that followed. "Idiot boy. But no, idiocy is not always damage, and Shen is no fool, to take offense at one boy's shivers. And he and his people have given us useful information indeed. Come on, then. There are things I must teach you, swiftly, if you are to be of use in our coming venture. You thought you were working before, boy?" Malech laughed, an unhappy sound. "Pray the silent gods we have time, before—"

Malech shook his head, and stopped, his mouth tightening into a thin-pressed line.

Before what? Jerzy wondered, but did not dare ask.

Chapter 12

*Y*ou are not *concentrating.*

It was less words and more a feeling of disapproval that came through, but Jerzy scowled up at the Guardian anyway. "Is it even possible to distract you?"

No.

"Then stop bothering me while I'm working to lecture me about something you can't understand."

The fact that he was talking—and getting a response from—an animate stone carving still made Jerzy blink, occasionally. Admittedly, his practical experience with magic was limited to the vines that his master specialized in, healing and fire, but none of his readings anywhere had mentioned a spell that gave motion and thought to stone. If life were less hectic, he would have asked Malech about it—it seemed rude to ask the Guardian, even if he thought it would answer—but in the two weeks since the Cooper Shen's visit, Malech had spent more and more of his time in his study, sending out messages via carrier pigeon, and entertaining *meme-couriers* at an increasing pace, all of them arriving and departing at all hours of the day until Detta and Lil both threw up their hands and merely left cold meals for them all. He came out of each meeting looking more and more worried, but still refused to tell Jerzy anything specific, instead exhorting him to push forward with his studies.

And so, Jerzy studied: morning to past nightfall. Some of that involved reading old texts, or memorizing charts and traditions, recited under the watchful eye and ear of the Guardian. However, a growing part of his education involved monitoring the vineyards, as Mid-Fallows passed, and the soil began to warm. In the southernmost enclosures, tiny leaflets were already beginning to bud.

By now, Jerzy could identify all four of their varietals at a glance, and determine if the growth was healthy or if steps needed to be taken to protect the vine. He had spent nights watching storms roll in, wishing that Malech believed in using weatherspells to moderate how much rain fell on the vines, and given orders to the various overseers on how much to prune back, where to fortify, and what to let go. Every move he made had an impact on what the yield might be, and there were nights he could not sleep for second-guessing his decisions. He was too young, too green to be responsible for such things. And yet Malech merely nodded when he reported his actions, and told him to continue as he saw fit, distracted in a way no Vineart should be from matters of the vineyard.

Driven by a lack of confidence, he dove with increased urgency into the historical reports of past harvests and pressings; what conditions created what results. Not only Malech's notes, but *his* master, Josia's, notes as well were included, going back almost a hundred harvests. Before then, another House had stood on these grounds, but all records were lost when that Vineart had died without successor and Josia had taken over.

Someday, if he didn't go off and start his own House, his records would be added to these notes. His successes, failures, and discoveries would be added to the weight of the years, the accumulation of knowledge.

The thought terrified him.

You are distracted again. The Guardian tilted its head to look down at him. *When the time comes, your notes will be written for the time, not the archive. Live now.*

The rebuke stung like one of Malech's head cuffs, but the sting was reassuring as well. Tradition was on their side, even if this urgency was not. Detta had taught him history along with his letters, and Master Malech reinforced it with his lectures. Once, every Vineart had been a student. Once, every student had been a slave. Like the vines, they grew best in stressed soil. That was how Sin Washer decreed it. Tradition kept you safe.

Jerzy stared at the paper in front of him and made a note on his own pad, ink blotting slightly as he scratched down another question to bring to Malech at evening meal.

"Guardian, I understand that the sun's warmth on the fruit makes the wine sweeter, but why does that also make healwine more effective, but do the opposite for firewine? Shouldn't heat be good for firespells?"

There was a not-unexpected silence, and Jerzy snorted in satisfaction. It might be that the Guardian felt no need to teach, but he liked to think the stone dragon wasn't quite as know-everything as it pretended.

He bent his head back to the text's comparison of harvesting techniques, and silence reigned in the workroom until the thudding of someone hammering on the door one level above them filtered down through the stones.

"Guardian?"

The stone dragon had already lifted its head. *Someone at the front door.*

Jerzy rolled his eyes. He'd figured that out already.

The man is not hurt, nor does he bear the sigils of a meme-courier *or a* negotiator. *But his horse is lathered and near foundering, and the human seems quite agitated. You should greet them, this is not something for the Household to deal with.*

Jerzy raced up the stairs, tugging at his plain tunic, to find that Detta had already opened the door. She stepped back with obvious relief when Jerzy appeared in the entranceway. "Young master, this is—"

The man shoved past her rudely, forcing his way into the House. He was a few years older than Jerzy, taller and broader in the shoulder, and his ruddy face was lined with exhaustion and his clothing was covered with dust from the road.

"My name is Jecq. I come on orders of Prince Ranulf, and I must speak to the Master Vineart!"

"It's all right, Detta," Jerzy said. To the messenger he said, "Master Malech's not here right now." In truth, he had no idea where the Vineart had gone off to that morning, save that he was not to be bothered short of fire or flood. "If you would follow our House-keeper, she can find you something cool to drink, and perhaps a light meal, while I arrange your meeting?"

"I must speak immediately with Master Malech! Prince Ranulf insists! Hundreds of lives are at stake!" Jecq didn't quite stomp his boot on the flooring, but Jerzy had the feeling that he wanted to.

Nothing short of fire or flood, Malech had said, his face stern. Jerzy ignored the man's rude tone, and instead looked in the eyes of the messenger and made his decision.

"Guardian. Go find Master Malech. Now."

From the workroom below their feet, Jerzy felt the dragon's slow acceptance, and, somehow, *felt* the stone wings rise and then push down as the carving left its perch.

"Go with Detta. When Master Malech returns, you will be informed."

The messenger looked like he was going to protest again, and Jerzy felt a sick turn in his stomach. If the other man insisted, what could he do? Sending the Guardian had been a wild guess, and while he had authority in this House, it did not include ordering his master around!

Jecq held himself very still and stared at Jerzy. His eyes squinted shut, as though the wind were still blowing grit into them, so that Jerzy could not tell what color his eyes were.

"A drink would be welcome," he said finally, dropping his gaze and turning away to follow a clearly relieved Detta off to the kitchen.

Jerzy returned to the workroom to tidy up the papers he had left scattered and to blot his own notes dry and store them safely for later. Then he returned upstairs, trying to prepare himself in case Malech did not return from wherever he was in time and the messenger became unruly again. His stomach ached like he had eaten rotted vegetables, and his skin was slick with sweat, despite the fact that the House was its usual comfortable cool temperature.

"Jerzy."

He yelped and jumped and turned a deep shade of red even he could feel on his skin when he realized it was only Malech's hand on his shoulder. Since the Cooper's visit, he had been more and more aware of people touching him. Malech knew that, and yet—

"Master. My apologies, I . . ." He gathered himself and his thoughts, and started again. "A messenger has arrived from Lord-prince Ranulf"—Malech might declaim about princelings, but until one was a Master, one gave respect even out of their hearing—"and demands to see you on a matter of some dire importance." He had only recently learned the word "dire," and had not had occasion to use it before.

Malech's narrow face was set in stern lines, but this time Jerzy was reasonably certain his master was not angry with him. "Indeed. Prince Ranulf is not a man to panic easily, nor is he one to ask for aid. In fact, this may be the first time he has ever come to me for anything other than his annual allotment of healwines. Dire, you say? So it may indeed be. Good that you sent the Guardian for me. If you would, please, collect this messenger and bring him—and yourself—to my study."

The tension of wondering if he'd made the right choice to recall Malech left Jerzy, only to be replaced by a new one; by the speed of his return, and his words, Malech was clearly concerned, and that did not bode well at all.

* * *

By THE TIME Jerzy collected the messenger and they presented themselves in the study, Malech looked as though he had been there all morning, awaiting their arrival. More, the wall of bottles that had so overawed Jerzy on his first visit was back, and there was a small table set upon the corner with an open bottle that—Jerzy sneaked a second look—that yes, had faint trails of steam rising up from it. Malech himself had changed into a dark red tunic, and pulled his hair back into a severe braid that emphasized the sharp lines of his face and the hawk-intentness of his gaze.

Despite the situation, Jerzy was amused. His master was as much a stage setter as any Player, when the occasion called for it.

"Please. Be seated."

Jecq took the chair closest to Malech's desk as a matter of right, while Malech seated himself behind it. Jerzy, unwilling to take up his usual bench, instead stood off to one side, behind the messenger but still with a clear line of sight of both Jecq and his master.

He looked up, and was reassured to see the Guardian had taken up a space over the lintel, mirroring its usual post in the workroom. It didn't fit the decor quite so well as it did downstairs, but its presence made him feel better, somehow.

"So, messenger. You have a message for me that could not wait?"

Jecq nodded, straightened his shoulders to board-stiffness, and began to speak.

"From Prince Ranulf of The Berengia: greetings to Lord Vineart Malech of the Valle of Ivy. This messenger comes to you with a request for your immediate assistance. Two days ago a monster rose up out of the sea and destroyed the entire village of Darcen. The entire village, near one hundred souls, gone in the time it took my prince's men to ride to their aid. Roofs were torn asunder, boats thrashed into kindling, nets ripped, and the people . . ." His voice didn't change despite the falter: he was still reciting a message, if not as adeptly as a *meme-courier* would have. It was not a question of saving costs, Jerzy thought, not for Ranulf, who had riches to spare. No, this message was urgent enough that the princeling could not wait, and dared not send a messenger-bird.

"The people were gone, Lord Malech. Not a corpse left, not even a babe in the cradle. Only blood, everywhere. And . . ."

"And?"

"And . . . chunks, Lord Malech. Chunks of some strange, fleshy matter, scattered over the remains of the village. As though whatever had come had also . . . left part of itself behind."

Jerzy, watching the messenger's face, would have laid coin he did not own that the chunks had been far more disgusting and disturbing than the messenger was saying.

"And your lord-prince would have me do what? I do not craft such spellwines as could be useful to you, if all are dead; I cannot defend your borders, or dispose of this . . . matter." There was something strange in Malech's voice, and Jerzy took a moment to puzzle it out. His master was not entirely taken by surprise, somehow, by this news. Malech wanted something, but was waiting to see if it was also what this prince wanted of him, and if not, how their desires might come together with the best advantage—or at least cost—to Malech. The dead could have been cows, or pigeons, for all the dismay his master showed.

The messenger looked disgusted, his mouth twisting as though he tasted something sour. "We had spellwines of Atakus to protect our coasts, and they failed. My prince requested a message sent to Master Vineart Edon, only to discover that Atakus itself . . . has disappeared. No captain can sail there but be cast back into unfamiliar waters, the skies overcast above them. It is as though a hole in the world opened and swallowed them entire."

Jerzy swallowed hard at that news, thinking it some new and terrible disaster, but Malech looked concerned and yet somehow unsurprised. Jerzy had only a moment to spare to wonder how an entire island might disappear like that, and why, before Malech was speaking again.

"Again, then, I ask: what is it you seek of me? To bury your dead? I do not craft spells of protection from weather nor beasts."

The messenger spoke, and Jerzy knew, somehow, that these were the man's own words, not a formal message. "Since the attack . . . none can pass through that village without coming down ill. Not with chills or fever, but a stupor they cannot shake. Already every worker sent to clear the rubble has fallen thus, unable to rouse even for their loved ones or to find cheer in any moment. My prince would ask of you a spell to cleanse the lands of this . . . disaster. A healwine for the spirit. Please, Master Vineart." He would not beg, not in so many words, but the tone was clear.

Melancholia was one of Malech's lesser known craftings, made from the fruit of a healvine, but richer and more delicate all at once than most body-healing wines, requiring the skills of a Master Vineart to craft. Jerzy had handled the grapes as they grew, learning their temperament, but it would be years yet before he would be able to craft such a decantation, if he was even capable of it.

"Indeed." Malech studied the messenger, but his thoughts were clearly elsewhere. "I cannot think of anything else that might do the trick. However, without knowing the nature of the melancholia it would be difficult to assign the proper bottling. . . . Ah." Malech leaned forward with the air of a man who has solved a knotty problem. "My student, Jerzy. He will travel with you, bearing a number of flasks, and once there will be able to determine the proper decantation, and thus instruct your prince in the usage thereof."

The messenger's back stiffened, and Jerzy had to quickly school his features to not give away his shock or excitement, lest the man look back at him. If Malech thought he was ready, then he would be ready!

"Lord Malech, are you certain this youth . . ." The messenger saw the look on Malech's face change from pleased satisfaction to a clouded sort of outrage, and backtracked quickly. Malech's reputation was not as a particularly harsh man, or a vindictive one, as Vinearts went, but neither was he to be trifled with or second-guessed, most especially by a lowly messenger, no matter how much money he was prepared to pour into the Vineart's coffers. If the Master felt the need to send his student with the messenger, then his student would go.

* * *

WITHIN THE HOUR, Jerzy was dressed and ready for travel, a horse—one of Malech's three riding animals, as opposed to the wagon-beasts—saddled and waiting next to Jecq's beast. Master Malech was affixing four wineskins to the saddle via a series of complicated straps.

"The decantations are ones you already know"—he glared at Jerzy, his stern expression no longer quite so terrifying—"or should, if your head has retained anything at all. Do not offer to explain anything; princes dislike being instructed.

"I do not know what you will encounter," he continued more quietly, this not for the messenger's hearing. "But what I have given you should cover all possibilities. You have never dealt with this part of our craft before: the magic-less think there must be ceremony. They do not understand that decantation has nothing to do with them, that magic is released from within the flesh of the grape only by our skills; that the spell-structure is merely a means, not the magic itself. Safer that way, to make them believe that they are part of it, to keep them from wondering too intently how we might be different from themselves, how we might indeed be the prince-mages' inheritors. This has always been our way, to protect ourselves."

Jerzy nodded, listening intently. One last lesson, one more thing to learn. He did not understand all of Master Malech's words, but the meaning came through: give Prince Ranulf the spellwines needed, teach him how to use them, and nothing more.

"Now go," his master said, stepping back. "And come home safe."

ONE OF JERZY's few vague memories of his life before the slavers was of being thrown on horseback and galloping into the wind, the feel of great muscles carrying him far and long. But he had been a child then, and the memory of how much his legs and arms and back ached after such a ride had long since faded. Cai's lessons had helped return some skill, but he was still no horseman.

It had not helped any that Jecq had pushed their pace to the fastest the horses could handle, a steady walk broken by occasional runs, allowing only a quick break to eat and then a few hours overnight to sleep, when it became dark enough that the horses could not pick their way along the road safely.

If he had been in less agony, and less concerned for the four wineskins slung onto the heavy saddle, Jerzy might have enjoyed the journey more: it was the first time since he had been sold that he had been off his master's lands, and back then he had traveled in an enclosed wagon with twenty or more others—there had been no view from inside the wagon, no scenery save the bodies of his fellow slaves and the rough hands and cool voices of the slavers.

Jerzy refused to allow those memories to resurface. That was a life that had happened to someone else, a story told and retold until he knew all the twists and turns but felt little of the emotions the players must have felt. It was Then. This, the aches and pains of his backside, the jostle and slosh of the spellwines on his saddle, the creak of the leathers and the clodding noises of the horses' hooves on the packed dirt road, this was the Now. Now he was no slave, but an apprentice Vineart on a mission of great importance for his master.

While the messenger had been checking the saddle strap of his own horse, Malech had lowered his voice ever further and given one last set of instructions. "Make an excuse, any excuse, to look over that village, to inspect those chunks, or whatever it is, left in the creature's wake if you have opportunity. But be careful—I don't want you falling victim to whatever malaise grips their villagers! A Vineart must always stand apart and never show weakness. Not ever."

Jerzy remembered those words as they came to the end of the two-day journey through the wooded hills outside his master's lands, the terrain slowly changing from the green rolling fields and tree-covered ridges of home to a rougher landscape of downward-sloping hills and marshy fields, studded with the occasional streamside mill. In the distance he saw darker splotches that might have been towns, but the road they followed cut sharply to the west, toward the horizon.

He heard the sea, a softly relentless roar, before he saw it, and smelled it before either, a sweet, salty mist that tickled the inside of his nose and made him think of green grapes, not quite yet ripe. His first sight of the sea itself came as they rode over a ridge and found themselves on the narrow cuff of a cliff. Behind them there was solid earth and rock. Before them, open sky and soaring birds and an endless expanse of ever-moving waters stretching out into a barely visible horizon.

It was magnificent, and terrifying, like falling and soaring all at once, and Jerzy fought off a sudden wave of dizziness, clutching the reins as though the horse would keep him in place.

Jecq paused just long enough to check the sun's placement against some marker in the distance, and then spurred his beast on along the path. Reluctantly, aware of the need, Jerzy followed.

Soon enough they were riding through a fisher village on the way to where Jecq said Ranulf and his men had camped while inspecting the damage in Darcen, a few hours' ride up the coastline. Here, the dirt road gave way to irregularly laid brown cobblestones and one-story stone buildings. It would have been attractive save that the streets were filthy with muck and the roofs coated with bird shit streaking the dark red tile roofs. Worse, the clean smell of the sea gave way to one more to do with flesh and sweat, although still tinged with the same salty mist. Jecq kicked his horse to a faster walk, and Jerzy gladly followed suit. Despite the recent attack nearby, the old men were sitting on benches with their net-mending, and old women were at their washing at the single stone fountain. As the two men rode through the town's upper level, they all stopped to stare, their dark gazes watching them pass by without a single word.

Even though his body ached, Jerzy forced himself to ride easily, sitting upright and strong, remembering Malech's parting words. He was a Vineart, bred of the stressed soil and blazing sun. He did not show weakness.

They had just left the village, with its low stone huts and the

overwhelming stink of fish, to ride up the path and into the encamp-
ment's gates, when a scream sounded from the rocky shore behind them.

"It comes! It comes again!"

THE WISE THING would have been to head for the princeling's camp
and let his men—trained fighters—deal with whatever "it" might be. A
Vineart did not partake of battle any more than they did of politics. But
Jerzy, a sinking feeling in his gut and the tang of something foul—far
more foul than old fish—hitting his nostrils, already knew that he, and
what he carried, would be needed down on the shoreline, not up the hill
behind canvas walls. Jecq was already wheeling his horse around, having
to saw heavily on the reins to get the beast turned away from home and
stable, so close to its destination. Thankfully, Jerzy's smaller brown mare
was willing to follow without fuss.

They hadn't gotten more than a few strides back into town before the
old men and not a few of the older women had dropped their chores
and grabbed makeshift weapons—long metal poles with hooks and
sharpened ends—and headed in the direction of the scream. They, too,
knew what had happened to the people of Darcen.

"To the beach," Jecq directed them—needlessly, so far as Jerzy could
see, and indeed they paid him no more heed than if he had been one
of the nets now cast aside on the ground. Jerzy started to follow, when
something tugged at his awareness. Not a smell, exactly, although his
nose twitched at it. A scent. An aroma. A familiar residue that tapped at
the side of his skull and beckoned him in a different direction.

Magic. Someone was casting a spell. He didn't know how he knew,
but he *knew*. It was inside him, drawing him down.

That pull led him not down to the rocky shoreline where the villagers—younger men and women pouring from shallow fishing barques
to join their elders—were bracing for battle, but upward, onto a slight
rise over the water. There, an older, close-shaven man stood, dressed in
wear-darkened leathers and braced by three fighting men, bareheaded

like their prince, each with long bows aimed up at the sky, faces set in ugly determination.

"My lord!" Jerzy didn't know how he knew, but there was no one else it could be, with bowmen at his side. "My lord, I am come from Master Vineart—"

"Have you anything of use?" The princeling demanded, turning on him even as Jerzy slid from the horse's side and rummaged for the nearest wineskin.

"My lord, I don't know—"

A roar filled the air around them, and Jerzy's hands faltered. He turned, as the bowmen swore and let fly the first round of arrows. The stink intensified, and the sky was blotted out until the pale blue surface became a distant backdrop for the nightmare that rose out of the sea in front of them.

Jerzy had looked through some of Malech's illustrated texts before they left. "Sea serpent" did not do the monster justice. A serpent was sleek, smooth, and supple. Sea serpents were supposed to glisten, to inspire as much awe as fear. This . . . thing was muddy brown and bulky, its scales mottled even under the afternoon sunlight, and the long neck was filled with odd lumps, like . . .

It took only that one look, seeing the lumps move, for Jerzy to realize that they were people, fishermen out on their boats, swallowed whole by that great, oxlike head. The thing did not tear or rend, but instead dipped its long neck to grab a terrified fisherman in its black-lipped maw and consume him in one gulp. Jerzy felt dizzy, his gaze sliding down the length of neck to the body, only partially visible under the waves. It had to be the size of a cottage—Jerzy watched it come forward, and revised his guess to twice the size of a cottage, impossibly large and muscled, and moving with a seemingly unstoppable if slow pace up onto the beach.

It was a monster, a sickening, terrifying monster. Where arrows struck it, bits of gray-brown flesh—the "chunks" the messenger had described, Jerzy guessed, dropped off and fell to the water, the waves boiling around each piece before it sank into the depths. And yet, that did not halt the beast. The villagers gathered on the sand, their metal hooks and fish spears at the ready, but clearly unwilling to enter the water where the beast was at an advantage.

"Boy, a spellwine, if you have one!" the prince demanded, even as two bowmen rearmed, and the third withdrew a sword and tried to urge the princeling to retreat back behind a large white rock that, despite its size, even Jerzy could see would be no defense at all.

His hand fell on one wineskin, even as his horse snorted and reared in fear, and then his hand slipped to a different one, taking it off the saddle hook without conscious thought. The moment he dropped the reins, the horse bolted, stopping, its sides heaving with effort, by the road, as though asking its rider why he wasn't mounting up and getting the hell out of there like a sensible creature.

The skin he grabbed had a dark blue band around the mouthpiece. Not the melancholia, then. What had blue been for? The trip had fogged his brain, and fear made it slow, and for an agonizing moment he could not remember what the spellwine in the blue-marked skin was for. Heal-aid, that was it: meant to soothe a wounded man or animal and send it into a deep sleep so that it could be safely treated by non-magical means. Why had he chosen that skin, of all the choices?

The prince, impatient, grabbed it from his hands. "How do I work it?" he demanded. "Tell me how to command it!"

Arrows sang again, soaring into the air toward the beast, landing and dispatching chunks of flesh, but with little effect on the monster, which continued its way toward the shore.

Jerzy couldn't take his eyes off the creature, but answered the question without hesitation. "'To the flesh,' then 'calm the flesh,' then the command." Malech's words echoed in his mind: the spell was a basic command-structure, yet important-sounding enough to make the user think the words were potent in and of themselves. The illusion of control. Yes, Jerzy understood a little better now.

The prince took a mouthful of the wine and turned to face the water, raising his arms as though to attract the beast's attention.

Jerzy knew that the spell Ranulf was about to cast might, at best, slow the monster down, so that the arrows and swords might strike more cleanly. But it was not a weapon, not the way the prince expected.

More people would die, eaten by that monstrous thing, before it could be killed.

Driven by some impulse he didn't quite understand, Jerzy took the wineskin back from the prince's upraised hand, and took a sip onto his own tongue.

The command he had given the prince would raise the soothing magics within the spell. But Malech's words . . . a Vineart worked the magic when it was in mustus, when it was unspecified *vina*. It followed, then, that a Vineart was not restricted by spell-structure. . . .

But Jerzy was no Vineart, not yet. He was a student, a slave, daring too much yet unable to resist the impulse growing within him. Even as the prince shouted the words of the spell, his voice muffled by the liquid in his mouth, Jerzy swallowed the spellwine, feeling the texture coating his throat, the aroma rising up through his palate, meeting the tickling sensation within himself. The impact made him stagger, but he did not lose control.

"Rise to the first spell. Rise!"

It wasn't a spell, but an order, torn out of desperation and fear, and yet it worked. Ordinary men could not see magic, only results, and so Jerzy was the only one to sense his spell rise and overwhelm the prince's casting. Jerzy held his breath and sent up a brief prayer to Sin Washer that he was doing the right thing. He drew a deep breath and said the final part, his voice in concert with the prince's.

"Go!"

The two decantations slammed into each other, twining even as Jerzy directed his casting, binding together and then slamming into the beast with a clap of sound and sparks like lightning hitting the tallest tree on a hill. The effect was immediate. The great sea beast roared, throwing its massive head skyward and letting a body drop from its mouth into the water below with a heavy splash. The serpent's head bobbed down again, swooping terrifyingly low, heavy-lidded eyes opening wide to reveal a blank, milky-white stare. The magic shimmered again, a pale red haze visible only to Jerzy's eyes, and the great beast shuddered.

"'Ware! Out of the way!"

The villagers scattered, holding on to their makeshift weapons even as they scattered back up the rocky beach, even as the great body swayed in the air, its maw of a mouth opening wider in a snarl that cut the air and echoed against the cliffs.

"Sin Washer save us," one of the archers cried, throwing himself down on his knees. His fellow guards stood and stared, their weapons held at shoulder or hip height, useless and slack.

"Washer, look at the size of those teeth."

Even as one of the archers muttered that, one of the teeth—in truth, fangs the length of a man's arm, yellow-white and curved like a cat's claw—fell from that open maw and splashed down into the wet sand.

Jerzy felt the air leave his lungs in a heavy gasp of relief. His twist had taken the spell one step further, sending the great beast not soothing calm, but such a deep relaxation the very bits of bone and muscle unwound from one another, the joints failing so rapidly that it could not remain upright, nor teeth remain in its mouth.

A man below them screamed as he narrowly missed being impaled by the fang. Upright in the sand, it was as tall, to Jerzy's eyes, as a young child.

The beast was, literally, falling apart as the spell rode down through the massive length of its body. It still lived, however, and still tried to feed, the body thrashing, swamping the remaining boats, the mouth relentlessly trying to reach the villagers on the shoreline. Those fisherfolk scattered and then returned, now prodding at the portions within reach with their staves and spears, drawing its attention at great risk to themselves.

"To arm," Ranulf shouted, drawing his own weapon, a sword that was dark and battered looking but still promised of sharp edges and

a heavy blow in his hands. The princeling did not wait for his men
to ready themselves, but ran down the path to the shore, leading the
charge. To their credit, the bowmen did not hesitate, even the one who
had fallen to his knees quickly rising. Two of them ran with their bows
at-ready, the third drawing a blade from his scabbard instead. In seconds, Jerzy was left alone on the bluff, watching as the battle was joined.

Even with the spell making the beast sluggish, it was no easy slaughter: the serpent beast lashed out with its massive head and knocked
half a dozen of the fisherfolk into the water, where they sank into the
waist-deep waves and were not seen again. Meanwhile, the remaining
boats were coming in to shore, not where the battle raged, but farther
out, along the rocky shoals, figures creeping onto the rocks and moving
slowly for home, trying not to attract the beast's attention. Jerzy felt the
wine sack in his hand, and wondered, desperately, if another casting
would help or not. Some spellwines could be used again and again, adding to the effect. Others merely faded once the wine was uncorked, until
they were nothing more than a whisper of power.

He didn't know which this one was. A surge of panic went through
him as he tried to remember if he had known and forgotten, or simply
never known. Why hadn't Malech better prepared him?

Because, a voice that sounded like his own told him dryly, *you aren't
supposed to be decanting spellwines, merely delivering them.*

"Disaster either way," he finally said, and lifted the spellwine to his
mouth again. The taste this time was muted, although he wasn't sure if
it was because he knew what to expect, or if the wine was fading already.
This time he noticed more subtle details; the touch of tartness on his
tongue, the lingering sense of sun-warmed flint surrounding it, the way
the liquid seemed to splash into his mouth rather than flow, and the
gentle, almost untraceable ribbon of creaminess that wrapped around
the flint and tart, binding them together. He had walked the soil of
this vineyard, felt the sun on the vines that had produced these grapes,
smelled the rain that nourished them, and the wind that cooled them.
He knew this wine, even if he had not created it, and that knowledge

triggered something deep inside him, tingling like a headache, only without the pain.

"Into the muscles, seep. Soften the flesh, soften." He whispered it around the golden liquid this time, then swallowed, feeling it slide down his throat. "Go." It was less a command and more of an entreaty, and he felt the magic within the wine following his desire.

He followed the flow of magic as it swooped down off the cliff, an invisible swarm of bees, a swirl of butterflies, streaking down to meet the beast just as it finally came up onto the beach proper, lengths of its body still coiling and uncoiling behind it in the water, thick, stumpy legs hitting the sand and leaving webbed prints behind. The neck seemed even longer and thicker, out of the water, and the head was terrifyingly close. Yet the prince stood stock-still as the mouth came down at him, closer, closer . . .

To those on the beach, it must have seemed that the princeling's sword blow decapitated the beast, the heavy blade sliding through scales and flesh without hesitation. Only someone watching the prince would see his reaction, his muscle awareness that he hadn't struck hard enough to land that sort of blow.

The beast wobbled, its voice cut off midroar, and the coastline resounded with that silence for a heartbeat before the huge head fell backward into the deeper water and the body followed, collapsing on its side, half on the sand, half in the water, sending wavelets racing back and forth and forcing the humans to retreat to a safer distance or risk being swamped.

The spell had done the work. The spell, and Jerzy's casting of it.

He had just enough time to feel a swell of pride before the fisher-folk were dropping their makeshift weapons and rushing toward their prince, shouting his name and cheering.

What did you expect? a voice crawled up to whisper in his ear. *Ranulf is the man with the sword and the circlet. All they know is you were the messenger, the servant, the slave. You did nothing. You earned nothing. No shouts for you. No glad praise or—*

Over the voice came the cool mental voice of the Guardian, impossible at this distance, and yet unmistakable. *You are Vineart.*

Jerzy cut the first voice off without real effort, and the Guardian's presence faded into a fine mist. He watched the celebrations below him with an oddly distanced eye, observing the details of how the serpent's flesh remained soft and pliable as the villagers and guards hacked at the body, even as others pulled the boats up onto shore and reclaimed the bodies of those fallen, pulling them a clean distance away from the monster's corpse.

"A bonfire," the prince shouted. "A bonfire to burn this abomination, and send a signal that we are not such easy prey for anything!"

At that, Jerzy blinked, and he cocked his head to study the beast a moment before collecting his horse—still waiting patiently, now that the fear was gone—and walking down to the shore to speak with the prince.

Chapter 13

*T*he stink of the beast was even worse up close. The last chunk of flesh—carefully wrapped in sailcloth, to keep flies away—was placed in the back of the small cart, and the guard who had overseen the loading drew one arm across his nose as though to block out the scent.

"You took this? Instead of gold?"

"I did," Jerzy said, checking the girth on his mare's saddle. She turned her head to look at him, as though wondering what he was thinking, and he patted the side of her neck reassuringly. The fact that she had carried him here, and not—unlike Jecq's horse—run away when the serpent beast attacked, had gone a long way to endearing her to him. He still wasn't looking forward to the ride back, however.

Agreeing to forego payment for the spellwines in exchange for selected portions of the sea serpent, and the cart and the donkey to ferry them home, had taken the last of Jerzy's strength. How dare he make such a decision? Yet, he had agreed, in Master Malech's name. The deed was done.

The guard shook his head and retreated, no doubt to consider the madness of Vinearts and all those associated with them.

It was perhaps madness. If so, Master Malech would punish him when he returned, and there was a part of Jerzy that quailed under that thought. Yet, the curiosity that overcame him when looking at the beast could not be constrained, and had his master not ordered him to take a look at what was left of the first beast? Surely a fresh sample would be even more useful, especially since the prince refused him access to the first village that had been attacked, deeming it too dangerous until the spellwine had thoroughly cleansed the area.

The small donkey attached to the cart made a chuffing noise and flicked one long ear, but otherwise did not seem perturbed. The cart was barely large enough for its gruesome burden, another canvas sail laid over it and lashed to the wood to prevent anything falling out—or anyone seeing what was being conveyed. Enough stories would come out of the day's events; Jerzy felt no need to add to them. Not until Malech had his say on the matter.

"Young mage."

Jerzy turned to greet the princeling—Prince Ranulf—now dressed in a sleeveless doublet of dark blue cloth and silver thread over a shirt of such whiteness Jerzy doubted it had ever been worn before, and most certainly not in any field or on any road, where dirt would find it like flies to split grapes. Two of his guards stood behind him, less ready than relaxed. Clearly, they thought their troubles had ended with the delivery of the spellwines and the seemingly effortless defeat of the sea serpent.

Jerzy, thinking back at the size and ferocity of the beast, wasn't so certain.

"I thank you again for your aid and assistance," the prince said. His face was calm, but his eyes showed a deeper shadowing. Unlike his men, Ranulf wasn't certain the spellwine would be enough, either. He knew that it had not been his stroke alone that killed the beast, although Jerzy doubted that the prince would ever admit it, even to himself. He needed to believe his superiority so that others would believe him as well.

"Master Malech is pleased to have been of assistance," Jerzy replied.

Whereas before, on the cliff, they had simply been two men among many facing danger, when Jerzy's training had been the more useful, here and now he had to fight the need to get down on his knees before the sole authority within these makeshift camp walls, to become as invisible as a slave could manage, and pray not to be noticed. Yet Cai and Master Malech had both taught him that a Vineart was equal to any princeling, maiar, or land's lord, and bowed to no mortal man. Instead, Jerzy inclined his head, acknowledging Ranulf's status and position, and the fact that they stood on his terrain.

The prince seemed satisfied by the gesture and came to stand closer, although still a distance away from the cart. Jerzy was amused, although he did not show it. In truth, the dead flesh did not smell any worse than the alleys of the village they had ridden through or a shit pot in the morning air. But it did remind him that he needed to be on his way, before the smell grew worse.

"If you have need of us again, send a messenger-bird or rider." Messenger-birds were faster than riders, but you could never be certain if one arrived at its destination or not until a reply came. Riders were slower, but more certain.

"Sin Washer protect us that it is not necessary. We know how to kill these beasts now, and have scouts posted a quarter's day sail out. We shall not be caught off guard again."

Jerzy thought the prince was too confident, but, bearing in mind what his master had said about the pride of princes, merely nodded solemnly, and swung into his mare's saddle. A guard handed up the donkey's lead to Jerzy, who tied it to the saddle, and put heels to the mare's flank, moving her forward into a steady walk. There would be no gallop home, not with the cart in tow, and his buttocks were deeply thankful for that.

The small crowd had already faded back to their other chores as Jerzy rode out of the prince's camp, the two-wheeled cart rattling behind him. He did not look back to see if anyone watched him go.

* * *

TRAVELING WITH THE wagon, it took almost half again as long for him to return home. By the time he passed the road marker indicating that he was on Malech's lands, his eyes were gritted with exhaustion, and he felt as though he had aged a year. The sight of the first vineyard he passed along the road washed him with relief, and he felt the passing urge to wave to the workers, but his fingers would not unclench from the reins. By the time the donkey cart rattled its way onto the stone-lined track up to the House midway through the third day of travel, Jerzy felt as though his hips were broken and his back bent in two, and the simple act of sliding off the mare's back nearly killed him.

A slave came up to take the reins from his numb fingers, and led the mare away to be fed and taken care of, without needing orders. Another unhitched the donkey and, making note of the ear tag that indicated who he belonged to, led him away as well. He would be fed and groomed, then returned.

"Bring the cart to the icehouse and unload it—do not open anything, or remove the bindings," Jerzy told a third slave, an older youth who looked vaguely familiar. A nickname came back to him: Mouser. They might have roughhoused together, once upon a time, or labored in the vineyard, tilling soil and pulling weeds. Another lifetime ago.

The slave ducked his head and shoulders to show his understanding of the orders and reached for the shaft of the cart, pulling it toward the small stone house. The cooler air there would keep the flesh intact until Malech had a chance to look it over.

"Welcome home, young one." Detta waited at the front door of the House, wiping her hands on a dish towel. The keys on her belt around her ample waist jangled as she moved, and they sounded like air chimes to Jerzy's ears, worn down by the sound of eight hooves and two wheels on too long a stretch of road. "Did you stop to feed, or were you so intent on coming home you forgot all else?" She read the answer on his face, and shook her head in mock dismay. "Vinearts, all the same. Not a one of them can bear to be away from their grapes a moment longer than they must. . . . All right, you. Come and be fed, else you'll fall over and Malech will be annoyed with me for not preventing it. And then you'll be for a washing, because you reek of horse and . . ." Her nose wrinkled, and she turned away, walking faster. "On second thought, Jerzy, you'll be washing before you're sitting down to any table of mine!"

He paused to sniff at himself, and frowned. He had thought the smell was coming from the cart, not him. Still, a hot bath would be welcome.

There was a new helper in the House since he had left, a young woman named Gert. She had long black hair tied up with a red kerchief, and pale skin and green eyes that made him wonder if she, like Cai, was Caulic. She carried the steaming water in for his bath, dumping and carting the empty pitchers out without comment or a second look, even as Jerzy was shedding his clothes and dropping them onto the cool slate floor.

"Her father's selectman in Blerton," Detta said almost casually, picking his clothes up and draping them over her arm. "She's four sisters older, so I've taken her on to teach her how to run a household, for a few months only."

Jerzy heard the threat implicit in the House-keeper's words, and slewed his head around from watching Gert's retreating backside to meet Detta's round, amused gaze. "I would never . . ." he stammered.

"Oh, you're too pretty by half for girl children not to notice, for all Gert's playing it casual. But you won't be cruel to her; you're not careless that way, no. I'll give you that much. You won't be trouble, not in that way, and eventually they'll learn to let you alone."

Jerzy stared at her, completely lost now. She thought that he would . . . or that the girl would . . . like Cooper Shen had . . . wouldn't he? Jerzy was suddenly, uncomfortably aware of his member, soft against his thigh. If it did not respond to fumblings in the sleep house, surely it would have done something now? But all he felt was exhaustion.

"Take your bath, sir, and then come down for your meal. Master Malech will want to speak with you directly after."

Jerzy was actually surprised that the Guardian hadn't been sent for him already.

He dropped his trou as Detta left the room and closed the door behind her, then stepped into the tub, sighing in relief as the hot water touched his skin, seeping into the aching muscles. If there had been room, he would have sunk his entire body under water and stayed there until his skin was as loose as the beast's, falling off the bone. But the tub was too small. . . . Jerzy frowned. The tub hadn't been too small before. Were they using a new one? He looked down. No, it was the same one as always. And yet, where once he could have stretched his legs out in front of him, now he had to bend them at the knees to sit comfortably, and the sides of the tub seemed to press in more than they had before.

He shrugged, and grabbed the soap. Sooner he was clean, the sooner Detta would feed him.

HE MET WITH Malech in the study, taking his usual place on the stool, now dressed in a clean shirt and trousers, barefoot for comfort. Self-conscious after the tub's revelations, the seat suddenly felt uncomfortable, and he couldn't quite get his legs to settle. His hair, still damp, flopped over into his eyes, and he shoved it back with a grimace. He would have to ask Lil if she could cut it for him again.

"So. You return with a cart and a donkey . . . and no coin."

"Master."

"Don't 'Master' me, boy. I can't see Ranulf cheating me, so whatever you did you must have had some reason to do. Don't hesitate now."

Malech sounded annoyed, but not angry. That allowed Jerzy to gather his heart up from where it had settled in his stomach, and try to explain.

"It was like nothing I had ever seen. Not a sea serpent as you described, not a familiar beast, but as though one such creature had mated with another, and then mated with a third, to create this thing. Body of a snake, yes, but the head was like a cow's, and the teeth of a meat eater . . . and the skin, where it was not scaled, was rough like a . . ." He hesitated, trying to find the right description. "It was rough, like an old vine," he said finally. That wasn't a perfect description, but it was the best one he could come up with, and the more he thought about it, the better it worked.

"And . . . ?"

"And it seemed to me that . . ." What had seemed so obvious at the time was less so, in the study, under Malech's cool gaze. "It seemed to me that something new, something dangerous, was something that we should not leave to a warrior, but inquire into ourselves."

He waited. After a half year and more, he no longer feared that the Vineart would send him back to the fields as a slave, exactly, but somehow not knowing the price of failure was worse than certainty.

"And you brought back a cart. Filled with this creature?"

"Parts of it."

"Well." Malech rose to his feet, and went over to the slender worktable, assembling an assortment of clear vials from a wooden box, and filling them out of the blown-glass flasks of various liquids. "Fetch my carry bag," he ordered, but Jerzy was already across the room, taking down the battered leather case by its strap. It held ten vials snug in a block of softwood, snug and secure against breaking or jostling.

"Now," Malech said, when the vials were filled, stoppered, and placed inside the case. "Come show me this treasure you've brought home."

The icehouse was set off to the side, into the hill, and guarded against the sun's direct rays; shadows were already gathering around the thick wooden doors.

The cart had been unloaded, and the contents placed, still wrapped in the canvas sail, on the planked floor. Surprisingly, cooled down, the remains did not smell bad at all, but rather something slightly familiar and not entirely unpleasant. He sniffed, the way he might to test a wine, and his nose reported back a combination of seawater, fish, and . . . mold?

Malech spit into his hand and held it up to the nearest wall. That was enough to trigger the mage-lights set there, and they flickered to life, pale blue lights cool enough not to disturb the blocks of ice shoved against the far wall.

"How did you do that?" Jerzy asked, fascinated.

"I hadn't shown you that?" Malech shook his head in disgust. "No, other things crowding my mind. My apologies, boy. That's the quiet-magic, what some call mage-blood. Remember I told you, the magic's in the flesh, not the words? It gets into our flesh, too. All the years of crafting and tasting and working with magic, some of it gets under your skin, stays in your blood. Some get more, some less. Enough, at least, to trigger a prepared spell, like that one. The firespell-lights were set into the walls by my master when he took over this property; any one of our lineage can trigger them."

"Even me?" Jerzy's eyes widened at the thought.

"Eventually. Now, show me what you bought with my gold."

Jerzy dropped to one knee and pulled back the edge of the canvas, tugging the heavy material until the entire load was displayed. Malech placed the leather case on the ground, and came closer.

"That . . . is a tooth?"

"A fang. When I changed the spell—"

"When you did what?" Malech stopped and turned, his gaze piercing Jerzy even in the dim light. "You young idiot, what did you do?"

Jerzy leaned away from his master's anger, all the confidence he had felt disappearing under that hard gaze. "I . . . we came on the creature, already attacking. I gave the healwine to Ranulf and taught him how to cast it, but . . . it wasn't enough. It wasn't going to be enough; I could tell that. It was too large, and . . . the spell wasn't affecting the beast the way it should. It wasn't slowing down enough. It was going to kill more people."

"And so you . . . did what?" His master's voice was too quiet, and Jerzy felt himself start to sweat even in the cool confines of the icehouse.

"I took some of the wine, and I changed the spell. Deepened it, so that it went deeper, into the flesh and joints, not just the muscles." With all his worries about trading the flesh for gold, he hadn't once thought he was doing anything wrong by enhancing the spell, once he'd felt the push to do so.

"And what happened?"

"The two spells . . . they wound together, acted together. My spell added to the first one, made the creature susceptible to physical attack." He should tell Malech about the second decantation. He knew he should. Even if his master was angry at him, he should tell everything, confess all his actions, and await punishment.

He said nothing further.

Malech sighed and shook his head, his narrow face creasing in deeper lines of worry. "My error, again, not to warn you. A Vineart's own quiet-magic interacts with spellwine, Jerzy. We are not . . . ah, no. No lectures, not here and now. Time enough tomorrow. Fortunately, you used the same spellwine, so the magics recognized each other. Had you used a different spellwine, without proper training . . . it could have been deadly to you, and those around you, not the beast."

"But . . . spells have long been used in support of each other." He had read accounts of such decantations in the books Malech had given him. "Wind and fire, weather and growth-of-crops . . ."

"Together, with two Vinearts of training, and only under great and dire need precisely because it is so dangerous. We take only a sip, use only one spell, for a *reason*." He sighed again, and Jerzy felt something in his chest tighten and sink at the disappointment in that noise.

"Forgive me, Master." He fell forward, face to the ground, and winced. His body was unaccustomed to such movements now.

"Ah, boy, get up. Up!"

Jerzy got back up on one knee, still averting his eyes, fearing not physical blows, but dismissal.

Instead, Malech's hand reached out, hovered over his shoulder, then dropped to the Vineart's side. "There is nothing to forgive. I sent you out into danger, without telling you what you needed to know. The fact that I did not know you would need it erases none of my responsibility. If need did not drive me so hard . . . But now you know. We have both learned, today. Now tell me what you brought back."

Jerzy still wasn't sure he could breathe, but he followed his master's command. "Flesh. And some of the scales." He reached into the box, held one up. It was the size of his palm, hard and yet flexible, glittering even in the low light like the inside of a seashell. "And one of the fangs."

Malech bent down to take a better look at the long white curve. Up close it looked even more impressive than it had in the beast's mouth, the length of a man's arm and just as thick. The Vineart reached a finger to touch the tip, but withdrew before actually making contact. "How many were there, two or four?"

"Four."

"Ah. Fetch my kit, and bring out the second vial from the left."

As Jerzy did so, he watched his master carefully. Maybe, if he had paid more attention, he would have known not to combine the spells. . . .

But then would the beast have been defeated so easily? Wasn't that worth the risk? Even if he had been wrong, had he been right?

The thought itched at his brain, but he forced it aside for later, and focused on what they were doing now. Malech had wrapped a scrap of cloth around his hand, and dragged a chunk of the flesh out, clear of the other items. Smaller than the others, the chunk was only about the size of a clump of grapes still on the vine, with smooth, almost slippery lines where it had come apart from the main body.

"It is all solid flesh," Malech murmured. "Is that a result of the spells, or was the beast created as such, meat grafted onto bones? Where are the muscles? How is the blood carried from one location to another?"

Jerzy came and crouched beside Malech, trying to look over his arm without being obvious or crowding his master.

"Do you see this? Here?" Malech prodded the chunk with one cloth-wrapped finger. "How solid it is?"

Jerzy looked. Under the thick skin, now a blueish-tinged black, either due to the lighting or death, the skin was a solid dark red. "It shouldn't be solid?" Slaves ate vegetables and grains, with the occasional hen stewed with *vin ordinaire*, or, as a treat, fish. Meat from a larger animal was still something new to him. This looked much like the pig Detta served, roasted off the spit.

"Not uncooked. Not even spell-cooked. There should be sinew and veins, and . . . blood. Jerzy, boy, was there blood when they hacked into this thing?"

It was so obvious, such a simple thing, that Jerzy felt like the idiot Malech called him, for not realizing it before. "Master . . . no. There was no blood." He paused. "What . . . what does that mean?"

"It means what we suspected is true. This is no sea serpent, no creature born of nature. Someone created this creature intentionally, and undoubtedly the one before it as well—and perhaps more, yet to attack. Here, uncork that vial and pass it to me, carefully! You don't want to spill that on yourself."

The warning wasn't needed; the moment Jerzy uncorked the vial, the repulsion was strong enough to make him want to fling it away. Forcing himself to control the instinct, he took a cautious nose of the aroma, the first step to identifying a spellvine.

A deep smell, like hipflowers in summer, dark purple and warm, with just a hint of spice. Nothing at all that should have repulsed. A deeper nose, still keeping the vial well away from his skin, brought the under notes, and he gagged, jerking his head away.

"Ah." Malech had been watching him, his deep-set eyes approving for once. "There you have it."

The smell—the *stench*—of death, corpses, and decay, hidden under the initial sweetness.

"What is it?" Jerzy asked, handing the vial over to Malech with a little more haste than was seemly.

"Nothing you ever want to tangle with," Malech said. "And yet, a very useful *vin magica*, on occasion. It is grown in the southern islands, high in the mountains where the sun beats down and cooks the grapes at the moment of ripeness. The juice is taken from them in that instant, a slave in each row waiting to capture the essence, and bring it immediately to the vats."

As he was instructing, Malech—rather than sipping the spellwine—sprinkled a few drops onto the flesh.

Nothing happened, and Jerzy felt breath leave his lungs in a disappointed sigh. Malech, on the other hand, seemed fascinated. "There. Did you see that?"

"I saw nothing."

"Exactly. If I were to cut a part of you away, and run the same test, those drops would have sizzled and sparked as it consumed the life-spark in that flesh, burning you in its excitement. Here . . . nothing. It soaked in like water to soil, no twist of magic whatsoever."

He sat back on his heels, careless of the dust and wood chips getting on his clothing, and looked expectantly at Jerzy. Clearly his student was supposed to say something to indicate his understanding of what had just happened. All Jerzy could think of was the way the top notes had smelled, the warm, living flavor of it. Living. Top notes. Underneath, death, decay. Lack-of-life . . .

"This flesh . . . it is dead." He knew that already. He had watched the guards cut it apart, taken it home. So, something more . . . "It . . . never lived?"

A flash of something went across Malech's face, too quick to be identified, and he handed the vial back to Jerzy, who stoppered it—carefully—almost without noticing the action. "Perhaps," Malech said. "Or if it lived, it was a very long time ago."

"But how . . ." Jerzy stopped. This was another test. "If it did not live, and still moved, and ate—"

"Or killed, at least," Malech said. "A thing without blood or life might not hunger, as we know it."

"Magic. You think this was made by magic." The thought of such a thing staggered Jerzy. Magic was for guiding the wind and rain, for healing bones and flesh and minds, for sharpening steel and hardening wood, for growing crops and strengthening vows. Giving life to things not living . . .

"I know that it was made by magic," Malech said. "The three questions we must ask are how, who . . . and why. Give me the fourth vial, and step back. And watch, carefully."

The fourth vial was filled with a thick white spellwine that smelled of resins and cold spices.

"Another gift of the southern islands," Malech said. "They produce little, but what they do is deep and potent. And dear—this small dose cost me as much as two casks of basic healwine in a bad Harvest."

You could buy five slaves for that sort of coin. Jerzy was pleased to see that his hands were steady as he unstoppered the vial, placing the wax cork carefully in the case and handing the vial to his master. Then, heeding the earlier warning, he scooted backward, putting more distance between himself and whatever Malech was about to do.

This time Malech did sip from the vial, barely a drop landing on his tongue. A hiss and a spark came from his open mouth, green and gold in the dusky air, and Jerzy could smell the magic, thicker than must and heavier, like burned spice bark and thunder after a storm.

Malech didn't seem to notice. "Taste deep," he directed the magic in that drop, then pressed his tongue to the roof of his mouth with an almost inaudible clicking noise. "Unto me, the seeing. Go."

Thanks to his lessons with Cai and an old skull his tutor had used as a teaching tool during their fighting lessons, Jerzy could almost track the liquid's path as it touched the upper palate, rising through the nose and into the eyes, so that Malech could *see* whatever he was looking for.

There was quiet in the icehouse, only the occasional drip-drip-drip of water melting off the blocks, and a distant hum of noise coming from outside through the thick wooden door and walls. Jerzy strained uselessly, anxious to know what Malech was looking for, what he was seeing in the dead flesh.

He moved his left hand over the flesh, then reached to take hold of the fang, grasping it carefully below the tip. He held his hand there, then reached down and picked up one of the scales, balancing it between thumb and index finger, grasping it loosely, as though it was fragile enough to shatter.

"Ah . . ."

"What do you see?" Curiosity trumped patience and manners, and Jerzy didn't flinch from the right-handed smack that landed on the side of his head. Even kneeling, distracted, and spell-casting, his master had a steady hand and almost perfect aim. "But what do you see?"

"Nothing." Malech put the scale back down on the sail and sat back on his heels. He took a sip from the hand-sized water flask at the belt that was always clapped around his hips, rinsing his mouth and spitting to the side, away from Jerzy. "I see nothing." He turned to stare thoughtfully at the remaining flasks, half hidden inside the case. His long, narrow face, the skin drawn roughly over the cheekbones, seemed faded somehow, scraped thin like thrice-used parchment. For a moment, his master seemed *ancient*.

"What . . . what was that, that you used?" Malech said he should question, and maybe if he had asked before, he would have known. . . .

"Magewine, boy." His face was old, but his voice sounded the same as ever, and Jerzy grasped onto that, looking down at his own hands and concentrating on that steady voice instead. "Magewine. Rare and potent, the only spellwine only Vinearts may use, kept secret and hidden from the outside world. It is crafted for one purpose only: to see into the heart of another spell, identify the legacy it came from."

That was enough to make Jerzy do a double take. "Master . . . there must be a hundred different legacies." Legend claimed that Sin Washer's blood dripped five and seven times into the soil, and five and seven times that it separated, one drop for each of the lands where the *vin* grew, to touch their roots and change them into something new, something less than what they had been before. From the First Growth had come the five elemental wines: healing, fire, aether, earth, and water—all potent, but none as powerful as the First Growth, the original flesh of magic. A single decantation that could identify all those second-growth vines . . .

"Not nearly so many changes boy, at least not at first. But as each new vine grew, it took on the characteristics of its surroundings, and each Vineart crafted his own style, and so now we have far more legacies than even Sin Washer might have dreamed. And yet," Malech said, "if this were crafted of magic, the magewine would tell me what soil it grew from."

Jerzy, drawn unwillingly, looked up into his master's face and saw there something he had never expected, something that mirrored his own emotion: confusion.

"The magewine did not know the legacy," Malech said. "The creature is made by magic—yet it is no spell we know."

JERZY WAS LEFT to rewrap the bits—"and tie them well, boy. I want nothing sniffing around, burrowing in, and taking bites from our beast"—while Malech went outside to the well-pump and washed his hands. Jerzy came out, blinking in the much-brighter air, and carried the case to where Malech stood, looking out across the road, into the hills. Jerzy followed his gaze, realizing slowly that the Vineart was watching, not the vines, but the tree line marching against the top of the ridge.

"Do we have pigeons in the hutch?"

Whatever he had been expecting Master Malech to say, it wasn't that. "I don't know. Probably."

"Fetch two, and bring them to me in my study."

THERE WERE SEVEN messenger pigeons in the hutch, and a single sleepy-looking slave, huddled in the straw for warmth, who scooted to the back when Jerzy entered. The boy child bowed down, straw stuck in his hair. The sight made Jerzy pause, even as he was reaching for a bird.

He had been that boy, once. Terrified of notice. Terrified of someone's hand being raised against him, terrified of doing something wrong, so he tried not to do anything at all. It was better here in the hutch, where you had space to sleep, birds to coo over, but you were still at the mercy of everyone else, from the overseer on down to anyone larger or meaner or faster than you were. And at this boy's age, everyone was larger and faster.

"Boy." His voice cracked a little, but he didn't think the slave noticed; he was so busy trying to hide his head in the straw. "Boy, I need two birds. Fetch them for me."

He had given orders to slaves before. He had told the house-servants what to do. He had even given direction to Detta, although carefully and knowing that she saw him as an extension of Master Malech. Never before had he tried so hard to make his voice sound right. Strong, but not cruel. Commanding, but without force. Like Malech when he decanted a spell, or the princeling when he gave an order to his men.

It seemed to work: the boy raised his head out of the straw and crawled forward, casting sidelong looks at Jerzy as though trying to determine if he was going to lunge at him or throw something. Jerzy kept as still as possible, his hands in plain sight, his shoulders relaxed, even though he wanted to shake the boy to make him move faster.

"Two birds, Master? Fast, or steady?"

Jerzy had no idea. "Fast."

The boy reached in and caught one of the birds and placed it into a waiting wicker cage, then went back for another, carefully not ruffling their feathers or getting pecked for his trouble. "This is Dag, and this is Ruffa. They're young but wise, and very fast." When speaking of the birds, he lost his hesitation, although he still would not raise his head to look at Jerzy.

Jerzy reached out to take the cage, and the slave flinched, but did not otherwise react.

Malech would have cuffed him for that reaction, and the overseer would have knocked him into the ground, not for showing fear, but offering insult by his fear. Jerzy merely took the cage and left, feeling sick in his own stomach. Not for the slave's reaction, but his own.

His shame, and Detta's words to him before his bath, came tumbling together, unlocking memories.

A dark room, the wheels rattling underneath. Taking them farther and farther away from where they had been, and toward somewhere else. He was sick, and bruised all along his arms and legs where others pinched and poked him. Not the slavers; they did not mistreat their cargo. The other boys, fighting for food, for air, for space, for some sort of ranking that would be destroyed the moment they were sold; they took their fists and feet to this new boy, small and scared.

"Boy. Come here, boy." One of the slavers, an older man. "Come here, I have a salve for those bruises, make them stop hurting."

Even then he knew to doubt.

"Boy, do you want to hurt? I can make no money off a limping, ill boy. Come here."

He did not want to hurt, and so he went into the slaver's grasp, the warm, hard hands that applied ointment, and did . . . other things, too.

The gut sickness made his bowels clench, and then he was out in the fresh air, the wicker cage clenched in his hand, aware only that Master Malech waited for him—his master, and a mystery.

Everything else was in the past, and the past no longer mattered.

THE CARRY CASE had been replaced, the vials emptied and left out to dry, by the time Jerzy came into the study, the cage held awkwardly in front of him. Malech was sitting behind his desk, carefully blotting a note before rolling it into a tiny scroll and placing it inside a small leather casing.

One of the birds, perhaps sensing it was to be let fly, batted its wings noisily inside the cage. Jerzy placed the cage on the stool, and waited.

"When was the last time I communicated directly with another Vineart, and asked for their help?"

It took no thought at all to answer that. "Not in the time I have lived in the House." Before then, Malech could have dyed himself green and danced in the hallways with a dozen other Vinearts, for all Jerzy would have known.

"Not in all that time, and seven years longer," Malech said. "So long, it has taken time to remember who yet lived, and who might have died."

He laughed, a slight exhale of sound, and made a rueful expression. "And so we follow the Commands. And so, now, I am prepared to break them. Come, boy, bring me one of the birds."

The slave had made picking up a bird look almost simple. The first hard peck against his hand made Jerzy jerk back with a yelp, and rethink that. A glance over his shoulder showed that Malech was busy writing a second message, and not paying his student any attention whatsoever.

A spellwine to calm beasts would be useful right now. But short of . . .

It stays in the blood.

Malech's words came back to Jerzy, almost like the flutter of a moth. Admittedly, he had been talking about a spellwine used hundreds if not thousands of times, over years . . . but it had only been yesterday when he drank the spellwine not once, but twice. Might not there be something left in him? But how to find it? And quickly, before the bird put a hole in his hand!

His thoughts churned madly before finally settling on one thought. Malech would sometimes ask him, midmeal, about a tasting they had done earlier that day. How did he recall those? He consciously made his mouth water, and thought back to the sensations he had felt when that liquid had been the spellwine. . . .

It was more difficult than those mealtime tests, because the impressions he got were of salt air, and exhaustion, and fear. But underneath it, a tang of something fruit and spice, sharp and full, crackling in his mouth the way only a commanded spellwine did.

Barely anything. Barely enough. Jerzy spit into his hand anyway, then reached with that hand back into the cage. "Bird, little bird, little bird, hush you now, hush, hush." He didn't add the command form at the end, but the contact of his damp palm with the bird's feathers seemed to be enough—or perhaps the bird simply recognized what it had been trained to do, and calmed of its own accord.

Triumphant, he cupped both hands carefully around the bird, and brought it over to Malech's desk, pushing the cage door shut with his foot to prevent the other bird from getting any ideas. The tiny heart thrummed under its feathered breast, reminding Jerzy of how delicate the creature was—despite the sharpness of its beak.

With an ease that could come only from experience, Malech tied the leather case to the bird's skinny leg with narrow thongs, testing them to make sure they were secure. "This one is to go to the watchtower of Armanica."

The birds could not simply be sent anywhere, of course. There were relay stations they knew, within their flying range. Once they arrived there, the message would be taken off and either given to a runner or placed on another bird to go the next distance.

Once the bird felt the weight on its leg, it settled down, and Jerzy was able to easily replace it in the cage and retrieve its companion, which was in turn fitted with a message, this one going in the opposite direction, south to the island of Corse, off the coast of Corguruth.

Jerzy visualized the tapestry hung in Malech's study, depicting the ancient *Lands Vin*. The second message almost certainly went to Vineart Corse, who had taken the name of the rocky lands he worked, as his master had before him, while the first . . . could be to either the Vineart Seisan or Master Vineart Denson. All were coastal vineyards, fronting the same waters as the villages that had been attacked.

The birds both back in the cage and the latch closed securely, Jerzy turned once again to Malech. "You asked them if they had seen anything like that beast?"

"In a delicate fashion, yes. Corse is . . . eccentric, but they are men I believe I can trust. And yet . . . we do not share well, we Vinearts. Our training is to obey Sin Washer's Command that we maintain our knowledge, but not reach for that which was forbidden, not overreach the boundaries given to mortal man. And so we have taken that to mean each should hoard his own knowledge, his own skills, his own magic, and not share with others. . . . Even if that sharing might be to our benefit."

Malech tapped the thin lines of his mouth with a forefinger, looking pensive. The gold band reflected the light, sending shivers of red along the rim.

"It's not a bad thing, over all, that we follow the Command thus. Sin Washer knew us, even then. We are not passive men, for all that the vines require our patience. The Command was made to save us from our arrogance, our need to do more, better, prove our spellwines the stronger. . . . It is good to know your boundaries, to be restrained, even as we tie up the vines that they might grow toward the sun and not into shadow and muck."

Malech stared at his desk and exhaled, an unhappy sound. "Yet, vines can be trimmed badly, and boundaries drawn too narrowly, and all things die without room to grow. I would not have wanted to live in such a time, but we are not given that choice. Enough. Take the birds and have them sent off, then you—" He looked closely at Jerzy, so much so that the boy squirmed a little under the inspection. "You have worked your body enough and your mind as well, these past few days. I think this evening you have earned a short respite."

The exhaustion Jerzy had not allowed himself to acknowledge swept in at those words. The idea of an evening where he had no duties, no lessons, no responsibilities . . .

"One evening only. On the morrow we will begin again, to make up for the time lost while you ran errands. You are taking initiative, making deductive—and foolish—leaps. It is clearly time for me to step up your training."

A heartbeat ago, Jerzy would have sworn that all he wanted to do was crawl upstairs to his room, shut the door and fall face-first onto the bed, and not move again until morning meal. Now he could barely wait for that time to pass.

Malech chuckled, and the sound wasn't entirely kind. "Go, enjoy your rest while you're granted it."

Jerzy ducked his head in gratitude and backed out of the room before the Vineart could change his mind.

* * *

AT BARELY PAST dawn the next morning, as Malech ordered, they began again.

"What do you taste here?"

There were seven decanters lined in front of Jerzy, each made of a smoke-dark glass that did not allow him to see the *vin* inside. Like that first day in the study, he was tasting blindly. Unlike that first day, he knew what to expect and—hopefully—what he was tasting.

He measured his words carefully before he spoke them. "It tastes like stone and lime, no softness at all. It's green, young. So it hasn't aged very long, maybe just went into the barrel?" It was a question, but he didn't wait for an answer that wouldn't come. "There was a tingling on my tongue, but no numbness, so it's not a healspell." Heal-spells were the most varied of the legacies; the red-black grapes were better for physical ailments, while the rose ones treated the humors, the emotional pains and mind-sickness. The one thing they all had in common was a rich, flinty taste, and the aftereffect of numbing the caster's tongue.

Malech merely sat in front of him, watching and listening. He was wearing a simple brown robe over the shirt and trou, similar to Jerzy's own, and his graying hair was tied back away from his face: what Jerzy now recognized as casual working attire. And yet, despite the familiarity, despite the relaxed pose, there was a mad sort of thought running through Jerzy's mind: this was the Master. This was the voice of life or death, the sole authority. And he . . . he was standing in the same room with him. Sipping spellwines, looking the Master in the eye and giving an opinion.

And he was afraid. Not of death—of failure. Of not knowing enough, not being enough, of being too slow, too stupid, to be consid-ered acceptable. Of having his master sigh the way he did, and turn away. To be cast away from the smell of the mustus, the taste of the rip-ened grape bursting between his teeth, the finished wine sliding down his throat, and the magic tingling through his body, causing the result he desired . . .

It was power of a sort he had never imagined. And he was afraid, so afraid he could barely swallow, much less speak.

And Malech still waited for his answer. The first two wines had been simple: a harsh berry-ripe healspell for bone-setting, and a gentle, spicy white that made his entire body quiver—that had been a growspell, likely used to make soil more receptive to seeds. He had blushed when telling Malech that, and the Master had laughed, but not said that he was wrong. That meant he had been right.

This one stumped him. Stumped, he could not impress Malech. If he could not impress the Vineart, he might . . .

He would not fail. He could not. The fear he seemed to feel all the time hardened into something hot and cold, inside. He had ridden all night to save a village, had done what a princeling could not, and been wise enough to trade gold for beast flesh. . . . He was no slave to cower before a challenge. He was a Vineart—or would be, once he proved himself. He must prove himself, until Malech was satisfied.

"A young, sharp wine," he said, thinking it through out loud. "One I've not tasted before. It's not one of ours—yours," he caught himself swiftly, and looked up from under lowered lashes to make sure the Vineart had not taken offense. "And yet, it is familiar. So it was grown in similar soil, similar conditions?" There were three other Vinearts in The Berengia, but one of them cultivated only the rare aethervine, and the other two had yards that did not match those of Master Malech's enclosures.

"Similar soil, and similar conditions . . . somewhere else." His mind raced, trying to remember where the conditions might produce a similar wine. The map flashed in front of his eyes, and he tried to focus on it, willing the right location to come into his thoughts. "Corguruth. The region of Aleppan is known for . . ." He had to search for the information. "Windspells. Windspells taste like healspells?"

"Occasionally," Malech said, and Jerzy felt some of the tension fade away. He had been right. "Your recall of locales is good, but that doesn't overlook the fact that you were not able to identify the core magic within the wine itself. That . . . is not good."

Jerzy braced himself for the inevitable lecture. Pointing out that he had never encountered a windspell before, to know what it tasted like, did not even occur to him.

"The fourth wine," Master Malech said, pointing to it with his bearded chin.

Jerzy had just poured the wine—a thick ruby liquid he already knew was going to give him trouble—when there was a noise at the door.

"Yes, Detta?" Malech said, a clear invitation to enter the room. There was no magic to that; only Jerzy or Detta would stand so outside the door, and Jerzy was already inside.

"A bird came."

Already? Both men turned their attention fully to the House-keeper, who offered up not one but two small leather packets. Malech stood and took them from her, and then waited while she left before returning to his desk and sitting down. He placed the packets in front of him, letting the tension build until Jerzy could feel his teeth gritting, and then he picked up the nearest and carefully slit open the wax seal, pulling out the scroll of paper.

"Vineart Corse has no knowledge of any spell that could animate flesh in that manner, and finds it distasteful that I should be inquiring about such a thing." Malech's voice was dry, but his mouth twisted in such a way to suggest that the note had not been so carefully worded.

"He thinks . . ." Jerzy felt outrage building at the thought, that his master should be questioned in such a way.

"It would surprise me if he didn't think such a thing. I only hope that I chose correctly in who I asked; that it does not in turn inspire him to dabble in such experimentation. That is the danger of an idea, Jerzy. Once planted, you cannot control where the roots may go." He smoothed the first message against the desk, then picked up the second packet and repeated the process. The message in this one was longer, and Malech had to squint to make out some of the writing.

"Again, Seisan claims no knowledge of any such spells, although there was something in his master's books that spoke of an old vine in the Mahonic that could be used to animate wood for a short period of time. Interesting . . . but not relevant. This was more than that, more than the Guardian spell.

"He does not seem to be as horrified by the thought as Corse. He is older, and has seen more of the evils in men's actions, so it may be that—"

"Or he may know something he is not sharing?"

Malech looked up and almost smiled. "Nine months ago that thought would never have left your mouth." When Jerzy stuttered out an apology, Malech raised one hand to stop him. "No. I am pleased. I told you then that I had no use for a broken slave. You need to be able to think for yourself, and speak those thoughts, else you will go nowhere with what I teach you."

The Vineart placed the second message on top of the first, and gestured Jerzy toward his usual stool. "To that, young one, I think it is time you knew the full nature of what we have discovered, and what we may face."

Jerzy sat, the wines untouched and forgotten.

"This concern of mine does not arise out of mist, nor have I been listening to rumors out of idleness. A year ago I received word from an old acquaintance, a Washer named Ishal who had visited the vineyards of a Vineart named Sionio during his wanderings. Sionio was young, only a few years of his own plantings, but well trained, and his plantings were old-vine foretells, a rare offshoot of growvine. These vines grow slow and yield little of their rich fruit, but crafted properly, the spellwines are potent and true—and expensive.

"This Washer arrived at the vineyard, and found only blasted root and abandoned buildings. No slaves, no beasts . . . and no Sionio. It was as though they had been scraped off the face of the land entirely."

Jerzy's mouth felt dry, and his throat was tight, although he was not sure if his horror was more for the fate of the men or the blasted vines. "What—"

"What could do such a thing? Ishal could find no answers that he understood, and so he sent me a sample of the soil, and the vines. At the time, I could find nothing. No trace of magic, no sign of disease or infestation. Merely death and abandonment.

"There are things in this world even we do not know, and things we were not meant to know. I long ago made my peace with what I am, and who I am, in the scale of the greater world, and the loss of one Vineart and his vines to whatever tragedy did not concern me overlong. Not until word came of other misfortunes, other disasters beyond the normal scope of a failed harvest or ruined bottling, and we ourselves were attacked—and now word has come that the island of Atakus has disappeared from the sight of man and magic.

"Even now, it should be none of our interest. We are Commanded to keep to our own vines, and not meddle in the greater affairs of the world."

Jerzy took a deep breath, refilling his lungs with needed air. "And yet, Master?"

"And yet . . . my curiosity is aroused, and my fear as well."

The thought of Malech being afraid made Jerzy blink, and the confidence that his master would always protect them felt a sudden chill.

Unaware of his student's inner turmoil, Malech continued thinking out loud. "The appearance of this sea creature here, similar to an attack reported in the oceans near now-missing Atakus, suggests that these malfortunes are more than random. There is little doubt now in my mind that there is something new in the world, Jerzy, a source of power we do not know, and it seems to mean us harm.

"We may not meddle—yet we need to know who our enemy is, and why. And, most important: how. How is he casting spells we do not know, cannot recognize, nor defend against?"

He tapped his fingers on the sheets of paper in front of him and smiled, a grim line not of happiness or satisfaction, but decision.

"And that, young one, may you forgive me, is where I plan to throw you to the wolves."

Chapter 14

espite Malech's ominous words, as the days grew warmer, Jerzy had little time to think about sea beasts or malevolent Vinearts or strange magics, or what role in all that his master expected him to play, caught up as he was in his first growing season as a Vineart.

The days were not as crazed as Harvest, but they were busy, starting well before dawn and ending, typically, with more lessons after evening meal. He barely saw Malech, the older Vineart traveling north to some of the smaller, younger fields, while Jerzy oversaw the main growth on the House lands proper. They passed at meals, which for Jerzy were often a small loaf of bread crammed full of whatever meat had been roasting on the spit, while Lil yelled at him to sit down long enough to eat, rather than cramming it into his mouth as he went, then turning her ire at Malech when he did the same thing.

The workroom lessons continued as well, Jerzy doing more and more of the actual work rather than observing, until he felt confident in his ability to incant the spell-structure into the *vin magica*, and to use it properly. But most of his days were spent walking through the yards until even in his sleep he could not rest, dreaming of endless rows of gnarled brown vines alternately reaching for the sun and dropping down into the soil, some filling with tiny green leaf buds, and others covered with shiny black beetles, or gray rot, or any of the countless other things that could go wrong every spring. After several weeks, he trained himself to wake before the dream became a true nightmare, just to save himself the shakes that would follow.

He was in the midst of just such a dream when a dry, silent voice broke into his mind. *Up*, it ordered him.

He opened his eyes immediately, noting first light filling the sky through his window.

Up, the voice repeated.

"I am up," he grumbled, splashing water on his face from the basin Roan had filled the night before. His connection was strong enough now that the Guardian did not bother to come to his window, but merely tapped him awake from his post over the workroom's door, three floors below. He could hear a clatter coming from the kitchen below where Lil was preparing the morning meal. Across the road, he knew, the slaves were being rousted as well. Three more slaves had died during Fallowtime, two from illness and one of injury, so they were shorthanded until Malech could arrange for more to be bought. Five, to replace all those lost.

Six, Jerzy thought suddenly. Six, to replace those who'd died, and himself.

He shivered, although the morning air was comfortable, and got dressed quickly and ran down to the kitchens for a quick meal before joining the slaves out in the yard.

The rough twisted vines were just beginning to set leaf, tiny green buds full of promise—and prone to disaster. The slaves were there to aerate the soil around the roots and make sure the soil was moist but not too wet, but it was Jerzy's responsibility to check each and every vine, to make sure that there had been no permanent harm from the root-glow or a previously unsighted bug or rot—in short, that his nightmares remained simply that, and not truth. It was slow, tedious work, checking every vine for soundness, but as he moved slowly down each row that morning, Jerzy could almost swear that he heard the vines whispering his name in greeting.

A fancy, of course. For all the magic in the fruit, they were merely plants. They could not speak, or recognize their growers. Could they? The thought unnerved him as much as the nightmares, and he quickly put it away.

He was trying to wash the dirt from under his nails before going in to lessons with Cai when Roan came out to the pump, two of the hammered metal kitchen ewers in her hands.

"Master was looking for you," she said, starting the pump up easily and aiming the stream of water into the first of the ewers.

Jerzy gave one last hopeless dig at his nails, and then nodded his thanks. He and Lil were old friends now, but Roan kept herself more distant, not indulging in jokes or teasing with him. "Do you know where he was heading?"

"Do I look like a Vineart?" Roan asked, splashing a little of the water onto her sweat-shined face, and wiped it down with her kerchief. "He just stuck his head in the kitchen and asked if you'd been through."

Jerzy made a logical guess, and went directly to Malech's ground-floor study, barely pausing to knock before he pushed the door open and went inside.

"Master Malech?"

The study was empty, but a map was spread out on Malech's desk, the colors brilliant enough to catch the eye from across the room. Jerzy let his curiosity get the better of him, placing the food down on the worktable and moving around the desk to see what Master Malech had been working on.

It was a map of the *Lands Vin*, not the tapestry map that Jerzy had studied, but a smaller drawing, creased and worn with use, and next to the red triangles that marked Houses, there were names inked in and then scratched off, over and over again, as Vinearts died and were replaced. Two of the names had black-stone markers next to them, and

Jerzy lifted them up carefully, trying to read the notes jotted down in Malech's careful labeling.

"Paerden of Leiur, and Giordan of Corguruth."

Jerzy jumped guiltily, but Malech kept talking as though he had been there all along, and invited Jerzy to look at the map himself.

"Paerden is a good man, very talented. A little too prone to trying to be everything to everyone, though, and that always hurts his wines. Giordan . . . difficult man. Stubborn. Crazy. Most Corguruthians are. Talented though. Weathervines, the ones you tasted. He's agreed to take you on."

The transition made no sense. "Master?"

"Giordan. He and I have agreed that you will go spend time with him, work with him for the rest of the growing season."

"You are . . . sending me away?" It was the Master's prerogative to do with slaves as he chose. But this . . . this was something he had not expected. "Have I displeased you, Master? Did I do something wrong yesterday—did I miss something?" Had he failed a test, just when he had stopped anticipating them?

"What?" Malech looked at him, startled. "Sin Washer, no, no. Jerzy. No. Sit, boy. Sit, and I will explain."

Jerzy sat, mainly because his knees were threatening to give way underneath him.

"These are strange times, Jerzy. Strange times. My entire life, I have followed the Command to mind my vines, craft my spellwines, and share them with the world for betterment, not war." Malech walked back and forth behind his desk as he spoke, his voice softer than normal, his head down, rather than up and alert.

"And yet . . . now we are faced with a situation that cannot be answered by the Command, cannot be dealt with directly, or by time-honored methods. The others I have spoken to, they tell me the same things: that there is a dangerous magic in the air, directed toward mischief, toward harm. This flies in the face of all we know, all we have been taught. So perhaps it is also time to let go of other things we have been taught."

Malech looked up at the doorway, as though looking for the Guardian. The dragon was not there.

"Sin Washer gave us the Second Growth, and commanded us abjure power, but only tradition keeps us isolated, never sharing the things we learn, and so never passing on knowledge that might be built upon, rather than standing endlessly upon the same ground. In these days, I begin to think that this tradition is dangerous, that it may cause harm rather than prevent it.

"Not all I have corresponded with agree. They claim that our specialization is the natural order of things, that each grape is likewise distinct and separate, and the magic in them likewise. They claim that sharing would bring back the dangers of the First Growth, of chaos and destruction through arrogance, and that is a greater threat than an unknown magic, an undiscovered spellwine."

His master's words had the sound of something well rehearsed. That did not make Jerzy any less upset; if Malech felt the need to rehearse his reasons before speaking to him . . . His master's next words caught him completely by surprise.

"You are a fast learner. A smart learner, with an instinctive understanding of spellwines that allowed you to improvise even before you knew it was possible. Traditionally, you would spend your entire study here with me, learning only what I know, crafting wines similar to what I craft. I think you can be more than that. I think—and Giordan agrees—that you would benefit from a wider training. That your spellwines someday will benefit from knowing more than I alone can teach you."

There was a silence after those words, Malech waiting expectantly, Jerzy feeling as though he had been kicked in the chest by one of the wagon-horses.

"I am . . . to study with another Vineart." Jerzy heard what his master said, but his awareness kept returning to that one simple fact. His master was sending him away.

Malech paused at the desk, pushing the black-stone markers across the map in a seemingly random pattern. "Yes. That is the story we are telling, anyway. In truth, I have a deeper mission for you, one I can trust to no other."

That managed to cut through Jerzy's focus, and he bit his lip, confused all over again. Malech sat down next to him, forcing Jerzy to focus on his words.

"Giordan is . . . a bit of a rebel already," his master explained. "He has no House of his own, but rather lives within the city of Aleppan, his arrangement with the maiar of that city a matter of old debate and not a few raised eyebrows. It suits them, however, and it suits our need as well. Aleppan is a hub of commerce and gossip, and Giordan's situation allows him access to many sources I do not have. While you are there, you will have an unprecedented opportunity to look around you, to see if this stain of danger extends beyond what has been reported, if it is being talked about openly, in the marketplace.

"Jerzy, listen to me. This is important. You must keep your own counsel, not tell anyone of this trust I have placed in you. If I am correct, and I pray I am not, then something great and terrible moves against us, and it is best it thinks us unaware, for now.

"And while you look and listen, there is much you can learn of the vine-arts. Giordan is not a Master, but his vinification techniques are impressive. More to the point, he is not bound so tightly by tradition that he will refuse a good idea simply for it being new, and not so wild that he would take a bad idea simply because it *is* new." Malech allowed a smile to crack through. "I trust him with you, and I trust you not to become too much a rebel in his training."

"Master, I . . ." His head was spinning, and the room seemed too warm, suddenly. What was he supposed to say?

"Are you willing to take this risk, Jerzy? Are you willing to do what has not been done in generations, to challenge traditions, to risk much in order to gain more?"

He did not want to, no. He did not want to be the focus of such a solemn question, so much weight, so much responsibility. Yet there was only one possible answer. This was to be the role he had to play, as Malech had told him, weeks before, and he could not question his master's decision. "Master, I am."

"Good, good." Malech seemed both relieved and concerned. "Now, there are some things I will need to teach you, before you go. Important things, and very little time to learn them in, so you needs pay close attention."

"Master?" He didn't think that Malech would cuff him for the question he was about to ask, but his head was already spinning so hard, Jerzy didn't think he would feel it even if he did. "You will still take me back, after?"

If he failed, if he did not please, if he made a mistake, or if Vineart Giordan threw him out—he didn't know which he meant, or if he meant all of them.

Malech stared at him, then let out a short bark of laughter.

"Yes, Jerzy. I will still take you back."

PART 3

Spy

Chapter 15

The weeks before Jerzy's departure passed in a rush of activity, allowing him little time to worry. Even as the leaves grew larger and darker, and flowers bloomed on the vines, more correspondence flew back and forth between Malech and Giordan, until the bird boy almost seemed to anticipate Jerzy's requests with a ready and rested pigeon the moment he appeared. Detta, seemingly resigned to the turn of events, fussed over his clothing, so he would, in her words, "look a proper scion of the House of Malech, not some gangling road-wanderer." Meanwhile, Cai was assigned to cram a few words of Corguruth into his skull, although Malech assured Jerzy that Giordan spoke fluent Ettonian and decent enough Berengian for them to understand each other.

By the end of the second week Jerzy felt as though he were one of the spent firestones they used to keep frost away on cool spring nights, flickering wanly, with no fuel left to burn. "Stress makes the Vineart," Malech would say when Jerzy flagged, and sigh; and the sound of that sigh made Jerzy get up and do one task more. It was no longer fear that drove him, but the desire—the need—to be perfect. He would not, could not, disappoint his master.

Curiously, as the language lessons progressed, Jerzy found other words coming back to him as well. They were harsher sounding than Berengian or Corguruth, as though he were speaking with a rock in his throat, but it felt perfectly natural at the same time.

"Ah," Cai said, the third or fourth time it happened. "So that's where you got that natural horseman's build, and the slant to your eyes. You were born in the Seven Unions." Cai shivered dramatically. "Cold nasty place, that. How in Sin Washer's name did a Vineart come out of Seven Unions?"

Jerzy could only shrug. The map showed little about the lands behind the Pariip mountain range save that it was, as Cai said, a place of cold, windy plains and snow-capped mountains, and his only memories were of faces and voices, and therefore of little use here and now.

It all seemed unreal to him; he had barely learned the patterns and expectations of the House, after the harsh security of the sleep house, and now he was being sent off to a strange place where he would know no one, with orders he didn't fully understand. Even with the serpent's stench still in his nostrils, the threat Master Malech spoke of seemed unreal, the thought that something could threaten his master enough to make him look so worried, impossible.

It was beyond him, and so he let events move him, learning what he was taught and doing as he was told, and letting others decide what was to be done.

Despite the additional work, Jerzy's other studies were not abandoned. In fact, it seemed to Jerzy that Malech now dragged him along on every small chore, and talked faster than he thought the older man could, trying to cram everything into the space in Jerzy's head that wasn't taken up with languages. The vines were well in hand and growing well, with nothing to do but watch and wait and hope for continued good rains and sunshine, but there seemed to be an endless number of things Malech needed him to learn that very instant, from ordering the right sort of barrels from the Cooper's Guild to arranging the acquisition and release of bud-bugs at just the right time to eat any grape-borers. Finally Jerzy just folded his legs underneath him and sat down on the vintnery shed floor, crossing his arms and staring at the wooden beams in the ceiling until Malech relented. The Vineart sat down next to him, his legs creaking awkwardly as he did so, and stared up at the beams as well.

"They need to be whitewashed," he said finally, and that was the end of that. The final few days, while still filled with the endless things that needed to be done, were almost relaxed, as though Malech no longer feared that Jerzy would not impress this Giordan. Jerzy, however, started to have nightmares where he was standing naked in the middle of a great hall, being asked endless questions about grapes he knew nothing about, and every time he answered wrong, a giant hand came out of the curtains and cuffed him on the side of the head, knocking him over. By the time everything was settled and a departure date was decided on, he was almost afraid to go to sleep.

THE MORNING OF his departure was a perfect dawn: pale blue skies and a freshening breeze carrying the smell of damp earth and ripe hillberries. In the vineyard, the flowers had faded and tiny green grapes were forming in their place, barely recognizable as the fruit they would become. There was a pain inside his chest at the thought of leaving, even as he tossed his packs into the waiting wagon, and tightened the girth on the mare he would ride down to the seaport, where he would catch a ship on to Corguruth, and the city seat of Aleppan. He liked riding no more now than he had a year before, but he preferred the mare's smooth pace far more than walking, or the jouncing of a wagon, the memory of the slaves pinned under the broken wagon still with him.

Cai had been waiting for him, sitting back on his heels, a small cudgel made of hardwood in his hand. When Jerzy had everything settled to his satisfaction, the weapons master approached. "Here. Gods willing, you will never need it. But . . ."

Jerzy accepted the weapon with a formal bow, student to teacher, and the Caulian returned it. "I will miss our lessons, Mil'ar Cai."

Cai shrugged, the beads on his mustache jangling. "You are a Vineart-
to-be, with Vineart's responsibilities. Soon, there will be no more lessons with Cai at all. So I will go take my meal from Lil and flirt with the
pretty girls before they throw me out for being a nuisance." He looked at
Jerzy a moment longer, then nodded once, and went on into the House
without a further word.

Jerzy felt the ache inside him ease a little as he held the cudgel, then
turned to tie it to the saddle, making sure the leather ties were secure.
He heard someone walking behind him and recognized his master's
steps.

"You're all set, then?" Jerzy turned again, nodding. His master's narrow face was drawn and shadowed, and Jerzy felt a stronger pang at
leaving now—even if for only a month. Now, when there was so much
work to be done, work he should be helping with . . .

"Here. Take this with you."

Jerzy took the disk from his master's hand. It was small, perhaps
twice the size of his thumbnail, with a hole cut in the middle. Letters
were etched around the edge on one side, while the other was blank.

"Keep it with you at all times when you are away from here. It identi-
fies you as a member of the House of Malech. Show it at any roadhouse
or ale station in The Berengia, and you will be fed and housed without
hesitation."

Jerzy closed his fist around the token, feeling the cool weight against
his palm, and nodded, a lump settling in his stomach that was all too
familiar. Suddenly he remembered Cai's words from months ago: *Think
you will always be within the safety of your Master's House?*

"You'll be back in plenty of time for selection, much less Harvest,"
Malech said, as though hearing his thoughts. "Learn what you can, both
of Giordan's skills, and what goes on in the city, and in the mouths of
her citizens. Do not fail me, boy."

"I won't, Master," Jerzy promised.

Malech stared at him, then looked out across the road and into the vineyard, and held up a cloth-wrapped package. "Normally, a Vineart would receive these when he set off to establish his first field. But . . . it seemed the right time, so long as we are already deviating from precedent."

Jerzy took the package. The rough unbleached cloth unrolled easily to reveal a small bone-handled knife, sheathed in a waxed leather case with a loop on it, to slide onto his belt when he was working. The ivory-white hilt fit easily in Jerzy's hand, and the narrow blade extended a finger's length beyond, glinting in the sunlight.

"You should never have to borrow another man's knife to cut the seal off one of your own bottles," Malech said matter-of-factly.

"Master, I . . ." His palm closed around the handle so tightly his skin whitened. Master Malech had a similar case hooked to his own double-wrapped belt, hanging next to the silver tasting spoon. Jerzy had never owned anything of his own before, had never been given a true gift. He looked away, then wrapped the knife up again and slid it into the pack on the mare's saddle next to the cudgel.

The wagon driver, a dark-skinned man who wore a white cloth wrapped around his head rather than the usual green straw hat most carters wore, came out from the vintnery, making sure that the slaves carrying three half casks of spellwine loaded them into the wagon to his satisfaction. The city lord, like all lords, had no authority to say nay to the exchange, but he could make things difficult while Jerzy was there, or cause trouble after, if not appeased. None of the casks were particularly strong vintages, but they would heal minor household ailments and the occasional sword cut, if handled properly. Fair enough exchange for compliance, Malech hoped.

Wagon loaded, the driver climbed up onto the bench and picked up the reins.

Malech nodded once. Nothing left to say, Jerzy mounted, and reached forward to pet the side of the mare's neck to cover his own uncertainty. The mare snorted and shifted, clearly impatient to be moving.

"Dar-up!" the driver of the cart cried, and flicked his whip at the horse between its braces. The horse started, wheels creaked and turned, and Jerzy rode away from the only home he could remember.

THE FIRST PART of the journey was a blur of trees and roads and fields just starting to turn green with crops, where workers would stop to watch them pass. They did not pass by any vineyards, although Jerzy could see, once or twice as the road rose on a hill, distant slopes marked with the familiar pattern of brown-and-green stems. Once they saw a Washer, his staff and dark red robes marking him clearly, who looked up from his roadside lunch and raised his hands in the cup-of-mercy blessing. Jerzy saluted him back, but they did not speak, and then he was gone, left behind in the road.

He saw a contingent of guardsmen marching ahead in a double row, their colors marking them as belonging to Prince Ranulf. Their captain gave a respectful salute as Jerzy rode by, the proper regard of a foot soldier for any man mounted. The lump in his stomach tightened even as he acknowledged the salute and rode on. He didn't understand why he felt so uneasy—he had been on the road before, when he was visiting other enclosures. The destination was different, but the travel itself was nothing new.

Except before, he had not been aware of any greater danger than failing a test, or disappointing Malech. Before, he had not known that there were forces and magics that could make even a Master Vineart worry.

Now the ditch alongside the road could hold dangers greater than muddy water or the random winter-hungry wolf, and Jerzy was suddenly aware that other than his cudgel he was unarmed, and the driver, while sturdy, carried no weapons at all. Cai had often lectured him that the first rule to staying out of trouble was not looking like you were looking for trouble, but Jerzy wasn't sure how that worked when trouble was already looking for you.

He lifted his face to the sunlight and tried to let those worries go. Cai had taught him how to defend himself, and he had a strong horse, and a sturdy companion. Nothing would go wrong.

The cart's driver was not much for speaking, and so the day passed in silence, broken by the two horses' hooves, the wagon's creaking, and birdsong winging overhead in the trees. Three times they passed through villages, mismatched assortments of rough stone buildings set at odd angles to one another, ringed by low-walled enclosures where small black goats and milky-white cattle grazed, but they did not stop until the sun was making a rapid descent in the west. Jerzy thought that his legs were going to wear through at the hip and his upper body would fall off, leaving only a pair of legs still clamped in the stirrups, pressed against the mare's side even in death.

Their destination was a squat, square building just off the side of the road. A roadhouse, Jerzy realized, and not a particularly nice one either, from the looks of it. Jerzy was too tired to care, so long as there was a place to sit that wasn't on horseback. He only dimly realized that they had left The Berengia at the last road marker, and were now passing through Leiur—it all looked much the same to him, no matter who ruled or how they pronounced words. He was not, overall, impressed with traveling.

He followed the driver, at the man's arm wave, around behind the building and into a small cobbled courtyard. The sound of hooves and wooden wheels rang out against the stones, and the mare came to a halt when Jerzy let the reins fall, dropping her head to her chest with an exhausted sigh, clearly understanding that they were done for the night.

The driver swung down from his seat, grimacing and rubbing his backside. "Boy, you have the Master's token?"

Jerzy touched his belt pouch and felt the reassuring weight of the lead token against his fingers. "I do."

The driver grunted. "Well, give it to the keeper, so we can get these beasts stabled and some food in our stomachs!"

A man emerged from the back door of the roadhouse. He was older even than Malech, his hair yellow-white and sparse over sun-leathered skin, and bent in the shoulders and hips, but his voice was steady and his hand quick as he asked for their payment.

"Here, Innkeep," the carter said, and nodded to Jerzy, who showed the token, holding the dark metal coin in his palm.

"Vineart, hey?" the innkeep didn't sound impressed. "Someone take these horses," he yelled, a surprising bellow from such a wizened chest, and a short, slender figure darted out from the shadows, slipping the reins of the mare out from Jerzy's hand without him feeling it.

"I'll care good for her, Master," the boy chirped, and the mare leaned forward to chew at his hair.

"And the cursed cart horse, too, fool," the keep ordered, plucking the token out of Jerzy's palm. "Come, travelers, come inside. There's dinner left, if you're hungry, and we'll find you a place to sleep for the night."

Jerzy took his bag and the cudgel off the saddle, noting the driver doing the same with his own belongings, and followed the keeper inside.

"The spellwine be safe on its own?" the driver asked Jerzy quietly, as the keeper signed their token in, and handed it back to Jerzy.

"Anyone who tries to break the seal on the tap will be unpleasantly surprised," Jerzy assured him, not bothering to keep his voice low. If the keeper was thinking unsavory thoughts, he would either take the lesson, or learn the hard way. Either road, the spellwine would be safe from greedy hands.

They ate their meal of grilled river-white and early spring greens, surprisingly good, and retired to the small room under the eaves they were given. There was barely room for the two pallets and a stool, but the door closed securely and the shutters over the window could be barred from within, so the driver was satisfied. Jerzy placed his bag under the flat pillow and the cudgel within easy reach, took off his shoes, and lay down, his muscles aching but his stomach, at least, full.

That was the pattern for the next five days: on the road with sunrise, a slow steady walk that ate distance without straining the horses, eating a midday meal as they traveled, and then stopping at a roadhouse for the evening meal and a few hours of sleep. Along the way Jerzy finally learned that the wagon driver's name was Ferd, that he was originally from a small town in southern Iaja, like Malech, and had traveled with the slavers for most of his life before settling down to take up carting through Leiur and The Berengia.

"I was a slave," Jerzy said. After Cooper Shen's visit, the thought sometimes came up, surprising him out of nowhere. He had been a slave. Was he still a slave?

"Yes." Ferd nodded. "You all are at one point, you Vinearts. You an orphan or your parents sell you?"

Jerzy shrugged. "I don't remember. Does it matter?"

"Not once you're sold, no," Ferd agreed. "Not once you're sold."

The rest of the day passed without conversation.

"I CAN SMELL it," Jerzy said on the morning of the sixth day. A shiver pricked his spine, remembering the last time that he had seen the ocean: the screams of the injured, the sweat under his arms and down his back, the cold clutch in his gut and the tang of spellwine, soured by fear in his memory. For a moment, he felt the urge to ride back the way they had come. What was he thinking, to get on a ship, to go out into the very waters that monster had come from? Master Malech thought there was little risk, but he had not seen the monster moving through the wave, its great mouth open and hungry. . . .

He shuddered, and cupped his hands for Sin Washer's kindness. There had been no reports of further incursions, no sightings along the coastlines. Master Malech was right. Whoever their mysterious enemy might be, he seemed to have moved on to another plan of attack.

Jerzy wasn't sure if that should be reassuring, or disturbing.

"I hate the sea," Ferd said, making a face. "Ships stink. Fish stink. Seabirds are thieves and sailors worse. You be careful on shipboard, boy. You're too pretty for the likes of them."

Jerzy laughed ruefully, even as a small hand clenched in his gut with this new thing to worry about, far more immediate than any monster. Shen had been courteous, but without Malech's presence to protect him, would others leave him be? All he wanted was to be left alone....

He closed his eyes tightly, and clenched his fingers around the leather reins, feeling the reassuring solidity of the mare under him, the regular pattern of her movement rattling his bones in an oddly comforting motion. He could stop her with a single movement, or make her go faster, or turn her to the direction he wanted. He was not helpless against her greater size. Malech had not punished him for turning down Cooper Shen. He could say no to something he did not want—with his cudgel, if need be, and he would not be punished.

Jerzy forced himself to relax his grip on the reins, before the mare thought something was wrong. Likely he was worrying for naught: after six days on the road his hair was lank against his scalp, his skin tight with grime, and he doubted he smelled of anything other than horse and sweat. Not even the loneliest of men or women would find him attractive right now, and if it would keep hands away, he would go without a bath for another five days, until he arrived at his destination.

As it turned out, he didn't need to worry. The carrack *Baphios*, named for one of the silent gods, was ready to sail, and more than willing to take on a Vineart's goods, and the boy accompanying them. The bill of lading was exchanged and, after saying farewell to Ferd, the mare tied to the back of the wagon for the return trip, Jerzy boarded the ship, went to his small cabin, and promptly became ill the moment the ship sailed out of the harbor and into the waves. The entire journey passed in a fog of turning his guts into a bucket, until there was nothing left to turn and his stomach felt as though it were folding in on itself from the strength of the dry heaves. He tried once to use a sip of healwine on himself, and couldn't hold the wine on his tongue long enough to set the spell in motion, instead racing to the pail and vomiting again. The sour, almost burnt taste it left in his throat made him decide to simply ride the worst of it out. The journey was only three days; how long could he be ill?

"Next time, young sir," the ship's mate said with a sympathetic smirk when Jerzy staggered out of his bed the third morning, "you might consider taking the mountain road instead. You've not the makings of a sailor."

Jerzy managed a weak grin of acknowledgment, and then threw up again, making the man dodge to miss the worst of it.

As QUIET AS Malech had tried to keep his communications, the Vineart knew full well that once Jerzy arrived in Corguruth, gossip would spread, and questions would be raised. All they could do was hope that by the time anyone took offense, the boy would be back home and any worries would be appeased. Fate planned otherwise, however, and word spread before Jerzy had set foot on the carrack, whispered into the very ears Malech had hoped to avoid: the Collegium.

Unlike the silent gods, whose priests tended only one congregation, the Washers wandered, and so the Collegium established stay-homes for them; places to gather, and to hear news of their order. Each was a simple house built of the local stone, each with the same simple floor plan: a main gathering space on the first floor, a matching space used as an open sleeping chamber upstairs, and a storage area below ground for the *vin ordinaire* they carried on their rounds, to bless the people and grant them solace as the Sin Washer himself had once done.

In one such gathering room in a stay-house near the river Mehnne in Upper Altenne, six men were huddled over a simple wooden table, intent on a recently delivered letter. The messenger, a young woman dressed in dark brown leathers with a single star burned into them between her shoulder blades, waited on a stool set just outside the door, a slender dog of the same dark brown patient at her feet. They watched the dusk scenery, ignoring the voices from within, the woman carefully sharpening a wicked blade twice the length of her hand and ignoring the cautious looks others gave her as they passed by.

"Master Vineart Malech is doing what?" A single voice was raised in outrage above the low murmur, ending with a screeching note.

The man who had been reading the message scanned it again, and repeated, "He is sending his student to live with another Vineart."

That broke the room into a flurry of shouting, each overlapping the other.

"That is impossible!"

"What is he thinking? It has never been done!"

"It is against the Commands!"

"Technically, it is not. Any of those things."

The final speaker was not older than his fellows, nor wiser, nor distinguishable in any way, particularly. They were all males, all between their fourth and sixth decade, their heads and chins clean shaven, and all wearing the dark red robes of Washers. Only this speaker's voice, deep and solid, gave him the ability to settle them, even for a moment. His name was Willem, and he did not pound the table, or stand, or even raise his voice further to demand their attention, but they all slewed in their seats to watch him as he continued speaking.

"The Commands never told them to keep their students close at hand, any more than it told them to raise them as slaves until their talents appear; it is merely a custom they follow. So it is neither impossible, nor against Sin Washer's instructions, merely not traditional. Vinearts are traditionalists above all; it takes much for them to break habit. So, we cannot assume that this has not been done before and simply not been recorded. Vinearts are not ones for sharing their habits, not even with us, and yet we must acknowledge that there are ample examples among other folk. Princes and lords send their daughters to be fostered, their sons are given as hostage-guests—"

"Those are matters of state and negotiation," one of his fellows—the one who had insisted that it was against the Commands—argued. "A Vineart partakes of none of those."

"Or should not," another said darkly. "There are reasons it has never been done, even if it is not specifically prohibited. Who is this Malech, that he flouts tradition in this way?"

The Washer who had been reading the letter originally

double-checked the page. "He is a Master Vineart, originally of the desert territories of Iaja, taken and taught in The Berengia, where he inherited his master's lands."

"A desert dweller in The Berengia?" The Washer to his left, the oldest at the table, snorted in amusement at the thought. "Clearly, Vinearts do travel."

"It is the nature of the slave trade, Brother Ae, to move the players around."

"Disgusting practice, that," Ae sniffed.

"More disgusting than sending a ten-year-old girl child off to marry a stranger in an Agreement of negotiation, as is the custom of your people?" Willem raised his hand to stop the discussion from going further. "It is all an argument of custom, brother. Custom, not Command. The question we should be asking now is not if he may do this thing, as clearly he has already made the arrangements, but *why.*"

There were mutters of agreement at that. Collegium training was clear on one point: that magic needed to be controlled and contained, not allowed free rein.

"He claims that the boy is a prodigy, a skilled learner whose talent would be enhanced by learning more than the narrow skills he, Malech, possesses. False modesty, perhaps, but it is a valid if unconventional claim." Willem sounded amused in that last bit, as though well aware of the impact such an unconventional act would have.

"And other Vinearts agree to this?"

"He needed only one, Brother Michel. Vineart Giordan of Aleppan, working in Agreement with the maiar of that city."

"And the maiar of Aleppan has agreed to this?"

Another brother, silent until now, snorted at his fellow's innocence. "Assuming the Vineart even bothered to ask? This is a matter of the Vines, not State. The maiar might fuss, but why? The lord-maiar of Aleppan needs his Vineart, as all maiars do."

Michel shook his head. "Why are we so upset, then? If the secular authorities have no problem with Vinearts trading students . . ."

"One student, between two Vinearts. Let us not make this into a situation more than it is," Willem interjected into their dialogue.

"Fine," Michel accepted the correction. "If two Vinearts agree, and the sole maiar involved does not object or feel threatened, then why are we even discussing it, no matter how our personal opinions might fall?"

"Because it is precedent. What might look innocent on the surface might have deeper layers beneath. As I asked before: who is this Malech, and what might he intend by this action? More, who is this student, so talented to require the breaking of tradition?"

Willem shook his head, as though saddened by his brother's ignorance. "You are new to the roads, but I would have thought they taught some history before they let you out of the solus. Master Malech specializes in healspells, including one that kept his region from being depopulated during the rose plague, before he had achieved Master status. More, he is the only Vineart in this generation to successfully craft *vin melancholia*, the mind-heal. We have used a number of Master Malech's spellwines ourselves, over the years. He has always treated fairly with us, and given no indication that he desires anything more than to continue as he always has."

"Until now," the doubting Washer said.

"Indeed, until now. It is a simple question, my brothers," Willem said, "and a simple solution: we must meet this young man, this young Vineart, and see if he, like his master, is an honest soul . . . or something else."

Chapter 16

After the quiet of his own cabin, the noise and chaos of the dock overwhelmed Jerzy, the shouting of men and rumbling of wagons on the land clashing with the hollow thudding of half a dozen ships of every size, their sides gently knocking against the quays. The moment he stepped off the gangway and onto the weather-beaten wooden planking, he narrowly missed getting knocked in the head by a sack being off-loaded, and when he ducked, he ran into a burly shoreman hauling up ropes tossed from the deck of the *Baphios*. He backed away, stuttering apologies, and bumped into another sailor, this one of a less rude temperament.

"To meet someone I go?" he managed to get out in badly mangled Corguruth.

The sailor pointed to the right, where people were gathered in a cleared area. "If someone's to meet ya, they'll be there." His Ettonian had a strange accent but was clearly understandable. Jerzy nodded his thanks, adjusted the strap of his carry bag over his shoulder, and ordered his oddly wobbly legs to take him in that direction. Sure enough, as he approached, a stranger stepped forward to greet him, effusive in passable Berengian.

"Ah, and you, you must be Jerzy, yes? You are!"

"I am," he agreed, moving carefully, trying to adjust his footing against land that seemed to rock underneath him. The stranger, who looked perhaps twice Jerzy's age, with thick black hair and a broad, tanned face that cracked open in a dazzling white smile, stepped forward as though to hug him. Jerzy held up an instinctive hand, warning the man away. "I . . . I did not have an easy trip," he admitted, taking a step back and stumbling slightly again. "And now the ground itself seems to dislike me."

The stranger laughed, the sound as open and welcoming as his smile had been, but Jerzy winced, his nightmare of being a fool in public coming back to him with a sudden flare.

"Sea legs," the stranger said soothingly in Ettonian, to Jerzy's relief. The accent was easier to follow in that tongue. "All will be well again once you've walked it off. So, you are Jerzy, and I am Giordan, yes?" The smile was back, clearly delighted with the fact of Jerzy being Jerzy, and himself being himself, and having it all sorted out so neatly.

"Yes," Jerzy agreed, more than a little overwhelmed by this man, so impossibly different from his own master. "You must be."

The Vineart was clearly a madman. But perhaps he had to be a madman to agree to this scheme. Jerzy's legs wobbled and his head hurt, and it was too much effort to do anything other than go along.

"Excellent," the Vineart declared as though Jerzy had spoken his thoughts out loud. "And so we will gather your things from this very fine ship, and take you home with us."

"Us" turned out to be two muscular slaves who were given the responsibility of handling the half casks, and a very thin man with a hook nose and thin lips, who leaned against the wall of a warehouse and watched the slaves work with a look of boredom on his face.

"That? Is Sar Anton." "Sar," Cai had taught him, was a title, not a name. It indicated someone of royal favor but no actual birthlines. The title was given for service or fondness or, Cai said, a suitable application of coin. "He does not approve of you. He does not approve of me, either. He approves of no one, save they are exactly like him, and few of them there are, more luck for us. And yet we must take him, and we must be nice to him, for he is much admired by my lord-maiar, who is otherwise a fine man who likes me well as well and therefore has excellent taste in who he chooses, yes?"

Sar Anton nodded acknowledgment of the strange introduction, but otherwise did not look away from the slaves, who were hauling the half casks onto a wagon of far finer construction than Ferd's, with a wooden bench running along the back and a raised, padded seat up behind the driver's perch.

Jerzy felt dizzy, and he didn't think it was merely the ground movement that was to blame. Why had an entitled man come to meet him? But there was no way to ask, even if he'd found the courage to speak.

His trunk was the next to be acquired out of the hold and loaded next to the half casks. When Jerzy nodded to indicate that everything was accounted for, the slaves clambered into the back, making themselves as comfortable as possible on the bench.

"You, up there, yes," Giordan directed him, indicating the padded bench. "For today at least you are my honored guest. Tomorrow, then we put you to work and we see what it is you can learn from me, and what I can learn from you, yes?"

"Yes," Jerzy agreed, taking up his cudgel and pack and climbing up into the seat. He tried not to notice how Sar Anton climbed in next to him, holding his thin frame stiffly, as though afraid to let his clothing touch Jerzy's and risk dirtying himself somehow.

Jerzy felt a fleeting, if unworthy, wish that the seasickness had not passed entirely, that he could have thrown up one last time upon Sar Anton's fine clothing.

Giordan kept up a rapid pace of conversation the entire trip to the maiar's House, which he called a palazzo. "I came here when my master sent me out. No wealth, no lands, for my master had none to give me. The lord-maiar here had lands, lands he planted with grain and grazed cattle on. Grains and cattle! I could feel it, the moment I trod down, crying out for the vines, and so it was done, although not easily, no . . ."

From his vantage point, still dizzy and overwhelmed by the seemingly endless prattle of his new teacher, Jerzy let the words flow over him and watched the countryside pass by. The road was narrow, not wide enough for two carts to pass each other, and the fields sloped down away from it on one side and rose up into hills on the other.

"Those are the Jurans?" he asked, pointing toward the hills. The tallest of them were still white capped, despite spring's arrival.

"Yes, they are, yes. You came from the other side of them, yes. Difficult travel. I did it once, when I was younger. Very cold even in the summer. Our ice comes from there."

"That's why we took the coastal route," Jerzy said in agreement. The roads might have been passable now that thaw was done, but they might also have been blocked with mudslides or other disasters, and no way to know until you were already there.

"And did you enjoy your voyage?" Sar Anton asked, his tone indicating whatever answer Jerzy might give, it would be wrong.

"No," he said simply. He had already admitted that, so there seemed no point in denying it now. "I am afraid that I am not a very good sea traveler."

Sar Anton looked sideways at him, those sharp dark eyes taking in every inch of Jerzy's frame. Suddenly the trou and doublet Detta had so lovingly made for him seemed shabby and ill-fitting, and his long arms and legs an affront against all that was decent. Sar Anton wore a formal half coat and leggings, and even Vineart Giordan's trou and doublet were of a finer cloth than Master Malech wore most days. Jerzy stared at his shoes and took some satisfaction in the fact that they, at least, were the equal of anyone's footwear, soft leather, with thin wooden soles flexible enough to walk all day without wearing down. Sar Anton's boots were polished and clean, but they were worn at the heel and ankle, and the laces needed replacing.

"And here we are," Giordan announced happily. "For you, your first sight of the palazzo of my lord the maiar of Aleppan!"

From the tone of triumph in his voice, Jerzy expected some great shining structure to rise before them, blinding in its wealth, surrounded by vineyards in full bloom. What he saw, instead, was a great stone wall rising out of a hill, with a single stone tower rising from behind it. Then the road rounded the hill, and spread out behind the wall were the familiar terraces of grapevines, sloping down a gentle grade to a ribbon of river half hidden by tall, angular trees. To the left, a grove of darker leafed trees grew, surrounded by small huts.

"What is your yield?" he asked Giordan, to hide his disappointment. The Vineart launched into an explanation of their harvesting process, with sideways swoops into how they alternated the grape harvest with the olives taken from the grove of trees. "The oil, it is very important to this land. We cannot cook without it. We cannot eat without it!"

Jerzy had tried a few of the brined fruits, at Malech's urgings, and not been impressed, but did not say so. Then they rounded the hill again and were riding under the arched entrance, and suddenly Jerzy understood why Giordan had been so excited and why Sar Anton looked down his long nose at a poor Berengian farmer.

Through the arch, the first things Jerzy saw were the buildings. Where his master's house was splendid in its isolation, these buildings were taller and far narrower, pressed up against one another and yet not seeming crowded at all. They were built of the same gray stone as the external walls, with dark red roofs that slanted down at the corners, so rain could drain off them and into gutters carved into the cobbled streets. The windows were small but the shutters were brightly painted in yellows and reds, making the stone seem not cold but welcoming, and almost every ledge boasted an overflow of flowers in the same yellows and reds and leafy green. He tried not to gape, but suspected his jaw was hanging open anyway. The people passing him by in the street were all as finely dressed as Sar Anton, although many of them were carrying their own packages and baskets, something Jerzy suspected the Sar would never deign to do.

"Welcome to Aleppan," the Vineart said, and Jerzy heard nothing but an understandable pride in his voice. "Indeed, it is a grand city, but our humble home, as well. My yard is outside the gates, and we shall spend much of our time there, but we are given the honor of housing with the maiar at his own palazzo, yes. It is a grand palace, worthy of the ancient founders. . . ." Giordan looked up at Jerzy and grinned. "And with their plumbing, as well!"

Jerzy started to ask what the Vineart meant by that, then the wagon cleared another, smaller stone archway, and came out into a huge courtyard filled with flowering trees and a huge white stone statue of a woman with her hand on the back of a stag, its head proudly upraised. He barely had time to take that in, when they were getting out of the wagon, the slaves taking it, and the half casks, away, and Jerzy had his personal belongings in hand and was being led up white stone steps into the palazzo.

"Gracious Lady," Giordan was saying to the woman who came out to greet them, making an extravagant bow that Jerzy wasn't sure he was supposed to imitate, not that he could have managed it without falling on his face. "May I present our honored visitor, the Vineart-apprentice Jerzy of the House of Malech?"

The Gracious Lady was a tall, elegant woman with gray hair swept up on the top of her head and hard, lean features that still managed to look feminine. She was dressed in a flowing green robe, and yet reminded Jerzy, oddly enough, of the overseer, although he could not have said why.

She offered her hand to Jerzy and, helplessly, he took it. The fingers were slender and cool and bore a single ring of gold and red stones that reminded Jerzy of his master's ring, although that had no stones. Acting on the whisper of Cai's voice in his head, Jerzy bent his head over that hand and raised it to his lips, not quite touching the powder-rough skin.

"My Lady," he said in what he hoped was passable Corguruth. "The pleasure is mine."

"Indeed it is," the woman said, but when he glanced up, her mouth was curved in a smile. "We hope that you are made to feel welcome in our home. Sar Anton"—and this was directed over his head to their erstwhile traveling companion—"attend me in my rooms." With that, she took no further notice of Jerzy, gliding serenely out of the hallway, Sar Anton in her wake. Giordan clapped his shoulder once, roughly, to reassure him. "She liked you, and of course she did. Go now, settle in, and I will see you soon." Giordan likewise hurried off to some destination of his own, and Jerzy was left standing, feeling like a witless fool.

A young woman dressed in a simple dark blue dress and a wide leather belt similar to Jerzy's own, her dark blond hair coiled at the nape of her neck, stepped forward out of the shadows. "We run at breakneck speed here," she said in Ettonian. "You will learn the pace of it soon enough. My name is Mahault. If you have any questions, you may ask me." She seemed young to be the House-keeper, especially of a place this grand, but perhaps she was the House-keeper's assistant. Unlike the Gracious Lady, her gaze was steady and her body language that of calm competence, very much like Detta's.

With a gesture, she handed him over to a young, soft-spoken servant of his own age, who in turn directed another servant, less grandly dressed, to take Jerzy's trunk, and gestured for the Vineart to follow him to his quarters. Overwhelmed with the sheer amount of people and stripped of Giordan's companionship, Jerzy complied.

The hallways were simple stone, covered by finely worked tapestries and lit by torches. Jerzy allowed himself a smidge of smugness—the torches burned with a strong smell and flickered in every breeze, and there were dark spots in the ceiling above, where they had scrubbed away accumulated soot. Malech's firespell candles were clearly superior in that regard, at least.

They made a turn and entered a different part of the house. The hallways were narrower here, and the walls of a less brightly white stone. It might have been less grand, but the difference made Jerzy feel immediately more comfortable.

"These are the Vineart's quarters," the servant said. His accent was not as good as the House-keeper's, but he spoke clearly enough. "You will stay here."

Jerzy wasn't sure if that was meant to be a command or merely in-forming him of where he would be sleeping, but all he wanted to do was find a bed that wasn't moving and lie down on it. Everything else could wait.

"These are your rooms," the servant said, as they came to the end of the smaller hallway. They paused in front of a dark brown wood door, then the servant reached out and, with a small flourish, opened it to display the space within.

The first thought Jerzy had was that the servant had made a mistake; surely this was not to be *his* room. But there, his battered trunk was in the corner next to a huge wooden cabinet, the doors open to show how meager his belongings would appear, once they were placed within.

The servant, his duties discharged, bowed himself out, closing the door behind him. For the first time in too many days, Jerzy was alone.

The silence disturbed his ears at first; after the constant sounds of the sea and sailors, and then the bustle of the palazzo, it was strange to be able to hear his own breathing. Soon enough, that silence became soothing, and he could relax. No fear of making a fool of himself here, alone.

The Vineart's wing might be less grand than the main palazzo, but the room was twice as large as his chamber at home. The floor was tiled in an irregular pattern of cream squares, while the walls were cool and rough to the touch, washed a pale green color that reminded Jerzy of bonegrapes ripening on the vine. There was a bed, draped in a darker green coverlet, and the clothing cabinet, and a heavy, raised table of the same dark wood that Jerzy surmised could also be used as a desk. The rest of the room was empty space, and it made him feel dizzy all over again.

He sat on the bed, noting as he did so that despite the height of the bed, his feet still touched the floor, and that the floor itself, rather than a rug, had colored stones set into the middle of the room to create a design of a sort. He squinted but could not determine what the design was meant to be.

It had been morning when the ship docked, and the journey from the docks had not taken long, but somehow Jerzy felt as though he had been awake an entire day, and the thought of resting was an appealing one, especially since he did not know if he was supposed to stay here and wait or go in search of Giordan.

As tired as he was, there was something yet he needed to do, and now was the time to do it. Going to his trunk, he spat into his hand the way Malech taught him, to waken the quiet magic, the mage-blood, and held his palm over the iron lock.

"Unlock," he told it quietly, and heard a small metallic click in response as the hasp swung open.

Inside, neatly folded, were his trou and shirts and jerkins, plus a few pieces that Jerzy did not recognize and, on closer inspection, turned out to be close-fitting pants similar in style, if not richness, to what Sar Anton had been wearing. Someone—Detta, Jerzy would guess—had been aware that styles were different. He held up the garment against his body and frowned. Maybe he would keep to what he was comfortable with, even if it did make him look like a hopeless foreigner.

Underneath the clothing, and placed above the boots and tools, was what he had been seeking. Lifting the cloth-wrapped bundle carefully out of the trunk, he laid it on the bed and unwrapped the fabric, revealing a precious mirror barely the size of his palm.

Malech had given it to him, with strict instructions on its use. If he were to discover anything, anything at all about a threat being directed against Vinearts, or heard of anything similar to what they had experienced—sightings of strange beasts or sudden unexplainable infestations of vineyards—he was to use that mirror to contact Malech rather than trusting to pigeons or human messengers.

Until then, Malech had told him, he was to keep the mirror hidden, safely away from prying eyes and possible breakage. "It cost me more than you did," the Vineart told him seriously. "Although at this point you would be more difficult to replace."

Jerzy was no longer certain in his ability to fulfill Master Malech's directions. This place was so much larger and more confusing than he had expected, so much grander—it was not as though he could wander the halls of this palazzo, asking strangers if anything unusual had happened recently, anything they thought might be suspicious, or dangerous. . . .

Giordan might know something. But Malech had warned Jerzy not to share his concerns even with the other Vineart. How could he ask, without betraying what he sought?

Jerzy's head hurt even more, thinking about it. For now, he would play the role he knew: student. He rewrapped the mirror and placed it back into the chest. He would have to find a proper place to hide it, soon, but it should be safest there for now.

He looked at the bed, but decided that if he slept now he would doubtless be up half the night. Instead, he took the opportunity to explore a little while he waited for someone to come fetch him. He went over to the single window in the room, a tall fixture that ran from floor to ceiling, and pushed aside the drape, only to discover that it swung open onto a small courtyard filled with more of the colorful flowers he had seen on the way in.

"Aha, there you are!" Giordan called happily from a chair and table set in the center of the courtyard, waving his arm in greeting. "They place you in very nice room, yes?"

"Yes," Jerzy answered, stepping through the window-door. "A very nice room."

"Good, good. It is a good thing."

Jerzy sat down at the table with him, awkward in the presence of this man who was a Vineart, and yet seemed to be given so little respect. Had any man acted so toward Malech as Sar Anton had . . . Jerzy could not imagine what Malech might do, because it was not possible such a thing might happen.

"Not all welcome you here, you know."

"No?" Sar Anton for one, Jerzy would guess.

"No. Others of our kind, they are, how do we say, vine bound. They do not want to ripen; they do not want to change. It would be better for you to fail than for them to see it can be different."

"Oh." Giordan meant other Vinearts, not people here. Malech had said the same thing, only it had been a distant worry then, overridden by other concerns. Giordan made those people seem more . . . unwelcoming, a threat rather than a worry.

"My maiar, he agrees to host you because I tell him it is good thing, will increase his status, not diminish it. He is much of status, he must stand to the council and be stronger than they, to control them. So we will do so, yes? We will make Giordan not a liar?"

Jerzy felt his throat tighten, and he suddenly wished that he was back on the boat, sickness and all. Why was Giordan looking at him like that? What did Giordan know? What did he want of Jerzy, in return? He was here to learn what he could, and to report back to Malech if he saw anything suspicious, and now this Vineart wanted him to be some kind of . . . commodity?

"Yes, of course," he said to Giordan. What else could he do?

WHEN JERZY RETURNED to his room a few hours later, after being shown the workrooms within their wing where Giordan did his blending and incantations, something looked different. A moment of puzzlement, and his heart leaped into his mouth when he realized that someone had been in his room and moved the contents of his trunk into the wardrobe. He shoved his hands into the fabrics, panicked, only reassured when his fingers encountered the mirror, still carefully wrapped, on an upper shelf. If anyone had looked at it, they would have seen only an expensive item, too expensive for a servant even in this place to risk damaging. No one could know what its actual use was. He forced himself to breathe normally. Master Malech said that quiet-magic was a secret. No one save another Vineart could possibly even guess, and Giordan had been with him the entire time.

Reassured, he pushed the package back under the pile of clothing and crawled into the oversized bed. He was exhausted, every handspan of his body aching and stressed, but Jerzy was certain he would not be able to sleep at all, in this new place, with so much newness around him, so much uncertainty. He believed that even as his eyes closed and his body gave in to the day, and he slept.

Chapter 17

*J*erzy woke well before dawn, his dreams filled with the sensation of tossing waves and a donkey that spoke with Giordan's voice but stared at him with Sar Anton's eyes and wore a golden ring round its neck.

He lay under the smooth-woven blanket, looking at the painted ceiling, and listened to the sounds of birdsong in the garden outside his window on his first morning in Aleppan. There was a pain in his breast, like something sharp was caught there, and he wondered what the Guardian was doing at that moment, if Malech was in his workroom, if Detta was working the shuttle of her loom, making new clothing for them in preparation of next winter, or if she was busy in her office, going over accounts and shipments—

There was a knock at the door, then it was pushed open and a tousled dark-haired head peered around. "Awake, yes?"

"Yes," Jerzy agreed, blinking at Giordan's cheerful face.

"Good, good. Dress and meet me in the cellar. No more will I wake you; you must be there yourself." With that, Giordan disappeared back into the hallway. Jerzy, oddly comforted by the brusque instructions, slipped out of the bed and rushed through his morning routine. The

Vineart had not given him a time, so he had to assume that he was supposed to be in the cellar immediately.

It was only as he was tying up the laces of his shoes that he realized that, despite their tour of the workrooms yesterday, he had no idea how to find the cellar.

The cellars turned out to be badly named—they were actually aboveground, built into the back wall of the wing, with a sliding door similar to the one back home, where workers would bring the casks in, after crushing. Giordan had no slaves, something Jerzy found difficult to comprehend but didn't feel was his place to question. Like Giordan's relationship with the maiar, it was strange, almost outrageous, and yet everyone here seemed to take it as perfectly natural.

The confusion and uncertainty that had attached themselves to Jerzy seemed to only grow, day by day. Giordan was an enthusiastic teacher, more than willing to share what he knew, but the way the Vineart shared his knowledge was not Malech's slow, show-then-try method, but rather an explosive dump of information that left Jerzy feeling staggered. Giordan would place a clay flask in front of Jerzy and rattle off the specifics of that vintage, then pluck another down and compare the two before Jerzy had the chance to consider the first. Worse, Giordan would ask Jerzy for a detail of how Malech did something, unleashing a stream of description of how Giordan might do something similar. Fascinating, yes, but there were terms and processes Giordan mentioned that Jerzy did not know, and the Vineart did not explain, leaving Jerzy near tears of frustration and feeling every speck the idiot Master Malech once called him.

Despite his frustration, Jerzy kept in mind both Master Malech's regard for Giordan's ability and the fact that he needed the Vineart's sponsorship to remain within Aleppan.

The first few days, however, every time he left their wing, be it to pick up their meals from the kitchen or to deliver something for Giordan, he found himself lost in the much grander, more confusing halls of the palazzo proper, often being escorted to his destination by an amused guard. After the second time, Jerzy realized that his reputation as a possible simpleton, while embarrassing, could be useful. The most obvious place to begin listening for gossip would be within the city's governance, the sars and citizens who came to see the city council, or the maiar himself. If the guards were used to him wandering, they would not think twice about him lingering to overhear conversations.

Unfortunately, while the servants quickly ignored him, they also had very little of interest to overhear, and the richly dressed courtiers stopped talking when a stranger lingered too long.

"You need to look less innocent."

"Beg pardon?" Jerzy had been trying to follow the conversation of three older men who were complaining about the recent storms off the coast, when they noticed him and moved away, down the hallways toward the maiar's private meeting hall. Unable to follow, Jerzy had slumped into a nearby bench and contemplated his shoes glumly, only to be interrupted by the unwelcome advice.

The speaker stood in front of him, bouncing slightly on his heels as though too full of energy to be still. He looked to be about Jerzy's age, maybe a bit older, with dark, almond-shaped eyes similar to Jerzy's own but a round face and straight, dark hair slicked away from his forehead, dressed in a dark gray shirt with a fine leather vest over it, and below that, boots that rose over his knees. "You look like a total innocent, a babe in the waters. Those sweet eyes and open expression . . . you could make a small fortune in the marketplace, no matter what you were selling. But here? Here, my friend, innocence is suspicious, not to be trusted. There is no true innocence here, so it must be feigned. And if it is feigned, they think, what is this handsome young man truly hiding?"

Jerzy started to reply, but the stranger continued after a quick breath of air. "Ah. And here you are, thinking; why should I take advice from this person, who may or may not have my best interest at heart?" He bowed, a florid gesture that cried out to be mocked. "I am Ao, of the Eastern Wind trading clan, here as part of a hopeful but so far luckless delegation to convince the lord-maiar to allow us to carry the work of his wool merchants. And you can only be the Vineart Jerzy, of whom everyone is whispering and none know the particulars of. So now we know each other and you may take my advice for exactly what it is worth."

"And what is that?" Jerzy asked.

"Whatever the market will trade me for it," Ao said, and then he laughed. Unlike Giordan's exuberant shouts of laughter, Ao's was quieter, more as though he were amused and despairing at the same time, at the world and himself as well. It reminded Jerzy of Malech somehow, and he felt a wash of loneliness. "For now, though, shall we call it a friendship gift? For you are an interesting fellow, Jerzy of the unknown, Jerzy of the innocent face and listening ears. And I? I am always interested in the interesting."

Malech had warned him to be careful, to confide in no one. And yet . . .

"I am Jerzy of House Malech," he said, formally accepting the offer and making room on the bench. Ao was more strongly built than Jerzy, more like a laborer than a trader, and had almost impossibly straight white teeth in a wide mouth, and a flat nose that looked like it had been cracked in two sometime before.

"I've never met a Vineart before," he said. "Which is strange, when you think about it. We travel everywhere, have contacts everywhere— and yet, no Vinearts. I suppose it's because we don't drink."

"You . . . what?"

"Don't drink." Ao shrugged. "Oh, we're not fanatics, don't worry. There are places, farther east and north, where they think vinespells are a sin, that magic is an abomination, and so on and frothing at the mouth like mad dogs. Me, I like magic just fine. It's a wondrous thing; the world would be a far harder place without it. But we never saw the need to partake; we get to where we're going on our own and don't rely on others to tame the winds or soothe the seas. And out of that I suppose we never developed the taste for your *ordinaire*, either."

Jerzy was confused, but fascinated. "So what do you trade?"

"A little bit of this, a little bit of that. Mainly cloth goods, now, and occasionally gems or fine metals. We don't handle livestock, thank the gods. Have you ever spent any length of time with sheep?"

"No," Jerzy admitted, feeling very sheltered and unworldly.

"Don't." Ao's eyes were bright with humor. "There, you have learned something already. This first, I give to you as a present. But now you need to learn how to be inconspicuous. Ah, where shall we begin?"

Jerzy started to protest, but Ao waved him down. "No, no, it's no bother, I'd been at loose ends a bit myself, not authorized to bargain on my own yet, and we're here for another three weeks, until we're due to meet with the others in Vlaandern." Ao shuddered slightly at the name. "Horrible place. Terrible food, worse bargaining. But we're not there yet, and anything can happen. And for fair trade, well, teaching reinforces the lesson for the teacher as well, so we're getting equal value."

He studied his new student with an expression that Jerzy recognized all too well, having seen it countless times before on Malech's face: an evaluating sort of assessment. "All right. To begin with, you need to learn how to ask a question so that it sounds like you already know the answer. . . ."

JERZY MEANT TO try his new skill out on Giordan, to test Ao's instructions, but when he arrived in the workroom the next morning, the Vineart had just taken possession of a new batch of shipping jugs, and the rest of the day was spent filling them with the previous Harvest's spellwines, sealing them with specially treated wax, and inscribing Giordan's name and the type of wine on the side, so that there could be no confusion at the other end of their journey. By the time Jerzy had a moment to rest, Giordan disappeared on another errand, leaving Jerzy on his own for the evening. Rather than remain in the suddenly-too-quiet wing, Jerzy ate a quick dinner in the kitchen, surrounded by familiar bustle, if not familiar faces, and then went wandering through the hallway, hoping to encounter Ao again. But the trader was nowhere to be seen, and when Jerzy dredged up the courage to ask a passing servant, the man could tell him only that the Eastern Wind delegation had been summoned to the maiar's appointment hall.

Jerzy had yet to meet the maiar or even see him except in passing at a distance. In fact, he had met very few people, as Giordan claimed most of his time during the day. The days went by with him learning a great deal about how to cultivate the delicate weathervines, but not of anything odd or unusual occuring—and not even a hint of a rumor of strange beasts or mysterious illnesses.

As that first week ended and Ao did not contact him, or appear anywhere Jerzy looked, he assumed that the trader had been pulled back into his clan's negotiations and forgotten all about his promise to teach Jerzy more on how to go unnoticed. Thankfully, Giordan seemed to settle down once the excitement of Jerzy's arrival wore off, and the lessons began to grip more of Jerzy's attention.

Giordan was quizzing him on the elements of location and its effect on mustus on an otherwise quiet afternoon, when a slender young woman appeared in the door of the cellar and waited, clearly there for a reason. A second sideways glance confirmed the fact that she was the House-keeper Jerzy had been handed over to on the first day.

"And in the mountains?" Giordan hadn't noticed the woman, intent on the lecture.

Even distracted by the new arrival, Jerzy didn't have to think about that, the response coming directly to his lips. "Brownstone and gravel. The grapes there are grown on the upper slopes, to catch the most of the sunlight, and allow the river to flow down past the roots rather than pool around them. The conditions create a ripe fruit that can be harvested early, before frost settles in, but because of that, the magic does not have time to come to ripeness, and only a strong Vineart can craft a spellwine from the grapes. The *vin ordinaires* of that region are in high demand, however, because of their sweetness."

"You sound disapproving," the woman said, breaking into the lesson without shame. She was still dressed in a simple gown, but today the color was brighter, the fabric more fine, and there were jewels on her fingers and in her coiled-back hair, making her skin seem even paler.

Jerzy blinked in surprise at the interruption, and glanced at Giordan for direction. The Vineart, however, merely made a subdued greeting and then seemed to be particularly fascinated with a nonexistent smudge on the wall, offering no help at all.

"There is nothing wrong with *vin ordinaire*, Mistress Mahault. My master himself serves it at his table." Occasionally, and only the finest quality. No need to say that. "And yet, a Vineart crafts spellwine. The magic is why we exist, our purpose in this world. *Vin ordinaire* is . . ."

"Common?"

Jerzy felt the walls close in around him like a trap. "My lady, I would not say so."

"But you would think so?" She stared at him, her eyes cooler than Malech's even when he was angry, and he shivered. "I am not a fan of the sweet wines, but do not ever presume that one without magic is without power, Vineart. Common, or no."

Jerzy realized, suddenly, that he had been wrong in his first assumption. This was no House-keeper, not dressed as she was, and speaking with such assurance and menace.

"Vineart Giordan. My mother would speak with you at your convenience. She expects a new shipment of spices today, and would welcome your assessment of their quality."

"Of course," Giordan said. "It would be my honor to lend my nose to such an event."

She nodded once to Giordan, who sketched a shallow bow in return, and exited the room with a sweep of fabric and the faint scent of autumn flowers. Jerzy shivered although the workroom was comfortably cool.

"Spices. Bah. I won't be able to work for an hour, after. But we do what we must. And you, you are a fool and a menace," Giordan said, shaking his head. "Malech is strong enough to spit in the face of the power, but do not think you are, no matter how talented you may indeed be. That was the lord-maiar's daughter herself you just crossed words with. She may not be a favored child right now, but her word could toss us both to the street, if she so chose."

The chill returned, this time bringing sweat. "But the lord-maiar—"

"Bah," Giordan said again. "The maiar is only the ruler outside his home, in the city, and over the people. Here, the lady-wife rules. Save my vines, all here is hers, and her daughter's after her."

Jerzy gaped at him.

"Close your mouth, you look the idiot you are." Giordan had the tone of someone about to explain that water was wet and the sun warm. "Ah, Jerzy you are talented, yes, but foolish, and your master's isolation makes him forget things. We Vinearts, we are exempt from the rest of society, but you must know how to live in it nonetheless, so learn this and learn it well. By law, a home, no matter the grandeur, is the woman's to hold and to manage. So it is in the prince's own castle and the meanest farmer's hut. Here, and in your own land as well. Only a Vineart, by Sin Washer's grace without a wife, might call his land his own. Thus has it ever been, in custom and in law."

Jerzy forced his jaw shut and bent his head, his cheeks flaming with the heat of embarrassment.

"Ah," Giordan said again, finally taking pity on him. "Worry not, for now. Women are complicated, and laws twice so. The vines, that is what we are made to focus on; the vines will never confuse us. Come"—he tugged Jerzy by the arm—"come and walk with me. Let the girl cool down and all will be well. It is time you met my children, anyhow."

The Vineart stopped long enough only to throw some items into a brown rucksack, then led Jerzy out, bringing him to a door in the garden wall Jerzy had not noticed before.

"There are times," Giordan said, that mischievous twinkle back in his eyes that made him look barely older than Jerzy himself, "when I do not wish to face the city dwellers and their noise and . . . bustle." He made a squinched-up face to indicate his distaste for that. "Thus," he said, and with a grand gesture, an arched doorway appeared in the wall. "A back door."

Walking through the archway, Jerzy discovered that they were now in the enclosure where the ponies that pulled the carry carts through the city were pastured, half a distance from the larger doors of the cellar. It took them time to walk along the wall to the main gate, and down the secondary road that led to Giordan's vines, but the Vineart refused to hear of taking a cart from the enclosure.

"Walk the ground, Jerzy! It is the only way you can truly know what you are growing. Sleep in the same soil, get your fingers into it, know its moods as you know the color of your eyes."

Jerzy couldn't disagree with the Vineart, but as he stretched his legs to keep up with the taller man, he could feel blisters forming on his heels and toes. The roads were narrow and rutted here, the result of decades of cart wheels digging into the dirt, and his shoes were too new still, and uncomfortable.

"Tell me about the maiar's daughter," he said, looking for something to take his mind off his discomfort.

Giordan laughed, a surprised whoof of a noise. "She's a bit old for you, boy, even if you were likely to do something about it."

Jerzy hadn't meant it that way, but Giordan's dismissal stung. "I've sixteen years," he said, scowling down at the ground and exaggerating only a little. He actually wasn't sure how old he was; slaves didn't celebrate birthdays, as Giordan well knew.

"And she's near three more than that, and set for a political alliance soon, no doubt." The Vineart's lively expression sobered for a moment. "Are you thinking of her that way, boy? Do your thoughts wander to a companion?"

Jerzy let a few steps pass before he answered. Detta had teased him that way, about the girl she was fostering, and Lil flirted with him, without harm. Roan was planning to marry a man from the nearest village, a potter, after next Harvest. He had seen them walking, hand in hand, on more than one occasion, Roan's head leaning against his shoulder.

And men and women . . . they went together, the way animals did, only in private, and not only in season. Did he feel like that about Mahault?

"I don't think so," he said finally. "I'm just curious."

"Curious is good," Giordan said, clearly relieved. "Be curious. But be careful. Sin Washer strips the urge from us soon enough, so steer any impulse you might have away from the daughters of men with power, or women with money. Your life will be simpler for it."

All other discussion ended when they reached the vineyard. Unlike the fields at home, the vines here were terraced down a straight slope, and planted in straight rows rather than clumps.

"We had a bad bout of leaf-rot about two decades ago," Giordan explained, when Jerzy asked about that difference. "In order to save the plants, each vine had to be individually treated, and we discovered that it was much easier if we planted them this way."

They walked along the rows slowly, allowing Jerzy enough time to investigate the way the vines were strung along a center post. It was too early for the grapes to have fully ripened yet, but the bunches hanging low on the branches were glossy and healthy looking.

"They're . . . beautiful," Jerzy said in awe.

"Are they not?" Giordan sounded like a doting parent, or a fond lover, but Jerzy couldn't begrudge him it, or deny that he had cause. The cluster of grapes resting in Jerzy's hand were still unripe, small and hard, but the skins shimmered in the sunlight with a pure green color that Jerzy found almost hypnotizing.

"I've never seen skins this color before. And when they ripen?"

"Like the sky at sunset, they are. Russet streaks like clouds running before a hard wind."

Giordan let his hands drop, grinning widely, as though aware that he was acting more like a poet than a Vineart. Jerzy's first opinion of him had been confirmed: the Vineart was a madman, but an amazingly talented one, to take these difficult, temperamental grapes to ripeness. Malech had been right: there was a great deal Jerzy could learn from him.

There were only two workers in the field, moving slowly along the rows and pausing every now and again to check something.

"You don't have a sleep house," Jerzy noted suddenly. He had known that, of course, and yet it had not seemed quite real. "No slaves, no sleep house, no overseer . . ."

"No, no. The maiar, he . . . does not understand, entirely, our ways. Our agreement, he gives me workers to help with the harvest, he loans them to me for when I need them, and in return I craft him wines he does not need pay for, and we each do well." Giordan shrugged. "It is not ideal but it serves my purposes. These lands—he grew grain, grazed cattle on them!" Giordan shook his head as though amazed still at such a misuse. "Perfect for my vines, perfect."

Suddenly, Jerzy understood why Giordan had agreed to Malech's plan; he had no slaves, and therefore nowhere to find a student. Did he think that Jerzy . . . ? No. He simply had the urge to show someone else, someone who would understand what he did. The Vineart was driven by ego, not a concern for the greater world, or the betterment of the vines themselves. The Command to tend only to his vines to the exclusion of power, the exclusion of wife or glory, became for him power and wife and glory itself.

Jerzy was starting to think that the world was even more complicated than he could have imagined. That thought made him shrink a little inside with the desire to go home, where things made sense and he knew whom to trust.

Giordan, meanwhile, was indicating the bunch that Jerzy was still examining. "Go on. Taste."

Jerzy hesitated: it was not forbidden, exactly . . . was it? Surely if it were, Giordan would not have told him to. He was acting with Giordan's permission; that was within the Command. He was not trying to take anything from the Vineart, not imposing his power over another . . .

He picked one of the grapes off the cluster; it resisted at first, then sprang free into his grasp. Unlike a ripe grape, there was no bleed of juice where it had been attached to the stem. The flesh was still firm, and the skin resisted his teeth slightly as he bit into it.

Tartness was the first impression, not unexpected with an unripe grape. Then a sensation of bittersweet juice, like a limon, only greener, fresher. "Grass," he said, barely aware that he was speaking. "Grass and wind, and the air after a storm."

The sound of clapping broke him from his taste-trance, and he blinked, seeing Giordan beaming at him. "Yes, you have the proper taste of it; your master was quite right! But now you must feel the result of such taste, as well. Come, come, the day is perfect for it."

Jerzy had no idea what he was talking about, until the Vineart pulled his rucksack off his shoulder and withdrew a leather wineskin.

"This most recent vinification," he said, uncorking the skin with a flourish. Jerzy wondered if the other man was capable of doing anything without a flourish. "Windspell, yes. A bit rough, but then, that's only to be expected, is it not? Come, come!"

They climbed to the top of the ridge, onto the low stone wall that ringed the enclosure. It would not keep anyone out, not even an ambitious goat, but it made for an excellent perch on which to see the entire scope of the vineyard slope, and back up the hill again to the city itself, with its own much higher, more strongly built walls.

"What do you see?"

Jerzy took the question as a lesson, meaning there was more to it than the obvious. He let his eyes scan the scene, soaking in everything he could. "The grapes are growing well, no brown or dried-out spots visible, and the leaf-cover looks full enough to protect the grapes from too much sun or rain. The road is dry." He had enough evidence of that on his shoes and pants leg, but the soil under the roots was damp. "You have an irrigation system?"

"Drainage, yes. But what do you see?"

"There is someone, no two someones, coming down the road, both on horseback. They are riding at speed. You don't have any trees in your vineyard—did you cut them down when you replanted?" That wasn't what Giordan had asked him about, so Jerzy moved on, scanning to see what might possibly be wrong. "The sky is blue, with a few clouds, and the sun is at a late-afternoon angle. We will be late for evening meal if we don't leave soon."

"Patience. A missed meal never hurt anyone, not even me. You say that there are clouds."

Jerzy looked at the sky again, just to make sure. "Yes." He almost started to say master, out of habit, but bit down hard before the word escaped. He would learn from Giordan, willingly, but he was not his master. "Small clouds, in the eastern distance." He suspected he knew where this conversation was going, now.

Sure enough, Giordan handed him the wineskin. "The fields are thirsty, Vineart. Call us some rain."

Before the root-glow, Jerzy would have frozen at such an instruction, to blithely attempt the most delicate and complicated of all spellwines. Before the serpent, he might have hesitated, doubting his own ability. Malech would not use weatherspells, calling them among the most difficult and dangerous spells to manage. Unlike healwines, which could be directed to a specific ailment and a specific result, calling rain meant meddling with a multitude of forces beyond the immediate result. Rain meant clouds. Clouds meant wind. Wind meant it came from somewhere else, and went on to somewhere else after it left the clouds. . . .

A windspell was mostly used out on the seas, to fill sails. To call rain, the rare waterspells would be more effective. Malech would frown on such a casual, pointless use.

Master Malech was not here. Giordan would not offer it to him if it were not all right to do. Jerzy took the wineskin and lifted it to his mouth.

The first mouthful was pure fruit, clean and fresh. Then the undertone hit his tongue and the roof of his mouth: deeper and greener, with an edge of bitterness. The taste of the unripe grape came back to him, the ability within him comparing the two tastes, sensing the similarities—and the differences. Unlike many of the spellwines Jerzy had helped Malech craft, these grapes did not change in the vinification, they *intensified*.

He closed his eyes and tried to recall the specific incantation. Changing the words slightly didn't change the effect, usually, but with the Vineart in question right there next to him . . .

"Rain come hither," he whispered. Almost immediately he could feel the moisture, pressing against his skin as though the very air were drenched in it. "Light onto this yard." He wasn't sure if "light" or "gently" was the proper term for what Giordan wanted, but the former seemed more in tone with the language of the invocation.

"Go," he whispered, and let the spellwine slip down his throat. He was more interested in feeling how the taste changed from initial mouth feel to notice the results of the spell, until a gust of wind nearly knocked them both off the wall.

"Ah," Giordan said, casting a glance upward. "Oh. That . . . was not good."

"What?"

A second blast of wind made him stagger, and he reached for Giordan to steady himself, but he was already off balance, and the next gust of wind knocked him forward. He landed hard, on his face in the dirt.

"Jerzy!" The Vineart dropped to his knees and began pulling him upright. "Are you well? Did you harm yourself? If you can walk, we must go, and hurry!"

"Wha—?"

Jerzy looked up at the sky as Giordan was getting him to his feet and almost sat down hard in shock. The sky, pale blue just moments ago, was now filled with dark clouds. Dark, wet-looking clouds.

"You said to call rain?" he asked hopefully.

"Rain, a gentle, soft rain. Not a storm!"

Even as Giordan shouted that, a loud crack sounded from the sky, rumbling down into the valley, and both of them started to run. They had barely made it out of the vineyard and back onto the road when the first rain began to fall, hard cold pellets that struck Jerzy's skin and made him wince. This was not good. Not good at all. The dry road turned to stone-filled mud, making footing twice as treacherous as before. Even as he minded his steps, trying to keep his vision clear enough to see, Jerzy was worrying about the damage this rain might do to the grape clusters, how much of the crop might be lost due to his carelessness. His heart sank, and his brain felt as sodden as his clothing. How could he have mangled things so badly?

The thought settled into his brain and every slam of rain only drummed it in deeper, the pounding of their feet adding another weight, until it was all he could think, all he could hear: *if the harvest is damaged, it will be all my fault.*

"Up you go!" a voice called out of the pounding rain, and before Jerzy could process it, Giordan disappeared. In the next instant, something grabbed him by the belt, and hauled him up as well. His feet instinctively tightened around the object he was dumped on, his arms reaching around to grasp onto the cloak of his . . . assailant? Rescuer? The horse seemed not to even notice an additional rider, galloping madly for the safety of the city walls, and its dry roofs.

The gates were open, and the market was in chaos as everyone scrambled for cover, although they rode past it too quickly for him to see details. Only when the horses thundered past the palazzo's inner gates and were hauled to a stop, servants racing to take the reins, did Jerzy catch his breath long enough to realize that he knew one of their rescuers.

"Sar Anton." They huddled under a canopy two of the servants brought over, moving to the better shelter of the side entrance. No grand arrival for Jerzy this time, and he was just as thankful.

"I take it this is your work, Vineart?" the courtier demanded, removing his sodden cloak with a grimace and handing it to a servant.

"Ah, yes, my lord."

"No." Jerzy felt like a significant idiot, but he would not hide behind another, nor let the Vineart take the scorn. "It was me. I . . . miscalled the spell."

"Hah." Sar Anton sounded as though he had expected nothing less.

"This," he said, turning to the fourth rider, "is the . . . youth we were discussing. Jerzy, of House Malech."

The man Jerzy had been riding with was tall, with broad shoulders and close-cropped hair that could have been blond or gray, it was difficult to tell. He wore an odd sort of cloak made of fine-woven wool that left his arms free, but then fastened underneath to protect his body, then hung loose again around his legs, dyed dark red and without any kind of decoration. Jerzy had seen the sort of cloak before.

The newcomer was a Washer.

"Ah," the man said now, blinking away rain and staring at Jerzy curiously. "And so he is."

Giordan rushed into speech. "This is not the time or place to be making introductions of a social nature, Sar Anton. Inside, inside! You, Arda! Sar Anton and his guest need towels and a place to rest themselves, and bring warm food as well, for they must be famished."

The servant made a quick bow, and waited for the two men to follow her.

"Jerzy and I shall take ourselves off to our quarters, yes, and rejoin you soon, once we are likewise dry and redressed," Giordan said, taking Jerzy by the soaked-through sleeve and leading him away even as he was chattering. "Yes, later."

As they went down the hallway, away from Sar Anton and the Washer, Giordan muttered under his breath, "much later."

The Vineart's wing had a small bathing space set aside for them, something Jerzy was thankful for right that moment. Unlike the bathhouse at home, the tub here was set into the floor itself, and two channels ran from the wall to the tub. You lifted the slide in the wall opening, and water flowed from the tanks into the tub itself. The left channel was for cool water, the right for heated.

Even better, there was a fire pit built into the floor next to the tub, so the room stayed comfortable no matter how long you soaked. Today, Jerzy was more interested in the fire than the tub, having already gotten wet down to his skin.

"I do not like this, I do not like this at all," Giordan was saying, even as they shed their wet clothing and hung them on the rack, shivering a little while the fire did its work. "I do not like that Sar Anton mentions you to others, and I do not like that the Brotherhood takes notice."

"Because my being here bends the Command?" Jerzy pulled the latch and watched while heated water ran down the channel, steaming a little. He sat on the edge of the tub, his bare skin twitching at the feel of the cool slate, and let his feet take in the liquid warmth. The older Vineart had an ugly scar across his back, running from one sun-darkened shoulder to the opposite hip: a lash mark. Jerzy's own scar from the overseer's lash was a small thing, a barely noticeable white scar against his skin. Giordan had made someone terribly angry, once.

If Giordan was aware of Jerzy's scrutiny, he gave no sign. "Bends, yes. Does not break, does not counter, but it is not the usual; it is not the norm. Washers, they are good men, they are well-meaning men, but they have their ways and they do not like those ways to change. Bah. It may be nothing; Sar Anton has news of your coming and he will sell it for whatever he may achieve, and Washers, they talk to people as we harvest grapes, no? It may be nothing. Still," Giordan continued, and sat down beside him to dunk his feet as well. "The Washers, already they look askance at me for my Agreement with the lord-maiar. They come to speak to me often, to test my obedience to the Command, and I cannot avoid them, but you should stay clear as much as you can, especially in light of the most recent little to-do."

As though to punctuate his comment, a clap of thunder sounded, audible even in the bath-space, and Jerzy flinched.

"I don't know what happened," he said miserably, reaching back to take a now-warm towel off the pile and drape it over his shoulders. "I thought I did the spell properly . . . did I misspeak it somehow? Did I take too large a mouth of the spellwine?"

"I do not think it was your wording, or the wine," Giordan said. "We all have our specializations, yes, and we train and grow with them. My own fault, for putting you to a task you could not but fail. No, no, there is no failure, only learning. Your master sent you here to learn how other vines are grown, to see if our ways might enhance your own, and perhaps teach us some of your ways. This we will do."

Jerzy's sense of guilt didn't go away, but he tried to console himself with the fact that Giordan didn't seem too concerned about the rain damaging the grapes, so he, Jerzy, should not steal trouble. There would be time enough tomorrow, when the storm was over, to go out and see firsthand.

"And the Washer? If he is interested in me . . . what do I do?"

"Answer his questions," came the answer, without hesitation. "Yes, answer his questions and do not shy away from conversation, but do not tell overmuch. Give him no reason to argue against the sharing of knowledge, in Sin Washer's name. If he has no cause for concern, he cannot cause trouble."

Good advice, Jerzy knew. But a more pressing thought came to him, even as Giordan warned him away. What had Giordan said, that Washers talked to people? Talked, and listened, as people gave their worries to Sin Washer. Jerzy hadn't gotten anywhere nosing around on his own. Maybe, while this Washer questioned him, he might also be able to question the Washer?

STORM PASSING OVER *the eastern ridge.*

Malech grunted, barely hearing the Guardian's comment. He was on his knees in the field, his fingers digging into the soil to reach the base of the root-ball. "Steady the post," he instructed the slave working with him, as he adjusted his hand slightly and poured a measure of spellwine over his fingers, letting it drip onto the dirt-tangled roots until the dirt was moist and he could feel the tingle of the magic starting to work. The rich red wine smelled of loam and new-mown hay and warm summer afternoons, and for a moment he could almost imagine that the potency was moving not into the plants, but his own tired body. . . .

"All right, there."

The post came down with a muffled thump, and Malech slid his hands away just in time. Only then did he look up at the sky. It was pale blue, without a cloud visible. He frowned. There had been clouds there that morning, when he'd arrived at the vineyard. The winds were not hard enough that the sky should have cleared that much.

A bad storm over the ridge, to the north and west of them, might have sucked up the clouds, but . . . why would Guardian have thought it important enough to mention?

Weathervines. And a storm moving toward Aleppan.

It might be coincidence, but he doubted it. He doubted everything, these days. Especially with the stone dragon bringing it to his attention. The Vineart had long suspected that Guardian kept a close eye on House Malech—even the members who were not currently in residence.

"Ah, Jerzy. Whatever it is you two are doing, I hope you're being careful. . . ." Giordan was a good Vineart, talented and open to new ideas, obviously, but Malech had been having second thoughts about allowing his student out of his sight for so long. More, the boy had not reported back; had the captain of the *Baphios* not sent back confirmation that the boy had been handed over into Giordan's care, Malech would not have known for certain he was there. Had he made an error? Was the boy too young, too green still for the responsibilities placed on him?

Idiot, he chided himself. The boy had been gone only a little over a week. If he had heard anything to report . . . if he had heard anything, it would mean the entire city was in uproar. That would have been far worse than silence.

Malech got to his feet, slowly and with more aching and creaking than he remembered feeling the year previous, the side effects of the spellwine fading quickly. This was a job for Jerzy to be doing, with his far younger bones. Thankfully, this was the only field he needed to reroot; the others were all well established and needed only a basic mix of fertilizer and spellwine to be scattered at the base. He should be done and home by nightfall, and still have time to go over the accounts with

Detta. He had been sadly neglecting those of late, and she was giving him meaningful looks that usually meant a lecture was forthcoming.

She had already lectured him on the folly of sending the boy away, thinking—as did all others—that it was merely a quirk of his mind, to give the boy exposure to other grapes.

Would that it were such innocent folly.

"What are you up to, boy?" he asked, louder than he meant to, and the slave looked at him, startled and fearful. "No, not you. The old man is talking to himself. Go pull the next mothervine and wait for me."

The slave ducked his head in acknowledgment and scurried a few feet away to the next grouping, while Malech stared into the cloudless sky again, his face creasing in worry lines.

The news from his messengers had dried up; whatever was happening—if anything at all was happening—had gone dormant for now. Either that, or they were not able to pass along word. Malech wasn't sure which thought disturbed him more.

A little over twenty years earlier the plague had struck Berengia, killing entire villages in a matter of days, leaving bodies even the carrion eaters would not go near, and no one knew until it was too late. Then, Malech had been able to study the symptoms and craft a healwine that stopped the plague from spreading. There was no spellwine that would work against an unknown enemy. He needed information!

Sadly, his mirror would not work beyond the limits of the House, and the smaller mirror Jerzy carried could be triggered only in person. He had no choice—other than sending a messenger directly—but to wait.

He would wait.

Chapter 18

*H*ave you known Sar Anton long?" Jerzy asked, as, baths done and better clothing donned, they left the Vineart's wing and made their way to the main hall.

"Since I first came to Aleppan," Giordan said. "He was not sar then, no, but a favorite of the lord-maiar and his lady, and held their daughter in his arms when she was a child. You are wondering why he came to gather you at the docks and takes such an interest in you now, yes?"

"Yes." It had seemed odd at the time, but so much had been happening, it had been crowded from his mind.

"Sar Anton plays many games, juggling the favors of one, then another, to keep himself forever foremost. It is not a vicious game he plays; I do not doubt his loyalty to my lord-maiar, and he has never given me cause to doubt his intentions toward me. But he sniffs the winds constantly, and anything new must be determined: is it threat? Is it useful? He does not yet know what you are. Once he does, all will be well."

Jerzy wasn't quite as reassured as Giordan intended. If Sar Anton caught Jerzy out, or found something objectionable in his questions to the Washer . . . could he cause trouble for Master Malech? Unlikely, but he would continue to be careful.

There was the sound of feet moving at a fast pace on the floor, and a voice hailed them. "Ah, Jerzy!"

"Ao."

The trader was dressed well, but his short black hair was ruffled as though he'd been running a hand through it, and his round face was flushed. "Ah, is it true? Did you call up this storm?"

Jerzy groaned. Ao's excitement just made him feel more like an idiot, especially if the story was spreading over the entire city so quickly.

"I had him call up rain, and things got a little overdone," Giordan said, trying to downplay it. "And who might you be, young master?"

Jerzy shoved his shame down long enough to make the introductions. "Vineart Giordan, this is trader Ao of the Eastern Wind trade delegation. Ao, this is—"

"Vineart Giordan! And now I have met two Vinearts! Most wonderful." Ao looked wide-eyed and enthusiastically innocent—exactly the expression he had chided Jerzy for, at their first meeting. "Vineart, if I may borrow Jerzy? We have not had a chance to speak recently, and . . ."

"Of course." Giordan was nodding as though this were the best suggestion he had heard in a tenday. "Go on. No, Jerzy, everything else can wait. I have been driving you hard, and it is good for a boy to have friends of his own age, yes. I will make your apologies to Sar Anton and his companion. They will understand, I know."

Jerzy thought that Giordan looked just a trifle relieved to be rid of him, but couldn't blame the older man at all. Despite his plan to use the Washer, he hadn't been looking forward to rejoining the other men, either.

As though worried Giordan might change his mind, Ao took Jerzy's arm and led him down the hallway, walking quickly.

"Are they really saying I caused the storm?"

Ao dropped the wide-eyed look once it got him what he wanted, and instead looked wickedly excited. At Jerzy's question, he shrugged. "Some are. Mostly they're impressed, Jerzy; why do you look so worried?"

"A storm like this . . . rain is good, but too much rain can rot the grapes, or flood the soil, or—"

"Oh." Ao's expression flickered to concern for a moment. "I hadn't thought of that. Still, the rain's almost stopped, so it wasn't that bad, was it?" He dismissed Jerzy's worries, and the spark of excitement came back. "And it did some good, because the presentation-of-goods ceremony I was supposed to be at was postponed, everything's been running late, so I was able to find you, the way I promised. Now come on, over here."

"Here" was a narrow wooden door set into a passageway. It had a lock on it, but swung open easily when Ao pushed at it. Behind the door was an equally narrow stairwell that led up to a gallery. It was dark and dusty, the only light coming in through a lattice against the far wall. A single bench set by the lattice suggested that at one time someone had waited there.

"A good snoop should always have at least one place where he can listen without being disturbed. I found this one my second day here—it's over the maiar's public rooms," Ao whispered, his voice barely carrying to Jerzy's ear, a handspan away. "You can sit here and not be seen, but hear everything."

Jerzy looked around dubiously, then back down the stairs. "Ao, if we're found—"

"Shhhh. If we're found, they'll skin us alive. Or just box our ears. What are you afraid of, Jerzy? It's not like we are listening on his bedchamber! If you don't risk, you don't earn!"

Jerzy wasn't quite sure that was true, but the lure of listening in on something he had been shut out of overcame any other hesitations, and he moved forward to join Ao at the screen.

"And so, my lord," a man standing several feet below them was saying, in the tone of someone who is summing up a foregone conclusion, "it behooves us to read closely into what the esteemed Negotiator is asking, and determine what it is that they truly desire."

"My lord-maiar! To imply that we desire anything other than—"

"Negotiator, we all want more than we ask for. The implication is a fair one, if not kindly phrased." The voice, deeper and older sounding than the others, had to belong to the maiar himself.

The Negotiator protested. "We ask only for what is fair and just, no more. What we may desire is of no consequence—all men have desires they do not bother to name, my lord."

"You have already been given what is fair. You ask now for more than is fair, and that is no treaty but a demand that cannot be met," the first man retorted, snorting with his disdain for the other man's words.

"They've been chewing over this treaty for a week or more, already," Ao told Jerzy. "Back and forth until even I'm dizzy with the talk."

"What is it a treaty for?"

Ao lifted his shoulders in a shrug. "Something to do with water rights between two villages. A spring ran dry, and now they have to share a single well until a new one is built, and arguments broke out, and so the smaller village brought a Negotiator to speak for them. Their taxes will go up for his hire, that's for certain. Someone must have near gotten killed, otherwise the council would have heard it, not the maiar. Aleppan will make money on this, no matter how it falls out."

"How? How do you know all this?"

Ao gave an exasperated sigh, and his whisper was louder than before. "I've been trading since I was fourteen, Jerzy. I told you, if you listen and watch, you can learn almost anything. Aleppan, as the maiar's seat, holds the leash on all negotiators in Corguruth. The maiar is not the sole authority—he has to deal with the city council on most things—but he has the final say, and the only say on matters of the villages surrounding the city, like these two."

Below them, the first man was speaking again, painting a picture with his words of a village being asked to give up their own rights to the fresh water for the benefit of others and not being compensated fairly in return. Listening, Jerzy thought that the man made a good argument, but something about it felt unfair, nonetheless. It wasn't the smaller village's fault that the well had run dry, was it?

"They're both going to be slapped down," Ao said quietly, listening intently. "They're both laying claim to the well, but neither of them actually built it. All the wells in Corguruth are from the days of the Empire. They've just been using them so long, they forget that."

"There hasn't been an empire in a thousand years," Jerzy objected. "So who does control the wells?"

"Whoever can back up their claim the best, usually. Since they had to come before the maiar to settle their claim, I'm guessing it's him. Aleppan's the bull in this field, like I said. Shhh . . ."

"Enough, both of you!" The maiar's roar cut across the other speakers' protests, and silenced them both, and the two hidden observers as well. His voice was raw and angry, but still controlled. "Enough with your useless pratter. Endless, endless nattering. You waste my time, while there are more important issues to be dealt with. Must I mount a guard to ensure that all have access to water? If I do, it will come out of your hides, and not anyone else's!"

The shouting below covered all other noises, so the heavy hand that clamped down on Jerzy's collar took him completely by surprise.

"Two snoops, have we?" The guard lifted them away from the screen, one collar in each hand, and dropped them both onto the bench with a hard thump. Jerzy thought that he recognized the man as one of those who had resteered him toward the cellar, but did not think that now was the moment to try to remind the guard of that.

Ao, on the other hand, seemed to feel no such hesitation.

"Ah, guardsman Theoduros, such a pleasure. I was only just saying to my companion that I was sure one of your cohorts would be able to tell us—"

"Shut it, trader," Theoduros said curtly. "Your clan will not be pleased to hear that you've overstepped your boundaries . . . again."

"I can't help it," Ao said. "Born curious, I am. Never a hallway I met I didn't find fascinating—"

"Trader—"

Jerzy flinched instinctively, anticipating the blow that was doubtless about to fall on his companion's head.

"Guardsman . . ." Ao said back in the same tone, totally unafraid.

"Someday you're going to run into someone who won't take your sass, boy, and then where will you be?"

"A good trader can always talk his way out of anything," Ao said. "And if he can't, he needs to be prepared to buy his way out. Fortunately for me, a guardsman of Aleppan would never accept a bribe, and is fair and courteous to guests within his master's house—"

Ao grabbed Jerzy's sleeve even as he was talking, and started moving toward the door. The guardsman let them go, but a sudden yelp and jump from Ao told Jerzy that the trader hadn't escaped without a well-placed boot to his backside.

They made it back down into the main hallway, where a passing courtier gave them an odd look but did not stop to question where they had been, or why. Hearing the guardsman's steps on the stairs behind them, the two dusted themselves off and sauntered, as quickly as possible, off and away from the scene of their crime.

"That is what you call not getting caught?" Jerzy could feel his heart pounding, and his knees felt weak, but Ao looked as cool and composed as . . . as Malech himself.

"I never said I didn't get caught," Ao said, as though they'd been in no trouble at all. "Did I ever say I never got caught? You need to *listen* when a trader talks, Jerzy, or you'll never go far in this world at all! Now come on, I don't have all day, and I can tell already you're a slow learner."

Jerzy meekly allowed Ao to lead him, the older boy talking all the while.

"Come on, the main garden courtyard is a perfect place to browse. Found it my first day—first hour, in fact. Nooks and seats everywhere, and you can hear a whisper clear across the way. Bad security if you're planning something, but smart if you're being plotted against. I bet the first maiar who built this place was a suspicious goat. Everyone thinks courtyards are the perfect place to have a private conversation. They're wrong."

Jerzy felt awkward hearing such things, as though forced into a skin not his own, but made himself listen closely. This, not wine-making, was why he was here.

Chapter 19

Captain. *Still no* sign."

The captain placed one hand down flat on the map table, and stared at the sailor as though his gaze alone could change the answer.

"It's there, damn it."

"Yes, sir. The maps agree, the stars agree . . . it is there. Except it's not. Sir."

The *Risen Moon* was a Caulic ship, a trim voyager built for fast travel and limited cargo. On this trip she was carrying a double-fist of crew and three scryers, bound for the island of Atakus. Or, more accurately: where the island of Atakus should be.

Should be, and was not.

The ship moved gently under his feet, surging forward with the wind in a rhythm as natural to his body as his own breath. Every creak of wood and sail, every shout, every slap of waves was as it should be, ordered and orderly. The sun shone overhead, the stars glittered at night, and entire islands did not simply disappear overnight.

Officially, he had been sent to offer aid, should something have gone wrong, if Atakus were under siege or laid low with a plague, but that was merely a cover. An island did not disappear without magic. It might be that the Principality had bought such a spell. If so, it was a game of some sort that did not bode well for seafaring, magic-disdaining lands such as Caul. If Atakus had not bought that spell, or had it forced upon it somehow, no matter who cast the spell it was an act of aggression by a Vineart in direct violation of the Command.

"The fact that we cannot see it does not mean it is not there. According to the maps, we should be nearing the harbor now. Slow to half speed and proceed cautiously. Even if they've masked themselves with magic, the scryers should be able to determine where they are."

That was what scryers did; they Saw. It was no magic; spellwines would not grow in Caul and so Caul would not use spellwines. The blood-robed Brotherhood bleated some story of a Caulic king turning from their Sin Washer and refusing solace, but he did not believe it. Sheer bad luck, that was all, to have soil that did not favor the vines.

But they had two things the so-called Lands Vin did not: scryers, and the heartwood trees, massive beasts whose trunks grew straight and strong, the exact wood needed to build ships like the *Risen Moon*. Caul boasted a navy that was second to none, ships, sailors, and navigators who knew the seas better than any other men alive. And he, captain of the *Risen Moon*, was best of them all.

And he had not one but three scryers at his command.

"Aye, sir," the sailor said in response to his orders, and turned to face the foredeck, shouting out demands and sending the rest of the crew scurrying. A scryer, her wizened body hidden from view by a heavy woolen cloak, stood in the bow with her arms held out in front of her, the other two huddled nearby. A trio of black corbies, they were, but their masters swore they could rip asunder the veil of magic, could See the length and limits of spells, and determine where and how they would end, and for that he could abide them.

It was not magic: scryers came by their skills honestly, a long-ago gift from when the gods still spoke to mankind. The secret of their training was kept by the Caulic navy, and only a dozen were in service at any given time. To have three on his ship was a signal honor—and a huge responsibility.

Islands did not disappear, even when they could not be seen. Atakus was there, dead in front of them. The Atakusians had gone too far with this latest magic of theirs, hiding their port and refusing access. What were they hiding? What mischief did they conduct, out of human view?

"We are the masters of the seas, not you," he told the unseen inhabitants. "We rule the waters, and we will not be denied!"

The scryers would break the spell, aye. The use of magic to interfere with matters secular had given Caul the right to do so. And then, by command of his king, he would lead the way for the warships sailing behind him, and they would break arrogant, magical Atakus, once and for all. The valuable port would be theirs.

And after Atakus . . . He smiled grimly. After Atakus, indeed.

JERZY OPENED HIS eyes, and was relieved to see sunlight streaming in through his window. After two days the massive, wind-whipped storm had finally passed. He lay in his bed with the coverlet pulled up to his chin, and debated getting up to look outside.

Not that the view into the garden would tell him anything. He wasn't going to know until he actually saw the vineyard for himself.

And if there was damage? If the hail that had slapped against the roof last night had destroyed the crop? Giordan wasn't Malech; he didn't have secondary fields tucked across the countryside. The fields surrounding Aleppan were his sole yields. If he, Jerzy, had damaged them through a miscast spell . . .

A faint whisper of denial crept through his brain. But Giordan told him to do it! It wasn't his fault, he hadn't been ready!

Jerzy wanted, very much, to listen to that voice. He was just a slave; what did he know? He hadn't even learned all of his master's vinespells, what right did he have trying another Vineart's work?

Was his being here breaking Sin Washer's Command to stay clear of entanglements, to tend to the Second Growth and not lust after more than was given? Was the storm his punishment for working a spellvine not his own, for experimenting with a spellwine not his master's crafting?

No. He had to trust Master Malech. The gods did not stir the affairs of mortals, not in a thousand and more years.

Jerzy rubbed his chin, surprised to find stubble there. He would have to ask Giordan if there was a barber he trusted near the palazzo, to take care of that. He had no desire to try to grow a beard just yet.

No, the idea that the storm came as some sort of reaction to his using Giordan's spellwine made no sense. Nothing forbade it. Vinearts did not restrict themselves to their own vintages. He had been with Malech when he used the spellwines of other Vinearts, and they worked exactly as they should. And yet, there had to be a cause, something he had done wrong, to create such a violent storm.

Might it be the simple act of his being here, learning from a different Vineart? Could Sin Washer have sent that storm to stop—

No. Guardian was too far away to reach him, but Jerzy could practically feel the cool, smooth words in his mind. *Sin Washer broke the vines, but he did not break us. That was not his Way.*

The only possible answer, then, was that he, himself, had caused it. That he was responsible. Jerzy's head ached and his limbs felt restless, the confusion taking physical form in his body. Unable to lie still any longer, he flung the bedcover off and padded across the room, pulling trou and a shirt from the wooden dresser. He might look like a yokel in the more fashion-conscious court, but today he took comfort from the familiar clothing.

Reaching for his belt, his hand brushed the hard form of the mirror, still wrapped in its protective cloth, and the guilt intensified. What had he accomplished in the time he'd been here? Nothing, really. Nothing at all, even with Ao's advice. He had to work harder, be more alert, take every advantage, no matter how uncomfortable it made him feel. Master Malech was counting on him. First, he needed to get out into the city. The palazzo was not offering enough opportunity. But how to do that?

Planning could wait. He needed to be student now, not spy.

Giordan was already outside in the courtyard, raising his arms overhead toward the sky the way he did every morning. Watching the slightly rounded figure go through the stretching motions: arms up, then out, then down again, in a flowing motion, Jerzy thought that it should have been comical, but the grace with which they were performed instead made it a silent dance. Not something Jerzy would have expected, on first meeting Giordan, but now was simply another aspect of his teacher. The open laugh was matched by a deep mind and a solid dedication to his vines.

"Ah. Awake and ready to go. Excellent, excellent." Giordan's tone was light, but the expression on his face, as he draped a towel across his neck and walked toward Jerzy, was of more serious mien. "You will walk with me to check on the storm's results?"

"Of course." Even with all his other worries, Jerzy was just thankful that Giordan would let him anywhere near the vineyard again, and hoped that the trust was not misplaced.

The road was muddy, but the sky was blue and the air fresh and clear, and Jerzy felt his spirits lifting as they walked, silently, out the side gate and down the road, retracing their steps of the ill-fated day. A bird flew overhead, circling gracefully in a decreasing spiral before it swooped to strike at its prey, then rose again. Jerzy could not see, at that distance, if it had been successful or not.

It seemed to take less time to arrive at their destination, and as they came to the edge of the enclosure, Jerzy felt his good mood plummet right back into his gut.

"I can't look," he said, almost to himself.

Giordan snorted. "Not looking is not a choice," he said. He placed one hand on the low stone wall and flipped his body over to the other side in a nimble movement that Jerzy, half his age, could not duplicate.

The first thing Jerzy saw when he clambered over the wall were the bunches of unripened grapes smashed into the dirt, vines torn from their supports, and the tightness in his gut became more pronounced. His head dropped, and he waited for Giordan's cries of dismay.

"Ah. Yes." Rather than dismayed, Giordan sounded . . . relieved?

Jerzy looked up, barely daring to breathe, and saw the Vineart crouched down in the dirt, looking down the rows of vines. "Yes. All right. You can stop your cringing, young Jerzy. The damage was no worse than expected, and far less than might have been. I've no need to beat you, none at all."

Shaken by the force of relief, Jerzy's knees gave way underneath him, and he sat down, hard, in the wet dirt, to Giordan's ringing laughter.

When Jerzy recovered, Giordan took two cloth sacks from his belt, and directed Jerzy to gather as many of the bunches as he could from the soil, using the knife on his belt for the very first time, to cut away damaged bits and pieces of twine.

"The cook uses unripe grapes to cook with," Giordan told him. "He crushes them himself, with his paddle-feet, and adds the juice to roasted fowl. Excellent, most excellent results. Normally he takes from the culling, but now he will have them earlier, no? There is very little bad from which good cannot be pressed."

Jerzy wasn't quite so certain, but, his arms filled with the harvest of his storm, he was not about to argue with the Vineart. After the grapes were gathered and sorted into the sacks, the two retied the vines that could be repaired, and cut the others away.

The walk back was more enjoyable, even burdened with the now-full sacks. They deposited their bounty in the kitchen, a massive, high-beamed room with five times the people and ten times the chaos of the kitchen back home, and escaped with a fresh cloth of cheese, a chunk of cured meat, and a loaf of newly cooked bread as their reward. Jerzy lingered a bit to thank the cook's assistant, remembering Ao's advice about being invisible to important people but liked by the servants.

"It is hard to believe you have been here a tenday already," Giordan said, tearing a bite out of the loaf as they walked back to the workrooms. "And a busy time it has been. Perhaps too busy? I think that we will keep you from active decanting for a bit yet, yes?" He shook his head, and for once his smile was not in evidence. "I was overeager to share my skills, and did not think through the possibilities of error and . . . overenthusiasm, rather than control. You learn quickly; we forget you are still very young."

Jerzy felt the urge to protest, and then thought better of it. His body might be filling out, his voice deeper, and his muscles harder, but Giordan was right. A Vineart's studies lasted years, not months, and control was essential to casting as well as crafting. Still, he felt as though he'd once again been found lacking, unable to be the prize student Giordan had hoped for.

Still, perhaps this might give him the chance to finally explore the city? His sense of failure struggled against the surge of desire to finally take action and prove himself worthy of Malech's trust.

"And so," Giordan continued, not noticing his companion's reaction, "we shall take a step back. No, not so far back, but only a step. Perhaps—"

"Ah. Vineart Giordan. And your young visitor. I regretted not being able to continue our too-brief acquaintance the other day."

"Brother Darian." Giordan did not sound thrilled to encounter the Washer. Jerzy felt the urge to move behind his companion, as though that would hide him from view, but his feet stayed planted firmly against the stone.

The Washer, now dressed in his customary dark red robe, the belt wound twice around his waist similar to a Vineart's save that he carried a small wooden cup where a Vineart hung a silver tasting spoon, fell into easy step with them. "It is rare in my journeys that I am given the opportunity to speak in the company of similar minds—companions in the blood, if you will. May I walk with you, this fine morning?"

Asked in such a fashion, with The Washer already matching their direction, there was nothing to do but give assent.

"You will be relieved to know that, with the passing of the storm, the talk of your involvement in it passed as well," Darian said to Jerzy. "I of course assured those who came to me that such a storm was nothing out of the ordinary—as it indeed was not."

"Indeed," Giordan said. "Spring storms often come up quickly, and the risk of hail is a normal one in these hills. Rare, but normal."

"I am originally from Etton," Darian said, "so our weather patterns are different, and we do not make use of weatherwine often enough to note their peculiarities."

"Ah, Etton. You have traveled far, to come to our humble city." Giordan's voice was odd, as though he were speaking through his nose. "Most of your fellow Washers stay within a tenday's journey of their placements. What brings you to these parts?"

"My own desire to see what is over the next hill, I am afraid. I met Sar Anton on the road, and he spoke of the wonders of Aleppan, and here I am. My Brothers despair of me, this wanderlust, and yet I find I meet the most interesting people in my journeys. After all, did not Sin Washer's blood travel to every land, and touch every soul? How can I do less than to follow that example?"

It was neatly said, but the answer didn't calm Jerzy's discomfort. He remembered, clearly, Sar Anton's words to Brother Darian scant days before: *the . . . youth we were discussing.* Giordan, on the other hand, seemed to relax, and his voice smoothed out into his normal tone. "I do envy you the ability to travel," he said. "We are bound to our vines, never to see beyond the extent of the lands we cultivate. And while I would not choose to be other than I am, still . . ."

"And yet, here is young Jerzy, traveling."

Giordan seemed to suddenly realize that he had led the conversation directly where it should not go, but it was too late.

"Do you not feel tied to your roots?" Darian asked, and the tone of his voice was casual, but the look in his eyes was not. Jerzy's mind scurried to find a possible response, something that would satisfy the Washer but not give anything away, but no words came into his mouth.

No one can call a Vineart to task.

"I go where my master sends me," he said finally, as though the stone-cool voice in his head had released the sounds. "His desire was that I see how Vineart Giordan planted his vines, as we had an outbreak of root-glow earlier this year, and he thought that the row-trellis would allow us to reach the roots more quickly, to prevent further loss."

It was a reasonable answer, had the advantage of being nearly true, seemed to satisfy Darian, and allowed Giordan to turn the conversation to a discussion of the Washers' needs for *vin ordinaire*, since he was thinking of adding another small parcel to his enclosure but did not want to commit to making more spellwine immediately.

They came to the garden courtyard, the same one Ao had shown Jerzy as being perfect for snooping, and strolled along the graveled path, talking about shipments and costings, things that Detta dealt with back home. Jerzy allowed his attention to wander, chewing on their make-shift meal and fretting over the fact that his sole accomplishment in his time so far had been learning how to skirt telling the truth to authority figures. When someone else entered the courtyard he tilted his head, hoping to be able to pick up some tidbit, but caught only mentions of a party that had recently been canceled and the uproar that was apparently causing. He had no idea if that would be a usual thing, or unusual, and his spirits sank again until he saw a now-familiar form across the courtyard, lifting a hand in greeting.

Speaking of lying and snooping . . .

"If you will excuse me?"

Giordan looked up and absently nodded permission for him to leave. Not waiting for the Washer to say anything, Jerzy walked quickly across the courtyard to where Ao was waiting.

"Ah-ha. Looked like hard talking going on there. I saw Pour-and-

Preach chase you two down the hallway, thought you could use a rescue." Ao's expression was so placid, an observer might think he was
merely wishing Jerzy a good afternoon, if they weren't close enough to
hear the mocking tone. He was wearing his usual tunic, this one dark
green, but there was a deep blue half cloak over one shoulder, giving
him a dashing look.

"You don't like Brother Darian?" Jerzy didn't, either, but he was curious why Ao had taken the Washer in dislike.

"Oh, I don't mind him. I don't mind most people, unless we're trading, and then I either love them or hate them, depending on how the
trade is going. He was just too obviously on the hunt, and anyone hunting a friend of mine, I watch carefully."

"Hunting?" *Friend?* he really wanted to ask.

Ao jerked his chin to indicate that they should start walking—away
from the direction Giordan and Darian were taking. "As I said, he was
following you two with the obvious intent to catch up with you. He's
only been in the city three days, and it seems as though every time I
turn around, he's asking after you. You, specifically, not Vineart Giordan. Why is he so interested in you?"

They took a left turn out through the archway and back into the
palazzo proper. As they walked, courtiers and servants passed by them,
intent on their responsibilities, their faces downturned and their body
language tightly closed.

"I don't know," Jerzy said. Could the Washer know why he was truly
there? How? Should he confide in the Washer, ask his help? No, he
could not do that. Giordan said they were already suspicious of him,
merely for working on the maiar's lands. If they thought that Jerzy was
somehow actively interfering in something they deemed not a Vineart's
concern, playing at secular things . . .

He did not know what they would do, but he suspected he would
not enjoy it.

"Ao? How did you see the Washer coming after us? I've barely seen
you anywhere. I thought you were dancing attendance on the maiar?"

"We were." Now it was Ao's turn to look away, crossing his arms against his chest. "That's how I heard that Washer asking about you. But after calling us here specifically two months ago, scheduling meetings and presenting terms, the maiar first leaves us to wait for hours, and then refuses to meet with us, or brings us in and then has a servant whisper in his ear and remember something else he must attend to, first. It's as though he's playing a game we don't know the rules to yet. Tan, our delegation leader, is ready to claw at the walls in frustration, and Ket just mutters a lot under her breath." Ao almost laughed. "Ket has a temper."

"How many of you are there?" He had been wondering about that—"clan" implied many, but . . .

"Only three, here. That's how we do it. One to lead, one to support, and one to play fetch-and-carry." Ao struck a servile pose. "Guess which role is mine?"

Jerzy laughed, despite his glum mood.

"There you go. The plus is, Tan's given me leave for the day, and now I've time to spend with you. Come on, we both need some fresh air after being indoors so long, and I have it on good authority that the ladies of the court are taking that same fresh air in the city gardens."

The gardens turned out to be a massive square a few streets over from the palazzo. In the time Jerzy had been in Aleppan, this was the first chance he had to be out on the streets proper, and while he tried to mimic Ao's seen-it-all poise, by the time they reached the tall hedge that hid it from street view, his jaw ached from the effort it took not to gape.

"It's all right, you know," Ao said, clearly amused. "They like it when they can make the provincials gawp."

He couldn't deny he was a provincial. But pride made him retort, "I wasn't gawping."

"But you wanted to."

"Did you see that woman?"

Ao looked back casually over his shoulder. "The one with the head-dress?"

"It was taller than she was!"

"Fashionable ten years ago. The well-dressed Aleppanese lady today has a cloth cap-and-band over her hair, which is coiled at the back of her neck once she reaches her majority, and in braids before then. And before you even ask, we carried a shipment of ladies' clothing last spring from Parta to the Southern Isles, and I had to learn every single style, in case someone asked me a question at the receiving end.

"Now, the woman there, with the girl carrying the basket? Quite fine, and I don't only mean her clothing."

Jerzy saw the woman his friend referred to, but couldn't say there was anything about her that put her above any other, and said so.

Ao snorted. "It's true what they say about Vinearts, then? You save your seed for the ground?"

Jerzy felt heat rise in his face. To cover it, he took a swing at Ao, who blocked it badly, taking more of the blow on his shoulder than Jerzy had intended.

"Oh-ho, the Vineart can fight," Ao crowed, seemingly undismayed by the bruise that was going to appear on his arm. "That's good to know."

"The best way to win a fight is to not get in one," Jerzy said automatically. "Are you all right? I didn't hurt you, did I?"

"Hurts like fire," Ao said. "Next time, aim for my face. Bruises work wonders for making the ladies sympathetic."

"Are you ever serious?"

"Constantly," Ao said, making a sweeping bow to a young girl and her older companion, who scowled back at him and pulled her charge away from the duo. "It's all a very serious business, playing the fool. There, I've told you a secret. Now you tell me one, and we'll have traded, fair and foul."

"I don't have any secrets," he protested.

"Everyone has a secret, Jer. Everyone. Sometimes it's a stupid secret nobody else cares about, but it's important to *them*."

"Oh." Jerzy was distracted from the conversation by his first sight of the gardens. He wasn't sure what he had been expecting, but as they walked around the tall hedge and entered the gardens proper, stones crunching under their feet, the blaze of chaotic color took his breath away.

Everywhere he looked, there was color: bright reds and deep blues, glossy greens and vibrant yellows, each contained within neatly tended beds. Small flowers and large ones, stems and vines and leaves setting off the explosion of colors.

"They say there are over a hundred men hired every spring to maintain it. Can you imagine, spending your entire life tending to flowers? The same flowers, in the same pattern, every single year?"

"Yes," Jerzy said simply, and Ao laughed. "All right, I am put in my place. But I would go mad."

While Ao was speaking, Jerzy suddenly realized what was wrong.

"They have no aroma."

"What?"

"These flowers. They have color . . . but no smell."

"They were magicked."

"'What?" The boys turned to face the speaker, a man with a face like an old apple, wearing a leather apron that covered him from neck to knees. He leaned on a wooden hoe, and nodded at the nearest flower bed. "The flowers. They was magicked. Years and years ago. So they don't smell. Smell brings bugs, don't you see? And the ladies who walk here don't like the bugs."

"That must have cost the city a small fortune," Ao said in appreciation.

"A large one," the gardener said, and laughed, a harsh, wracking noise. "But the ladies, they like it, and so do the dandy-men as meet them here."

"Then how do they propagate?" Jerzy asked. "If no insects find them . . ."

"Ahhh." The gardener nodded his head wisely. "Young but not stupid, you. More magic."

"A growspell," Jerzy said. "For a garden? For flowers, that were spelled not to grow in the first place?"

"That's a bad thing?" Ao looked back and forth between the two, his nostrils practically flaring with interest.

"It's a waste," Jerzy said. "Growspells are meant to encourage life; they enhance harvests so we don't have another famine. They allow women to bear healthy children, and animals to thrive. This—"

"Is there a shortage of growspells? Are they rare?" Ao asked.

"No," Jerzy admitted. "One that would do this, a very basic fertility decantation, is the most basic. Expensive, but not rare."

"So then? How can it be wrong?"

"The young Vineart did not say it was wrong," a cool, feminine voice said. "He said that it was a waste. Common, even."

Jerzy bit back a groan even as they turned to face the maiar's daughter. "I never said common," he said. "Not now, and not then." He was exasperated enough that he added, without thinking of whom he was speaking to, "And don't tell me that I thought it, because you have no idea what I think."

Mahault blinked, her expression almost as surprised as Jerzy's at his outburst. "Right now you think that I am an annoyance of a female and would gladly see me sunk headfirst in the nearest pond," she replied tartly.

Jerzy felt his lips twitch, even as he tried to scowl, but the look of astonishment on Ao's face was too much, and the laugh escaped. Honors were about equal, he decided, and from the slight warming in her expression, he determined that she had decided the same.

"My lady Mahault," Ao said, ignoring his friend with as much dignity as he could manage. "We met, briefly, as I was pacing in one of your father's antechambers. Ao, of—"

"The traders, yes." Her cool gaze turned to him, assessing. "My father has not yet seen you?"

"No, my lady. Perhaps you might—"

"My father does not see fit to take my advice, Trader Ao."

Something Giordan had said, about her not being a favored child, stirred in Jerzy's brain at the faint bitterness in her voice. "An angry person says more than a happy one." Another of Ao's words of advice.

"Trader Ao was offering to show me about the gardens," he said, taking a chance. "But you, who live here, surely could show us both the best views?"

Mahault did not look displeased at the suggestion, although her gaze sharpened as though she knew he had ulterior motives. "Of course."

"Ahem."

Mahault looked back at her companion, an older woman with ruddy skin like Cai's, and gray hair almost hidden under her cap-and-strap, who had made the unhappy noise.

"These are guests within my mother's house," the maiar's daughter said strongly, her chin jutting stubbornly. "It would be discourteous to refuse them such a harmless request."

The woman looked over the two boys as though she were considering their purchase and nodded grudging permission, not looking particularly happy about it. While a Vineart was not to be scorned as a companion, a trader was less so, and neither of them were anywhere near Mahault's social level. Jerzy had no doubt that the companion would just as soon not allow her charge to speak to them in the first place, had she been given a vote. Mahault, however, clearly did not care, any more than she had seemed to notice that her dark blue gown and sturdy boots were drab compared to those of the women strolling past her.

"The centerpiece of the gardens is the sculpture of Alagatto," Mahault said, moving forward, the two of them flanking her, and the companion trailing behind like a disapproving watchdog. "The roses there are the only ones that do have a scent. You will like that, Vineart Jerzy."

"If my master heard you calling me that, he would cuff me so hard your ears would ring," Jerzy said. "Jerzy, please. I can't claim the title until my master says I've earned it."

"Is it true you are—were—a slave?" Mahault asked, her eyes widening. Jerzy noticed then that they were outlined with a dark smudge, making her skin seem paler, and her eyes larger.

"Yes."

"Was it . . . terrible?"

Jerzy was puzzled by the question. Cooper Shen had assumed so, also: that slavery had been terrible. "I had a place to sleep, two meals a day, I worked hard, and the overseer was not a man who punished for no reason."

"But you . . . were a slave," Ao said, picking up the conversation. "You couldn't choose your master, or where you would live, what you would do. You weren't free."

Jerzy simply shrugged. "I don't know what free is."

"Free is being able to *choose*. To go where you want, do what you want," Ao said, gesturing madly for emphasis.

"To make your own decisions," Mahault added, with a guarded, sideways glance at her silent, disapproving companion.

"And you can?" Jerzy asked, feeling a little overwhelmed by their urgency. He found his hand going to his belt, touching the bone-handled knife that hung there, next to his purse, as though for reassurance.

"Of course!" Ao said immediately.

"You could just walk away, tonight? Your clan would understand, and welcome you back when you returned?"

"Yes." Ao's voice was a little less certain there, though.

Jerzy's comment struck home with Mahault as well. "He is right. The painful truth is that while we might have the illusion, none of us are free," Mahault said as they came upon the sculpture she had mentioned; a man in robes, made of white and red marble. "At least Jerzy will be, someday, once he becomes a Master. Vinearts do what they will. I envy you that."

Ao looked as though he wanted to protest, but something in Mahault's voice said that the discussion was ended. Jerzy leaned forward to smell one of the deep red roses that were planted around the statue. True to her word, the flower gave off a soft, warm smell that reminded him of mustus.

"My father used to grow these roses," Mahault said. "In the courtyard outside our private rooms: ones with fragrance. He said . . . he said they were the roses of justice, that's why they were planted here. Brother Alagatto stood against the first maiar of Aleppan, back in the founding years when all was chaos, and called him a dictator. They killed him for it. But, like Sin Washer, his blood ran into the ground, and turned the white roses of the maiar's coat of arms red."

"That's blasphemy!" Ao said, scandalized. "Isn't it?" he appealed to Jerzy, who looked at Mahault, who looked back with those cool eyes.

"I don't know," he said. "I'm not a Washer. It's probably just a story. If it did happen . . . how can a miracle be blasphemy?"

Ao looked as though he was going to argue the point, then dropped the subject and turned back to Mahault. "What happened to the roses? You said he used to grow them?"

She touched a pale finger against the crimson of the petals, and Jerzy was struck by how delicate the flower looked, and how strong and capable her hand was, not what he would have expected from the daughter of a maiar, at all. He wasn't sure what to expect from Mahault. She reminded him, again, of Detta, or the Guardian, stone-made-flesh, although he couldn't say why.

If he were drawn to a woman, it would be Mahault. But his body felt nothing.

"He tore them up late last year, all the roses, every bush," Mahault said. "I woke one morning, and there were only bare holes in the ground."

"And you didn't ask why?" Ao said.

Jerzy snorted. Ao would have asked Sin Washer himself why, and expected an answer.

Mahault did not look at either one of them, stroking the petal like it was the most precious and delicate of glass, and would shatter if breathed upon. "My father . . . no longer welcomes questions, Trader Ao. Best you remember that, if he ever grants you an audience. Aleppan is no longer as it once was."

The trader's face went from one expression to another, like the shifting of clouds across the sky, but Jerzy could not identify what the changes meant. In a determinedly casual change of topic, Ao instead asked Mahault about the type of stone used for the statue, and if it was locally mined or imported. Mahault responded in kind, and the conversation moved on to discussions of quarrying and local artisans, leaving Jerzy feeling as though he had missed something important.

He truly was not cut out to be a spy.

Chapter 20

lthough the conversation remained in his mind, Jerzy had no chance to follow up on Mahault's odd comment about her father, or what it might mean, because, seemingly overnight, the grapes reached first ripening, and Giordan and he spent the next two days in the fields from dawn to dusk, inspecting the fruit, removing subpar bunches to allow others more room to grow. Malech did not preselect, but weathervines were more jealous of their growing space, or so Giordan explained it, too many together "like clouds colliding, and storms arising." It could not be accomplished alone, of course, and so while Giordan identified the grapes for culling, Jerzy found himself working with the servants the lord-maiar supplied to do the actual pull.

"No, no, like this!" Jerzy showed a worker the proper way to work around the gnarled and twisted rootstock for the third time, and bit back an impatient swear. The overseer would have laid a slave out flat by now, for such incompetence. How did the Vineart work with such useless hands?

"Patience, Jerzy," Giordan said, coming up behind them as Jerzy sent the man back to work. He took off his hat, a particularly misshapen straw form that looked like it had been nibbled at by mice, and wiped his forehead with a scrap of red cloth, then tucked the cloth back into his belt. "They do their best, but they have no feel for the vines, the way we do."

Jerzy wiped his own forehead and looked out at the field. It had taken them two days to accomplish what would have been a morning's chore back home, with trained slaves. "And you think this is a better way to work?"

"No. I think it is an acceptable compromise for what I get in return: excellent lands, work, and living space someone else maintains . . . I know it's not traditional, but the vines are worth it." And that was all Giordan would say on the matter.

Back at the palazzo, Jerzy sluiced the sweat and grime off his skin in the bathhouse and contemplated going in search of Ao, or heading out into the city again, but exhaustion won out each night, and he ate a light meal in his rooms and fell asleep soon after.

The third morning brought with it a light, almost misty rain, and Jerzy found his way down to the workroom, planning to continue in his study of the yield patterns of healvines versus Giordan's weathervines, a project the Vineart had suggested, to determine if the other Vineart's trellis-and-row method actually showed an improvement in yield. If he could not carry out Master Malech's orders to gather information, he could at least bring *something* of value back to the House.

Giordan had a kettle of tai and steaming-fresh bread waiting, to ward off the unusual chill, and Jerzy headed for it with no small feeling of gratitude.

"Good morning. Before you begin, I found a journal of my master's I thought you might find useful." Giordan indicated a large, leather-bound book resting on the workbench. Jerzy opened the book, and was struck by the delicate ink drawings within. Little text, but page after page of leaves and grapes, birds and insects, all rendered in a careful hand and labeled with names and details.

"This is . . . amazing."

"My master was not a very good Vineart," Giordan said, returning to the calculations he was making on a vintage chart. "I learned as much as I could from him, and then set out on my own. I suppose that is why I don't hold much with traditions. But he loved the vines, and noticed details in the natural world most of us would overlook. That journal is only a few years' worth of notes, and it holds more than most people could see in a lifetime."

Jersey turned another page and, enthralled, sat down on the floor, drawing the bench toward him to better look through it.

"It's yours."

"What?" Surely he had not heard Giordan correctly.

"The journal. When you go, take it with you." The Vineart looked at Jerzy, his normally smooth features creased. "I have been . . . thinking, recently. About my Agreement with the maiar. You have seen it yourself. I have no slaves. I will have no student, no one to pass this along to. I made that choice and I do not regret it, but . . . I don't want that to end up in the maiar's collection, stored and never looked at save as a curiosity, and whoever takes over my vines when I am gone . . . no. I would rather you have it. A gift, one Vineart to another, in honor of this quietly momentous exchange we have shared."

Seeing Giordan was serious, Jerzy merely bowed his head in acceptance, and put the book away, feeling oddly uncomfortable now, as though he were taking the gift under false pretenses.

The rest of the day passed quietly, the only sounds the scratching of Giordan's pen and the rustle of pages. It was interesting work, and useful work, but Jerzy felt a twitch between his shoulder blades that only became worse, the longer he worked. Giordan's words, about leaving his master and going out on his own, had sounded in him like a stone dropping into the well. He had been waiting for an opportunity to fall into his lap; no more. Vines did not harvest themselves; if he wanted information, he had to go find it himself.

That afternoon, when Giordan left him to run some errand of his own, Jerzy made his way into the main hallways of the palazzo. He did not have enough time to go into the city, but the garden would do almost as well.

By now he knew some of the courtiers by sight, and they him, and the guards were often willing to stop and chat, if they weren't on watch. As he walked through the cool white hallways, however, he became aware of an odd feeling to the air, like a storm about to fall—or one that was threatening. The now-familiar faces were stern, warning him off from approaching them, and the courtiers he saw had a furtive, worried look about them. Jerzy's pace slowed, and he had to fight the urge to go back to his wing and bury himself in the old journal all evening.

When he saw Washer Darian walking down the hallways toward him, however, he let his caution push him back into a small alcove, keeping his body as still as possible so as not to attract the man's attention. The last thing he wanted right now was to explain why he was wandering aimlessly, rather than sitting at lessons. When he saw those dark red robes go through the double doors that led into the maiar's antechamber—the one Ao had complained about wasting so much time in—his curiosity got the better of him, however, and he moved forward, even as a messenger in the maiar's household colors of blue and brown came out through those doors with a leather packet in his hand and the mark of a newly formed bruise on his face.

"Be careful, young master," he said softly, seeing Jerzy. "Now is not the time to be anywhere near here, if you can avoid it."

Before Jerzy could ask what the man meant, he was too far down the hall, never pausing in his steady pace or in any way indicating that he had even noticed Jerzy, much less spoken to him.

"Always listen to servants," Ao had said. "Always."

Before he could decide what to do, there was an outburst of noise, and the door the Washer had recently gone in was thrown open, and three men came out.

Two of them wore the brown surcoats of the Aleppan Council. The third was an older man, with night-dark skin and a bald head, in much finer clothing.

Jerzy quickly leaned against the wall next to an alcove and thought hard about if he wanted to sit there and think for a while, or move on. Thus apparently distracted and harmless, he was able to watch the activity at the end of the hall without calling attention to himself.

"You cannot do this! This is not right!" The older man was shouting not in Ettonian, but Corguruth, meaning that he was probably a local, and a well-off one, if Jerzy could tell anything from his attire. From the way the guards were handling him, firmly but without violence, and with almost a hint of deference, he had some status in the court as well.

Or, had once had status, Jerzy amended. Clearly, he was not well-regarded by the maiar right now.

The man was struggling, although not enough to do damage. "The maiar is not himself! You must allow me—"

One of the guards, finally tiring of the noise, placed a large hand over his mouth, turning the complaint into a muffled yelp. Jerzy couldn't hear what he said to his prisoner, but the man stopped struggling immediately and allowed himself to be marched off without further complaint, in the opposite direction the servant had gone.

The door to the antechamber swung closed, as though someone had pushed it, and the hallway was silent again.

Ao's clan, summoned and then insulted. Mahault upset, saying her father had changed. Servants and guardsmen worried enough to change their behaviors. And now courtiers being removed, forcibly, from the council room, saying that something was wrong with the maiar . . .

Ao might have had the courage to forage on. Jerzy, all too aware of how tempers could flare and bad things happen, turned on his heel and fled for the safety of the Vineart's wing, and his own room.

Tucked into bed, the journal open on his lap, Jerzy fought with his shame and guilt. Something was happening outside, perhaps even the very thing he had been sent to discover, and he had fled. Ao would have talked someone into giving him answers. Mahault would have stayed. He had hopped away like a rabbit, and hid.

He did not sleep well that night, at all.

THE NEXT MORNING Jerzy rose, determined that he would not be squeamish again. Time was half gone. If something was happening, Master Malech needed to know about it. And if he could not get near the maiar or the council rooms themselves, he would do the next best thing.

It was midmorning when the opportunity came about. They were sitting in the courtyard garden, with seven tasting spoons of weather-wine lined up in front of Jerzy. He was supposed to taste each one, a sip only, and tell Giordan what each one was for. The trick was, Giordan crafted only three different spellwines: wind-bringing, rain-controlling, and one that should raise or lower the warmth within a specific range. That meant that at least four of the wines were either duplicates, or something else entirely.

As Giordan fussed with the placement, Jerzy sat in his chair and tried not to let his anxiousness show through. Out of the corner of his eye he saw a figure moving slowly through the open walkway at the far end of the courtyard. It was Mahault. Jerzy raised a hand in greeting, but she either did not see him, or chose not to respond. Giordan clearly saw the aborted exchange, but did not make mention of it.

"You were right," Jerzy said, as though suddenly coming to a realization. "Master Malech's independence leaves me woefully ignorant about the larger world. Tell me . . . oh, tell me about the lord-maiar and his family?"

"Test first. Gossip later." Giordan's temper was sharp this morning. Whatever he had gone off to do the day before had, apparently, not gone well.

"It's not gossip, it's interest. Master Malech sent me here to learn other ways. . . . Your relationship with the lord-maiar is another way from how we live back home. I may end up in a situation closer to yours than Master Malech's, so I should know how to go about in such company, yes?"

Jerzy was rather pleased with his talk-around. Ao might get him into trouble, but he was as good a teacher in his own way as Cai back home. And while Malech would have whapped him for the flummery, Giordan merely tsked, and pointed again at the wines. "Taste, and I will tell."

Jerzy lifted the first tasting spoon. Not as fine as Master Malech's; these were little more than hammered silver depressions with a curl on the side to lift by, and while deeper red wines glimmered in such spoons, the yellower tones of weatherwines merely sat there unappealingly. Jerzy knew better than to make that observation out loud, however.

He raised the spoon to his nose, and sniffed, delicately. "Straw, and . . . sunberries? Ripe sunberries." Without waiting for a yea or nay, he took a sip, holding it in his mouth and letting the flavors fill his senses. He remembered the first time he had ever tasted spellwine, when it had exploded all at once in his mind, no subtlety or distinction. Now he could find the threads of flavor that matched to and indicated the magic contained within. And still, the more he learned, the more he became aware that he did not know. Giordan had spent his entire life learning to harness the magic within a single grape, and Master Malech said he was considered near-Master level. Jerzy was . . . simply Jerzy. Jerzy who brought thunder and hail when he was tasked for a gentle rain.

"Less thinking. More tasting." Giordan scowled at him, an expression the Vineart had trouble maintaining. "You are letting your head overcome your senses. So, what is this?"

"Straw and sunberries are not hallmarks of one of your vines. There is magic here, but less subtle, more forward." He let his tongue run over his teeth, and followed the taste. "This is a growspell, but not one I am familiar with."

"For children," Giordan said. "For babies born too soon, or ill, to bring them back to health. The vines grow on the rocky hills of Carcel, where the sea winds blast them with spray, and the sun is fierce but quick. I trade a cask of my wines for one of theirs every year, and pray it is not needed. And now the next."

The second wine was darker, unappealingly the color of bloody urine, and smelled like well-worn leather, a deep, musky nose. When Jerzy tasted it, the magic almost knocked him off the chair, swooping through his body like a storm.

"Windspell. Yours. Stronger than the one I tasted before." There was a sense of motion to it, of racing from one place to another. . . . "A sea wind, to fill a sail and send a boat flying."

"Well done. Yes. Sailors come on the sly and buy much of each vintage. Even some from the Caulic islands," Giordan said with a smirk. "They may scorn us in public, but their coin fills coffers within all Aleppan while they are here, making a satisfying association for all concerned. They are arrogant, for a people with no magic of their own, but they pay well for ours, and their ships undeniably are among the finest on the water."

Jerzy bit back a smile. Cai would be heartbroken to hear that not all his fellow Caulians were willing to go without the assistance of magic.

Jerzy lifted the third spoon. The wine glimmering in the spoon was a clear golden color, like morning sunlight, and smelled of warmed stone. He inhaled, and placed the spoon back down, untouched. "*Vin ordinaire.* Should I try to identify where it is from, or was the test merely to see if I recognized it for what it was?"

The words came out of his mouth as though Ao had spoken them, brash and confident, and somewhere part of him cringed, anticipating the blow he had just earned.

"If you could not recognize *ordinaire* you would still be breaking your backside under the vines," Giordan said sharply. "Finish the exercise."

The words stung as hard as a slap, and Jerzy meekly picked up the spoon again. "The mouth is . . . stone. Warm stone, carrying over from the nose. I . . ." He took another tiny sip, and let the liquid roll around in his mouth, able to focus purely on the taste without the distraction of magic in his mouth, then opened his mouth slightly and drew air in over the wine, trying to open it up. It was lovely, smooth and cooling, delicate and yet thick at the same time. "I . . . it was grown in a porous soil, and a gentle sun but . . . I can't identify it. I am sorry, Magister."

"Confidence is a good thing. Pride is a failing. We craft what the vines give us, but we must also give the vines an understanding of what we want. We are no more, no less than our work." Giordan let his words linger in the air for a moment, and then reached for a small clay shipping flask. "This is the wine you were drinking."

The wax seal on the side was that of the Valle of Ivy. His own vineyards.

"Bonewine." Once he knew, it was obvious.

"A year came, not so long ago, that the vines did not give up their magic. A bad year, that. Some Vinearts panicked, dug up their vine and replaced them with another, or hoarded their stores as though the world might fall down in flames. Your master calmly set about making a *vin ordinaire* that was, in a word, magnificent. Not magic, but magical. A spellwine lasts a year, perhaps two, once it is made. An *ordinaire* might last two or three years, if stored properly. That wine, Jerzy, is almost ten years old."

He replaced the flask carefully, handling it the way another man might his weapon, or his lover. "My master was . . . a good man, a wise man, and a mediocre Vineart. Your master? Is a magician. Never forget that."

The thought, rather than reassuring Jerzy, made him more anxious. "Giordan?"

"Yes?"

"Do you ever . . . do you ever actually feel like you know what you are doing? Or is it all . . . someday, someone's going to find you out, and . . ."

"And?" The Vineart looked at him, his open face showing nothing but an honest curiosity. Jerzy could have asked anything at that moment, anything at all, and Giordan would have answered it, in apology for his unusual burst of temper. Jerzy lowered the spoon, and stared into the remaining wine as though it might speak for him.

"And send you back into the fields?" Giordan finished the question for him.

"Yes." He didn't question how the older man knew; it might have been a question that every student asked, or it might have been a lucky guess, or it might not even have been the question he would have asked, but needed the answer to, nonetheless.

Giordan sighed, the first time Jerzy had ever heard him utter such a sound. It wasn't enough to make him look up, however. Looking down was easier. There was less risk of seeing whatever punishment was coming.

"Our lives seem easy to those outside. They are not. Magic does not come to those who are not . . . tested, and once it comes . . . we pay a price for it, every day of our lives.

"We never escape the fields, Jerzy. We are always in the fields. We are always slaves. The only difference is that now we know what we are slaves *to*."

There was silence, and then Giordan pushed back his chair and Jerzy heard his soft boot steps pace across the room. Had it been Master Malech, he would have known where he stood, and what sort of response would be forthcoming, be it a slap or a scold. "Go," the Vineart said, finally. "This test is done. Spend the afternoon somewhere other than here."

It was an order, not a suggestion, and Jerzy left without asking any of the questions that were now simmering in his mind.

The unease he had felt the day before still lingered in the halls of the main building, to the point where courtiers no longer lingered in hallways or courtyards, chatting, and even the servants were keeping out of sight. Jerzy went back to his room and changed his soft boots for harder-soled ones, wrapped his belt around his waist, added his leather purse to it, and followed his teacher's orders.

"Going out, young master? Mind you avoid the southern market. Horse market's today, and there's always a fight or five the town guards have to break up. Best to avoid it entirely."

Jerzy acknowledged the door guard's advice, even as a small, annoyed voice inside wanted to tell him that he, Jerzy, had faced down worse things than a market brawl. The urge to go directly toward the southern market followed, and was likewise firmly squelched. Instead, he headed into the center of town, following the circular streets that curved away from the palazzo at the northern point of Aleppan, past narrow gray stone houses pressed up against one another like Giordan's vines, resting their walls on one another for support. Members of the Aleppan Council lived here, he knew now from Ao's chatter, within the beck and call of the maiar. The only other people on the street were servants, on their way to or from errands for their Houses. A single older man walked an unsaddled gray horse, possibly coming from the market.

The neighborhood in the next, nearest section out from the palazzo belonged to the Perfumers' Guild, and the smells from their shops that afternoon were wafting on the breeze, making his nostrils twitch. The maiar might find them appealing, but Jerzy couldn't quite rid himself of the desire to sneeze; it was too much, too thick, and he walked more quickly, hoping to escape before his head began to ache from the confusion.

The cobbled stone streets broadened slightly as he moved into the next neighborhood, and the smells were thinner but less pleasant, bringing a note of overcooked meat and clay on random wafts of air. The buildings here were made of the same gray tone, but were wider, and occasionally had narrow alleys between them, leading to glimpses of greenery hidden out of public view. The sight made him think wistfully of the open skies and wide fields of The Berengia. The city was exciting, but it was also confusing, and complicated. Jerzy decided that he would not want to live here, not even for the comfortable surroundings and secure living Vineart Giordan had negotiated with the maiar.

There were more people in sight here, gathered in groups of three or four, either pausing to look at a storefront or talking amongst themselves. Good pickings, to harvest gossip.

One group in particular caught his attention, although he couldn't have said why. Four men, dressed in the half coats and hose he knew now indicated a high level within the maiar's court, were standing near a small gray stone fountain: a likeness of Sin Washer with the water running from his elbows down into the basin at his feet. Drawn by a tickle of something in the back of his thoughts, Jerzy walked closer, trying to keep his path as seemingly random as possible, thinking casually that the fountain seemed a good place to sit and rest awhile, perhaps while waiting to meet a friend. The men kept talking as he drew near, and he was able to see that two of the men wore a palm-sized device sewn onto the breast of their half coats, an archway picked out in silver thread. Jerzy had seen that mark before. Like the Coopers' bronze barrel, the silver archway was a mark of guild membership; in this case, the Carters' Guild. Detta dealt with the cartsmen, making arrangements for Master Malech's spellwines to go to his buyers, and for supplies to come back in return.

"And half our shipments never arrived," one of them was saying, his voice thin with displeasure. Jerzy knelt against the fountain, just out of sight of the men, and looked out across the street, as though he were searching for someone. "No sign of pirates, no report of wreckage, just disappeared from the ocean's skin like the air itself ate them. And then we are expected to make good on our Agreement, and we have no one to turn to for compensation ourselves! This will bankrupt us within a year, if the maiar does nothing."

"Nothing is exactly what he means to do." A lighter voice, tight and hard. "I was to see him the halfweek before, to plead for a reduction in the taxes he has placed on us. Impossible, to pay such a fee, and no reason for imposing it. The metalwrights are always willing to do our share, but there need must be a reason for it! He cripples us to build his treasury, and forces honest men to find work elsewhere."

"The day I meet an honest metalwright, I'll eat your hat," a third voice said. "But you have the right of it, otherwise. He brings forward taxes and fines that he claims are needed, yet will give us no satisfaction when we ask for reasons. There are those who whisper he is in the pay

of another city, to beggar us so that we would be easy pickings for an-
nexation."

"It's not only the guilds that are suffering. Have you seen the markets
lately? Fewer traders, fewer goods, fewer supplies coming into port. And
the one trading clan that is in court has been made to cool their heels,
rather than being begged to negotiate. It makes no sense; it's madness."

Jerzy's ears perked up at that. It wasn't what he had been sent for, but
he could all too easily imagine the fate of a vessel, laden with supplies, if
confronted with one or more sea serpents, in the open waters. . . .

"Fewer traders and goods in the market, perhaps." The fourth man,
who had not spoken until then. "But money flows through the city, in
goods and coin. And all of it comes from elsewhere, via strangers with
easy access to our beloved maiar. . . ."

"Ahhhhh," the second speaker cautioned, his voice lowering. "The one
thing you don't want to do right now is speak ill of the maiar, even in
jest, even among friends. He has a chancy temper, and even the court
familiars are watching their step around him now. Grumble all you
want about conditions; he does not seem to care. But against the man
himself, stay quiet, and keep such thoughts to yourself."

Jerzy was distracted by whatever response was made to that by a familiar figure coming into view.

"Ah, there you are! Excellent, I was worried I'd be wasting my entire
afternoon trying to decide which fountain you had meant. Come on,
we'll be late." Ao took Jerzy's arm even as he was speaking, and pulled
the Vineart forward, walking away from the statue at a steady but un-
hurried pace.

"What are you . . . I was listening back there!" Jerzy was indignant at
being taken away, just when he had finally gotten somewhere.

"I could tell. And doing a good job of it, too. But you'd been there
long enough for one of them to notice you, and then they would have
shut up anyway, even if they didn't decide you needed accosting, or
maybe even a quick dunking off the piers, to wash the snoop out of
you."

"Oh." Jerzy had thought he was doing well. "How long have you been there? Did you follow me?" It was ridiculous, but how else could the trader have found him, in the entire city?

"Of course I did. And don't look so downcast; you're absolutely getting better, didn't I just say so? It's entirely possible, if they were merely passing the time of day, that they would not have looked at you with suspicion at all. Did you hear anything useful?"

"I don't know," Jerzy said plaintively, not even bothering to protest being followed. "How can you tell if something's important, if you don't know what's going on or even what you need to know?" The moment he heard those words hit the air, his jaw snapped shut, and he felt like an idiot. Why had he said anything? Malech would be angry with him for letting even that much out.

Ao clapped an arm around his shoulders and, thankfully, didn't respond to the question. "You, my friend, are in need of something to drink. And, lucky us, I know just the place to get exactly that."

The "place" was down two long streets and around a corner, in a neighborhood that obviously catered to a less affluent customer. The wooden placard over the door showed a badly drawn goblet lying on its side and a crescent moon over it. Jerzy hesitated at the doorway: other than the roadhouse he had stayed in during the trip down to take passage here, he had never been in a public house. But Ao gave him a friendly shove, and he was inside.

"Two ales," Ao told the woman leaning behind the bar, and put a coin down on the surface, keeping his fingers on it just enough to ensure it stayed there until their drinks arrived. Jerzy let his gaze flit around, not sure what to expect. In truth, it looked a great deal like the dining hall back home, although the ceiling was lower: a long wooden table with an assortment of benches pulled up to it, a fireplace down at the far end that, although unlit, looked like it had seen long years of hard use, and a plank floor that was worn down with the countless shuffle of countless shoes.

Ao handed him a mug of some dark brown liquid and pointed to the far end of the table. "Over there."

The liquid turned out to be thick and strongly bitter, as unlike a *vin ordinaire* as could be and yet satisfying for all that. Jerzy took another long pull and decided that he approved.

"The first time I tried to listen in on a conversation I shouldn't have been near," Ao said thoughtfully, clearly reliving the memory, "I almost got my ears cut off. They were Eopan riders, fierce as the wind and smelly as twice-dead fish, and I thought to learn something to aid my elder in our negotiations."

"And they caught you."

"By my aforementioned ear. Held me up by it and trotted me back through camp until he came to our tent, then bartered my release for a double-fold of cloth and a new saddle for his oldest daughter. And the worst thing? I spoke maybe ten words of Eopan, so anything I heard would have been gibberish, anyway!"

They finished their first ale, and Ao waved at the bartender for another round. By three mugs, he was in full storytelling mode, to an appreciative audience not only of Jerzy, but two other merchants and a kitchen boy who had snuck out from behind the bar to listen.

"And then we had to make amends with the Dyers' Guild, but they got over it. Eventually. But it took another month before they would resume discussions with us."

The others hooted with laughter, while Jerzy stared at his friend in disbelief, amused despite himself. "How, in Sin Washer's name, do you make a living, the amount of trouble you're constantly in?"

"Ah, that's not trouble," Ao said with an airy wave, "that's trading. Give and take, bicker and barter; it's all a game, Jerzy. It's how you determine a man's limits, and learn what he respects, by pushing and pulling a little here and a little there. At the end of the day we all know that the goods are the important thing; they trust us to carry them safely back and forth, and we trust them to give us quality, and a fair price so we make our own profit on the transaction. It's all deadly serious but that doesn't mean it has to be *dull*."

He lifted his mug—his fourth now, to Jerzy's two and a half, and used it to point at his friend, leaning forward to exclude the others from his conversation. "Like you. You're deadly serious like the Red Plague"—Ao spat on the floor to ward off bad fortune—"and yet there's a tension in you, an air of secrecy and urgency that I can't resist, no more than a dog cannot not chase a hare."

"I . . ." Jerzy looked at his fingertips. Normally they would be stained red working with the Berengian grapes, but weathergrapes were paler, and the juice left no mark. He could smell it, though. His vinery's mark ached lightly. "I don't know what you mean."

The merchants, sensing the stories were over, went back to their own conversation, and the serving boy slipped back into the kitchen, unnoticed.

"Cut loss, Jer. Just because I never met a Vineart before you doesn't mean I don't know about them. First off is that they don't share students. You're more guildish than any guild, secretive and standoffish and never ever ever getting involved. But here you are, studying with another Vineart, and sniffing around trying—oh so badly—to hear what's going on beyond your reach, like your next deal depended on it."

Ao looked up at him, his round face woeful. "And yet you won't share what you're trying to learn. Don't you trust me?"

"As far as I could throw this barrel," Jerzy said, thumping the side of a nearby cask with his heel.

His friend gaped at him. "Now that's the way to do it!" he said in delight. "Jer, I'll make a trader of you yet!"

"I'd sooner drown in my own wines," Jerzy grumbled.

Ao just laughed and ordered another round.

Chapter 21

"You had a good time last night, hrmmm?" Giordan said, looking at Jerzy from across the worktable. A pot of something that smelled delicious waited on the table, but no food, for which Jerzy was thankful. He wasn't sure he could handle the smell of anything even slightly greasy.

"I guess." He lifted the lid of the pot and sniffed cautiously. Not tai, nor—thank the silent gods—ale.

"You guess? You do not remember too much?"

"Not much, no," Jerzy admitted. He did, actually; every painful, off-tune, staggering moment of it, right to the moment he threw up in the courtyard and staggered into his room, to fall facedown onto his bed with barely enough awareness left to take his shoes off before he collapsed. Master Malech had warned him against drunkenness, but he had only considered wine, had not known of the thick, bitter brew that made his head feel like stone. "Ao bought me ale."

"Quite a lot of ale, one presumes. Ah, to be young and stupid once again." Giordan chuckled, then clapped Jerzy on the shoulder. "Drink your potion and feel well again. Enough time, and the quiet-magics will make sure you are never so again."

"It will keep me from getting drunk?" That was the best news Jerzy had heard in weeks.

"No. It will take away your taste for ale. Drink; I need your thoughts clear today. Today, yes. We have only a week or so left, and the most important is yet to come. Today I teach you how to refine!"

Jerzy looked at Giordan blankly. In all the steps he had gone through with Master Malech, from Harvest through to incantation, he had never heard of refining. Fining, yes . . . but refining?

"Weathervines only," Giordan said, enjoying his student's confusion. "A thing no others know."

Considering he had shown a complete and utter lack of ability to handle them, there was no reason for him to learn that process, and yet the thought of learning something new, something that even Master Malech did not know, proved impossible to resist. Despite his aching head and sour stomach, Jerzy poured a cup of the odd-smelling brew and drank it willingly, only gagging a little at the hot, grassy taste. "What is this," he asked when he could breathe again.

"Potion," was all Giordan would say. "Very strong potion. Now that you can think, follow me, and pay attention."

Jerzy obediently got up and followed the Vineart through a heavy wooden door that closed silently behind them. They were now standing in a small room bare of any furnishings but a low slab made of the same whitish-gray stone as the statue the day before. The surface was smooth, save for two narrow ridges that ran parallel down the length, a fingertip deep; Jerzy assumed they were to keep the half cask on top of the slab from rolling off.

Giordan changed, somehow, when they entered that room. He was still the same . . . but there was a stillness in him, a seriousness, that once again reminded Jerzy that this was a Vineart, one who would likely someday earn Master status for his skills.

"This I tell you: from teacher to student it is shared, and no others."

Part of Jerzy didn't want to hear more: he was not Giordan's student, he had been bought by the House of Malech, those were his vines, not these . . . but he could feel the touch of the weathervines brush against his senses, and the desire to know more overwhelmed the warnings in his head.

"Weathervines are old, very old, and were very far away from Sin Washer when he changed the vines. That is why they are so green, even when ripe, not completely red. They do not grow well here, take longer to incant. This you know. Now you learn that they are not to be commanded. They do not like being told what to do." Giordan patted the quarter cask on the table in front of him the way he might a dog who had done good work. "And now that you know why we must refine them, you will learn *how* we refine them, so they accept incantation." He looked at Jerzy, and for a moment there was an uncanny resemblance between Malech and Giordan, although neither man looked anything like the other. "The telling characteristic of weathervines, what is it?"

"Delicacy," Jerzy responded instantly, sure of his answer.

"No, no. Delicate, yes. Delicate as you know, but what else do you know of them? You who have walked in their soil, handled their leaves, tasted their fruit, in all its stages: what is the telling characteristic? Not what your teachings tell you—what does the *vine* tell you?"

The answer came, this time, not from his head but that awareness Malech had first identified, the Vineart's Sense. "Stubborn. Weathervines are stubborn."

"Ahhh. Yes. And how do you coax a stubborn vine to give what you want? How does a Vineart bring a vine into agreement with its purpose, with its noble destiny?"

Jerzy stared at the wooden slats of the cask, trying to imagine that he could look through them, into the wine stored within, tracing its path from flowering to fruit, from juice to mustus to *vina*. What would bring a stubborn wine to the next step, into *vin magica*?

There was silence in the little room, just him and Giordan and the cask of wine, all waiting for his answer. Jerzy could feel his heart speed up, his stomach tighten, the skin on his arms prickle as though cold air had touched them, his entire body reacting to . . .

His entire body. That was it. House of Malech was Malech—and so he, Jerzy, was House of Malech, and part of the vineyard itself, connected to the rootstock of every vine that felt his touch. Giordan was no less part of his yard, and the yard was part of him, so . . . He could feel the vineyard, even at a distance, like the faintest brush of leaf against his skin. And, if he opened himself to it, another, fainter brush: the weathervines, closer physically, not his, but not unwelcoming, either.

How did that awareness translate into convincing a stubborn wine? What did his senses tell him? How could he know?

Once he looked, the answer appeared.

"You have to believe it's necessary," he said slowly, thinking it through. "You have to incant your own certainty into the wine, so that it has no choice but to accept. Or that it wants to accept. But, Master . . ." The first time he had ever given Giordan that title, and it slipped out without fuss. "Master, vines are not aware. They are not alive. So how can a wine be stubborn, or coaxed, or . . . ?"

Giordan shook his head and raised his arms in an enthusiastic shrug. "Nobody knows. It is magic."

A surprised snort escaped Jerzy at that happy admission of ignorance. He supposed, reluctantly, that it was as useful a response as "because it is traditional."

"So," Giordan said. "Thanks to the studies of my master and my master's master, I know what this wine must do, to release its magic. And so I share that knowing . . . thus."

The ridges weren't to keep the cask steady. They were to collect the blood that dripped from the cuts Giordan made in his left arm, slicing with his knife a line from palm toward elbow. Jerzy bit back an exclamation, his attention caught by the slow, steady drip of crimson blood falling onto the white stone, enclosing the cask with two narrow lines of blood. It took forever, it seemed to Jerzy, watching the drops fall and collect, but Giordan never wavered, and his expression of concentration never changed.

"So Sin Washer bled to change the First Growth, so do we bleed to craft our spellwines. There is no magic without sacrifice. There is no growth without change. There is no gain without price."

Jerzy thought at first that Giordan was explaining it to him, but the words had a rhythmic feel to them that came only from constant repetition, and even as he realized that, he felt the pressure in the room increase, pushing against his chest and filling his mouth and nose. This was a magic unlike any he had learned from Malech; neither greater nor less, merely unlike. The pressure built, and held, until he thought his chest might break and his heart stop, then the spilled blood steamed in the cool air, and then evaporated, leaving the channel dry and unstained.

"Only so much blood, no more," Giordan said, wrapping a cloth pad over the cut and raising his arm in the air to stop the flow. "Only enough to share your conviction, to renew the bond."

"The blood . . . it's in the wine? You have to do that for every cask?" Jerzy tried not to be horrified, but the thought of Giordan' arms after an entire bottling made him shudder.

The Vineart laughed. "Ai, no, no. Not all my mustus becomes spell-wine—only the very best, the most potent. These wines are rare not because I do not make enough but because there is not so much that can be made. And, as you rightly said earlier, delicate, yes. Very delicate and subtle. And so this medi, this half cask, we will bring to the vats and add a little in, each to each, so the purification is shared among it all. Only a little bit, a little bit and it is done. Subtle and simple, when you are working weathervine and weatherwine. Subtle and simple, or as you learn, a big rain comes down on your head!"

Jerzy had a flash of comprehension, the touch of the vines and the scent of the blood mingling into something he could grab at: he had not failed to bring the rain because he could not work the vinespell, but rather because it had responded *too well*. But why? What had he done, to pull so much power out of a basic decantation? The thought faded back into faint smoke, and was gone, even as Giordan sluiced water across the stone, washing away the last traces of blood.

* * *

THEY CAME OUT of the room to find that the cup and pot of potion had been removed, and the sun's rays now slanted across the single window in Giordan's workroom, rather than streaming in. More time had passed than Jerzy had realized, in that small room. Giordan sent Jerzy off for the rest of the afternoon, claiming that both he and the half cask needed to rest before they moved on to the next and final step.

Feeling better—and suddenly hungry—Jerzy decided to stop by the main kitchen, and see if a pitiful expression could get him a few slices of meat he could take with him into the city.

The palazzo's kitchen was three times the size of the kitchen back home, with a great stone fireplace at one end and an iron stove at the other, both in use. Jerzy had become accustomed to the noise and bustle, and avoided both ends of the room—tempers were always inflamed by the heat there—and instead edged toward the huge table in the middle, where three women were busy cutting piles of white vegetables into smaller chunks of vegetable with frightening efficiency.

The first woman looked up without missing a chop of the cleaver. Her eyes were startlingly blue, so like Malech's that Jerzy had a sudden and unexpected burst of homesickness. "You. What do you want?"

"Something to eat," he ventured, trying his best to look helpless and hungry.

"Hmmmph." The second woman looked up as well, her eyes narrowing in a dark brown face as she surveyed Jerzy. "Doesn't look like a starveling."

"Magician's boy," the third said without even looking up. Her slender hands gathered a handful of chopped vegetables and scraped them off the table into a bowl at her feet, and the bowl was taken away by a kitchen child. "They didn't take a meal this morning. Young men shouldn't miss meals. Give him something before he falls over and dies on our floor."

All three went back to work, dismissing Jerzy entirely. He stood there feeling stupid, when he felt something being pushed into his hand. Looking down, the kitchen child smiled up at him and then scampered off under the table to whatever chore it was supposed to be doing. The "something" turned out to be a large oddly shaped fruit the size of his palm, stuffed with cheese. Deciding that was the best he would get, Jerzy ducked his head in thanks to the three women, and retreated out of the overheated chaos.

Looking for a place to sit and eat his meal, Jerzy headed for the nearest courtyard. There were three within the palazzo itself, two large ones inside each wing, and this smaller one behind the main hall. The shape was the same, however: a square of garden and grasses, surrounded on all sides by covered pathway. On each side there was a small alcove, about shoulder high, with a bench set inside for gossip or—conveniently—eating a quick meal. One of the alcoves was empty, and Jerzy claimed it, sitting with his back against the side wall so that he could look out and see the deep blue sky overhead. The dark-fleshed fruit was surprisingly delicious, sweet and meaty, while the cheese added a sharpness that reminded Jerzy of ale. The thought wasn't entirely pleasant, but he was hungry, so he ate the entire thing, letting his mind rest on what he had learned that morning, not trying to consider any one aspect, but instead letting it seep into him like water into soil.

As he wiped the crumbs off his hands, he realized that someone—two someones—were walking through the garden, their voices coming closer, on the other side of the alcove.

"An entire land, gone? Hah! I would pay half my worth to be able to disappear thus. Leave it all behind, these voices constantly muttering in my ear . . ."

"My lord-maiar, you must not be fanciful. These are dangerous times, dangerous days, and you must be alert to danger, within and without."

"Trade-lands, and the actions thereof, are my concern, not yours, Washer."

"Indeed, my lord-maiar. And yet such an action speaks of magics, and perhaps not well-used or well-disposed ones, and that is very much our concern. It is why I have come here, to warn you, to be alert—"

"Alert, alert. Bah. I am forever alert for these dangers you warn me of.

What are they, my lord Washer? Where are these dangers you whisper so sweetly of, this stranger and that trusted friend and ally . . . would you have me advised by none but yourself? I think not."

The two kept walking, passing beyond the alcove. Jerzy, frozen between the desire to hear more, and fear of being caught, hesitated just an instant, then moved off the bench as quietly as he could, planning to keep low, below the half wall, and follow the conversation.

That was until he left the alcove itself, and came nose to nose with an equally surprised Mahault.

The maiar's daughter stared at him, her brown eyes wide. Before he could make a sound, her hand came up and clamped over his mouth, and she was dragging him back into the alcove.

"What did you hear?" she demanded.

"N-nothing. Nothing, really. The maiar, your father, he was speaking with someone. I did not—"

Her face twisted, the calm expression finally falling away. "You were trying to follow them. Why?"

Jerzy shook his head, not having to play dumb. In the face of her anger and fear, he couldn't think of a thing to say.

"Something is happening," she said insistently, leaning in close enough that he could smell a pleasant, woody flavor to her breath. "Something from the outside, threatening the city, threatening us. My father won't tell me what it is. He tells me not to worry, then he yells at me, calls me foolish, and sends me away. But I'm not foolish, and I won't sit here while something bad comes! It's bad, isn't it? You're from outside, you know! Tell me!"

"My lady, I—" He faltered at the tears forming in her eyes, and shook his head, falling back on the brutal truth. "I know nothing I can tell you."

She released him, leaning back in dismay, and he fled, not caring if anyone saw him or wondered at his haste.

ALONE IN HIS room, his hands still shaking, Jerzy unwrapped the mirror and placed it on the table in front of him. The reflective surface showed him nothing but his own face, dark red hair pulled back with a cord, darker eyebrows straight lines over his eyes, nose peeling from too long in the warmer Aleppan sun, and mouth a discontented frown.

All he had to do was spit onto the surface and press his mark to that, and the spell would be cast that connected this mirror to Master Malech's in his study.

Jerzy hadn't thought before of what might happen if Malech was not there when he cast the spell. Perhaps Guardian would know and report his message?

"And none of that matters, since you haven't found out a thing to report to Master Malech yet, have you?"

Had he?

Jerzy stared at the mirror and thought about what he *had* learned.

Ships had disappeared. Even he knew that was not unusual, when storms came up or pirates attacked, but enough had gone missing that the Carters' Guild was concerned. Commerce was down, building unease and tension among the citizens, and raising doubts about the maiar's competence.

The maiar, when he should have been acting strongly, was instead acting strangely: not responding to the complaints of his citizens, ignoring a trader delegation he had requested to see, having members of the council forcibly removed from his presence, leaving the entire Household on edge and his own daughter sensing a threat. At least one guildsman implied that the maiar was being influenced by an outside source—and was warned by his fellows to keep his suspicion to himself.

And now this most recent revelation, a Washer warning the maiar of dangers "inside and outside"—the same Washer who was asking so many questions about Jerzy himself.

Jerzy had hoped that the Vineart might be helpful, but Giordan seemed oblivious to all of these things . . . or was doing his best not to notice. Because he feared for his vineyards—or because he was involved?

Jerzy did not want to follow that thought, but could not dismiss it, entirely. The Washer was following the scent of misused magic, but he had not mentioned the Vineart specifically. They had been speaking of a place that had disappeared. . . . Master Malech had said something . . . no, it had been Ranulf's messenger, speaking of the island that had disappeared somehow.

Jerzy let out a huff of air, annoyed at himself for not having anything more specific. Discontent and rumor could be placed at the feet of a dozen causes. The maiar might have innocent reasons for his words and actions, or might indeed be mad, but from some innocent cause. Giordan could be exactly as he seemed, a Vineart placing his vines before politics, as was commanded. Mahault could be trying to use him in a family argument, or to further her own plans. There was no way around the fact that he did not have enough information.

Malech had been too long inside his own House, protected by the Command. The world was too complicated for one person to understand. And yet, *tell no one* had been his master's command. *Tell no one.*

Jerzy chewed on his upper lip, torn between the two orders—discover, and keep secret—until the tender flesh cracked and bled into his mouth. Mahault's words, her expression, haunted him. He needed someone with more sense of what was normal for a city this busy, a court this complicated, someone who knew the outside world as well. He needed someone like, oh, a trader, who had contacts everywhere, could ask anything.

He had no choice but to take Ao up on his offer.

Jerzy thought it would be simple to find the trader—it seemed as though every time he turned around, Ao was there, lurking nearby. Now that he needed him, though, Ao seemed to have disappeared. Jerzy was annoyed that he had never thought to ask Ao where in the palazzo he was housed; it would not do to go poking around the private quarters, yelling Ao's name. And yet, how else was he to find him?

He supposed if he waited until the evening meal, he could find Ao then . . . assuming he wasn't off in town, carousing in another tavern.

Grumpy and yet vaguely intrigued by the thought, Jerzy went back to his room to put on sturdier shoes and to throw his few coins into his pouch. Ao had paid the night before, but he couldn't expect . . .

Jerzy paused, realizing that he had no idea how much a tankard of ale cost. At home, Detta handled all the expenses, and here . . . it had never been an issue, with the maiar's House servants supplying whatever they needed.

"Giordan is right," he said to himself in disgust. "We are sheltered."

That thought in mind, walking off the palazzo's grounds into the city streets was a different experience. What had been bright and different and exciting days before now had a more ominous overtone, and Jerzy couldn't quite shake the idea that people were looking at him. Not to mock, as he had first feared, with his unstylish clothing and odd accent, but to scorn—or plot against him and his ignorance. Using the smaller side gate, with the trickle of servants and tradesmen, Jerzy hung back a moment, trying to gather his thoughts and his courage.

"Vineart!"

Jerzy jerked his shoulders, his body's instinct to respond warring with his brain's instinct to flee, but managed to change it halfway into a semigraceful greeting.

"Guardsman." It was the same guard who had hauled him and Ao out of the galley. His face today was not scowling, but Jerzy was cautious.

"You are looking for your trouble-companion? He and his folk were in the antechamber again this morning, but the lord-maiar was called away by one of his aides and did not see them, and their leader, he was not happy. They left this way at the start of my watch, and have not come back as yet."

Jerzy bit back a sigh. Maybe he would have to go wandering, and just hope that Ao found him again.

"You might try the Cockerel's Egg," the guard suggested. "The owner was a tradesman himself, and many trader folk go there for news and such. You know how to get there?"

Jerzy grinned a little sheepishly, aware that his reputation for being able to lose himself in a single room would outlast his actual stay there. "You will draw me a map?"

A few minutes later Jerzy found himself walking down an unfamiliar street in the wake of an off-duty servant the guard had roped into service. The boy, perhaps two or three years younger than Jerzy, moved with complete assurance through the crowds, often looking back to make sure that his charge was still with him. If asked, there was no way Jerzy could have said how they got there, or how to find his way back.

"Here you are," the boy said, gesturing down the street, which ended with a low, windowless building blocking the way. The red-painted door was open, and a large, scruffy gray cat sat in front, washing itself rudely.

The cat looked up as Jerzy approached, as though judging his worth to enter, then went back to its grooming.

Thus dismissed, Jerzy entered the Cockerel.

Inside, rather than the noisy, low-ceilinged room he had expected, Jerzy was confronted by a space that would have fit in well at home. The walls were whitewashed and the ceilings high enough, despite its being only one level, that the space felt larger than it was. There was no bar, but an open doorway in the back where, even as he watched, a woman came out bearing a tray of covered plates and several mugs. There were tables, but they were lower than expected, and placed at angles to the groupings of chairs and benches where men and the occasional woman were gathered, all talking intently over their mugs and plates.

This, he realized, was less a place of drinking than one of business. What right did he have to be here? He was no trader. . . .

It was as though Malech were standing next to him, the mental slap was so real. Or maybe it was the memory of Guardian's voice: *You are Vineart.*

Only slightly more resolved, he looked around again, but did not see Ao. "Excuse me," he said to the serving woman as she passed by, her tray now empty. "I am looking for the Eastern Wind traders?"

The woman gave him a once-over remarkably similar to that of the cat's, and pointed with her chin to the back of the room.

"Thank you," he said, but it was to her backside, as she headed for the kitchen.

Approaching the indicated group, Jerzy finally saw Ao perched on a bench, for once staying very still and quiet as two older men and a woman argued vehemently about something in a tongue that managed to be both guttural and flowing at the same time, like water over sharp rocks. The woman and the older man both had similar features, with rounded faces and broad noses, and were dressed like Ao in soberly formal attire that made sense if they had meant to meet with the maiar today. The third man, however, had much darker skin, wore a sleeveless leather jerkin trimmed with white fur, and his long black mustache was braided, giving him a wildly exotic look. He was the one doing most of the talking, while the others seemed to be disagreeing with him.

Uncertain again, Jerzy paused, and at that moment the woman looked up. She was old, with white hair and deep wrinkles around her eyes and mouth, but Jerzy got a sense of strength and determination from her. Mahault, he thought suddenly, would get old like this woman.

The trader woman paused long enough to tap Ao with her elbow, and direct him toward Jerzy's direction, saying something to him in an undertone. Ao looked up, then looked back to the woman, replying in an equally low tone. The man—the delegation's leader, Jerzy recalled—said something over the both of them, and the woman shook her head, tapping Ao again, more firmly this time. Ao's expression did not change, but he was clearly hoping that the woman would prevail.

Finally, the man made a gesture with his left hand, and Ao shot up out of his seat and came forward to join Jerzy.

"Out, quickly, before he changes his mind and makes me sit through more useless complaining about things that can't be changed!"

Once out in the street, Jerzy looked at his friend suspiciously. The trader was bright-eyed, without any hint of the shadows or puffiness Jerzy had seen on his own face that morning.

"What?" Ao touched his wide, scarred nose as though expecting to find something stuck to it.

"You told me you don't drink," Jerzy said suddenly. "Your people, you said they had no use for drink. But you had ale with me, and in there. . . ." He wasn't quite able to accuse his friend of lying to him, but the suspicion came through in his voice.

"Oh, that was truth, true enough; my people have no truck with your Vineart's ways. An occasional ale, though, now that is needful to business discussions. It soothes the throat and loosens the tongue and makes the work seem ever so much more social. For the other person, that is." Ao hooked his arm in Jerzy's companionably and started walking down the street, still talking. Bemused, Jerzy followed along without protest.

"The first thing you learn," Ao said, without apology, "is when to drink . . . and when to let half of your mug find its way elsewhere. The tavern we were in last night, did you notice the floor?"

Jerzy tried to remember, then shook his head.

"Softwood. Very popular in places like that; it soaks up liquids, so there's less cleanup to do when they close. I only drank half my first tankard and dumped most of the rest when you weren't looking." Ao chuckled, clearly proud of himself. "I wanted to see what you might say when you were foam-faced."

"You . . . I . . ." Jerzy stopped dead in the street, forcing Ao to stop as well. "You—"

"And you said not a word, not sober or drunk. I say again, I could make a trader out of you."

It was so clearly meant as a compliment, Jerzy couldn't find a comeback this time.

"But you did not come down here to learn my secrets," Ao said. "So, what is it?"

"I did, actually. Or, not to learn your secrets. But to learn my own." Jerzy stopped, aware how jumbled that sounded. "I need your help."

Ao looked at Jerzy, all joking gone, and in that moment the few years' difference in their ages seemed closer to a decade. "We need to talk. No, not here. Somewhere you are comfortable."

* * *

THAT "SOMEWHERE" WAS the stone fence enclosing Giordan's vineyard. The flesh of the fruit was starting to swell with juice, and Jerzy felt a pull inside to be home, watching their own vines. He shivered, and Ao mistook it for cold.

"Are you sure you don't want to go inside somewhere?"

"No. Here is better." The sun had warmed the stones, and the breeze was fresh coming off the hills. Looking at the vines, even if they weren't his, gave him the courage he needed to speak.

"You asked me before, what I was here for. I told you the truth, I'm here to learn from Vineart Giordan. My master sent me for that purpose."

He paused, looking out into the vines. "That purpose . . . and another." It was harder to say the words than he had thought, enough to make him wonder if Master Malech had incanted him somehow, to prevent the secret from being shared. But no, there were no spells that could do that against a person's will.

Or so Malech claimed. Might he have lied about that?

Jerzy forced the doubts away. "Over the past year, my master has been hearing rumors, stories. A Vineart disappeared, mysteriously. Protection spells faltered, vattings failed without cause . . . our own vineyard was attacked by an infestation out of season—something that could not happen on its own."

Ao looked interested, but not concerned. "All those things, could they just be coincidence, a run of bad luck, or a decantation somehow gone awry?"

"They could. My master says that most of those he heard from assumed they were, each individual thing happening only to them. But then . . . Ao, in your travels, have you heard of sea serpents?"

"There is no such thing as sea—" Ao stopped. "Are there?"

"I've seen one."

That stopped Ao cold for a second.

"Sea serpents. Creatures of magic. They are attacking coastal towns, two at least, but there are likely more, unreported."

He waited for Ao to make the connection.

"Merchant ships? The cargos that are delayed . . . You think . . ."

Jerzy made a helpless gesture. "My master fears that this is all part of a single attack, that someone is using magic to attack."

"Against Vinearts? Another Vineart? But why? I mean . . ." Ao frowned, working it out aloud. "Princes go to war for power, or land, or sometimes just because the other insulted them. Vinearts . . . why would a Vineart war on another? For his vines? I thought that they were handed down, that they stayed within your . . . family lines, or whatever you call it?"

"If a Vineart has secondary yards, he usually deeds them to his student," Jerzy agreed. "There are only so many places the vines grow, and attempts to move them . . . rarely succeed." Jerzy stopped, unwilling to say more. Malech had taught him that *vin magica* required three elements: vines, soil, and weather. If one was missing, there was no mustus, and if there was no mustus, there was no *vin magica*, and no spellwine. That wasn't a secret, exactly. But something kept his tongue still. Bad enough, that he had shared as much as he had with an outsider.

"So if there is some threat—why are you here? Why aren't you defending your master's lands like a good student? Except, against what?" Ao answered his own question. "You don't know who is behind it or why, you have no proof, so anything you do will be seen as an act of aggression, of power gathering . . . exactly what you're forbidden to do. And if the princes see that . . . they could use it as reason to break the Commands as well. Steal your vines, use violence . . . take magic for their own."

Ao let out a low whistle and stared out into the vineyard, too. "Sin Washer, there's a problem and no mistake. And your master sent you here"—he answered his own question again—"because Aleppan is a trade city. There's no gossip that's not repeated here, at some point. That's why you've been trying to listen in—and why you came to me. Because my people travel widely, hear more than you ever could."

Ao's voice had gone flat, and for a moment Jerzy was afraid that his friend was angry, or felt used. "I . . . I am sorry. I didn't know . . . I didn't mean to—"

"Blessed Joran's wheels," Ao said, and Jerzy realized the trader was laughing. "Jerzy, stop apologizing! I'm honored! Now"—he leaned forward, his voice dropping to a conspiratorial tone—"what do you need me to do?"

Chapter 22

Jerzy woke, feeling strangely ill. He lay still, the high bed and oversized chamber as familiar to him now as his bedroom back in The Berengia, and waited for the feeling to subside. The sun was barely slipping through his window, which meant that there was still plenty of time before he needed to join Giordan for their morning meal.

The journal the Vineart had given him lay on the table by his bed, and Jerzy reached over to touch the pebbled leather cover. He had fallen asleep the night before studying sketches of different vine leaves, comparing the subtle differences in shape and color, and his dreams had been filled with the stink of serpent flesh and the crackling of fire, until the stink had been banished by a hot, dry wind. The combination of fire and wind were terrible omens; merely remembering the dream made his stomach hurt worse.

He forced himself to think of something more comforting. Ao had agreed to help. Simply having someone to talk with had eased a great deal of Jerzy's unease. Having a trader scouting for more rumors, more disquiet, could only be useful. And if that trader had no use for magics,

scorned their use of spellwines, then none could say he, Jerzy, was ma-
nipulating power, could they?

Malech would not approve.

"Then I won't tell him," Jerzy said. The words, spoken into the cool
stillness of the room, were shocking, and he flinched a little but did not
take them back.

You are green, still, Malech had said. *Not ready. But I have no choice.*

Neither did Jerzy, not anymore. Not if he was to do what was needed.
And the dream lingered in his memory, making his stomach roil again.

Forcing himself to move, despite the nausea, Jerzy threw back the
covers and looked outside to check the height of the sun. Deciding there
was time, he went down to the washroom. Even without Detta there to
remind him, the weekly bath had become a habit, and more, the deep-
seated tub of hot water was a small luxury he would be sorry to give up.

Later, his hair slicked back and tied at his neck with a leather strap
and his skin freshly scrubbed, Jerzy walked the hallway to the antechamber where he and Giordan took their morning meal. But before
he reached the open archway, he stopped, hearing another voice coming
from within.

The Washer.

Manners told him to hang back and wait: if this were Malech's study,
he would not even think of entering unbidden. Curiosity pushed him
forward. But even as he came to the lintel, the voices stopped, and he
heard the sound of a chair being pushed back against the stone floor.

"Vineart Giordan?" Formality seemed reasonable caution, considering what he had overheard in the courtyard the day before.

"Ah, Jerzy." Giordan was standing, his back to the far wall. Washer
Darian was still seated, looking comfortable as a cat with a rat well
trapped. The door to the workrooms behind Giordan was closed, which
was unusual. Jerzy took all this in with a quick glance, and then cast his
eyes down like a good, obedient servant.

"I believe it is time now for Jerzy to resume his studies, Brother Darian. Perhaps we can continue our discussions another time?"

"Yes." Jerzy could feel Darian's gaze on him, but did not look up. Ao said his face was too honest; he could not risk letting the Washer see anything there, not now that he had something to hide.

"Indeed," Darian said, and for a terrifying second Jerzy thought the man was responding to his own thoughts. But no, he was talking to Giordan. "It appears as though you two have much to go over. You are only here for a little while longer, no? I am sure that you will have much to report back to your master, when you return."

The Washer's voice was calm, almost jovial, but Jerzy could feel the knife hidden inside. He didn't look up, and the Washer didn't force the issue.

When they were alone, Jerzy raised his gaze to see Giordan had moved to the worktable, fussing with the sheets of tasting notes. "I want you to go down to the yard and check for mite damage."

Mites set on the underside of the leaves, chewing them into lacy tatters. They were also a mostly harmless nuisance, not something he should be spending time on, especially not now. Jerzy started to protest, but the words died in his throat. Giordan's body language was different. The careless, almost lazy way the Vineart held himself normally, which said "come in, be welcome, no harm," had been replaced by a coiled anger, drawn in every muscle of his body. A casual observer might not see it. A servant might know something was wrong. A slave knew to get out of the way, now.

A year of freedom was nothing against the instincts of a lifetime in the sleep house. Jerzy left without a word, returning to his room only long enough to change to thicker soled shoes, and, on a whim, add a small skin of water to his belt, hooking it next to the knife Malech had given him, and a pair of thin leather gloves that covered his palm but left his fingers free to work. He looked down at the belt and, despite his concerns, smiled. A Vineart's kit: all he lacked was the hook-handled tasting spoon.

Following that same instinct, he used the side exit through the stable enclosures, rather than going out through one of the public doors. It took slightly longer to walk to the vineyard that way, but fewer people used it and, unlike the doors to the cellar, it was not identified with Vinearts. Right now, that suited him.

A young mule colt decided to follow him along the length of the fence. Its dam watched calmly, unconcerned even when Jerzy pushed the colt's head away, when it tried to chomp on the gloves. It was a cute beast, though, and Jerzy paused to scratch behind one of its floppy, furry ears, inhaling the fresh, healthy smell of animal, straw, and sweat. Some of the tension that coiled in his stomach, the remains of the morning's ill-feeling worsened by seeing the Washer, and by Giordan's obvious dismissal of him, eased slightly at the animal's uncomplicated pleasure.

"It's not a bad life," he told the mule. "Stand in the sun, eat your grass, pull the wagon when they hitch it to you, let them worry about what's in the cart or where it needs to go."

The colt reached over the fence and nipped again at the gloves with its large, flat teeth, clearly agreeing with Jerzy's assessment. He could, he supposed, simply not go, instead walk into the city proper. . . . But the idea of rebellion came and went quickly. Giordan had told him to do something. He would do it.

Walking with the air of someone with an unpleasant but necessary task ahead of him, Jerzy saw only the occasional traveler on the road, exchanging passing nods as they each went their way. His mind kept replaying the scene in Giordan's rooms, and the Washer's overheard words the day before, about dangers within as well as without. By the time he hopped over the low fence and felt his feet touch the dirt, his mood had not improved—but he did have a second, more important reason for checking on the vines.

A quick survey of a double-handful of random plants turned up only an occasional mite-bitten leaf, certainly not enough to warrant the labor of washing down each row. His obligation taken care of, Jerzy picked a spot deep within the rows of green-leafed vines, and knelt down, letting the leaves of the vines rest on the bare skin of his arms and shoulders. The air was still morning-chill, but that wasn't why he shivered. Again, there was the touch of the vines against his awareness, faint enough to dismiss as his imagination if he hadn't been waiting for it.

Something had happened between the Washer and Giordan. Something that made Giordan not want to teach him—perhaps not want to spend time with him, want to get him out of the way with a useless chore. Why? The Washer was chasing after something . . . and if Giordan knew something, or had heard something, or was somehow, some way, involved . . .

Ao had promised to dig out what he could in the maiar's court itself, but if Giordan was somehow tied into it now, there was one thing only he, Jerzy, could do.

The soil pressed against the knees of his trou, his fingers digging down into the soil, feeling the texture between his fingers, the weight and heft of it against his skin. His fingertips encountered the gnarled roots, sliding up along the nearest stem, feeling the rough skin of the vine, the pulsing beat of life within the hard flesh matching his own life-pulse.

This was not his vineyard. These were not his wines. But Giordan had brought him in, allowed him to take part in the crafting, and the vines recognized the touch of their own within him.

Lifting one hand, he spat into his palm the way he had seen Malech do. The spittle glistened against his skin, mixing with the dirt to make a muddy smudge. The worm of doubt wriggled in again. He was too young to have enough quiet-magic yet, too green to be able to do what he was doing.

Green. Untried. Unready. His failure with the weatherwine haunted him. The fear of failure snarling at his back, hot breath on his neck.

"I did not fail. I will not fail. Master Malech sent me. Master Malech trusted me to do what needed to be done."

There was no reason to doubt that. No reason to doubt his master at all.

Reaching with the muddy hand, he lifted the leaves until he found what he was looking for: a small cluster of early-budding grapes, still small, but filled with juice and starting to show faint red streaks along their skin. Plucking one bulb from the bunch, he let it rest against his skin, then closed his fist around it, squeezing hard until the skin split and the wet pulp mixed with the spittle.

Opening his palm, he didn't let himself hesitate, but licked his palm clean, taking back his spittle and the harsh bitter flesh of the grape.

Weathervine. Not the vines of his master. These had not accepted him, had placed no mark upon his skin, and yet . . . Giordan had allowed him to participate in vinification; he had let their juice sit on his tongue, felt the change as vinification forced the magic from potential into truth.

"Let me in," he asked the vines, not even aware that he was speaking. "Let me know . . ."

His fist clenched, even as his arm spasmed and he fell forward, hitting his head against the vine, knocking it askew. Every handspan of his body felt like a thousand grubs were wriggling against it, digging into the meat, stinging and biting in a way that was sharp but not actually painful.

Holding the sensations with half of his awareness, Jerzy reached for his memories of the sea serpent, the smell and feel of it moving through the water, the stink of the chunks of flesh, the tingle of magic as Malech tested the remains.

Master Malech had not recognized the magic that created the sea serpent. The magewine had not recognized the legacy it came from. And yet Giordan himself spoke of how unique this soil was, how subtle and powerful . . . and how little others knew of how it was crafted.

And something was wrong here in Aleppan. Something that brought the Washers here, curious enough to make Giordan angry. Was it only the Brotherhood questioning Giordan's actions in taking in the student of another? But Giordan had knocked down those questions before, without hesitation. Something new had occurred. It might not have anything to do with the conversation Jerzy had overheard between the maiar and the Washer in the courtyard. . . .

But it might.

And that connection might lead back to the attacks elsewhere, the things Master Malech worried about. Might. Maybe. No proof, no certainty. But something—some tingle in his blood that whispered for trust—told him it was so.

Only magic spoke like that. If it was Giordan's magic, if his host was involved, then Jerzy had to know.

He concentrated, letting the feel of the magic settle into his awareness. Soil, weather, vine, Vineart. Four elements of magic, each recognizable in the final issue. Here, in the rawest, purest sense, without vinification redirecting it, Jerzy could find not the slightest echo of the fire-root infestation, or the more overt "stink" of the sea serpent's flesh. No decay or death, only the clean aroma of rain and wind.

These vines—he would risk enough to say weathervines anywhere—could not have been at the root of the magic they had encountered so far.

The relief he felt was not a surprise—he had not wanted to think that Giordan could be involved. Underneath that, though, there was a niggle of dissatisfaction and disappointment. If there had been a connection, he would have been the one to find it, the one to solve the mystery, the one to hand the solution to Master Malech. He would have been . . .

Jerzy's imagination failed him at that point, and the rush of the magic began to drain from him, leaving his limbs heavy and aching. He tried to sit up, feeling a wave of dizziness hit him worse even than being shipboard, a disorientation that was not helped by a hard hand closing around his arm and roughly yanking him back onto his feet.

"What have you done!" Brother Darian cried, pulling him away from the vines by force, his voice pitched not for Jerzy's ears, but those of the others standing on the other side of the fence, unwilling to step over that border into a Vineart's lands. Jerzy was able to focus enough to see that the Washer was wearing formal robes, and that his eyes had a wide, almost maniacal gleam to them.

Sar Anton, standing just on the other side of the fence, reached over and grabbed Jerzy from the Washer, hauling him forcibly onto the road. "Witness!" he cried, shaking Jerzy until he thought his eyes might be jolted from his head, and the words spoken over his head became a jumble of noise. "Sin Washer bear witness, this boy has used magic not given unto him, has usurped another Vineart's rights, and broken Commandment!"

THEY MADE A strange parade back to the palazzo, Sar Anton and another man on horseback, Brother Darian and a third man driving a small cart, with Jerzy behind them, his hands and feet bound with rope they pulled from the cart. People stopped and stared at the grim-faced men, but otherwise fell back and gave them room. Jerzy stared out at the passing scenery, the rush of magic having given way to a coldness deep in his bones, and all he could think was how disappointed Malech would be in him.

They pulled him from the cart, loosening the ties at his legs enough so that he could walk, and moved him up the stairs he had arrived at a month before in such different circumstances. The maiar met them at the front entrance, flanked by two guardsmen and an aide, and Jerzy had the sudden feeling that none of this was by chance.

"What are you doing? What is going on? What? What?" Giordan raced up to them, out of breath and clearly agitated. Whatever was happening, he had not been informed ahead of time. The earlier unease and discomfort had been replaced by confusion and anger as the Vineart reached for Jerzy, only to have Sar Anton push him away.

"Enough, Anton!" the maiar barked, and the nobleman glowered, but stepped back obediently.

"I warned you, Vineart," Darian said, his hand like an iron band around Jerzy's forearm. "I warned you to stay within the Commands, and not let your pride blind you to the dangers you invoke. Now is no time for your rebellious studies. And here is the result—your ill-advised student, taking powers that were not given unto him, using magics he has not earned!"

Giordan blanched, his normally lively expression going still.

"I did not!" Jerzy protested, stung by the accusation into forgetting his precarious situation, and Darian knocked him across the chin hard enough to make his jaw snap. To someone not used to such blows, it would have been a felling stroke. Jerzy staggered under it, but stayed upright, ignoring the pain stinging his face. A sideways glance at Giordan's face, catching the slight shake of his head, and he subsided. Master Giordan would take care of this.

"Brother Darian, enough." The maiar's voice was stern, almost angry. "The boy has transgressed, I agree with you. But there is no need for unseemly violence. Put the boy somewhere secure, so we can hear your accusation, and judge its merit."

"You have no authority over this," Darian retorted, but he allowed a guardsman to take Jerzy from him. The ropes around his legs were untied, but his hands remained bound behind him, and the guardsman's grip, although looser than Darian's, was still enough to keep Jerzy still. "The punishment for breaking a Commandment cannot be argued; it is all that has kept our world safe for generations. He is apostasia."

Jerzy almost fell to his knees, even as he heard a woman's gasp of shock. The punishment for apostasy, for a Vineart turning from Sin Washer's Command, was no mere beating, but death.

The maiar was taken aback as well. "That is a serious claim, Washer Darian, a very serious claim."

"And it is a Washer's solemn obligation to find such things, and root them out, before irreparable damage is done," Darian said. "I will insist—"

"Insist?" The maiar's voice dropped, becoming dangerously soft. "You are not the master here, not of them nor of me, and while you are indeed the guardians of our virtue, you do not have sole authority to pronounce guilt. Unless I missed a pronouncement come down from the heavens?"

"No." The "my lord-maiar" that was added after a guardsman stepped forward was only grudgingly said, through gritted teeth. Jerzy could not keep track of what else was happening, too dizzy with his own dilemma, wondering what was to happen to him next.

The maiar turned to look at Jerzy, then reached out and unhooked the leather belt, handing it to Giordan, whose hand trembled as he accepted it.

"Take the boy to his room, and keep him there. Vineart, Washer, come with me."

Jerzy was led off in the other direction, two more guardsmen falling in behind them. Servants pressed to the walls to let them go by, and looked down at the floor, as though a touch of sleeve or glance of eye might implicate them in whatever trouble Jerzy had found.

They came to his room, and one of the guardsmen went inside first, to check around, while the others waited in the hallway. He came out with a pitcher of water in one hand, and a wineskin in the other.

"Just these; the rest of the room's clear. If he's hiding magic, it's smaller than a thimble."

Jerzy was led into his room, his arms untied and the rope tossed onto the table. One of the other guards produced a thick leather cuff with a heavy chain attached to it. The cuff was buckled around Jerzy's leg, and the chain attached to a post of the bed frame.

"Sit and wait, and this will all be dealt with." The first guard was a heavyset man with the patient look of a man who had seen and done everything, twice. "Don't cause trouble and the maiar will sort this out in time for dinner."

The door closed behind them, and Jerzy was up off the bed, testing to see how far the chain would allow him to move. He could reach the wardrobe, and the desk, but not the door or the window, and every move he took resulted in the clanking of the metal against the cool stone floor.

The dizziness had faded, as though being chained down literally steadied him. The Washer had not appeared in the vineyard—with witnesses, and a cart!—by chance. Jerzy had, perhaps—no, probably, he admitted to himself—overstepped the boundaries placed on them by strict interpretation of the Commandments, but there was no way that the Washer could have known that, simply by watching.

Unfortunately, Jerzy had no way of proving he was innocent, either, even if anyone were willing to listen. Worse, he was not the only one at risk: Giordan might be held responsible for his actions, and Master Malech as well.

He had to warn Malech.

Wrapping the chain around his hand once, he lifted it enough so that he could move without too obvious a clanking noise, and stepped carefully to the wardrobe. With one hand, he opened the door and shuffled through his folded clothes until his fingers touched something hard.

The mirror.

He retrieved it, and stepped just as carefully to the table. Only then did he let the excess of chain rest at his feet, and used both hands to unwrap the mirror.

Placed flat on the desk, the silvered surface reflected the ceiling, a textured white plaster. The temptation to look into it was easily put down: Jerzy suspected that his face would not fill him with confidence.

Without the water pitcher or his winesack, Jerzy had to work to gather enough spit to make a decent puddle in his palm, and when he did, there was a pink tinge to it that told him that Darian's blow had done more than bruise the outside of his face.

"Well, Malech did say they once called it blood-magic," he said, trying for humor. The words sounded flat, spoken out loud, and he didn't feel amused at all. Still, the words of the decantation came to him letter perfect.

"Respond to my will. Carry my words to the maker-glass. Go."

As he chanted, Jerzy placed his wet palm down against the glass, and pressed hard.

"Stop him! Guard! He works magic!"

The voice sounded inside the room itself, and Jerzy looked up just in time to be knocked over by a body crashing through the courtyard window.

The boy—hazily, Jerzy recognized him as one of the servants whom he'd passed countless times in the hallway, one of the pages attached to the Aleppan Council—grappled for the mirror, trying to snatch it out of Jerzy's hold, even as the two slammed onto the floor, elbows and knees swinging for maximum impact. "No, don't," Jerzy cried, and their hands both clutched the mirror, battling for possession. The servant was small but tough and wiry, and Jerzy struggled to remember Cai's lessons for defeating a smaller opponent.

The door slammed open, and Jerzy heard bodies rushing in, the heavy steps and cold snick of drawn metal identifying the guardsmen who had been placed outside. Panicked, Jerzy stopped trying to regain possession of the mirror, and instead brought his hand down hard, dragging his assailant's arm with him, and smashing the mirror against the stone floor. All he could think was that Malech's mirror was broken and the spell on it destroyed. Nobody could tell now, for certain or sure, what it had been.

A shred caught in his hand and he winced, the thin cut seeping blood almost immediately.

"He works mage-magic!" The servant was wild-eyed and gesturing madly, his face twisted in frustration. "I will show you! I will prove it!" He dove for one of the larger shreds of mirror, grabbing it as though to wave it as proof—or shove it between Jerzy's unprotected ribs.

And then Sar Anton was there, standing between Jerzy and the servant. The nobleman's left arm rose, came down, and then pulled back, the blade sliding from the body with a thick, wet-sounding *thwick*.

Jerzy stared at the blade, its length now coated in red grue. He had seen men—even children—die before. He had seen them killed in the heat of passion and the cold deliberation of judgment. But he had never seen death come for him, and land instead on another.

His head stung where the dead boy had hit him, and his ribs ached from the fall to the hard floor, and the echo of the boy's last shout fading in his ears.

Mage-magic.

He could only have meant mage-blood, the quiet-magic. The ability no one other than another Vineart should know about, recognized by an outsider, shouted about to outsiders. Jerzy felt as though one of the boy's kicks had landed in his chest, depriving him of air. How? How could he have known?

His worries were disrupted by an angry shout. "You killed him! He was a witness!" The lead guard was outraged, kicking the servant's body with a booted toe in his frustration.

Sar Anton fixed him with a disdainful glare. "The boy was mad. Do you see any spellwine, any vials or cups? Did you not see the maiar take his tool belt from him?"

"But he cried out—"

"Phah." Sar Anton's voice was filled with scorn. "He cried gibberish. A servant? Who knows what a servant might be thinking. Perhaps they fought over a sweetheart, or squabbled over this frippery, and he thought to use the boy's disgrace to his own ends." Saying that, Sar Anton's heel came down on the remaining shard, cracking it into glittering dust.

When Jerzy made an involuntary noise of protest at the destruction, Sar Anton hauled him upright, yanking him farther away from the collapsed pile of bloody meat on the floor. His other hand still held the blade, and Jerzy tried not to flinch away from it. "Say nothing, boy," Sar Anton hissed at him, his head bent low to Jerzy's bleeding ear, quiet enough that none of the others could hear him. "Say nothing and you may yet live through this day."

Chapter 23

There was a flurry of activity in the hallway even as the guards were dragging the body of the servant away, and Giordan appeared, with Ao breathless and sweating in his wake. They shoved their way into the room, where Giordan focused his attention not on Jerzy, but the remaining guardsman who had accompanied Sar Anton.

"What goes on here? Is this our Aleppan justice, or conspiracy?" Giordan asked. "The boy was to be kept safe, not attacked in his own room, under the nose of those who were to be guarding him!"

The guardsman opened his mouth to rebut the charge, then shut his jaw with a snap. The bloody floor and broken window was evidence enough that the accusation was valid.

"You dare make accusations against loyal guardsmen?" Sar Anton shot back, still gripping Jerzy's shoulder with one hand. Only Jerzy noted that the swordsman's hand was shaking, most likely from anger, although his voice remained steady. "This is too much coincidence for my liking, Vineart, this attack on him, in your own wing, under your own doubtless magical protections. Where did that servant come from, to be passing by at such a convenient moment, to accuse a shackled boy of some new crime? No, this reeks of something foul—some other hand casting shit to distract from the true source of the smell." Sar Anton took a breath, and stared intently at Giordan.

"This boy is guilty, but even were he the prodigy you claim, he is not versed enough to get into such mischief on his own; more, he cannot be held responsible for such chaos as has come to this city the six months past. I accuse you, Vineart Giordan. I accuse you and his master as well, of being in league against our most noble maiar, of plotting against him, of enspelling his only daughter to spy upon him, and plotting against this House for your own magical gain, against every Command ever given. I accuse you of apostasy."

Jerzy almost collapsed under this additional, unexpected blow. This was madness! But the men surrounding them nodded grimly, accepting every word, even though a landsman, not even a titled one, could not make such an accusation on his own.

"Guardsman, take this man into custody, and bind him for judgment by my lord-maiar and the Washer Darian."

The guardsman moved to take Giordan's arms behind his back, binding them with the same rope that had been around Jerzy's limbs not an hour before. Unlike Jerzy, Giordan resisted, swearing at the man until he took another length of rope and tied it across the Vineart's head, fitting the length into his mouth so that he could not close his lips enough to form coherent words.

"There will be no further decanting within these walls, not until judgment has been passed," Sar Anton said with grim satisfaction. "You, boy. Why are you here?"

"I heard the commotion, and saw Vineart Giordan running," Ao said, giving his best innocent expression. "You know, Sar Anton, that young Jerzy is an acquaintance of mine. I was worried for him, in light of rumors floating throughout court this afternoon. He is not the best bargain in the bunch, but an honest one—I will attest to that in front of the silent gods themselves, if need be."

"Trader boy of the Eastern Wind clan, are you? What's your profit in this?"

"None, Sar Anton. Save if you are correct, then saving the maiar from his enemies may lead my clan to more favorable terms."

Sar Anton sniffed in disgust, but did not bar Ao from accompanying them, even as the guards shuffled Giordan and Jerzy out into the hallway and down to the main hall, down to where the maiar and Washer—and judgment—were waiting.

THE AUDIENCE CHAMBER was not as large as Jerzy had imagined it, sitting in the gallery overhead listening to voices from below. But what it lacked in size it made up for in grandeur. They entered through a door at the side, and walked into a pool of colored light thrown down from the round window overhead. Jerzy was immediately able to sense the firespell illuminating it—it might, in fact, be one of Master Malech's own spellwines, although he could not tell for certain. Day or night, rain or shine, the entrance would be illuminated—and anyone entering the hall would be seen clearly by anyone already present.

That fact filtered away, as Jerzy noticed that there were, in fact, very few people already there. The benches that lined the hall were of a deep red wood that glimmered warmly, bare of the courtiers or messengers he would think normally sat there, waiting their turn. The guards did not give him a chance to gawk, moving him up the gray stone floor, onto a narrow carpet patterned in the brown and blue of the Aleppan Council. A small gathering of adults moved aside, and out of the corner of his eye, past Giordan's frame and the arm of his guard, he saw a tall, white-faced figure.

Mahault. She wore blue again, and her blond hair was pulled back severely, and then she was lost from view as he was pushed forward to stand in front of the maiar's chair.

The maiar looked . . . ordinary. Neither short nor tall, his hair was dark and his beard trimmed to his chin, and the rest of his face set in lines that suggested exhaustion rather than age. He wore a heavy robe of deep brown, and a dark blue mantle over it, both spilling over his shoulders and hiding the chair itself from view. Three men and a woman stood next to him: two of the men were older, unfamiliar. One was Washer Darian. The woman was young, straight and stern, dark skinned and dressed in thick, padded trou over heeled boots, a worn leather surcoat without any design or sigil on it over an equally plain woven shirt.

A solitaire, one of the female soldiers-for-hire. Jerzy had never seen one before, but no other woman would stand so, dressed so. What was she doing here?

"Not one, but two Vinearts, brought for judgment," the maiar said, resting his chin in one hand and staring, not at the prisoners but over their heads, at something at the other end of the hall.

Jerzy fought the urge to turn, to see what so held the maiar's attention.

"This is indeed a serious moment. Serious, yes; a moment I have not, in my life, faced. And yet, here it is.

"Our civilization rests upon three legs: the wisdom of the Collegium, the skills of the Vinearts, and the authority of the Land's Lord. By Sin Washer's actions, no one has power over another, but two in concert may judge a third. You, Vine-student Jerzy, and Vineart Giordan, have been brought forth on the most dire charges of apostasy by Washer Darian. I am here as second, to hear the charges, and the defense.

"These three"—he gestured to the men—"are members of the Aleppan Council, here at my request for witness. Solitaire Gennet will carry out the verdict, if necessary."

Jerzy swallowed, all too aware of what that verdict would be, since it was doubtful anyone would dare speak in their defense.

"Sar Anton. Your charges?"

The killer who had casually killed a boy and whispered cold-blooded warnings was gone. In his place appeared a worried, almost distraught nobleman, his rich clothing merely a cover for deep concern about his fellows. "I was traveling with Washer Darian, discussing matters of history, of which we both have interest, when we saw the boy in the vineyards, unaccompanied by Vineart Giordan. He appeared to be weeding, or some such acceptable task, and at first we assumed him to be on an errand from Vineart Giordan. But then he appeared to go into a trance, and Washer Darian recognized the signs of incantation, the attempt to manipulate another Vineart's holdings, in direct disobedience of the Command."

It was such an obvious lie, Jerzy felt a protest rise in his throat, but the ropes around his hands reminded him that his voice would not be heard. Not here, not against these charges. He had not been incanting, not as Sar Anton charged. He had been guilty, yes—only not of what they claimed, and there was no way he could explain what he had been doing, or why it was necessary. Not without admitting to equally dangerous acts, and making public his mission—exactly what he had been ordered *not* to do. His only hope lay with Vineart Giordan. He could not believe the Vineart had sent that servant to betray him. It made no sense . . . the vines had told him that Giordan had not worked the magic that created the serpent.

"Vineart? Is this true? Has this student attempted to influence your vines? Do you have knowledge of this?"

Giordan went down on both knees, his back straight but his voice pleading. "My lord, I swear to you. I knew nothing of this. I have been prideful, perhaps, and too eager to show off what I knew, but all without malice and no thought at all to break Commandment! Whatever this boy did, he did alone—or at the behest of his master!"

The hollow feeling in Jerzy's stomach surprised him, and then he was surprised at the surprise. Whether or not Giordan was guilty of anything else, the Vineart had been the one to bring Jerzy here, to allow him access to his vines, and that would naturally make him the villain in the Collegium's eyes. That was what Sar Anton had meant—if he let Giordan take the blame, the Collegium might excuse him as the innocent tool of men who should have known better.

Giordan knew that, too.

Jerzy understood saving your own skin. The sleep house taught you the truth: you could depend only upon yourself. He could not blame the Vineart, who had grown in the same hard soil. But he could not allow it, either. A cold, grim determination grew inside the hollowness. Master Malech had sent him, trusted him. He would not allow himself to fail, and certainly not to let this Vineart besmirch his master's reputation.

"I swear to you," Giordan was saying, his words coming hot and swift. "I did not allow the boy to do anything beyond watch, to help in the tasks any slave would do. If he learned anything of my grapes it was through sneaking and—"

"The Vineart is his vineyard; the vineyard makes the Vineart," Jerzy said. His words were a direct quote from Sin Washer's Lessoning of the Mages, a quote he had read during his lessons with Detta a dozen times or more. The words had the same cool hard feel to them in his mouth as the Guardian's thoughts, and he took strength from that. "Within his enclosures, the Vineart is supreme and all-knowing, and none move there save he allow it."

Unlike Giordan, he remained upright. He would kneel before his master, but none other. A Vineart stood apart, and showed no weakness.

"The boy speaks better than the man," the Washer said, with a touch of what Jerzy would have sworn was relief, confirming his suspicion. This was not about him. He was only the bait to lure the fox out—the hook to catch Giordan.

But if Giordan was not guilty, why would Sar Anton, much less the Washer, so badly want the Vineart disgraced and dead? What game was being played here?

"Indeed," the maiar said thoughtfully, leaning forward on his gilded chair. His cloak of state slipped off one shoulder, and an aide stepped forward to fix it for him, as though he were too feeble to do so himself. Jerzy frowned. Had the aide's hand touched the maiar's skin, where neck met shoulder? The gesture was similar to the one he had seen

Master Malech use, had used himself, on the mirror, and yet that aide was no Vineart but servant . . . and there was no spell that could influence a man, save he allowed it. . . .

And there was something . . . familiar in the air. A scent, almost too faint to catch. No, no a scent, a taste . . .

Without thought, a part of him cut itself away from the trial taking place around him, searching the air for that tingle of magic.

"Vineart Giordan," the maiar continued, seemingly not noticing the aide at all, "we have long been in Agreement. I would not think you guilty of anything beyond arrogance, but arrogance was what led to the downfall of the prince-mages of old, and woe to me for overlooking that."

"Lord Ma—"

"Silence!"

Giordan quivered once, and stopped speaking.

"The lands you till are under my domain, yours only under the terms of our Agreement. Your actions have put me at odds with the Collegium, which is breach of that Agreement. For that, I declare the Agreement void and done. The vines you have tended, the spellwines you have crafted, remain yours. But you will remove them from my lands."

Vines uprooted need to be replanted swiftly. Without a ready new home . . . the way Giordan swayed and almost fell, he knew what it meant. Jerzy could not spare a thought for his former teacher, even as the maiar went on to argue with the Washer over the punishment to be meted out to Jerzy himself. That magic, that taint, it was so close; faint but he knew it, and knowing it, he could follow it . . .

His head jerked up and he stared into the face of the aide who had touched the maiar, into his eyes and down a deep dark hole, an endless falling tunnel of swirling reds and blacks, thick with a familiar-yet-unfamiliar stench. Soil. Stone. Pulp and juice . . . but something more. Something darker, more dire. Heavy and weightless, smooth and slick, and the very touch of it even in this no-space made Jerzy's flesh crawl, and his heart sorrow.

The same scent—stench—he had looked for in the vineyard earlier that day. The stench that he had sensed on the shores of that fisher village when the sea beast towered overhead, and then again in the ice-house, while Master Malech tried to identify the remains . . .

"Blood," he gasped, falling to his knees at last while the stench over-took him. "Blood and flesh, ash and bone."

"What did the boy say?"

"Nothing. He is overcome, overwhelmed." Sar Anton, his face close in front of Jerzy, too close; he tried to pull away but the nobleman would not allow it. "Be silent," he said urgently. "Be silent or you will share the Vineart's fate. It is not too late for you, but you must remain silent!"

"Even now he works magic, trying to influence the lord-maiar!" Gior-dan cried, flailing his long arms at Jerzy, despite the guards' hold on him. He was literally frothing at the mouth, like a terrified horse. "He and the trader boy! It was not me, I did nothing wrong, it was him!"

The maiar stood, and Sar Anton swore, pushing Jerzy aside as he turned to deal with the maddened whirlwind that was the Vineart. And then, the whirlwind was literal: an impossible burst of wind knocked over several of the guards, shoving Jerzy onto the ground and rattling his teeth.

Windspells. He felt them, knew them, knew the touch of Giordan in their casting, that it had been done with the quiet-magic of a lifetime, built up and released all at once. Another gust nearly knocked over the men standing by the maiar, even as guards scrambled to position them-selves between their master and the Vineart.

"Do not kill him!" the maiar shouted. "Take him alive!"

A hand grabbed Jerzy by the back of his collar and he struggled, re-sisting, until a vaguely familiar hand covered his, clenching hard enough to get his attention.

Mahault. With surprising strength, she dragged him toward the door, somehow remaining unchecked by any of the guards running to her father's aid.

Ao met them at the door, untying the remains of Jerzy's bindings even as they hurried down the hallway. None of the servants paid them any attention; the sight of Ao and Jerzy was common enough, and word had not yet spread of Jerzy's disgrace. Certainly, even if they had, none of them would be brazen enough to stop Mahault, striding ahead of them as though she, not her father, ruled those halls. In her blue gown, her hair falling from the wooden pins holding it back, she seemed as much a creature of the winds as anything Giordan had ever wrought.

The three did not speak until they were back in the Vineart's wing, and through the exterior gate to where—to Jerzy's muted surprise, two horses waited, saddled and hobbled, ready to go.

"You . . . you planned this?"

"When you were taken. Ao came to find me," Mahault said calmly, unhobbling the horses. "We had to assume that they weren't simply going to let you go, not after such a fuss. We knew you were innocent, but my father . . . he does not trust anyone, these days." Her voice turned bitter. "Any accusation of wrongdoing or betrayal would find belief in him."

"We didn't expect such a fuss to help us in the rescue, though," Ao said. "Was that you, or . . . ?"

"Giordan," Jerzy said. "He panicked. They will kill him now, for sure."

"You were both dead the moment you were taken," Ao said. "And so are we, now, once someone remembers our part in all this. I know it wasn't the plan," he said to Mahault, as though expecting debate, "but too many people saw us. You can't go back."

"I know. Jerzy will ride double with me. Battus can carry us both." Mahault was matter-of-fact, putting her hand on the neck of the nearest horse, a thick-bodied black.

"You never intended to go back," Ao realized. "You planned to flee with us, all along?"

Mahault didn't look at either of them. "There isn't anything for me here. There never was, only I kept hoping . . . my father would return to himself. But he won't." She looked at Jerzy then, her face still and without hope. "Will he?"

He didn't know why she was asking him or even what she was asking him; he didn't know anything.

"A woman with sense, praise the silent gods. Get on, let's go," Ao said, reaching for the reins of the other horse, a lighter-built brown. "No telling how long the chaos will last, and then they'll realize Jer is gone, and come looking, if they're not already. Whatever was going on, those two needed him for it, so we need to not be here."

Mahault put her foot in the stirrup and hiked her gown up enough to swing into the saddle unencumbered, and Jerzy looked away from the flash of bare leg. "Come on," she said impatiently, holding out a hand. "Ao's right, we need be gone, now."

Still bewildered, feeling as though he had fallen into some kind of dream where all his intentions turned into disasters, Jerzy took her hand, and scrambled into the saddle behind her.

Chapter 24

Jerzy had no idea where they were going, letting Mahault guide their horse, Ao riding close behind. They did not gallop, but instead picked their way in a steady, unremarkable trot and walk pattern that covered almost as much ground, and attracted far less attention. They left the main road quickly, turning onto a narrower dirt track. Heavy ruts in the center of the track indicated that it was regularly used by wagons, but they saw no other traffic as they wound downward out of the Aleppan hills.

Mahault was surprisingly easy to hold on to; although the saddle was not built for two, Jerzy found that if he pushed back onto the leather rise, and kept one arm hooked around her rib cage and the other balanced on his leg, the horse's motion kept them upright and steady, even at a fast trot.

He didn't want to think what might happen if they were forced to run.

Ao suddenly trotted on up ahead, disappearing from sight. Jerzy had a moment of worry before the brown horse came back into view.

"There's a creek around the turn," Ao said. "We should follow it down, wash our scent off the track, then find a place to pack down for the night, and hope whoever's after us decides we've gone another way."

The spot Ao finally decided on was up from the banks of the creek, sheltered from view by trees but clear enough that there was no worry about building a fire. Mahault hobbled the horses and removed their saddles, while Ao quickly gathered fallen branches for a fire. Jerzy stood stupidly, watching them set up camp with casual competence, suddenly painfully aware that the familiar, comforting weight of his belt was missing, and along with it all of his tools.

"I don't suppose you could just magic us up some food and fire?"

The request made Jerzy flinch, and Ao took a step back, his rounded face showing dismay at having, somehow, put his foot wrong.

"He doesn't have spellwine with him," Mahault said. She sat on a fallen log and spread her skirts out, frowning at the soaking-wet hems. They were all muddy, tired, damp, and on the edge of spoiling for a fight, without actually wanting to argue. "He's useless."

"Hey!" Ao started to defend him, but Jerzy held up a hand, stopping him mid-protest.

"No, she's right. I am. I'd be in chains, or dead, if you hadn't dragged me out of there. I gave them the excuse they were looking for, and wasn't smart enough to take Sar Anton's warning, and failed every step since my master sent me—" He stopped, aware they were both staring at him.

"What warning from Sar Anton?" Ao asked, even as Mahault wanted to know. "What excuse did you give them?"

Jerzy swallowed hard, and sat down on a rock opposite Mahault's log. Letting Ao in on his mission had been bad enough, and look how he had tangled that even with help. Telling Mahault . . .

She had helped him. For her own reasons, he was sure, but she had helped him, maybe even saved his life. For good or ill, whatever yield this harvest brought would be hers as well.

He answered Ao first. "Sar Anton told me to stay silent and let Vineart Giordan take the blame. And . . . I think he killed the servant who attacked me, as part of a setup to make Giordan look guilty. I just don't know *why*, or who actually sent the servant, or how any of it ties in with . . . what I was sent to find."

He bent down and dug his fingers into the dirt, feeling the cool texture against his skin. It wasn't vineyard soil, but he could almost feel the energy pulsing below, the endless root-path of Sin Washer's blood still holding the world together. He thought of the vines of Aleppan, and wondered what would happen to them now.

"What excuse? What happened to start all of this, anyway?" Mahault asked. A cool breeze touched her skin, making her shiver in her damp clothing.

They had saved him. He needed to take care of them now.

"Gather the wood," he told Ao. "There, between us."

Ao did so, and stepped back, watching curiously. Jerzy sucked at the inside of his mouth, willing moisture to come forward, and then spat onto his palm, cupping the small amount of spittle protectively.

He had not worked firewines enough to have them in his system. But he knew the taste, the smell, the depth of the grapes, the shape and color of the leaves, the touch of the soil that fed their roots.

Was it enough?

"Fire, come." The most basic firespell decantation. "Fire, come. Flame to fuel." He placed his hand on the topmost branch, and barely let the command slip from his lips, a faint blowing whisper. "Go."

It was barely a crackle at first, so faint he wasn't sure he heard it, then the log warmed under his touch and when he removed his hand, a flicker of steady blue flame appeared in its place, dancing up and down the branch. It caught, moving from one bit of wood to another, until a small but cozy fire burned in front of him.

"Not so useless after all," Mahault said, and Jerzy felt as though the fire was warming inside his chest as well.

"There are things both of you need to know," he said, sitting back down on his stone and waiting while Ao sat next to Mahault on the log. They seemed strangers—they *were* strangers, unfamiliar faces made even more distant in the hazy air above the fire.

"You can trust us," Mahault said. "On my honor, if not that of my father's." Ao said nothing, merely waited, his hands resting on his knees, his face calm and unworried, his dark gaze sharp even through the haze.

"It began almost a year ago," he began. "When my master first heard rumors of strange disasters that could not be explained by normal means. . . ."

When he had finished bringing Ao and Mahault up to date with everything, from Malech's first voiced concerns all the way through to the death of the servant boy in his room, the last of the sunlight had disappeared. The only illumination came from his little fire, still crackling merrily over the wood it was not consuming.

"You think that's why he would not see my delegation?" Ao asked. "Because whoever was influencing him told him not to? But why? To what profit?"

"And he would not . . . would not be rational, would not listen to anyone who had counseled him fair in the past, because . . . someone was telling him otherwise, as Sar Anton claimed? But how does that tie into what you were sent to find?" Mahault was trying to put the pieces together in a recognizable mosaic, and failing.

"I don't know," Jerzy admitted. "My master sent me to harvest what news I could find, of strange doings or disasters aimed at Vinearts, against magic itself. Instead, I find—"

"That it's not just Vinearts," Mahault said, the pieces clicking for her, even as Jerzy saw the pattern in his own mind. "It is power itself that is being attacked. My father . . ." Her face could have been carved from the same stone her city was built from, once again cool and strong. "My father is being manipulated by those he trusted, coaxed into decisions that are not good for Aleppan. I don't know if that Washer had anything to do with it—but Sar Anton certainly did, I would swear to it."

"Intrigue," Ao said. "Court intrigue . . . only rising from servants, not courtiers. From within the House itself, not external. If the maiar is being manipulated by an aide, was he set there by Sar Anton? Or the

Washer, Darian? Washers are deep, and their Collegium has fingers in every pot. But what would be their complaint against Vineart Giordan? No, it makes no sense."

Jerzy held up a hand, unconsciously imitating a pose he had seen often enough from Malech, when his master was thinking something through and did not want to be disturbed.

"What made you think something was wrong?" he asked Mahault. "You were following them, listening . . . and you've accepted everything I've told you without hesitation. Why?"

"My father . . . was a strong man, but a fair one, and he knew that there was a role for every soul born. 'Like Vinearts,' he would say. 'They end up where they're supposed to be.' I had thought, when I told him I wished to be a solitaire, he would be proud. It is a seemly career, if not one often taken by the daughter of a maiar."

"He refused you permission?"

"He refused permission, and set that . . . hound of a watchwoman on me, to ensure I did not leave without consent, and my mother would not gainsay him, too afraid of his uncertain temper. Without their dowry, or some great act of courage on my part, the solitaire would never accept me."

"So you used us to make your escape," Ao said.

Mahault looked up, but Ao was grinning, not at all annoyed. "Brilliant," he said. "Brilliant. What a solitaire you'd make!" He sobered then, just as suddenly. "Not that I can offer any dowry to ease your way. My own clan . . . I'll have caused them loss of face, taking something that belonged to another without compensation. It will take something equally brilliant to make them accept me again."

Jerzy leaned back, starting to feel as though he were back where his master wanted him to be, after all. "Something like discovering who— or what—is trying to influence princes, and to what end? And you, Mahault . . . would finding those who tried to harm your father, and bringing them to light, be considered an act of courage?"

Ao's expression was still solemn, but a hint of his usual mischief returned in the way his eyes crinkled slightly at the ends. "Oh, yes, indeed," he said, even as Mahault turned his offer over in her quiet way.

Jerzy watched the two of them, coming to Agreement over the flickering tendrils of spellfire, and felt something twist in his gut. Serpents attacking shorelines, ships destroyed, Vinearts disappearing, and a trade-city's ruler and the local Vineart both undermined . . . Giordan, the maiar, perhaps even Washer Darian: the touch of magic he had felt twice now, it came from none of them. That aide to the maiar . . . it was his unknown master who was the greater enemy, the cause of the unrest and distrust being sown across the Lands Vin.

And it was an enemy they could warn no one against. Without a name, or a reason, no one would believe their misfortunes were not caused by a visible enemy, an attackable foe. Panic would be the enemy's ally, not theirs.

And if he returned to the Valle . . . they would take him there, him and his companions, and perhaps Master Malech as well. But he needed to warn his master. He had no mirror, no messenger birds, or coin to hire a *meme-courier.* . . .

The three of them, against an unknown force of unknown strength and purpose. The student, the trader, and the fighter.

That thought triggered a memory, and it was as though he heard Master Malech's voice, too distant to be true and yet real as the fire in front of him.

"Magic, and knowledge, and strength," he said, feeling a sense of impossible calm settle over him. "Those are the three things we need . . . and the three things we have. Ao, can you find us a ship? I have a plan."

THE CAULIC FLEET struck during a night-storm, prows rising and falling over the white-capped waves. The storm itself was natural, although he knew his crew believed the scryers had called it up through some dire arts; not ideal weather to sail through, but a useful screen against their own actions, should anyone be watching for them.

The scryers stood, as they had for days now, in the bow of the *Risen*

Moon, three shadowed figures sodden and whipped by the storm, but solid as though planted in the planks of the ship itself. At the helm, the captain put his hand on the pilot's shoulder. "Steady and true, boy. Steady and true. Through to dawn, and we'll be in the royal bedchambers by midday."

They had been lurking for days, waiting until the damned scryers said the time was right. They were short of supplies and long on nerves, but he had faith in his men, and they trusted him. Caulic skill and Caulic steel were a match for any Vineart's tricks.

"Steady," he said again, as the ship rocked in the wind. "Steady . . ."

"Firespouts!" came the cry from the scout's mast, where a young sailor was lashed to his nest. "Firespouts ahead!"

The pilot swore, hauling hard on the wheel, and the *Risen Moon* shuddered under the sudden change of direction.

"A pox on their mothers," the captain swore. "In this weather?"

As though in answer, a geyser of flame slammed up through the waves to the starboard, flickers reaching out toward the sails. The captain slammed his hands down hard on the rain-soaked rail. There were no firespouts near Atakus, not in any reports ever made of the well-traveled lanes, not in a hundred years.

"More damned trickery," he muttered, swiping the back of his arm across his face in a useless attempt to clear the rain from his eyes. The band holding his hair from his forehead was soaked and likewise useless, and he pulled it off with another muttered oath, tossing it down to the deck. "They cannot blind us, so they think to singe us. But we shall not have it! We will not be denied. Steady on, lads!" he yelled into the storm. "Steady on and strong!"

Sailors raced to the side, hands pulling on ropes, tugging the sails out of harm's way, but another firespout to their rear caught a barrel of spellwine, and the crew was split between trying to protect their cargo and their means of propulsion.

"Steady," he said again to the pilot, and went to help his crew, even as another firespout hit them dead-on.

In the bow of the battered ship, the three scryers never once took their gaze from where the shoreline of Atakus should be.

"KAÏNAM. KAÏNAM, WAKE. Wake quickly."

Kaïnam sat upright. He had been reading an old text, and fallen asleep at his desk, when his sister's voice called to him, urging him to rise.

"Am I late?" he asked her, rubbing the exhaustion from his face—and then remembered. Only a dream. Thaïs was dead, his father gone mad, his home cut off from the outside rather than face his sister's killers, hiding in fear rather than demanding justice—

"Kaïnam, look!"

A dream, following him into his half-awake state. But the voice was so urgent, he found himself following its urgings, rising from his chair to the balcony of his bedchamber, looking out over the dark, rain-slicked night seascape.

A seascape blasted by sudden, short-lived pillars of flame.

"Sin Washer be merciful. . . ."

Barefoot, wearing only a robe against the night air, Kaïnam flung open his bedchamber door and raced down the stairs, knocking aside the servant who had come to rouse him. His father was already dressed, standing on the open portico, only slightly protected from the rain. He was accompanied by his ever-present guard, and even as Kaïnam came up beside him, the guard who had been stationed outside his chamber door slipped into place to his left.

Master Vineart Edon, a constant visitor in the months since the barrier went up, joined them within minutes.

"What further madness, what insanity is this?" Kaïnam demanded of the Vineart. "What spells have you encircled us with, to cause this?"

Firespouts were deadly, the bane of any shipping port; no captain would dare wend his way through them, not when a single burst could destroy his entire ship. To cause such a thing, even in defense, was to doom them to isolation and poverty forever, for no matter what the future brought, none would ever believe the harbor safe again.

"Master Edon, is this your doing?" Erebuh asked, staring out into the night, where columns appeared and disappeared without visible pattern.

"Of course it is," Kaïnam shouted. "Firespouts don't simply appear where none have been before, not without magic—"

"Kaïnam, I swear to you." Edon's voice cut across Kaïnam's, even without raising his own tone. "To create that many firespouts is a skill beyond any single Vineart, even a Master. Whatever happens out there, it is not my doing."

"There's a ship out there," one of the guards said, looking through a viewscope. He handed it to Kaïnam, who looked as well.

"A Caulic-built vessel, by the lines," he said. "Coming straight for us, as though they knew exactly where we were."

"Could the fires be theirs?"

"Cauls?" That surprised a laugh out of Edon. "Not unless they've found a river that runs of gold, to buy the firespells and waterspells needed, and the Vinearts skilled enough to decant them. And why would the Cauls cast firespouts around their own ships?"

"Two enemies, come so close in one night, attacking each other?" the prince asked. "But who would come to our aid thus?"

"Our aid?" a quiet voice mused in Kaïnam's ear, an impossibly familiar voice from out of his dream. "Our aid, or our downfall? This, too, we shall take the blame for, however it falls out."

Kaïnam alone heard the Wise Lady's voice speaking his innermost fears, and he alone felt a shiver in his spine.

THE NEXT MORNING wreckage spread across the shallow waters of the bay, driftwood bobbing on the waves, barrels and spars drifting in the tide, while the stink of burned, bloated bodies rose from the shore. Kaïnam guided the salvage operation, as befitted his father's heir, but the bile in his mouth came not from the scene, but what he dreaded lay beyond.

None of this had been accident, or coincidence. He knew that, deep in his gut. Someone had set the killer to prick them, push them into the ill-advised use of magic with withdrawal from the world. Because of that, someone had sent those ships to discover them—for good or ill, it did not matter now, because someone—the same someone? A different enemy?—had used magic again to create firespouts, making it look as though Atakus, not content to simply disappear, had used spellwines to kill.

Princelings using magic to wage war, to kill. Forbidden, by Sin Washer's Command. No one would ever believe their innocence, not now. Not after what they had done. Someone had done this to them, planned and prepared the way. But for what? What purpose, what plan?

"We took the bait, Thaïs," he told the dream voice, now silent. "We took the bait, and sealed our own doom. But I will not let it go unanswered. I swear to you; your death, our loss of honor—though it cost me everything, it will not go unanswered."

The harsh cry of a seabird overhead was the only response to his vow.